Indian Ethos and the Western Experience: A Study of the East-West Encounter in Raja Rao's Fiction

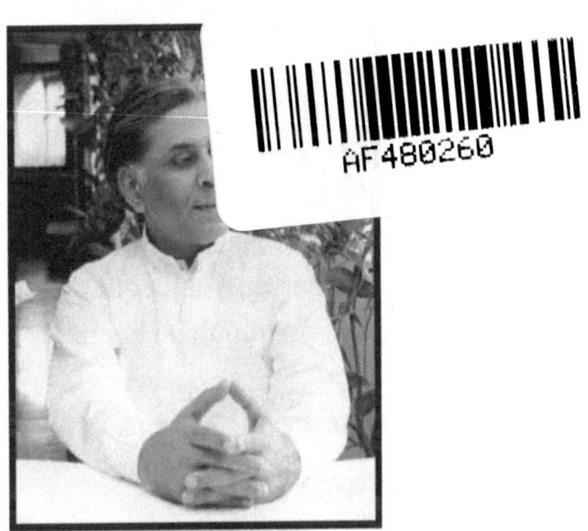

Dr. Madhulika Singh

Rajmangal Prakashan

An Imprint of **Rajmangal Publishers**

Price : 269/-

ISBN : 978-9394920408

Published by :

Rajmangal Publishers

Rajmangal Prakashan Building,
1st Street, Sangwan, Quarsi, Ramghat Road
Aligarh-202001, (UP) INDIA
Cont. No. +91- 7017993445
www.rajmangalpublishers.com
rajmangalpublishers@gmail.com
sampadak@rajmangalpublishers.in

प्रथम संस्करण : नवम्बर 2022 – पेपरबैक

प्रकाशक : राजमंगल प्रकाशन

राजमंगल प्रकाशन बिल्डिंग, 1st स्ट्रीट,

सांगवान, क्वार्सी, रामघाट रोड,

अलीगढ़, उ.प्र. – 202001, भारत

फ़ोन : +91 - 7017993445

First Published : Nov. 2022 - Paperback
Printed by : Thomson Press India Ltd, Repro India Ltd & Manipal Tech Ltd.
eBook by : Rajmangal ePublishers (Digital Publishing Division)

Copyright © Dr. Madhulika Singh

ACKNOWLEDGEMENTS

Raja Rao's writing is premised upon several key perspectives which my book analyses. What has fascinated me about the work of Raja Rao is that due to his background he treats his work as a sadhana, which is what centrally becomes the Indian-ness in his fiction. It is incredible that despite living in the west as part of the great second wave or generation of Indian diaspora, his roots with India were never severed. Raja Rao, and many other spiritually charged authors, who have kept alive a rich tradition of India's spritual prosperity contribute the multicultural and reflective ethos now conspicous by its absence.

Through studying this aspect of Raja Rao, I wanted to explore his ideas at the cusp and intermixing region between the East-West Connection which is Raja Rao's favourite theme. Whether he sees both these meta-cultures as complimentary or contradictory is amply expressed in his writing. The dialogue between these two cultural identities shaping the immediate post-second world war world in which many ex-colonial nations gained their independence never ceases nor grows stale in his work. Yet his literary exploration of this cultural frontier is set deep in his personal life, his loves and estrangements, his thought, craft and skill with which he embarks on a journey of self-discovery through his works. He sees India as something pristine in which we are all born and reborn, continuously seeking moksha or liberation. it is my fervent hope that in discussing his writing from such a perspective, I shall have contributed something towards keeping alive the spiritual narrative tradition and genre in contemporary times and milieus when material culture(s) tend to supersede and obliterate spiritual ones.

I am beholden to Dr. Satyabrata Singh, Head Department of English, Faculty of Arts, Bhagalpur University, Bihar for introducing me to the works of Raja Rao. He helped me devise the basic structure of this study. I wish to thank my doctoral supervisor Dr. P.K. Singh, Head, Department Of English, Faculty of Arts, Kashi Vidyapeeth, Varanasi, without whose help I could not have completed this work. Without his able, kind, and most benevolent guidance, this work would never have seen day. My husband, Dr.Ajay Pratap, Professor, Department of History, Faculty of Social Sciences, Banaras Hindu University, also helped with valuable technical support, without which completing the book would have looked more complex than actually.

My loving parents, Shri Durgesh Prasad Singh, Public Pleader, District Court, Munger and Khagaria, and Shyama Singh, and my sisters Minoo Singh and Mamta Singh, constantly urged me to finish this long overdue work. My daughter Amrita Pratap and son Siddhant Pratap provided an extremely congenial atmosphere leading to the completion of this work.

My late mother-in-law, Dr. Kusumlata Singh, a scholar of Sanskrit and Hindi literature, Senior Teacher at Mount Carmel School, Bhagalpur, Bihar, and late father-in-law, Prof. Udai Pratap Singh, Former Head of the Department Of Psychology, Tilka Manjhi Bhagalpur University, Bihar, and Ex. Vice-Chancellor, S.K University, Dumka, Jharkhand, provided considerable and constant encouragement and whose last wish was to see my Ph.D complete. I sincerely appreciate my sister-in-law, Dr. Varsha Rani, for her valuable suggestions, frank critical comments and help in improving and completing this work.

To all the forgoing, I owe the merits of this study while the work's shortcomings are mine alone. To my colleagues at Sunbeam College, Bhagwanpur, Varanasi, to whom I am beholden for their support and assistance. I am also indebted to The Sunbeam College Library, the Banaras Hindu University Library, The Tilka Manjhi Bhagalpur University Library, and A.N. Sinha Institute Library, Patna, and the Patna University Library for providing me with invaluable source material.

The photograph of Raja Rao on the book's cover is courtesy of www.beaninspirer.com.

Madhulika Singh
Varanasi

Glossary of Terms

Advaita – Non-dualistic philosophy of a single God.
Ananda – Bliss, ecstasy
Anandmaya – Verb of Ananda, a blissful mind
Annamaya - Concerned with worldliness
Atman – Soul
Ayurveda - Indian science of health and medicine
Bhakta Prahalad – A legendary devotee symbolizing the power of unquestioned devotion found in Indian mythology in the story of Narasimha avatar of Vishnu
Bhakti - Devotion
Bhakti Yoga – human deliverance through complete devotion and surrender
Bilva – Banarasi colloquial for the woodapple
Brahman - God
Chitta - Heart
Drasta – A seer, visionary, or a wise man
Dvaita - Dual
Gunas - In Indian parlance, the properties or attributes of the primordial matter, such as Sattva (purity or light), Rajas (luxury and attachment), and Tamas (ignorance and darkness), constitute the human personality. It also corresponds to the three states of human consciousness Jagriti (waking), Swapna (dreaming) and Susupti (sleeping).
Guru – Master, teacher
Gyana - Knowledge
Gyani - An enlightened one
Jiva - A living thing, Human being
Kailasha - The mythical mountain abode of the Lord Shiva
Kaliyuga – The age of kali or decline in the four-fold Hindu calendar of the cycles of time
Karma – Action
Karma yoga – Spiritual deliverance through action
Khadi – Homespun thread and cloth introduced as a symbol of nationalist struggle against British colonialism in India
Koshas - Stages of the Mind

Kusha – A type of long-bladed grass used in worship
Marjara Nyaya - Philosophy of the Cat
Markata Nyaya – Philosophy of the Monkey
Moksha - Salvation
Mana - Mind
Manomaya Kosha –The sum of issues of the mind
Mantra – Sacred chant
Mukti - Liberation
Nirgun - Attributeless, a school of philosophy considering the creator to be formless
Pralaya - Apocalypse
Pranmaya - Mortal life
Purush - Male or the male principle
Prakriti – creation, or feminine principle
Sabdabrahman – The word as embodying God
Sadhaka – A spiritual initiate
Sadhana - Penance or meditation
Sagun – God as possessing specific attributes
Shakti – Force, power, primordial energy
Sat – Truth
Satyagraha – Urge for truth, Gandhi's famous idiom of non-violent struggle against oppression
Siddha - Spiritual Master
Sthala Purana – literally the "place chronicle' or the record of a place
Shivoham – "I am Shiva" or personification of the supreme God in sanskrit
Til – Sesamum seeds
Vedanta – The Indian philosophical corpus
Vedantin - A follower of the Vedanta or Vedantic principles
Vignanmaya - A mind full of knowledge
Vishista Advaita – a kitten-like surrender to the divine will
Yoga – The science of fitness
Yuga – Epochs of time according to the Hindu calendar – satyuga, tretra, dvapar, and kali

Contents

CHAPTER I: Introduction

The following chapters introduce our analyses of Raja Rao's works to examine the impact of his experience of the west upon his writings through the main themes underlying his work. This introductory chapter of the work summaries of the chapters of this book as well as an introduction to it. In chapter one we trace the growth of the art and the artist from inception to culmination in a historical sequence through biographical highlights and thereafter the main currents of his thought followed thematically in separate chapters.

Chapter two The East Vs. the West outlines Raja Rao's family background, the significant events, experiences and influences which shaped his mind, thought and writing akin to art, making him the metaphysical genius in the world of English fiction.

Chapter three Towards India's Freedom discusses how Raja Rao negotiates a contemporary and critical political issue within his writing and illustrates his first attempt at a novel. Written in France in (1938) Kanthapura, also called the Gandhi Purana, represents the microcosm of the Indian subcontinent of the British days and the Mahatma's initiative to overthrow the foreign hegemony. The novel also explores human relationships in an orthodox and decadent socio-political and economic milieu. Though it was his first attempt, Raja Rao displays complete mastery over various aspects of the novel as a form of art. Kanthapura is the first of a series of the trilogy written to explain the Indian ethos of human deliverance through karma yoga or selfless action preached by the Hindu philosophy. It depicts how Gandhi struggled not only for political empowerment but total deliverance of India in the form of social, economic, cultural and spiritual regeneration. Kanthapura represents an archetype Indian village as all that was happening in Kanthapura was being enacted in the countless other villages and cities of pre-independent India.

Chapter four entitled as The Discovery of Self deals with Raja Rao's magnum opus, The Serpent and The Rope. Written in

(1960), which explicates the second Hindu precept of deliverance through Gyan Yoga or self-knowledge, which enables us to delineate between illusion (serpent) and reality (rope). The theme of the story is the meeting and separation of two ardent lovers from diverse backgrounds. Through the union of the main protagonists, the meaning of Advaita or principle of non-dualism propounded by the great sage Sankara is revealed, in which rope symbolizes the reality and the serpent the illusions of life. The story's theme distinguishes the love rope from the serpent of hatred. The novel indicates the breach between the knowledge of the truth and the fascination for the untruth or the unreal, occasioned by differences in intellectual convictions, spiritual perceptions, cultural rites and religious practices, and the need to chalk out a clear and direct path from this mundane world for union with the sublime.

In chapter five, Faith and Surrender, analyses his work The Cat and Shakespeare written in 1965, elucidating the third Hindu principle of bhakti yoga, which exhorts human beings to seek deliverance through complete devotion and surrender to the Almighty. The novel explores human relationships in a temporal world through the life of two friends and neighbours, highlighting the philosophy of vishista advaita propounded by Saint Ramanuja who believed that a kitten-like unconditional surrender to the mother cat of divine will ensures protection and salvation in return in unknown ways.

Chapter six, Alienation and Integration, considers Comrade Kirillov, published in 1976, and explores existential dilemmas depicted through the crisis of adopted identities. It narrates the story of an Indian Brahmin, Padmanabha Iyer, who is disillusioned with the state of affairs in resurgent India and yields to an alien political ideology of marxism which he thinks will redeem humankind. Tremendously impressed by Dostoevsky's character – Kirillov, Iyer adopts his name. The story revolves around the consequences of this psychological impersonation, especially the inner conflicts and contradictions of an atheist, Kirillov, who disbelieves traditional ways of spiritual deliverance, negating the concept of an Absolute. His attempt to find redemption through alien human ideologies fails miserably, leaving him with a divided consciousness and unresolved conflicts.

Chapter seven Raja Rao and the Short Story elaborates on Raja Rao's vision of rural life in such novels as The Cow of the Barricades and Other Short Stories (1947). The Policeman and the Rose (1978) and On the Ganga Ghat (1989) have also been included in the study for analyzing complex existential issues such as Hindu-Muslim unity and the contradictions of the Indian and western lifestyles.

In his book, "The Hindu View of Life", Radhakrishnan rightly says, " The Hindu culture possesses some vitality which seems to be denied to other more forceful currents. It is no more necessary to dissect Hinduism than to open a tree to see whether the sap still runs"[1] For all the critics of this religion, Hinduism remains an enigma and, to all the followers, a liberal all-encompassing way of life. The pessimist perceives India as a cauldron of "economic, political and social malaise,"[2].

In contrast, the optimist staunchly believes that " Indian culture has a surprising power of phoenix like regeneration, the secret of which lies at least partially in its tolerance, comprehensiveness and adaptability. Within the "ordered complexity" and "harmonized multiplicity" of Hindu culture can be seen a universe in miniature which can absorb widely different even conflicting faiths and doctrines and still retain its identity."[3]

In this book, we have attempted to study how Rao, who spent two decades in France and almost four decades in America, took up the challenge of creating something authentically eastern to reconcile different cultures and worldviews, to give a timeless message of deliverance to humanity. However, that this was synonymous with exploring the diasporic literary and intellectual, cultural space between India and the west is reflected in the fact that many of his characters tend to struggle in the subliminal diasporic space. They attempt to resolve interpersonal, intellectual,

---

[1] S. Radhakrishnan, *The Hindu View of Life,* London, George Allen. 1960.p. 12

[2] O.P. Mathur, "The Indian Protagonist and the Western Experience," *Modern Indian English Fiction*, New Delhi: Abhinav Publications. 1993.p.1.

[3] Ibid., p.1

philosophic and even civilizational dilemmas between themselves. To that extent, his works are also an ethnography of the west and westerners as actors in Indian cultural and social realms, an ethnography he, as an author, performs surrogately through his western characters.

Follies of Indian orthodox and liberal life, society and philosophy do not escape his attention. However, his unique position as a diasporic author also places him adequately for an ethnography of the east, of his native realms when explored from the vantage of living overseas. Nevertheless, this ethnography of two worlds results in a history of morality, the intellect and spirituality of the east and west documented from the mid-twentieth to the early twenty-first century. Other than in the Kanthapura, most of the leading characters of his novels, like him travel abroad, hoping to make their fortunes there. Like him, they try to marry into both local society, philosophy and worldly life with varying degrees of success in various different parts of the American, British, Western and Eastern European worlds. Raja Rao has a view of all these worlds, which is what makes his works a historical ethnography performed through the means of his novels.

For many prodigal sons, who travel across the seven seas, the glitz of western materialism presents a stunning spectacle for the first time. They appear to be "noticeably shaken by the glamour and power of modern western civilization."[4] Raja Rao admits that he chose France for his spiritual studies thinking that "France was a place where people spoke the truth. So I went there. But it took me about a week to find out that it was not so. I became Indian immediately afterwards."[5]

His complete disillusionment was evident from his statement, "I wanted to become a Sanyasi"[6]. Settling down in this alien milieu includes a "process of adjustment of the timeless East to the new cultural values and norms of the West"[7] and this process

[4] Ibid., p. 1
[5] Raja Rao, quoted in E.M. Forster: *A Tribute*, ed .K. Natwar Singh. Delhi. 1964. p. 17.
[6] Ibid., p. 17
[7] O.P. Mathur, "The Indian Protagonist and the Western Experience," *Modern Indian English Fiction*, New Delhi:Abhinav Publications. 1993.p.2

"can perhaps be best studied in the crucibles of the souls of those sensible and thoughtful protagonists of Indo-Anglian fiction who visit the West throw out their tentacles of intellectual, moral and spiritual exploration and through their own dilemmas, explicit or implicit arrive at their personal equilibriums and fulfillments."[8]

Sooner or later, the temporal existential illusion of the West dissolves, giving way to the East's metaphysical reality and spiritual superiority. The Indian consciousness is imbued with the greatness of its ancient civilization. Therefore its new cultural values, which have been traditionally reinforced by its archetype mythical protagonists' confronting new intercultural norms, have resulted in the insightful writings of the expatriates. Thus "the pull exerted by ones native ethos has been rendered in deeply human terms and not superimposed artificially"[9] by creative writers whose western sojourn ultimately concluded on the Eastern threshold. "This pattern of an alternating cultural diastole and systole finds its objective correlative in the circular movement of a journey that brings one back to the strength of one's beginnings."[10]

Raja Rao undertook the daunting task of stunning the West by revealing the innate greatness of Indian culture and civilization and the unique Indian Ethos, becoming one of the greatest Indo-Anglian novelists and an acknowledged literary genius. His writings which capture the spirit of India, reveal his profound vision of humanity and his synthesis of the traditional Indian culture and wisdom with his intimate knowledge of the various western cultures. He, therefore, talks about Hinduism, Buddhism, Islam and Christianity, the major religions of the World and how they prospered in India. International travels and multi-cultural experiences enabled Raja Rao to perceive the dualities of the western civilizations, realizing the importance of India and the essential Oneness of the East. Through his literary works, he

---

[8] Ibid.,p.2
[9] Ibid.,p.2
[10] Ibid.,p.1

presents this India to the world, making India significant not only for Indians but for the world as a whole.

The present study intends to explore Raja Rao's prime quest for the truth of life as a metaphysical being and the redemption of his self by union with the Absolute as fictionalized in his works. The present study explores Rao's East-West experiences, his impressions of Eastern and Western perspectives of life, and how this intermingling moulded the characters that enacted his life drama. Embedded deeply in the Indian ethos, they reveal Rao's unity of vision through their private responses to the Western influences, traditions and culture.

Raja Rao's Western encounter first left him awestricken, ending in great disillusionment. His most intimate relationship, his marriage to a French woman, brought him in direct collision with western culture and attitudes. It threw up countless dualities, which helped him formulate his two central concepts of illusion and reality- the undercurrent of all his works. He belonged to a traditional value system where truth, loyalty, simplicity, love, compassion, and universal brotherhood is interwoven in the Indian geographical, cultural and intellectual fabric, forming the core of an ideal life. They not only regulated man's worldly pursuits but took him beyond his mundane existence to selflessness and eternity. The egocentricity of worldly Western life did not appeal to Raja Rao's compassion and wisdom. However, with the characteristic Indian openness of mind, instead of opposing the Western cultural onslaught, he harmonized the diverse currents of Eastern and Western thought to create a unique body of literature, which projects his universal vision of harmony transcending the boundaries of the East and the West.

In the process, Rao realized that he had a unique Indian identity and could never abandon India. In turn, his Indianness never failed him. He continued to live in alien land as he admits, "by force of circumstances purely accidental and sentimental I have lived abroad. My roots are in this country. I live abroad but I am chained to my country."[11] This love for India intensified no matter

<hr>

[11] R. Parthasarthy, "The Future World is being made in America:An Interview with Raja Rao" *Span.*

where he stayed, motivating him to make repeated trips to India to rejuvenate his mind, body and soul, "He became a compulsive visitor, returning to India again and again for spiritual and cultural nourishment indeed in a sense, Rao never completely left India."[12]

His English publications began with his short stories collection *The Cow of the Barricades* in 1947. The first novel *Kanthapura* which became a landmark in Indian writing in English, followed in 1938. His second novel, *The Serpent and the Rope,* his magnum opus, which brought him great acclaim, was published twenty-two years after *Kanthapura* in 1960 and *The Cat and Shakespeare* in 1965. *Comrade Kirillov* was first published in French in 1965; its English version came out in 1976. The same year his second short story collection, *The Policeman and the Rose,* was published. *The Chessmaster and His Moves* followed in 1988, which got him the prestigious Neustadt International Prize for Literature awarded by the University of Oklahoma USA. Another short story collection, *On the Ganga Ghat,* was published in 1989.

Besides novels and short stories, Rao also wrote essays, travelogues and biographical sketches from leading contemporary publications. He edited two anthologies of essays *Changing India* (1939), *Whither India?* (1948) and Jawahar Lal Nehru's book Soviet Russia: Some Random Sketches and Impressions (1949). Some of them were collected in the book *The Meaning of India,* published in 1997.

To understand Rao's art from a proper perspective, one must first comprehend the framework and intricacies of his creativity. It is a daunting task for Westerners unfamiliar with India's social, cultural, linguistic and philosophical traditions. It is not easy for an uninitiated Easterner to understand his "mystique" and comprehend Rao's idea that "silence is more important than the spoken word, the vacant space in the book more significant than the printed page! This is not what is seen but what is to be seen. Upanishadic illumination is a matter of flashes, not the steady light of the day."

September. 1977. p. 30
[12] Makarand Paranjape, *The Best of Raja Rao,* (selected and edited).New Delhi, Katha Classics, 1998.p.v

Thus this staunch metaphysical view of creativity is a spiritual exercise, and the need to convey something which was essentially very Indian but carried a universal message led him to structural and linguistic innovations for his works in the English language. The process was not easy for Rao himself, "The telling has not been easy. One has to convey in a language that is not one's own the spirit that is one's own. One has to convey the various shades and omissions of a certain thought movement that looks maltreated in an alien language. I use the word alien yet English is not really an alien language to us. English is the language of our intellectual make up like Sanskrit or Persian was before- but not of our emotional make up ……We cannot write like the English. We should not. We cannot write only as Indians. We have grown to look at the large world as part of us. Our method of expression therefore has to be a dialect which will someday prove to be as distinctive and colourful as the Irish or the American. Time alone will justify it."[13]

Rao's most significant concern regarding his style was "that the tempo of Indian life must be infused into our English expressions…. Our paths are paths interminable. The Mahabharata has 2,14,778 verses and the Ramayana 48,000. The Puranas are endless and innumerable………we tell one interminable tale. The episode follows episode and when our thoughts stop our breath stops and we move onto another thought. "[14]

With a vision and commitment to creating something uniquely Indian that would become his identity, he devised his form of the "Indian" novel in English, synthesizing the East, cultural and philosophical traditions of the East and West. Through various narrative techniques and Indianized English, he tried to convey his ideas of wisdom and the universal message of deliverance for humanity. His creative expanse was astounding as it encompassed diverse languages and dialects, which included Italian, Latin, Provencal, English, French, Sanskrit, Tamil, Greek, Hindi, Hindustani, and Urdu. Imbued with literal and symbolic meaning,

---

[13] Raja Rao, Foreward to *Kanthapura*, Delhi, Orient Paperbacks. 1970 p. 1
[14] Ibid., pp.1-2

from this context, specific lexical churning and aphoristic use of language emerged in his unique poetical and metaphysical discourse, which, through stories, anecdotes, songs, myths, legends and philosophical discussions, conveyed his deep insight into both the Western and the Eastern though and life. The sophisticated scenario of France or the rustic rural site of Harihalli all come alive, touched by Rao's magic wand. From America, England, China and Moscow to Delhi, Banaras, Bombay and Bangalore, from Indian History to European history and all the central philosophies and ideologies of the World, Hinduism, Buddhism, Catholicism, Marxism, Taoism, Gandhism, Darwinism, Nazism and Islam, Rao's erudition is unmistakable.

All this stupendous effort is directed towards establishing a simple Indian phenomenon of *Advaita Vedanta* - i.e. the realization of the true purpose of our lives and finding refuge in the Divine, thus securing liberation or *Moksha* from this illusory, mundane world of human existence. The lives of all Rao's protagonists, Moorthy, Ramaswamy, Govindan Nair and Padmanabha Iyer, reveal this spiritual pursuit despite their social work, academics, politics, and administration engagements. While Moorthy and Ramaswamy are still seeking the Ultimate Divine Reality, Govindan Nair, with his unflinching faith in the Absolute, is the only one who finds the Truth and lives by it. The quest of Communist and atheist Comrade Kirillov, who negates the existence of the Supreme Being, ends in failure forcing him to live a life full of contradictions bordering on annihilation.

Rao regards Literature as *Sadhana* and himself as its devotee or *Sadhaka* His central theme of the 'Quest for the Absolute' becomes a novelty in Indian English fiction. Perhaps no other novelist, poet, or dramatist is seized with this idea as much as Rao. Absorbed in metaphysics, Rao sets his class apart, not only by revealing the Indian ethos to the Westerners but also by reviving this dormant ethos within the consciousness of Indians themselves. Narasimhaiah comments perceptively, "A very challenging beginning for a novel – challenging to the novel 'form' which invariably evokes in its first pages the spirit of a place or a time, but what is summoned here to our imagination is neither place nor time but something that transcends both – it is, what has made the great Indian tradition and sustained it through the vicissitudes of history: the Vedas, Upanishads, Brahmanas, Sutras, The Gita, the Great Teacher and their lineage, these again made alive to us by their modes of life - wandering to 'mountains and distant hermitages to see God face to face' and death burnt by tank or grove or meeting of two rivers (the confluence of rivers as hallowed by tradition) – and brings the immemorial tradition quite up-to-date, to the present, to himself, and the faith by which he 'feels' them in him. Such is the vitality of a living tradition, inarticulate but accessible to those who 'feel' it in them- it flows in their veins and now is brought to the surface by one who belongs to it."[15]

In Raja Rao's works, the 'formless form' of the novel Narasimhaiah perceives the real spirit of real India, initially considered strange both by the English world and the world of Indo-English Fiction. He recognizes the truth that transcends time and space, which only a *Sadhaka* realizes at the culmination of his *Sadhana* (devotion). The commoners and the intellectuals, applying logic and intellect, failed to comprehend this quest for truth which is the real goal of all human life. Woven in the Indian fabric of life, prominent saint, Kabir, portrays this metaphysical world lucidly as a place beyond time and space, with no sun, moon, or stars. Neither has its day nor has its night. If it rains there, that rain has no water, and that water is neither salty nor sweet and tasty.

To the western authors, this idea appears alien because, like Rao, they are not seeking the Absolute after annihilating mundane dualities of life, "To the western man, to the Englishman in particular, literature is all that concerns man, society, civilization and his concern with these made, as one could expect for social morality as a central preoccupation of the English novel. However, turn to American fiction, Melville especially and how inadequate becomes the social yardstick with which to measure the spirit of man. As Arthur Miller remarked, Raja Rao knew how to measure the giant's boots but could not look you in the eyes. Moreover, for

---

[15] C.D. Narasimhaiah, *Raja Rao. Indian Writer's Series.* Sterling Publishers. New Delhi. 1988 p. 80.

an Indian, the centre of interest shifts from both the moral centrality of the British and the transcendental ego of the American to, if one may venture a tentative generalization, Man, World and God-the last manifested variously as the Truth, the Absolute, the Brahman.[16]

Thus Rao's quest sets him apart in his class. While Rao focuses on the mortal Self and immortal Soul, his western counterparts explore the human psyche or individual Ego. While Rao's metaphysics explores the inner spiritual consciousness, the westerners dabble with the science of Psychology to examine the unconscious and subconscious levels of the human mind. Rao's distinction in the literary world is established because of his metaphysical beliefs, which according to Ahmad Ali, is the omnipresence of the Vedantic point of view, while Narsing Srivastava feels that it is the quintessence of the Bhagavad Gita. Comparing Stavrogin from Fyodor Dostoevsky's *The Possessed* with Ramaswamy, the protagonist of *The Serpent and the Rope* (1983), Iyengar explains the factor which lends superiority to Rao's belief and style. Iyengar observes that "although Stavrogin shows the way to others – to Shatov, to Kirillov, to Pyotr Verhovensky – he is himself bare of all support in the end; love might perhaps save him still, but his "experiments with truth" have exhausted him, and he takes the surer way out of the mess – suicide. However, Rama is the Hindu Brahmin; for who the way would be not what Rajam Iyer has called 'bodycide', the putting out of the body's life, but the real suicide - the killing of the ego, the ending of the illusion of individuality. Thus, Rama seeks out his Guru.[17] He will teach him through *sadhana* how to kill his ego and cleanse his soul from the evils of mundane values or *sanskaras,* and then the authentic self (the rope) will emerge, bringing real peace and tranquillity. This is how he can work out his salvation and cross the bridge of life to attain the Absolute.

This thought establishes Raja Rao as a unique writer striving to find his metaphysical "being" in the world of English fiction. Prominent western metaphysical poets like John Donne

---

[16] Ibid. pp. 81-82.
[17] K.R.S. Iyengar, *Indian Writing in English.* Delhi. Sterling Publishers Pvt. Ltd. 1983. p.402

(2011) also echo his concern, but only partly when he states in *Death Be Not Proud*:

> And soonest our best thee do go,
> Rest of their bones, and souls' delivery.
> Thou art slave to fate, chance, kings and desperate man,
> And dost with poison, war and sickness dwell,
> And poppy, or charms, can make us sleep as well,
> And better than thy stroke; why swell's thou then?
> One short sleep past, we wake eternally,
> And death shall be no more; death thou shalt die.[18]

The poet is not afraid of death, for it is a long, restful sleep from which there is finally waking up. However, he does not look beyond it. The quest for God or attaining the Ultimate Reality is not his calling. George Herbert (1963), in his poem, *The Pulley*, does not exhibit any such concern either:

> When God at first made man,
> Having a glass of blessings standing by..
> When almost all was out, God made a stay,
> Perceiving that alone,
> Of all his treasure, Rest in the bottom lay…
> For if I should (said He), Bestow this jewel also on my creature,
> He would adore my gifts instead of me,
> And rest in Nature, not the God of Nature:
> So both should losers be.
> Yet let him keep the rest,
> But keep them with repining restlessness;
> Let him be rich and weary, that at least,
> If goodness lead him not, yet weariness,
> May toss him to my breast.[19]

---

[18] John, Donne. *Death Be Not Proud: The Complete English Poems*, Penguin Classics Paperbacks. U.K. 2004.
[19] George, Herbert. *The Pulley: The Complete English Poems*, Penguin Classics Paperbacks. U.K. 2005

Herbert (1963) shows how God blessed man with everything except for satisfaction thinking dissatisfaction, if not better, would bring him back to the Divine. Thus Herbert's metaphysics is restricted by merely mentioning God's name and making his Will supreme without allowing man the scope to redeem himself by his efforts. The mystique of the western metaphysical poets like John Donne, George Herbert, Henry Vaughan, Richard Cranshaw, and Thomas Trahern, as manifested in their poems, was only to be in close communion with God, as they believed that the material world was a mere shadow and the spiritual world - a reality.

The Hindu belief is that the human body is a medium and the human life an opportunity to transcend the illusion or Maya of the world and attain union with the supreme. Raja Rao did not restrict himself to a mere realization of this fact but, following Hindu metaphysics based on Vedantic truth, exhorted the individual to endeavour to attain the Divine. Raja Rao's quest is, therefore, unique, and his art is unchallenged in the world of English fiction.

Even distinguished novelists like Mulk Raj Anand and R. K. Narayan, part of the same cultural tradition, do not parallel Rao as they do not consider literature a sublime pursuit and salvation through writing is not their goal. Walsh comments illuminatingly, "If Anand is the novelist as reformer, Raja Rao the novelist as metaphysical poet, Narayan is simply the novelist as novelist.[20] He reiterates. "How different in every particular from Mulk Raj Anand is Raja Rao, a member of an old Brahmin family, born in Mysore in 1909 and roughly a contemporary of two senior novelists, Mulk Raj Anand and R. K. Narayan. He has, however, a completely different literary character. 'He is not, like Anand, a politically committed writer, and he is very different from Narayan being poetic, metaphysical, Law-rentian.[21] Paranjape feels that "neither their stylistic and poetic depth nor dexterity can compare with the best of Rao's writing. Formally and stylistically, he is the most

---

[20] William Walsh, *R. K. Narayan: A Critical Appreciation.* Allied Publishers Pvt. Ltd. New Delhi:1983.p. 6.
[21] Ibid. p.5.

adventurous of the three. Thematically too, Rao is somewhat different from Anand and Narayan. He is a metaphysical novelist whose concerns are primarily religious and philosophical."[22]

Raja Rao's self-perception reinforces Walsh's stand considerably, "….my quest for Absolute is essential for me. I am always with this inner quest…I do not rate myself as a writer or novelist. I am only a seeker or a Sadhaka, though I teach at Texas University. I have students to whom I try to convey my ideas and impress upon them the need to go inwards.[23]

Thus Rao steers clear of his ilk quite clearly. His art has a novelty quite unsurpassed by any other novelist, whether compared to the stream of consciousness novelists like Virginia Woolf, James Joyce, Dorothy Richardson and Marcel Proust or novelists of Indo-English Fiction like Anita Desai, Manohar Mulgaonkar and Arun Joshi. Both groups indulge in introspection, exploring the inner recesses of the human mind, thus working merely on a scientific psychological plane. He stands drastically apart since, as a Sadhaka, he transcends the various existential stages or *Koshas* viz. *Annamay* and *Pranmay are* the worldly levels, and the three stages of mind or Mana which is *Manomay, Vignanmay, Anandmay Koshas according to* Vedanta. Surpassing worldly vicissitudes and crossing the bridge of existence, the real Sadhaka attains Oneness with the Absolute, experiencing eternal bliss. This stage of *Isness* or *Self Recognition* where all duality ceases has been depicted in *The Serpent and the Rope*:

> "Isness is the Truth", she answered
> "And Isness is what?"
> "Who asks that question?"
> "Myself."
> "Who?"
> "I".
> "Of Whom?"
> "No one"

[22] Makarand Paranjape, *The Best of Raja Rao*, (selected and edited). New Delhi, Katha Classics, 1998.p.ii-iii
[23] Shakuntala Balu, "Eternal Quest of Raja Rao." *The Times of India*, Patna, 30th January.1987

"Then 'I am' is."
"Rather I am "
"Tautology!" She laughed :
"Savithri says Savithri is Savithri."
"And you say Savithri is What?" She begged.
"I"
And the moon and the silence seemed
To acknowledge that only the
 I" shone.
There is no Savithri", I continued
 after a while.
"No, there isn't. That I know."
"There is nothing", I persisted
"Yes", she said, "Except that in
 the seeing of the seeing there's a seer."
"And the seer sees what?"
"Nothing", she answered.
"When the I is; and where the nothing
 is, what is the Nothing but the 'I'"
 "So, when, I see that tree in that
 moonlight that cypress, that pine tree,
 I See I-I See I-I see I."[24]

This ultimate truth of the East, the backbone of all Indian ethos, has been repeatedly revealed by Raja Rao graphically through what I.A. Richards calls 'emotive language'. Through dialogues and discussions, through symbols and situations, through description and evocation, through myth and metaphor is explicated, the all-absorbing truth of *Isness* and *Self-recognition* and how to attain it through conventional Indian precepts. Adhering to them under the guidance of a Guru can enable human beings to transcend time, space and ego, leading to the attainment of the eternal self and salvation or Moksha. This 'European' Brahmin, wherever he goes, does not abandon his goal of finding God. He

---

[24] Raja Rao, *The Serpent and the Rope*. Orient Paperbacks. New Delhi 1968 pp. 130-31

confesses unabashedly, "I get up around 6 and I meditate."[25]All his protagonists are infused with his spirit. Time and again, he tries to reveal this principle through them, who like the characters of Charles Dickens, Emile Bronte, George Eliot, Tolstoy, Hemingway, and D.H. Lawrence, are the personifications of the authors.

The protagonist of *Kanthapura,* Moorthy, seeks salvation through *Karma Yoga* or selfless action. Oblivious to the fruits of his endeavours, he works for the welfare of others people. Through sacrifice and service unto the downtrodden, in the teeth of severe oppression, even losing his mother, he realizes the divine within himself, " Shivoham, Shivoham' i.e I am Shiva. I am Shiva, Shiva am I"[26]

Madeleine, the female protagonist of *The Serpent and the Rope* redeems herself through *Gyan Yoga* or self-knowledge. Transcending physical, emotional and intellectual fascination for her husband Ramaswamy, she gradually becomes conscious of her true nature. Striving towards spiritual perfection, she then divorces Ramaswamy marrying her true self. Like Maitreyi and Yajnavalkya, this love was neither for the wife nor husband's sake but for themselves, which is reflected in the other. This very self transcends all else to attain spiritual perfection.

Shantha, The Cat and Shakespeare's female protagonist chooses the path of *Bhakti Yoga* or self-surrender for liberation. Though a mistress, her love for Ramakrishna Pai is unconditional and her surrender to Pai is like a devotee's surrender to the supreme will, who is assured of divine protection. Shanta worships Ramakrishna Pai and sacrifices all her worldly possessions to enable Pai to realize his dreams as she believes that they are the same and all that belongs to one belongs to the other, " What belongs to you belongs to me, what belongs to Lord alone belongs, for Woman is belonging to me. You can only shine of light. The

[25] Shakuntala Balu, "Eternal Quest of Raja Rao." *The Times of India*, Patna, 30th January.1987
[26] Raja Rao, *Kanthapura*, Orient Paperbacks. Delhi. 1970 p. 92

shine shows its light, but to whom does the Light belong? Light belongs to light."[27]

Light symbolizes the wisdom of this mutual relationship of giving and take between the devotee and his God as embodied in the Vedas, Upanishads or the Bhagawad Gita, which belongs to all. However, only those who have risen from the carnal to the sublime plane can attain it. When all actions of the mundane world are silenced like the turbulent waves of the ocean and going beyond his non-self, when the spiritual aspirant becomes calm and serene like the sea, he attains the ultimate reality.

Padmanabha Iyer, the protagonist of Comrade Kirillov, trying to find deliverance through alien ideologies like Communism, realizes his folly, "Go, go, Mara', Kirillov would say, "I know of your doings. I know the dialectic of Feurbach, and the state and the revolution of Lenin. Marx has been suppressed by hagiography, and Lenin is in his tomb. Go, you many mouthed, many-armed, you multiple monster, Mara!"[28] But so long as Kirillov remains an atheist and non-believer of the Divine principle, Mara symbolises foreign thought and is bound to torment him, creating that divided consciousness that prevents him from attaining the truth.

Only in the character of Govindan Nair Rao's quest for truth culminates successfully. Nair is a perfect example of a person who has attained the truth himself and helps others attain it. Considering the world as real while others continue to rejoice in joys and withdraw in sorrows negating the divine will, Nair negates the world as illusory, considering only union with the Absolute as the fundamental goal of human life. Nair lives Rao's Advaitic conviction that "the world can be negated even as we participate in it, just as it can be negated when we withdraw from it."[29]

Thus, Raja Rao proves to the western world how creative writing is not merely an intellectual pursuit but a spiritual exercise which enables both the writer and the reader to become

[27] Raja Rao, *The Cat and Shakespeare*, Delhi, Hind Pocket Books. 1971. p.34.

[28] Raja Rao, *Comrade Kirillov*, Orient Paperbacks. New Delhi 1976. p. 92

[29] Makarand Paranjape, *The Best of Raja Rao*, (selected and edited).New Delhi, Katha Classics, 1998.p.xxv

metaphysical Beings. His works have successfully revealed deep insight into the ethos of eternal India. The Western prism imparted great clarity to his vision of the East, as compared to many contemporary novelists who still see India through western eyes only. Rao is convinced that "India is not a country, like France, or England...India is a state of being... India is an idea, a metaphysic ...open to whoever can attain it, wherever they may be."[30] India, therefore, is not something which can be barely seen but has to be felt. This is the challenge that Rao throws to the West.

The present study thus tries to explore how Raja Rao depicts the Indian ethos, especially after his encounter with western values. His works give an insight into his creative mind, exhaustive knowledge, aesthetics, wisdom, and the nature of intercultural influences acting upon him – all of which have gone into the creation of his complex and artful narratives, which try to resolve contradictions and conflicts. The intention here is to understand the man whose pen captures the spirit of India and whose vision reveals the essence of India. Thus Raja Rao is "undoubtedly, one of the most widely acclaimed Indian English novelists by virtue of his wide range of thoughtful content – philosophical, intellectual, political and social and his command of the fictional form, language and technique. He deals with Indian philosophy, the metaphysical and man's spiritual quest for liberation."[31]

So multi-dimensional was he that some regard Raja Rao as a philosophical writer, some a Vedantist, some a Tantrist and some a Gandhian. Some think he writes like a European others think that he is essentially an Indian. "Well Raja Rao is all of these",[32] according to Mallikarjun Patil and probably more. P. Dayal concurs, "his expatriation to the West is purely an accident, he is essentially an Indian in regard to his personal propensities and artistic preferences and his novels primarily revolve round Gandhism, Vedanta and Tantra."[33] Malikarjun Patil rightly

---

[30] Raja Rao, *The Serpent and the Rope*. Orient Paperbacks. New Delhi 1968 p. 376
[31] Kaushal Sharma ,*Raja Rao: A Study of His Themes and Technique*, New Delhi, Sarup & Sons. 2005.p..3-4.
[32] Mallikarjun Patil, "Raja Rao: A Philosophical Novelist." in Rajeshwar Mittapalli & Pier Paolo Piciucco, Ed. *The Fiction of Raja Rao: Critical Studies*, New Delhi: Atlantic Publishers :2001. p.1
[33] P. Dayal, *Raja Rao*, New Delhi: Atlantic Publishers, 1991.p.4

considers him "a Raja of the Indian English fiction…His literary product and philosophical stand has brought him the status of a classical writer."[34] His creations combining realism and fantasy, reveal the impersonal truth beyond cause and effect, logic and reason, mind and intellect. He beckons Seekers wherever they are to experience the spirit of this vibrant and eternal India of the Vedas and the Upanishads, of the Mahabharata and the Ramayana, of Sankara, Ramanuja and Kabir, of Aurobindo and Gandhi and chalk out their deliverance.

---

[34] Mallikarjun Patil, "Raja Rao: A Philosophical Novelist." In Rajeshwar Mittapalli & Pier Paolo Piciucco. Ed. *The Fiction of Raja Rao: Critical Studies*, New Delhi, Atlantic Publishers : 2001. p.1

CHAPTER II: The East Vs. the West Experience

Raja Rao was an ocean of ideas generated after birth, upbringing, Eastern heritage, cosmopolitan education and multicultural encounters in the West. Ramaswamy, the protagonist of *The Serpent and the Rope* personifying Rao, reveals how important ideas were to him, " And thus I tried to formulate myself to myself. I like these equations about myself or others, or about ideas, I feed on them." [35]

India also dawned upon him as an idea while he was in self-exile for studies in France. In his book *The Meaning of India,* he asserts that India is not a country desa but a perspective darsana." This darsana or philosophy was the Advaitic Vedantic principle to gain spiritual perfection by becoming one with the divine from which all life emerges and ends. Interpreting his idea Paranjape rightly observes that for Rao, "even if there was no India in the physical, material sense, India as an idea would always exist." [36]

The idea of India motivated Rao to become a "Thinker, Meditator and Seeker of Truth."[37] Rao called himself the 'holy vagabond', and wherever the protagonists of this spiritual wanderer went, they tried to seek and teach the eternal Indian values. Only atheist and Communist Padmanabha Iyer, the protagonist of *Comrade Kirillov,* is an aberration. Digressing from his tradition and delving deep into Marxism, he soon realizes that as he thought, it is not a panacea for all ills. According to Paranjape, this reflects that his "Communism is only a thin upper layer in an essentially Indian psyche."[38] Kirillov's wife Irene confirms it, " he is almost biologically an Indian Brahmin and only intellectually a Marxist."[39] Rao principally chose to align with Shakespeare's Hamlet as his

---

[35] Makarand Paranjape, *The Best of Raja Rao*, (selected and edited).New Delhi, Katha Classics, 1998.p.xx
[36] Ibid.,p. xxiii
[37] Ibid.,p. xii.
[38] Ibid., p. xiv
[39] Ibid. xiv.

staunch belief was "There is a divinity that shapes our ends, Rough hew them how we will."

Unlike the female protagonist of *The Serpent and Rope,* westerner Madeleine who is looking for the truth outside of herself, Rama the Easterner believes that "the self is identical to truth as the wave is a part of the sea, and that all separateness is an illusion, like the illusion in which the rope is mistaken for a serpent."[40] From this main idea ensued Rao's East-West vision which enabled him to perceive the dualities and Oneness in both cultures, eventually convincing him that the goal of human life anywhere was the same. Moreover, this goal should be the deliverance of man from his illusory existence by striving to unite with the Absolute. "For Raja Rao the only reality is the Absolute, "there is no world "and individual existence is completely illusory."[41]

It is imperative to probe the mind and influence of Raja Rao, which motivated him to embark on this soul-searching journey, this eternal quest of truth whose experiences are portrayed in his sublime works. Like his protagonist, Govindan Nair from The Cat and Shakespeare, who lives his philosophy of unconditional surrender to divine faith and lifts the veil of ignorance from his neighbour Ramakrishna's eyes leading him to truth; Rao also practised his philosophy and went through the creative process to universalize his prime belief. Thus the East-West interactions establishing the spiritual supremacy of India over the materialistic cultures of the West propelled Rao also towards his resurrection. India ultimately proved to be a panacea of all ills to him, beyond doubt.

Born in an elite Brahmin family on November 5, 1908, at Hassan, a small town in the erstwhile princely Mysore State now Karnataka, he was called "Raja" for just at his birth, the then Maharaja of Mysore was standing at the door of his house, and his father was receiving him in the ceremonial way."[42] His mother believed that Rao was a prince in his past life. This made Rao very

---

[40] Ibid.,p. xii

[41] Esha Dey, *The Novels of Raja Rao, The Theme of Quest.* New Delhi.. Prestige Books. 1992. p 144

[42] Raja Rao, in *The Illustrated Weekly of India,* September 25, 1966. P.15.cited, M.K. Naik,, *Raja Rao ,* Twayne's English Author Series. New York: Twayne, Publishers,,1972 ,pp 16-17.

proud of his birth. He was equally proud of being born as a Brahmin as much as being the eldest son's son, which gave him a privileged position in his orthodox social milieu.

Rao, barely four, was struck by the biggest tragedy of his life, his mother's death and could barely cope with it, "Whenever I stand in a river I remember how when young on the day the monster ate the moon and the day fell into an eclipse, I used with *til* and *kusha* grass (emphasis mine) to offer the manes my filial devotion…So with wet cloth and an empty stomach with devotion and sandal paste on my forehead I fell before the rice balls of my mother and I sobbed."[43] The angst of being an orphan stayed with him for life, "I was born an orphan, and have remained one. Am I always going to be an orphan?"[44] Though he learned to cope with death, it always remained an enigma for him leaving its stamp of melancholy on Raja Rao forever.

Around this time, Rao's grandfather, an orthodox Hindu scholar, initiated him into great philosophical and spiritual learning embodied in *Advaita Vedanta* propounded by Sankaracharya in (788-820 A.D.). Thus he began reading the Upanishads at age four, had his sacred thread ceremony by age seven and knew Sanskrit Grammer and *Brahmasutras* as a young boy. Rao was also a descendent of the illustrious sage Vidyaranya Swami, "the greatest teacher of Advaita Vedanta after Sankara, and the mentor of Harihar and Bukka, who founded the southern kingdom of Vijayanagar, which was the last Hindu state to fall to the Mughal onslaught in the sixteenth century.[45]

Rao spent part of his childhood with his grandfather in his native village Harihalli, which gave him a keen insight into rural India. Though Rao was born in an orthodox Hindu family in Karnataka, where Kannada was his mother tongue, he was forced to spend his formative years in the state of Hyderabad, where Telugu and Urdu were spoken. For long before Rao was born, his family had taken refuge there due to the escapades of his grand

---

[43] Raja Rao, *The Serpent and the Rope*, New Delhi, Orient Paperbacks, 1968. p. 101.
[44] Ibid., 100.
[45] M.K. Naik, *Raja Rao*, Blackie & Sons. Madras. 1982.

uncle. When Rao was born, Kannada as a language was in severe crisis as the British, for their political convenience, were trying to break up the land of the Kannadigas and subject portions of it to other linguistic groups. "Thus right from his birth so to say, Raja Rao had become "an exile, linguistic, religious and cultural."[46] Rao's father was a teacher in Nizam's College, Hyderabad, so Rao joined the Salar Jung's Madarase – Aliya School in Hyderabad and was the only Hindu boy in his school. In the preface to the book *The Policeman and the Rose,* he admits that the British teachers impressed him most.

He went to Aligarh Muslim University, where he simultaneously completed his matriculation and learned Muslim theology. It was here that he came in contact with a minor poet, painter and Visiting Professor, Eric Dickinson from Oxford, who brought out the artist in Rao by inculcating in him the love for – Michaelangelo and Santayana and the language of France, the centre of all European movements in art and literature in the 19th century. Rao admits, "He impressed me very much. I have been made by him. My literary sensibilities were formed by him."[47] Raja Rao thus grew into a versatile intellectual with firsthand knowledge of all the world's important religious and philosophical systems. He returned to Nizam's College, Hyderabad, and completed his graduation in English and History, two typically modern and western subjects. In 1929 he embarked for France after being awarded the Asiatic Scholarship of the Government of Hyderabad to study the "Mysticism of The West." He aimed to explore India's influence on the West as he firmly believed that Buddhism drove Cathars to the Albigensian heresy. However, he was destined to drift to literature and then to philosophy and finally metaphysics which was to influence and shape his mind and vision and initiate the quest for Truth, which would never abandon him for the rest of his life wherever he would be - East or West.

Transiting from a new culture with orthodox ideas to modern western life with progressive ideas, Rao travelled abroad

---

[46]Esha Dey, *The Novels of Raja Rao, The Theme of Quest.* New Delhi.. Prestige Books.1992. p 16.
[47] Ibid., p. 16.

to escape the miseries of an enslaved person in India. He had left behind a decadent system due to their noble descent and smooth talk. The Brahmins, he felt, had been enjoying innumerable privileges. He was disgusted with his society which had " no use for intelligence. It has use only for bright limbs and slick tongue."[48] He was fully aware of the shortcomings and strengths of his own high and holy Hindu caste, which had been shamefully suppressing its low caste brethren. Travelling to France, he hoped that he would find his land of truth and initially "was so much overawed by the Western civilization that he was planning to preach its magnificence to his countrymen for the rest of his life,"[49]

Within a week of his arrival he discovered the inadequacies in the 'materialist' life in the west. As his initial euphoria waned, Rao regained his Indian fervour " India is not a country like France is... or like England, India is an idea, a metaphysic."[50] Naik is convinced that Rao "appears to have 'discovered' India only after going abroad."[51]. However, so disillusioned was he with the materialist West that after regaining his intense spirituality, he wanted to renounce the world and become a Sanyasi or recluse.

He was barely nineteen years old and had to complete his studies. He was a student at the University of Montpellier when these East-West encounters awakened the Orientalist patriot and the cosmopolitan Occidentalist in him, and both motivated him to interpret Indian life and values in the Western world and European life and culture to the Eastern world. For the moment, the East-West exposure had left him with the divided consciousness of his protagonist *Comrade Kirillov*. Split between materialism and spiritualism, he began to formulate his ideas to reveal the eternal truths of India. After he married Camille Mouly, a highly educated French woman who taught French at a lycee in Menton, his efforts were fructified into concrete work. Rao shifted to the University of

---

[48] Raja Rao, *Comrade Kirillov*, New Delhi, Orient Paperbacks, 1976.p.11,
[49] Raja Rao, *The Serpent and the Rope*, Orient Paperbacks, New Delhi 1968, p.15.
[50] Ibid.,p. 376.
[51] M.K.Naik, *Raja Rao* Blackie & Sons. Madras. 1982

Paris in 1931 to conduct research on *The Influence of India on Irish Literature* under the guidance of Professor Cazamian.

Camille played a crucial role in Rao's development as a writer, encouraging him to write in his own language Kannada. From 1931-1933 he wrote three essays and one poem in Kannada for the journal *Jaya Karnataka*. The response was rather lukewarm, so he began writing his first stories in English, later published in *The Cow of the Barricades* in 1947. In 1933 he visited Pandit Taranath's Ashram in India in search of self-realization *Kanthapura* followed in 1938, becoming a landmark in Indian English Fiction writing. Mouly herself became an ardent admirer of the Indian culture and religions, especially Hinduism and Buddhism. Raja Rao rightly admits that she "played a very important part"[52] in his life until they unfortunately divorced in 1949.

Rao was a descendant of the legendary late historical period southern Indian Hoysala dynasty of Karnataka, which was clan endogamous and had an influential position as the eldest son's eldest son in a patriarchal Hindu society. This probably explains Rao's decidedly superior bearing, which eroded his marriages. Upon losing his spouse, a distraught and disoriented Rao returned to India and first went to Banaras, where according to Mehta: "he shut himself in a room for a number of days, trying to decide whether he should become a Sanyasi."[53] To soothe his restless soul, he visited various Ashrams and saints and was tremendously influenced by their thoughts and philosophy, which eventually shaped his vision and writing. In *1939 he* went to Sri Aurobindo Ashram in Pondicherry. Sri Aurobindo's writings greatly influenced his views on life, literature and aesthetics. In 1939-40 he also met Sri Raman Maharishi in his Ashram at Tiruvannamalai, and in 1940-41, he visited Narayan Maharaj at Kedgaon in Maharashtra.

The freedom struggle raging in India infused great nationalist fervour in Rao, who plunged himself into several

---

[52] M. K. Naik, *Raja Rao*, Blackie & Sons. Madras. 1982 p.19.
[53] P.P .Mehta, *Indo-Anglian Fiction: An Assessment*.. Bareilly, Prakash Book Depot.. 1979.p.197

academic, social, political and cultural activities in India. He edited the magazine *Changing India* (1939) with Iqbal Singh, which carried articles of modern intellectuals from Raja Rammohun Roy to Jawaharlal Nehru. In 1941 he met Mahatma Gandhi at Sevagram, where he translated many of his Kannada stories into English, later published in the collection *The Cow of the Barricades* in 1947. Meanwhile, he also came in close contact with radical socialists participating in the Quit India movement of 1942. In 1943-44, he co-edited a journal called *Tomorrow* with Ahmad Ali, published in Bombay. He started the organization, Sri Vidya Samiti, to rejuvenate ancient Indian values and culture, which unfortunately did not last long. In 1946 in Bombay, he also became a member of a cultural organization called *Chetna,* which propagated Indian culture and values.

All this happened while Rao's tormented soul searched for a spiritual preceptor. His quest ended when he met Guru Atmananda at Trivandrum in 1943. While he immersed himself in the study of philosophy, analyzing the reasons for his break up, his Guru resolved all his existential conflicts initiating him into eternal wisdom. He dissuaded him from becoming a recluse advising him to remain a writer.

As a scholar, philosopher and seeker, meditation and yoga became an integral part of Rao's life, from which he banned non-vegetarian food and drink no matter where he was. Rao was convinced that only self-discipline through Yoga would lead to self-enlightenment and holistic development of humankind. Having realized and imbibed this principle strengthened his resolve to seek the divine for deliverance. Rao wanted to settle down in Trivandrum, but Atmananda died in 1959, and Rao returned to France, creating his magnum opus, *The Serpent and the Rope,* in which Ramaswamy and Madeleine became his and Camille's literary counterparts. According to Dey, Madeleine's character is probably, "the most profound and sensitive portrayal of a white woman by an Indian writer."[54]

---

[54] Esha Dey, *The Novels of Raja Rao, The Theme of Quest.* New Delhi. Prestige Books.. 1992. p.16.

The Serpent and the Rope, published in 1960, after a hiatus of twenty-two years of *Kanthapura's* Gandhi Purana, was hailed as Rao's major epic or Mahapurana - and was regarded as "the most sophisticated exploration into the ambiguities of an intercultural encounter."[55] Rao, the philosopher himself, believed that the novel's theme is 'the futility and barrenness of man in human existence when man has no deep quest and no thirst for the ultimate. Man's life here in *Samsara* is an august mission to find the Absolute."[56] Through Ramaswamy, the hero experiencing an intense urge for the quest of the Absolute, Raja Rao advocates Vedantic principles, which lead us to divine Union - the Ultimate truth of Life (the rope). All else is an illusion (the serpent).

The *Serpent and the Rope* won wide acclaim, and Rao received the prestigious Sahitya Academy Award in India in 1964. The Indian Government also awarded him the Padma Bhushan in 1969. He received invitations for lecture tours to various institutions in India, France and the U.S.A. He finally settled in America, teaching Indian Philosophy at the University of Texas, making it his second home. In 1965 he married an American stage actress Katherine Jones from whom his only son Christopher Rama was born. This marriage also ended in a divorce, and he was subsequently married to Susan, another American woman. The 10th Neustadt prize awarded the prestigious international award by the University of Oklahoma, came to him in 1988 for his classic *The Chessmaster and his Moves.*

In our view, the best way to understand Rao's art is to develop a rapport with 'his mind' and the historical-cultural contexts of his work. Essentially rooted in the Indian tradition, Rao's search for the Absolute is the eternal search of all Sadhakas in India from time immemorial. They have all embarked on a similar journey of discovery and found the metaphysical truths at the end of the rainbow. These truths, which form the core of pristine Indian values, have been revealed to Rao as he walked in the

---

[55] Ibid.,p. 18

[56] Raja Rao's letter to M'K.Naik quoted in Mallikarjun Patil, "Raja Rao: A Philosophical Novelist." Rajeshwar Mittapalli & Pier Paolo Piciucco Ed. *The Fiction of Raja Rao: Critical Studies*, New Delhi: Atlantic Publishers 2001.p. 5

footsteps of the renowned Indian sages for enlightenment and are not the outcome of mere academic interest in philosophy. In Kanthapura, Rao's philosophical quest was at its seminal stage, which gained predominance, becoming a high tide in The Serpent and the Rope; flowing upstream in The Cat and Shakespeare, it finally became an undercurrent in all his other works.

Rao, therefore, regarded man as "a metaphysical entity" and his writing as "a consequence of a metaphysical life." He firmly believed that "the idea of literature is anything but a spiritual experience",[57] which demands total concentration. Before embarking on his literary journey, he therefore seemed to face a dilemma, "I had this conflict in me, should a man be a writer first, then a man, or a man first and a writer afterwards?" [58]The writer succumbed to the philosopher as his passion for metaphysics overpowered him.

A decade after the publication of *Kanthapura*. Raja Rao confessed to E M Forster, " I have not written a book for ten years because of my study of metaphysics."[59] However, he continued writing metaphysics in fiction. No wonder his characters in *The Serpent and Rope,* despite their diverse cultural backgrounds, reciprocate amiably to each other thoughts, beliefs and lifestyles and are not politically hostile to each other as the characters of *The Passage to India.*

Rao considers literature as s*adhana* or spiritual experience and himself as a Sadhaka or devotee. Word is a mantra which sublimated through human consciousness and becomes writing, a consequence of his metaphysical life. Illustrating his notion, he writes. "I really think that only through dedication to the absolute or metaphysical principle can one be fully creative. Literature as sadhana is the best life for a writer. The Indian tradition which links the world with the absolute (*shabdabrahman*) has clearly shown the various ways by which one can approach literature, without the confusions that arise in the mind of the Western writer viewing life

[57] S.V.V. "Face to Face." *The Illustrated Weekly of India* ,Jan 5 1964, pp 44-45.cited M.K. Naik *Raja Rao* Blackie & Sons. Madras. 1982. p.23.
[58] Esha Dey, *The Novels of Raja Rao, The Theme of Quest.* New Delhi.. Prestige Books. 1992.. p.18
[59] A.P. Oberoi, "Meeting Raja Rao", *Prajna,*2.(2) 1966. p. CLXXXI

as an intellectual adventure. Basically, the Indian outlook follows a deeply satisfying, richly rewarding and profoundly metaphysical path."[60]

Following this wisdom, the protagonists of all his significant works mostly autobiographical, remain south Indian Brahmins closely "devoted to truth and all that" with their staunch belief that a "Brahmin is he who knows Brahman..." Madeleine's ecstatic statement reveals her love for Ramaswamy and the influence of his India on her, " Oh, to be born in a country where tradition is so alive",[61] She exclaims, " India is a paradise" and is greatly delighted at the prospect of dying in India by virtue of her marriage to an Indian."[62]

Raja Rao is explicitly proud of his elite descent and rejoices his birth into the highest caste of one of the world's oldest civilisations. Having imbibed the hoary yet thriving Indian traditions and being the custodians of all sacred knowledge and highest learning, his caste had enjoyed being spiritual mentors and guides to royalty and commoners alike. From time immemorial, they had been showing them the path of salvation or *moksha*, the ultimate goal of man's life. Rao only seemed to further this tradition.

The spiritual orientation perceived in all his works which had begun early, stayed with him for life as his quest for truth culminated in finding a Guru who resolved his existential conflicts. According to Kumar, "Rama was proud about his ancestry and his upbringing in the tradition of Brahmanism .with a sage to begin his genealogical tree and a guru to end the cycle of birth and death."[63]

Not only do the main protagonists share Rao's archetypal concern of finding the truth of the Absolute, but his other characters also mirror his attributes and cultural and mystical beliefs. They confronted almost similar situations in life, and their responses were also identical. Concretizing his abstract ideas, revealing his

---

[60] Raja Rao quoted in K.K. Sharma, *Perspectives on Raja Rao*, Vimal Prakashan. Delhi.1980. p. 11
[61] Raja Rao, *The Serpent and the Rope*, Hind Pocket Books, Delhi 1968. p.19.
[62] Ibid.,p. 88.
[63] G. Thirupathi Kumar, *Conceptualising Tradition: A Study of Raja Rao, R.K. Narayan and Mulkraj Anand..* New Delhi. Research India Press. 2007.p,74

attitudes and unfolding important events of his life through them, Rao transformed mundane personal happenings into impersonal art objects.

His spiritual progression following the central precepts of Hindu philosophy *karma marg* or selfless action, *gyan marg* or self-knowledge *bhakti marg* or self-surrender was reflected in Moorthy, Ramaswamy and Govindan Nair, respectively. This shows that though in self-exile, thousands of miles away in France, Raja Rao was only physically and not emotionally or spiritually removed from India. In his Trilogy, It was his patriotism which was revealed in *Kanthapura* through Moorthy, it was his love for traditions which was reflected in *The Serpent and the Rope* through Ramaswamy, and it was his ardent belief in divine benevolence which was exposed through Govindan Nair in *The Cat and Shakespeare*.

The dilemma of communist Kirillov was the dilemma of the staunch Brahmin narrator 'R', who personified Rao himself. Rao temporarily vacillated between the dual identities of Padmanabha Iyer, a contemplative Indian mystic and Communist Comrade Kirillov, seeking to redeem his suffering fellow citizens through Marxist principles. The 'vertical' Brahmin 'R' and the 'inverted' Brahmin Kirillov are the same personality split into two. They symbolized "an individual in whom the East, an inalienable part of his intellectual and spiritual heritage, survives overwhelming waves of Western ideologies making him an alien wherever he goes and creating in him a despair that is in marked contrast to the conscious levels of faith at which he operates."[64]

Naik is convinced that Kirillov was "the projection of a suppressed element existing in Raja Rao's own mental make-up, which had inspired him during his stay in France to be closely associated with the socialist movement in Paris, particularly with French trade union leaders and Trotskyites."[65] Unlike Kirillov, Raja Rao, the Europeanized Brahmin, never converted to Marxism,

[64] O.P. Mathur, "The East West Theme in Comrade Kirillov", *Modern Indian English Fiction.* New Delhi, Fp in India.1993. .
[65] M.K.Naik, *Raja Rao* Blackie & Sons. Madras. 1982 , p. 18

holding steadfastly to his Indian values, despite his travels and multicultural experiences in the West. Adhering to conflicting ideologies, Kirillov became a bundle of contradictions, yet being an atheist and communist, he did not forgo his fondness for India and Sanskrit, even visiting Sri Raman Maharishi's ashram like Rao. Though their logic was different yet their identity was one.

Rao chose to align with ' R' Kirillov's double, who suffered no dichotomy in his personality, harmonizing his orthodox spiritualism and progressive liberalism very well. Rao closely resembled 'R', an enlightened intellectual and pious metaphysician perfectly capable of balancing the duality of eastern and western thought. 'R' had been endowed with a unique syncretism to perceive mundane things' reality and recognize the metaphysical truths concealed in them. Irene candidly states, "His stronghold is metaphysics…He floats in metaphysics as I float in figures…. He is straight and simple as a child and like most Indians magniloquent." [66]

The east met the west when Ramaswamy and Madeleine entered matrimony, and though divorced, the East had won over the West when Madeleine renounced the mundane world and chose to progress towards spiritual perfection. The east and the west met again when Rao married a second time. This union became complete when his American stage actress wife, Katherine Jones, gave birth to their only son Christopher Rama. This incident is reminiscent of *Comrade Kirillov,* who married Irene, a Czech communist nurse, who gave birth to a son called 'Kamal Bathoska'. Both these marriages were an attempt by Raja Rao to synthesize the eastern and western philosophies, thoughts, cultures and lifestyles. His sole aim was to reconcile the materialism of the west and the spiritualism of the east, promoting a better understanding between the two.

The first and foremost influence in the Eastern context that moulded Rao's spiritualism and formed the substratum of all his works emanated from the tenets of Sankara's *Advaita Vedanta.* There are two other schools of Vedantic thought *Vishista Advaita,*

---

[66] Raja Rao, *Comrade Kirillov* .New Delhi, Orient Paperbacks, New Delhi. 1976.

propounded by Ramanuja (1067-1137), and *Dvaita* by Madhavacharya (1197-1276). All the three theories "are related to *jiva-brahman* relationship prescribing different paths for man's spiritual elevation. Vedanta in general prescribes surrender of the self, devotion, meditation, ascetic rigour, annihilation of the Ego, non-attachment to worldly possessions. All this has to be done for man's *mukti* (liberation) from the cycle of birth and death. Brahman alone is the creator, preserver, and destroyer of the universe."[67]

Therefore sublimating life's mundane events as a creative art, Rao viewed literature from a metaphysical perspective as he firmly believed that "all creation is entirely impersonal."[68] or transcendental. "The great writer sinks....into the depths of impersonality" and "this comes not by contrivance but insight and perception and vibrant experience at the time of writing."[69]

Rao's idea that the 'word' originates and ends in 'the absolute' is derived from the vedic tradition and its proponents Sri Aurobindo. The Vedic poets of India had interpreted *Mantra* as "an inspired and revealed seeing and visioned thinking..." and believed that "poetry is mantra only when it is the voice of the inmost truth and is couched in the highest power of the very rhythm and speech of that truth."[70] Sri Aurobindo also regards Word as Mantra because it is the "highest revealing form of poetic thought and expression."[71] Raja Rao concurs with him that the creative writer needs to become a saint-poet and the reader needs to elevate himself to the supra-mental level, for only when his communion with the absolute is complete can he receive the full impact of the word as a mantra.

Delivering a lecture on "*The Critic and the Creator*" at the Banaras Hindu University and explaining his aesthetic sense inspired by Sri Aurobindo's philosophy that literature has emerged from supra-rational activity, Rao stated, that, "In difficult moments suddenly a word comes from somewhere as if by magic, not

---

[67] Kaushal Sharma ,*Raja Rao: A Study of His Themes and Technique*, New Delhi: Sarup & Sons 2005.p.3.
[68] A.P. Oberoi, "Meeting Raja Rao", *Prajna*,2.(2) 1966. p CLXXXII
[69] *Ibid.*, p. CLXXXIII
[70] M.K. Naik, *Raja Rao*, Madras, Blackie and Sons, 1982. p. 281
[71] Ibid. p. 280

something you thought of ……that is the final word – yes, the final words. No writer comes by deliberation to the final word……a word………..gives the vibration of the object. The object is strongly felt, and the word brings it out. So creation is the pure vibration of a human being in concentration…Yes, this is the delight...of words. They group themselves ……but it is the impersonal which constructs the series of statements."[72]

Rao felt that without devotion and worship, "Pratilabha or Bhakti"[73] as explained by Coomaraswamy, the right word or the perfect expression could not be achieved. Rao was convinced that words emerged and merged in the impersonal Absolute, and their ultimate goal was silence, "without this entrance into the absolute, no greatness can come"[74] He reiterated this contention in the article on *The Writer and the Word,* "Therefore, my argument is, unless, the writer, could go back to the changeless in yourself, you could not truly communicate with a reader……..Unless the author becomes a upasaka (devotee) and enjoys himself in himself which is rasa (aesthetic experience) the eternality of sound……will not manifest itself, and so you cannot communicate either. Man faces himself when he seeks the word. The word as pure sound is but a communication that comes from silence…Unless the word becomes mantra no writer is a writer and no reader, a reader.[75]

In an article on *Books which have Influenced Me,* published in *The Illustrated Weekly of India* (February 10, 1963, p. 45), Raja Rao talks about both Indian and western literary influences which had profoundly augmented his mystic thought and philosophy, his artistic viewpoint and vision of life evident both as content and form of his books.

The epics Ramayana and Mahabharata which he believed epitomized Indian tradition and wisdom along with the Brihatstotra Ratnakara an anthology of religious verses in Sanskrit, compiled by Vasudeva Shastri Panshikkar, which cast a mystic influence on his philosophical mind involved in the quest for reality through his

---

[72] A.P Oberoi, "Meeting Raja Rao". *Prajna*, 1996 , p . CLXXXII
[73] A.K. Coomaraswamy, *The Figures of Speech or The Figures of Thought*.London., Luzac Co. 1946,p. 144.
[74] A.P Oberoi, "Meeting Raja Rao." *Prajna*, 1996. p. CLXXXIII.
[75] M. K. Naik, *Raja Rao,* Blackie & Sons. Madras. 1982, p. 25.

creative medium. Appreciating the Ramayana thoroughly, he states, "What could be more glorious, more sacred, more fantastic, a book of books – showing every beauty and treachery of our tragic-comic existence, absurd, inhuman, gentle, devout, noble, cruel, yet not altogether felt as of this world, described for our terror and our joy and final wisdom – than the Ramayana.[76] Raja Rao was immensely influenced by the Buddhist texts "with their poetry and rich humanity"[77]

The traditional Hindu vision, wisdom and spirituality of illustrious saints, mystics and aestheticians all cast tremendous formative influences on Rao's creative ideas. His devotion and metaphysical ardour were reinforced by the writings of the 12th-century Kannada saint-poets known as Vachankaras, followers of the Lingayat faith, and Kanakdasa and Purandaradas – the followers of the devotional cult of Dasas. He quotes profusely from the hymns of Bharthrihari, Jagannatha Bhatta, Sankara, and Meera, and Sanskrit classics such as Raghuvansh, Meghdoot and Uttarramacharitam and from the works of many other writers.

Tantricism also influenced Rao considerably, and it is expounded as the Feminine principle in his works. In this belief system, spiritual perfection is achieved through sensuality as only the gratification of the carnal desires can lead to the attainment of the sublime. All creation has a divine origin from the sexual union of the male (Shiva) and female (Shakti), representing two sides of the same reality. Therefore both in Hinduism and Buddhism, women are deified as Devi, Mahadevi, Adishakti and Shakti and worshipped as Mother Goddesses in the form of Parvati, Durga, Kali, Saraswati, Lakshmi and Tara. Rao regards them as the 'priestess of God'[78] in *The Serpent and the Rope*. No wonder Raja Rao's principal characters idealize their beloveds and worship them as the emblems of the Female principle.

Patil is convinced that Rao's " belief that woman is the source of sensuous and aesthetic pleasure to man has Tantric

---

[76] Ibid..,p. 28.
[77] Ibid. p..29.
[78] Raja Rao, *The Serpent and Rope* , New Delhi, Orient Paperbacks. 1968. p. 57.

contours."[79] Furthering his argument, Patil even regards *The Cat and Shakespeare* as a carry forward of the Tantricism of *The Serpent and the Rope*. He considers it "an enigmatic work for it combines both comic and serious and amorous and metaphysical."[80] Ramaswamy, a Brahmin who has europeanised considerably, finds it challenging to practice sexual abstinence as a Vedantist. Ramaswamy regards sex as a physiological necessity but does not attach great importance to it. P. Dayal says that since Ramaswamy "suffers from sexual repression, he follows the path of Tantra which promises the fulfilment of his carnal love as well as the attainment of truth."[81] Gandhian autobiography elaborates the Mahatma's philosophy of love, truth, non-violence and purity of means and ends highlighted in Kanthapura, also had a tremendous impact on Rao.

However, it is the art historian Anand Coomaraswamy whom Rao regards as the true representative of India and Indians in the West. Since Raja Rao himself was a part of the great second wave of Indian diaspora, he perhaps looked up to Coomaraswamy and his work as exemplary in this regard. Perusing his writings, he comments, "one was discovering an India that one may have 'felt' but could not have 'named'.[82] Interpreting Indian art and aesthetics, Coomaraswamy not only exhibited his deep insight and intense knowledge but gave easy access to the Westerner to these treasures of the East.

His concept of art and artist and the spiritual significance of art and beauty are envisaged in his scholarly works "Figures of speech or figures of Thought", "Literary Symbolism", "Samvega – Aesthetic Shock", "Hindu view of Art", " That Beauty is a State" and "The Dance of Shiva." influenced Rao profoundly. His idea about the impersonality of the artist seems to be derived from Coomaraswamy's view that "more perfect the artist becomes, the less will his work be recognizable as "his", only when he is no

---

[79] Mallikarjun Patil, "Raja Rao: A Philosophical Novelist." In Rajeshwar Mittapalli & Pier Paolo Piciucco. Ed. *The Fiction of Raja Rao: Critical Studies*, New Delhi: Atlantic Publishers. 2001.p.7.
[80] Ibid.,p. 8
[81] P. Dayal, *Raja Rao: A Study of His Novels*, New Delhi, Atlantic Publishers. 1991. p. 31.
[82] M. K. Naik, *Raja Rao*, Blackie & Sons. Madras. 1982, p. 280.

longer anyone can he see the shortest distance, or my real form, directly and as it is."[83]

Coomaraswamy felt that only artists with "penetrating vision,"[84] who can sort out the sublime from the mundane, will find this distance to the absolute reduced. The Hindu tradition believes in the threefold significance of real art. i.e "Love, Truth and Beauty, which are also the three phases of the Absolute, manifested equally in the little or the great"[85] This process involves participation, imitation and expression. Participation is a mystical and metaphysical experience, "The form is in the work of art as its "Content", but we shall miss it if we consider only the aesthetic surface and our sensitive reactions to them, just as we may miss the soul when we dissect the body and cannot lay our hands upon it…."[86]

Tracing Pandit Taranath's significant influence with whom Rao lived closely for a short while, Naik states, "The Master in the short story Narsiga, in *The Cow of the Barricades* and other stories is perhaps Taranath who was a remarkable man, doctor, social reformer, freedom fighter, writer, musician, philosopher and yogi."[87] Apart from his extraordinary personality, his profound ideas on art and aesthetics influenced Rao's psyche and literature. Taranath strongly believed that real art had a spiritual genesis and functions, for it is "whole and wholesome in origin and effect, raising from and appealing to the whole Chitta", which "Not caitiffs but only kings of the spirit can produce or appreciate…" and which "can surely be recognized as the stepping stone to spirituality."[88] Taranath is convinced that " only he whose expression is the perfume of the heart in blossom is an artist."[89]

Among the countries of the west and their influence on Raja Rao, the impact of France, the centre of all modern developments in European art and literature, was first and foremost.

---

[83] A.K. Coomaraswamy, The *Figures of Speech or the Figures of Thought*. London. Luzac Co., 1946. p.138.
[84] A.K. Coomaraswamy, *The Dance of Shiva*. New York. The Noonday Press. 1952.. p. 42
[85] Ibid. p. 42.
[86] A.K. Coomaraswamy, *The Figures of Speech or The Figures of Thought*, London. Luzac. Co, 1946. p.138.
[87] Ibid., p. 30.
[88] Ibid.,p. 31
[89] Ibid. p. 31.

In the preface to The Policeman and the Rose, Rao admits himself, "A South Indian Brahmin, nineteen, spoon-fed on English, with just enough Sanskrit to know, I knew so little, with an indiscreet education in Kannada, the French literary scene overpowered me."[90] The existentialism of Sartre and Camus had still not arrived. Maurice Barres's *culte de moi* or concentration of Ego as nationalism and Charles Peguy's Roman Catholic Humanism and Gallicism were the flavours of contemporary France which also infused Rao with nationalistic fervour.

Motivated enough to adore the Indian ethos, he evolved his core philosophical principle of the metaphysics of India by merging Hindu nationalism with Advaita. Roman Catholicism influenced Rao immensely, "What I like in France is the Roman Catholic it springs up in every intellectual and literary discussion… it is the background of France." Charles Peguy, who finds repeated mention in Rao's works regarded as a repository of French Catholic Humanist thought and ideals, also influenced Rao significantly. Rao considered him "the human embodiment of the living force of Europe."[91]

The Holy Bible influenced Rao profoundly too, and so did Shakespeare, who symbolized the "universal" as his "vision transcends duality and arrives at a unified view of the world."[92] T. S. Eliot's contention of divine inspiration as a "pre-condition of artistic creation or a "unity of being,"[93] also clearly perceived in the works of W. B. Yeats, was wholly aligned with Rao's philosophy. The other western writers who influenced Rao include Plato, Ignazio Silone, Maxim Gorky, Paul Valery, Andre Gide, and Franz Kafka. Rao considered Romain Rolland a "mystic and metaphysician, the "great sage of the West" and his novel *Jean Christopher* with its "overtones of Indian philosophy,"[94]as the Gita of mankind"[95] Both of them believed that true love could not be shackled by possessiveness.

<hr>

[90]Esha Dey, *The Novels of Raja Rao, The Theme of Quest*. New Delhi. Prestige Books.1992. p..20
[91] Ibid.p. 20
[92] Makarand Paranjape, *The Best of Raja Rao*, (selected and edited).New Delhi, Katha Classics, 1998. p. xiii
[93] T.S. Eliot,"Tradition and the Individual Talent", *Selected Essays*, Faber and Faber, London, 1951, p. 21
[94] Kaushal Sharma ,*Raja Rao: A Study of His Themes and Technique*, New Delhi, Sarup & Sons 2005. .p. 6.
[95] Quoted in M. K. Naik, *Raja Rao*, Blackie & Sons. Madras.1982..

Rao shares his metaphysical thought with Rainer Maria Rilke, who in Seventh Elegy says, "Nowhere beloved can world exist but within."[96] Like Charles Baudelaire, Rao believes a man is incomplete without a woman, but fidelity in love is unnecessary. Rao's concern for the soul and the spiritual development of man in *The Serpent and Rope* and *Comrade Kirillov* is inspired by Fyodor Dostoevsky's *The Brothers Karamazov and The Possessed.* Both the authors explore the complex psyche and divided consciousness of their characters. Fyodor Dostoevsky's metaphysics which elevates an ordinary crime story of *The Brothers Karamazov* to a sublime level, influenced Rao so immensely that he felt "as if it had happened all around."

Rao could not hold himself back from repeating references to Dostoevsky's characters in *The Serpent and the Rope* and even titled the novel Comrade Kirillov after one of his famous characters. The divided consciousness of his characters, whether Kirillov, Nair or Pai, derives their pattern heavily from Shatov. Rao's thought, "that the Indian novel can only be metaphysical in nature," finds resemblance in the Russian master's disciple, the French novelist Andre Malraux who influenced Rao intensely with his belief that a novel "is an instrument of metaphysical consciousness."[97]

These philosophical and literary influences endowed Rao with a mystical and realistic vision and went a long way in establishing him as a metaphysical writer. His simple narratives conveying the realities of life, reinforced by profound thought, were invaluable pieces of literary art. They set him in a class entirely apart from the other great writers of Indo-Anglian fiction, such as Mulk Raj Anand and R. K. Narayan.

Like the great philosophers of the East and the West he is endowed with enormous descriptive, interpretative and intuitive powers which enable him to see things in a unified perspective and make profound revelations of the universal truths of life. Juxtaposing the metaphysical with the realistic, he had the perfect

---

[96] Quoted in Esha Dey, *The Novels of Raja Rao, The Theme of Quest.* New Delhi.. Prestige Books. 1992. p. 21
[97] Ibid.,p. 22.

ability to present with great finesse two contradictory elements e.g.The Serpent and the Rope and reveals two independent yet interdependent realms of existence. Thus his creative thinking reveals his firm grasp on philosophical abstractions and concrete reality equally.

The intellectual, religious and spiritual initiation Rao received in his childhood profoundly impacted his mind in formulating his philosophical ideas, which fructified successfully in his adulthood. Creative thoughts imbibed from several literary sources also shaped his personality and attitudes, making him Raja Rao –the celebrated artist, the novelist of ideas. Thus a philosopher par excellence, through an alien western medium, went ahead to lucidly interpret Indian culture, traditions and thoughts to the world.

Dressed in a Jodhpur close-collar coat, Rao looked every inch a traditional Indian scholar or a learned Orientalist to the Westerners. To his people, he was a cosmopolitan expatriate with great love for everything Indian. His belief that the Indian novel could " only be epic in form and metaphysical in nature"[98] and India's image as a spiritual entity in the West guided his literary endeavours perfectly. Thus his life and literature made Raja Rao a cultural emissary of India in the West – that India which was "infectious, mysterious and infectious."[99]

Mathur rightly points out that Ramaswamy's statement that "India absorbs everything and makes it her own".... proves the strength and resilience of Hindu culture and *Samskarus* as aginst the mundane life of the West, which is focused on the visible and the concrete ever in a state of flux. However, in *Comrade Kirillov* the conclusion is reached only after the West has been given its due in full, and there is no tipping of the scales." No matter what, "the Indian strain is so persistent that it can never die."[100]

---

[98] G. Thirupathi Kumar, *Conceptualising Tradition: A Study of Raja Rao, R.K. Narayan and Mulkraj Anand..* New Delhi. Research India Press. 2007.p.67.

[99] Raja Rao, *The Serpent and the Rope*, New Delhi, Orient Paperbacks.1968. p. 40..

[100] O.P. Mathur, "The East West Theme in Comrade Kirillov," *Modern Indian English Fiction.* New Delhi, Fp in India.1993.p.116.

Chapter III: Towards India's Freedom

This chapter deals with how Raja Rao contextualizes India's struggle for freedom from the British yoke in terms of what happens when a scholar steeped in traditional Indian values receives western education and travels abroad to gain further knowledge? What happens when this exposure intensifies his love for his own country? What happens when an diasporic milieu infuses him with a nationalist urge to support freedom fighters struggling to liberate their land from foreign domination? Detached from his native soil and yet attached to its well-being, when his inner turmoil finds creative expression – the result was Kanthapura.

Living and writing in France, yet wholly attuned to India, Raja Rao, in his first novel, gives a detailed insight into the life of Indian villages and cities and their role in the freedom struggle of the 1930s. Naik informs that Raja Rao wrote Kanthapura in a 13th-century castle in the French Alps belonging to the Dauphins of France and he slept and worked on the novel in the room of the Queen."[101] Kaushal Sharma feels that the " The Indian village life came live to him in the castle. The gracious spirit of the queen appeared to have inspired the author to make the grandmother his narrator."[102] Called Achakka, she symbolizes the eternal spirit of Mother India, waiting to be redeemed from alien domination. Her first-hand experience of participating in this fight for freedom unfolds in the novel.

According to Narasimhaiah, Rao's sojourn abroad gave him the "necessary perspective and detachment"[103] to portray his vision of the crisis and the strength of rural India. "This emotional attachment and intellectual detachment enables Raja Rao to create an objective and balanced record of a people's movement full of narrative vigour."[104] The other literary stalwarts like "Mulk Raj

---

[101] M.K.Naik, *Raja Rao*, Bombay, Blackie & Son Publishers Pvt. Ltd. 1982. p. 57.
[102] Kaushal Sharma, *Raja Rao: A Study of His Themes and Technique*, New Delhi, Ist edition, Sarup & Sons. 2005..p.8,
[103] C.D. Narsimhaiah, Raja Rao, New Delhi :Arnold Heinemann, 1970 . p. 43
[104] Quoted in Niranjan Rout, The Fictional Work of Raja Rao: A Study of his Mind and Art, Ph.D. Thesis. Magadh University.1995

Anand is known for his social concerns, R.K.Narayan is known for his mythological evocations of social life, while Raja Rao writes about Indian life in a historical perspective. His philosophical viewpoints exposed here and there in Kanthapura may not be quite rich as in his later novels but they do suffice in the historical context…Nothing in the history of Indian English fiction is as significant as Raja Rao's Kanthapura."[105]

The novel deals with nationalism, one of the most challenging ideologies of the 20th century, which aimed at the social, political, economic and spiritual emancipation of humanity from colonial subjugation. Unfolding the saga of a village in the wake of freedom struggle, the novel reveals "at least three levels of experience…the first is political struggle – a struggle for securing freedom to the country, the second is the religious life – a life that highlights Indian life; and the third social concerns."[106]

Kanthapura's drama was enacted in the Indian subcontinent, but the world found its *Mahatma* the saint, whose policy of non-violence heralded a new "ism" in world politics. *"Gandhism"*, no wonder Rao believed was" the future of the world,"[107] and Gandhi was an "emblem of divine power as well as a great reality."[108] Thus "Gandhi's axiom of non-violence presents an astonishing paradigm for the whole world,"[109] as it is a "war without violence and battle without hatred."[110] It is an amazing principle also because it believes that "good ends can be achieved only by good means."[111]

What inspired Rao most was that Gandhi, a prodigal son, had been waging a lone battle to drive the invaders away from his native soil. This set him on a quest to decipher the Truth, which motivated Gandhi to give up his legal profession and work towards ameliorating the condition of his oppressed brethren. Rao realized

[105] Mallikarjun Patil, "Kanthapura : A Portrait of Village Gandhi," *in* Rajeshwar Mittapalli &Pier Paolo Piciucco. Ed.*The Fiction of Raja Rao, Critical Studies*, New Delhi: Atlantic Publishers 2001.p.112.
[106] Ibid.,p. 112.
[107] Raja Rao quoted in Ratna Rao Shekhar, " Seventy Six Years of Solitude." *Society* August 1985. p. 30 .
[108] Uday Shankar Ojha , "Gandhian Ideology : A Study of Raja Rao's *Kanthapura.* " *in* Rajeshwar Mittapalli &Pier Paolo Piciucco Ed.*The Fiction of Raja Rao, Critical Studies*, New Delhi, Atlantic Publishers, 2001.p.110.
[109] Ibid.,p. 109.
[110] G. Ramachandran, "Promotion of Gandhian Philosophy," Mysore 1973.p. 33 .
[111] Ibid.,p. 34

that Gandhi was not fighting a mundane political battle to set his country free from foreign domination but also trying to purge its decadent socio-economic system, which allowed opportunists a chance to divide and rule. "Gandhi wanted all the people, the opulent and the indigent, to lead a dignified life sans exploitation of any sort."[112]

Exhorting Indians to set their own house in order without which the intruders would not exit, Gandhi introduced *satyagraha* – the urge for truth which implied spiritual regeneration or soul searching by its believers. Only after exercising their inner self could they plunge into action for political and economic freedom. Raja Rao wanted to convey to the West that Satyagraha was not a mere intellectual pastime but a profoundly satisfying mission of furthering the profound metaphysical tradition of India. Karma yoga, or the path of selfless action preached by the Bhagavad Gita, which had inspired the spiritual ideal of Satyagraha, was - one of the central precepts of Hindu philosophy. It believed that selfless action was the path to the Absolute.

For Raja Rao, as the Mahabharata was fought in Kurukshetra, the Indian Independence movement was also fought in Kanthapura. The struggle against colonial rule in India's million's of villages was nothing less. It was a quintessential conflict between good and evil, freedom and slavery, love and hatred, truth and untruth both at the internal and external planes - internally with ones orthodox spirit and externally with the colonialists. Satyagraha was not merely a political tool; Gandhi's principles evolved from his experiments with truth. These ultimately became the guiding light for Raja Rao, a seeker of truth, who embarked on a long, solitary and arduous journey to showcase the Indian ethos to the western world. For Gandhi, satyagraha was a sadhana. Raja Rao documented that sadhana, through writing, for he believed that literature too as sadhana is best for a writer. "Gandhi is a vast symbol of ideal life code, of a holy and noble

---

[112] Uday Shankar Ojha. "Gandhian Ideology : A Study of Raja Rao's *Kanthapura*" *in* Rajeshwar Mittapalli &Pier Paolo Piciucco. Ed. *The Fiction of Raja Rao, Critical Studies*, New Delhi: Atlantic Publishers, 2001.p.110.

person."[113] To Raja Rao, "he is a symbol of a veritable God. ……. a Narsinga …..endowed with the heavenly power of doing away with the so called enemies of freedom. …a spiritual leader who has the skill of oration like Krishna in the immortal Gita."[114].

Documenting Gandhi's sadhana, Rao revealed to the world the intricacies of Indian, "life which comprises various levels of consciousness", making it his aim "to delineate life in its totality."[115] Raja Rao strongly believed that "India is the kingdom of God, and it is within you, India is wherever you see, hear, touch, taste, and smell. India is where you dip into yourself and the eighteen aggregates are dissolved."[116] Therefore in writing Kanthapura, he was not merely chronicling a political movement but providing a view of what the east and India stood for. Gandhian values were not merely political tools for achieving political ends but pristine Indian virtues with the power of transforming the entire human "Being". Thus Kanthapura "explores both the dimensions of the freedom struggle and Raja Rao's philosophical concerns with the Gandhian thought.- Non- Violence, Untouchability, Truth – and his fascination for Vedanta."[117]

India's struggle for independence which gained true momentum under the leadership of Gandhi, taking the country by storm, also impacted Raja Rao's literary sensibilities intensely, "His search for an appropriate narrative technique, suitable for the portrayal of Indian life, Indian sensibilities and his philosophical concerns begins with his first novel."[118] "Thus Kanthapura becomes an epic of freedom struggle, encompassing India's vastness within its artistic structure of a work of fiction especially the grand battles fought on the field of the villages, the role of the villages in freedom struggle has not, hitherto, been adequately appreciated by historians. It is a marvel of narrative technique, a

---

[113] Kaushal Sharma ,*Raja Rao: A Study of His Themes and Technique*, New Delhi, Sarup & Sons 2005.p.23,
[114] Ibid,, p, 22
[115] Ibid.,p. 25.
[116] Raja Rao, *The Serpent and the Rope*, New Delhi.Orient Paperbacks, 1968, p.389.
[117] Kaushal Sharma ,*Raja Rao: A Study of His Themes and Technique*, New Delhi, Sarup & Sons. 2005..p.8,
[118] Ibid.,p. 8.

blend of puranic style, symbols, myths, religious metaphor and linguistic experiments."[119]

Being a Brahmin and a deeply spiritual person, Raja Rao uses myths, legends, symbols and religious metaphors abundantly as literary devices, which enable the contextualization of mythical characters in a modern milieu making the narrative effective. Rao knew that "Indian people were very close to their myths and felt the inadequacy of the western model for portraying true Indian ethos and sensibility and thus resorts to traditional Indian form....Raja Rao emerges as the foremost exponent of the Puranic model of storytelling the oldest technique of narration"[120]

Narrating the "confrontation between the static archaic existence of a Hindu village and the historical reality of the present in the form of the Gandhian socio-political agitation, Rao manifests the Indian ethos which has always, "consistently attempted to perceive a historic fact, the existential reality of an individual life, in the mould of a set legend or myth so that the historical person may be annihilated in the archetype which is eternal."[121] "The use of the religious metaphor also helps Raja Rao's narrator to explain the subtleties of the freedom movement." [122] "For the illiterate villagers the contemporary problems like those of the freedom struggle can be explained through scriptures which form the psyche of the Indians. The appeal of these religious books has the efficacy to inspire the simple villagers to join the Satyagraha."[123]

Gandhi striving to liberate India was thus compared to Rama who "leaves his home, roams the length and breadth of India and passes his banished life,"[124] and one day would undoubtedly kill the "Ravana (Redman). As a reincarnation of Krishna, he would kill the poisonous snake Kaliya (the British government). When Gandhi leaves for the Second Round table Conference, the narrator comments, "They say that Mahatma will go to Redman's

---

[119] Ibid.,p. 25.
[120] Ibid.,p. 20.
[121] Esha Dey, *The Novels of Raja Rao, The Theme of Quest*. New Delhi. Prestige Books. 1992.p.26.
[122] Kaushal Sharma ,*Raja Rao: A Study of His Themes and Technique*, New Delhi, Sarup & Sons. 2005.p..22.
[123] Ibid., p. 23,
[124] Uday Shankar Ojha , "Gandhian Ideology: A Study of Raja Rao's *Kanthapura.*" in Rajeshwar Mittapalli &Pier Paolo Piciucco Ed. *The Fiction of Raja Rao, Critical Studies*, New Delhi: Atlantic Publishers, 2001.p.108.

country…he will get us Swarajya…come back with Sita on his right in a chariot of air."[125] Sita here is a symbol of freedom.

Kanthapura is an archetype Indian village peaceful, pious and traditional, with its own culture and history, were protected by "the tremendous and bounteous, legendary and timeless Goddess Kenchamma, people of various castes, crafts and ideologies reside. It follows the orthodox caste hierarchy with the high caste Brahmins the beneficiaries of the conventional socio-economic system at the top and the deprived and depressed pariah at the lowest rung of its social ladder.

Ungrudgingly the villagers carry on with their lives till initiated spiritually in his dream by Mahatma Gandhi. Moorthy, a young university dropout Brahmin lad, returns to his village Kanthapura, vowing to involve it in the freedom struggle and then sweeping the nation. Experiencing spiritual power and feeling blessed after receiving instructions in political ideology by Gandhi himself, Moorthy aptly states, "There is in it something of the silent communion of the ancient books." There is but one force…God of all."[126] So it is through Moorthy, the main protagonist, that Raja Rao tells the story of the rise and fall of Kanthapura, his own village Harihalli a sleepy Kannada hamlet, which symbolizes thousands of other villages of pre-independent India.

The theme of *Kanthapura* centres around the political domination of India and an open fight by the villagers, who are denied their human rights and dignity, to wake up from their slumber of slavery to overthrow the British yoke. The storm called Gandhi propels them towards their goals, who, according to Nehru was like, "a powerful current of fresh air…like the beam of light that pierced the darkness and removed the scales from our eyes, like a whirlwind that upset, many things but most of all the working of people's minds."[127]

Moorthy is a man of action. From organizing Harikathas or Jayantis to revolting against orthodox conventions, his village

---

[125] Raja Rao, *Kanthapura*, New Delhi, Orient Paperbacks. 1971. p.251.

[126] Raja Rao, *Kanthapura* ,New Delhi, Orient Paperbacks. 1971. pp.52-53

[127] Jawahar Lal Nehru, *The Discovery of India,* Bombay Asia Publishing House.1961..p. 358.

reforming activities eventually made him a role model for his people. A transformed Moorthy now faces the challenge of proving his efficiency as a leader at every step, unlike Ramaswamy of The Serpent and the Rope, a man of ideas. In sharp contrast to him is the city-bred young man Dore who neither clears his examination nor joins the freedom struggle.

Moorthy's pure and immaculate personality becomes an embodiment of the Gandhian virtues of love of mankind, non-violence, self sacrifice, truth, equality of castes and social harmony. Challenging Brahmin orthodoxy and British colonialism, Moorthy discards his western attire adopting *khadi* clothes. All his actions, movement and planning, are aimed at strengthening the Congress movement, which will enable the claimants of power – the followers of Gandhi to wrest their rights from the possessors of power, the anti-national British imperialist forces; who will understandably brutally suppress all such efforts. However, the villagers have nothing to fear since to redeem them through Moorthy, his replica, Gandhi, like Lord Krishna, has taken an *Avtar* or reincarnation, "Whensoever there is misery and ignorance, I come, For I, says Krishna, Am the defender of Dharma "[128] "Thus, as a God, Gandhi is endowed with the heavenly power of doing away with the so called enemies of freedom,"[129] and end the suffering of mankind.

Raja Rao has successfully demonstrated how religion which is an integral part of Indian life, mainly in rural India, is an effective medium for a social and political resurgence. Comparing it to Ignacio *Silone's Fontamamra,* Narasimhaiah points out, "The organized religion of Fontamara had, in contrast, alienated the sympathies of people; indeed had become a menace to life...."[130] Religion in Fontamara generates fear and does not establish affinity with people, whereas in *Kanthapura,* it touches almost all the villagers, becoming a substratum of their lives and cause.

---

[128] Inner title page, Raja Rao, *Kanthapura*, New Delhi, Orient Paperbacks. 1971..
[129]. Kaushal Sharma, *Raja Rao: A Study of His Themes and Technique*, New Delhi, Sarup & Sons. 2005..p.22
[130] C. D. Narsimhaiah quoted in Narsing Shrivastava : *The Mind and the Art of Raja Rao*, Prakash Book Depot, Bareilly (India), 1980 p. 48.

Moorthy, the pivot around which all the action revolves, stands testimony to this fact. A modern progressive and spiritual leader Moorthy, at times, becomes a *Bhakta Prahalad* (emphasis mine), a messiah of the pariah, a symbol of new life in Kanthapura and at other times … a valid symbol of Vedanta, stating, "There is but one force in life and that is Truth, and there is but one God in life and that is Love of mankind, and there is one God in Life and that is God of all."[131]

Inspired by Gandhi's selfless action, Moorthy staunchly believes that tremendous penance prepares one for better action. This preparation is the highest act of wisdom and the attainment of the most profound reality. Through meditation and yoga Moorthy comes closer to truth, realizing that he tells Seetharamu that by practising meditation, he would always experience divine grace: "Thoughts seemed to ebb away to the darkened shores and leave the illumined consciousness to rise up into the back of the brain. Light seemed to rise from the far horizon, converge and creep over hills and fields and trees, and rising up the Promontory, infuse itself through his very toes and fingertips and rise to the sun-centre of the heart."[132]

He recalls similar spiritual fervour from his childhood when seated by the river, with his mother washing clothes. He had closed his eyes and murmuring his prayers felt like child Prahlada who had said Hari was everywhere, and he said to himself, 'I shall see Hari, too'. In this dream, he also saw himself floating away, "like child Krishna on the Pipal leaf." from a flooded temple sanctum. Feeling light and airy he opened his eyes later to see an all-pervading brightness over a mountain top and cool, blue light spreading and entering his limbs. Every evening after this vision, he told his mother "now you can throw me down the mountains", and she asked, "Why, my son?" and he answered, "Why, mother," because Hari will fly down and hold me in arms, as I roll down the mountains…. for, Mother, I have seen Hari….. he had caught a

---

[131] Raja Rao: *Kanthapura*, New Delhi, Orient Paperbacks. 1971.p 161
[132] Ibid.,p. 92-94

little of that primordial radiance and through every breath more and more love seemed to pour out of him.[133]

Experiencing divine ecstasy again, he says, "I shall love even my enemies… The Mahatma says we would love even our enemies", and closing his eyes tighter, he slips back into the fold less sheath of the soul and sends out rays of love to the East, rays of love to the West, rays of love to the North, rays of love to the South, and love to the Earth below and the Sky above. He feels such exaltation creeping into his limbs and head that his heart begins to beat out a song, and the song of Kabir comes to his lips:

> The road to the city of Love is hard, brother, it is hard,
> Take care; take care, as you walk along it.

Singing this, his exaltation grows, and tears come to his eyes. Moreover, when he opens them to look round, a great blue radiance seems to fill the whole earth, and dazzled, he rises and falls before the God, chanting Sankara's 'Shivoham, Shivoham. I am Siva. I am Siva. Siva am I."[134]

Moorthy experiences the same childhood bliss after seeing Mahatma in his dream, for the novel presents Gandhi not in person but as a divine invisible force inspiring and guiding the people of Kanthapura.. Emulating Mahatma's ideals preached by the Gita, Moorthy and his followers consider Gandhi a reincarnation of Lord Krishna,"You remember how Krishna, when he was but a babe of four had begun to fight against the demons, and had killed the serpent Kali. So too our Mohandas began to fight against the enemy of the county."[135]

Gandhi's satyagraha is a religious ideal converted into action, purifying the subject by revealing the ultimate truths to him. Moorthy's religious consciousness makes him accept Satyagraha as a sacred religious ritual. He motivates people to participate in this observance for the liberation of the motherland. When Moorthy organizes a "Harikatha' in Kanthapura, the priest Pandit Jairamachar talks about Gandhi as a divine incarnation on this

---

[133] Ibid, pp.92-94
[134] Ibid.,p. 92-94
[135] Ibid. p.22

earth meant to destroy the evil forces and reinstate *Dharma* which is truth and righteousness. Mahatma's words, accepted as divine discourse, become the perfect means to self-purification and eventually attaining freedom.

Rao portrays religion as a dynamic force which propels the freedom struggle and how by transcending the self, a spiritually integrated person, through truth and non-violence, can selflessly serve his oppressed brethren. So even an economic activity like spinning becomes a religious act," To wear cloth spun and woven with your hands is sacred," says the Mahatma , and "spinning is as purifying as praying."[136]

From religious faith, the villagers derive the strength to fight the Britishers. "That is why religion and politics are interwoven in the novel. The importance of independence is delineated in a religious metaphor."[137] According to Narsimhaiah "the novel delineates the dynamic power of a living religious convention.....religion seems to sustain the spirits of the people of Kanthapura."[138] From daily invocation of the benevolent village Goddess Kenchamma to observing the various village festivals and participating in the Harikathas and Bhajans, religion is an integral part of the life of Kanthapurians.

Conventional mythology coincides with contemporary reality when lights are lit throughout Kanthapura because the villagers believe that in the auspicious month of Kartik, Gods walk on the lighted village streets crossing even the potters' and the weavers' quarters. So Satyagraha very quickly becomes another religious ceremony for the Kanthapurians, who observe it with intense sacred fervour. Rao regards the freedom struggle as a conflict between the divine and the devil. Iyengar aptly comments, "The reign of the Red man is Asuric rule, and it is raised by the Devas, the Satyagrahis. The characters sharply divide into two camps: The Rulers(and their supporters)on the one hand and the

---

[136] Esha Dey, *The Novels of Raja Rao, The Theme of Quest.* New Delhi. Prestige Books. 1992.p. 27.
[137] Uday Shankar Ojha , "Gandhian Ideology : A Study of Raja Rao's *Kanthapura."* *in* Rajeshwar Mittapalli &Pier Paolo Piciucco. Ed. *The Fiction of Raja Rao, Critical Studies,* New Delhi: Atlantic Publishers . 2001.p. 110.
[138] C.D. Narsimhaiah, *Raja Rao*, New Delhi, Arnold Heinemann, 1970 . p. 47.

Satyagrahis (and their sympathizers) on the other."[139] The villagers strongly feel that the battle of independence cannot be won without divine grace. So, "Temples are used to recruit members for the Congress, and they administer the oath of allegiance to the party and its ideologies particularly of Ahimsa, Love and Truth in the sanctum sanctorum."[140] Thus elevating the Gandhian movement to a mythological plane, Rao finally opines that Gandhi has been incarnated to free Mother India, the "Goddess of sapience and well-being, the enslaved daughter of Brahma from the bondage of foreigners."[141]

Following the Gandhian dictum before plunging into political action, Moorthy, a Brahmin, has to first purge himself from the hereditary supremacy of his caste and the fear of its pollution. So Moorthy denouncing untouchability begins interacting with the poor lower castes in the village and the half-naked and starving coolies of the neighbouring snake-infested British Skeffington Coffee Estate, who tolerate all kinds of humiliation because of poverty. The British overlords pick up their women for sexual gratification, and the fear of joblessness makes them accept even this disgrace. Moorthy preaches the Gandhian ideals to these have-nots, mingling, eating, spinning and fasting with them. Visiting the village elders from the most esteemed Range Gowda to weavers' Elder Ramayya and Potters' Elder Siddayya, he advises them, "One cannot become a member of the Congress if one will not promise to practice Ahimsa, and to speak truth and to spin at least two thousand yards per year."[142] Thus, all his moves aim to break the Brahmin British colonial nexus that conspires to oppress the downtrodden Indian further.

To uplift the lives of his village folk, he also teaches them the alphabet, Grammar, Arithmetic and Hindi. He focuses primarily on spinning, weaving and using Khadi as a means to economic self-sufficiency through cottage industries, which according to

---

[139] K,R,S. Iyengar, *Indian Writing in English,* New Delhi, 1962. p. 391
[140] Ibid.,p.23.
[141] Uday Shankar Ojha , "Gandhian Ideology : A Study of Raja Rao's *Kanthapura."* in Rajeshwar Mittapalli &Pier Paolo Piciucco. Ed. *The Fiction of Raja Rao, Critical Studies*, New Delhi: Atlantic Publishers, 2001.p.108.
[142], Raja Rao, *Kanthapura* ,New Delhi, Orient Paperbacks. 1971.. p. 103

Gandhi's vision, is a pre-requisite for removing foreign rule. Moorthy laments that "Our country is being bled to death by foreigners…(the village weavers) buy foreign yarn and foreign yarn is bought with some money and all this money goes across the ocean."[143] The producers cannot enjoy the fruits of their labour as, "There on the blue waters, so they say, our carted cardamoms and coffee get into the ships and no Redmen bring and, so they say, they go across the seventh oceans into the countries where our rulers lived."[144]

So Moorthy exhorts the villagers to stop this drain of money and resources, which could have fed and clothed the hungry and poor in their own country. "Both Gandhi and Marx held the opinion that the root of permanent happiness and prosperity lay in the improvement of economy. But they advocated different means to achieve this goal Marx stood for industrialization and use of machinery, whereas Gandhi advocates self- reliance and simple life."[145] He said, "Don't be attached to riches…for riches create passion, and passion create attachment and attachment hides the face of Truth."[146].

Moorthy, a true disciple of Gandhi, who has imbibed his spirit of selfless action detached from the fruits of their efforts, vociferously preaches Gandhian ideology of truth." Truth must you tell, he says, for truth is God and verily, it is the only God I know,"[147]This statement reinforces the message of Bhagavad Gita, which exhorts man to make truthfulness a part of his behaviour. So when Moorthy is charged with this "fire of Truth (satyagraha), even men of straw become heroic men of action, capable of embarking upon *nishkama-kriya*, or non-involved-dispassionate action for the sake of the action, of the kind Krishna enjoins upon doubting Arjuna in the Bhagavad-Gita."[148]

---

[143] Raja Rao, *Kanthapura* , Delhi, Hind.Pocket Books 1971..p,16.
[144] Raja Rao, *Kanthapura* ,New Delhi, Orient Paperbacks. 1971.p. 32
[145] Kaushal Sharma ,*Raja Rao: A Study of His Themes and Technique*, New Delhi, Sarup & Sons. 2005.p. 12.
[146] Raja Rao, *Kanthapura*, New Delhi, Orient Paperbacks. 1971.p.22
[147] Ibid.,p. 22.
[148] J.B.A Karkala, cited in, D.S. Maini. 1980. *Raja Rao's Vision, Value and Aesthetic*. in Sharma, K.K. (Ed.) Perspectives on Raja Rao. Delhi, Vimal Prakashan. p.81

Following non-violence, Moorthy explains, is to erase hatred from one's heart and love one's enemy. He preaches universal love to Ratna "The greatest enemy is in us. If only we could not hate, If only we would show fearless, calm affection towards our fellow men, we would be stronger."[149]   Before beginning his self-expiatory fast once, he tells Rangamma, "The fault of others, Rangamma, is the fruit of one's disharmony and silently he walks down the steps and walks up to the temple, where, seated beside the central pillar of the Mandap, he begins to meditate."[150] Then turning to himself, he says, "I shall love even my enemies."[151] For Gandhi says so, "Fight, says he but harm no soul. Love all says he, Hindu, Mohammedan, Christian or Pariahs, for all are equal before God."[152]

No wonder Seetharamu willingly accepts the torture of the British government, and Range Gowda abstains from settling violent scores with Puttayya for unjustly diverting all the canal water to his fields. When violence erupts in Kanthapura, and Rachanna's tormented wife cries, wondering what they should do, the Gandhian volunteer pacifies her thus, "Monsters, monsters, yes, they may be, but are we out to convert them, the Mahatma says we should convert them, and we shall convert them, our hearts shall convert them. Our will and our love will convert them. And now let us be silent for a while, and in prayer send out our love that no hatred may live within our breasts. And brothers and sisters, the battle, we will win…[153].

Rangamma, on the other hand, also motivates the Satyagrahis to face the police action fearlessly, "No, sister, the sword can spilt asunder the body, but never the soul ."[154] Not only the locals but even the freedom fighters that flock to Kanthapura from other parts of the country inspired by the same philosophy take the movement forward fearless of death. .

---

[149] Raja Rao, *Kanthapura* ,New Delhi, Orient Paperbacks. 1971.. p. 96
[150] Ibid., p. 92.
[151] Ibid., p 22
[152] Ibid.,p.22
[153] Ibid..p. 170
[154] Ibid.,p. 153.

Thus from initial hesitation to final conversion, Moorthy's following grows, and villagers learn and emulate his ways. In his short leadership, he is venerated as the village Gandhi for his compassion and concern and his portrait is hung in every household. He is no longer a mouthpiece broadcasting his master's voice but a real character with an authentic voice. He is Gandhi personified and therefore accepted as a universal leader of his worth. Range Gowda fervently says, "You are our Gandhi, and ignoring people?" chuckles and continues, "There is nothing to laugh at, brothers. He is our Gandhi."[155] Despite earning the epithet of the Village Mahatma, Moorthy is human enough to understand and be understood by the villagers.

Like Gandhi, Moorthy sacrifices all his pleasures, even his silent and secret love for Ratna, "She seemed something so feminine and soft and distant, and the idea that he could ever think of her other than as a sister shocked him and sent a shiver down his spine. But Ratna looked at him sadly and shyly and whispered, 'Is there anything I can do?' and Moorthy answered, "Pray with me that the sins of others may be purified with our prayers."[156]

Moorthy an incorruptible man, an ideal leader, and a selfless individual, has numerous admirers and detractors. The city-advocate Sankar fondly states "I love him like a brother, and I have found no better Gandhist" Rangamma remarks, "Why, he is the saint of our village?"[157] Moorthy was undoubtedly, "A brave soul and a holy soul,"[158] hankering for the divine truth. Goldsmith Nanjudia comments, "Oh let them do what they like. Our Moorthy is like gold – the more you heat, purer it comes from crucible."[159] Cajoled by the city advocate and devout Congress leader Sankar, Rangamma is overwhelmed by talking about, "Moorthy the good, Moorthy the religious, and Moorthy the noble and she had found no more words, as she had come down from the platform, and begun to shiver and tears had come into her eyes."[160]

---

[155]Ibid.p.109
[156] Ibid., pp. 94-95
[157] Ibid. p. 135.
[158] Ibid., P. 125
[159] Ibid., p. 136
[160] Ibid., pp. 144-45

However, Moorthy faces stiff opposition from the orthodox upper castes represented by the premier Brahmin moneylender Bhatta and the foreign authority invested in police officer Bade Khan. Even narrator Achakka belonging to a Brahmin family, laments, "He even goes to the Potters' quarter and the Weavers' quarter and the Sudra quarter, and I closed my ears when I heard he went to the pariah quarter. We said to ourselves he is one of these Gandhimen, who say there is neither caste nor clan nor family and yet they pray like us and they live like us. Only they say, too, one should not marry early, one should allow widows to take husbands and a Brahmin might marry a pariah and a pariah a Brahmin. Well, well, let them say it how does it effect us? We shall be dead before the world is polluted. We shall have closed our eyes."[161]

The village high priest Swami vested with religious authority, instantly excommunicates Moorthy. Unfazed, he established the Congress Committee of Kanthapura, which became a part of the All India Panchayat - a territory ruled by a parallel government. Bhatta begins to charge high-interest rates of eighteen to twenty per cent on credit given to Congress members, who can ill afford to pay it. Arrested for seditious activities, Moorthy is sent to jail, but on his release, he motivates his followers to now join the mainstream of the freedom struggle, the civil disobedience movement.

Under the leadership of Moorthy, the villagers followed the national agenda of prohibition by picketing toddy fields and shops, burning foreign clothes, opposing British laws, establishing a parallel government and refusing to pay taxes levied deliberately to punish the rebellious. Like everywhere else in India, the *satyagrahis* of Kanthapura give a tough fight to the British government and are completely unstoppable, "But the volunteers go on, Yes, sister, yes, the Government is afraid of us , for in Karwar the courts are closed and the banks closed and the Collector never goes out."[162]

---

[161] Raja Rao, *Kanthapura* , Delhi, Hind Pocket Books. 1971.. p. 9
[162] Raja Rao, *Kanthapura* , New Delhi, Orient Paperbacks. 1971. p 228.

The slogans *Vande Mataram, Inquilab Zindabad, Mahatma Gandhi Ki Jai* reverberate in the air constantly. The jubilant crowds sing and dance, "Lift the flag high, O lift the flag high, Brothers, sisters, friends and mothers, This is the flag of the revolution." The mere presence of Moorthy in all these activities and the involvement of the entire village provoke the British government no end and Moorthy is arrested and sent to Karwar jail. Hereafter the women Rangamma and Ratna spearhead the movement further.

The furious British Government pours extra police force into the village, violently suppressing all freedom activities, inflicting great physical atrocities, killings and attachment of properties. Giving up passive resistance, the Satyagrahis also retaliate most aggressively in revenge by showering dung, slippers and broomsticks, pelting stones and burning houses, mainly of Bhatta, the exploiter of the poor. In the climax, there is extreme violence where a "hand to hand fight" ensues, revealing great hatred and animosity, "men grip men and men crush men and men bite men and men tear men."[163] As the Gandhi Irwin pact is signed, the agitation is called off. However, the very identity of Kanthapura is effaced forever by the British, who unleash severe penal action by auctioning all of Kanthapura's land to wealthy outsiders. Having ultimately sacrificed their assets and lives, only those who survive death and destruction, primarily middle-aged widows, take refuge in the neighbouring village Kashipura to begin life afresh.

Moorthy, utterly disillusioned with the fate of Kanthapura and Gandhian ideology, says "have faith in your enemy, he (Gandhi) says, have faith in him and convert him. But the world of men is hard to move and once in motion it is wrong to stop till the goal is reached."[164] Moorthy joined the socialist camp with his followers, but not without planting the seed of nationalism, which eventually flowered into the tree of Indian independence in 1947. Gandhian ideologies stood the test of time. His experiments with

---

[163] Raja Rao quoted in Esha Dey, *The Novels of Raja Rao, The Theme of Quest*. New Delhi. Prestige Books. 1992..p. 29
[164] Ibid., p. 31.

truth have inspired thousands of little Gandhis across the country, whose selfless actions changed the destiny of India forever.

Dey, and other critics, feel that the story fizzles out towards the end, as the mythical and realistic clash, trying to negate each other, "This sharp juxtaposition of the historic reality of vindictive violence and the ideal of non-violence and love indicates the deep gulf that separates the mythical category of action, where such blatant contradiction is unthinkable and the concrete existential reality which is always a web of human complexities."[165]

The reason they advnce is that "living thousands of miles away not even a spectator to those happenings a verisimilitude of which he seeks to present", Rao is alienated from the "actual scene of action and therefore from the interrelated problems of the contemporary Indian reality….. Therefore his "telling" belongs to a mythical plane, and the historical theme gets lost in generalized abstraction, a contradiction in itself and a deviation from the literary convention that he has adopted earlier that of detailing, concretization and firm focus." [166]

Although this criticism is valid in so far as Raja Rao's writing was influenced by his diasporic vantage, however, Srivastava puts up a strong defence. Eulogizing the idea of selfless action in Kanthapura, he says, "But an intelligent reader interested in the plot and also conscious of the aesthetic demands of its structure will understand that whatever was needed for winning the freedom has been done; the sacrificial fire is lit and yajna performed. Nothing is tragic on the altar of the Goddess Liberty; everything is a sacrificial offering or worship. We have to bear in mind always that *Kanthapura* is a novel of selfless action, and that is why it ends with action and not with the fruit thereof. This idea of the Gita can be befitting motto of this novel. The lasting effect of *Kanthapura* emerges as much as out of the powerful depiction of the suppressions and exploitation of a foreign rule, which sought to rob Indians of their humanity, as out of the vivid portrayal of

---

[165] Esha Dey, *The Novels of Raja Rao, The Theme of Quest.* New Delhi. Prestige Books. 1992..p.29
[166] Ibid.,p.39.

characters as these freedom fighter represent the group will – the unified will of a nation, struggling to change their condition and be master of their own destiny. The will of the leaders identified with the will of the people in a mass movement, does not represent the will to endurance and survival at the physical and material planes alone; their fight is for total deliverance."[167]

Pallan too is enamoured with Rao's narrative and presents an interesting analysis, "The end of novel is like the end of *kaliyuga* with the *pralaya* or inundation engulfing the whole village. All the villagers leave Kanthapura to settle in Kashipura. Range Gowda, the onetime head of the village, goes to Kanthapura only to find "there is neither man nor mosquito in Kanthapura." This is undoubtedly a change from one *yuga* cradling into another, and *pralaya* indicates the end of cyclical civilization, and the preparation for the new beginning and the trumpet call of change."[168]

Showcasing Indian ethos, Kanthapura thus presents a realistic model of national resurgence, where political revolution and social renaissance combine on the rural stage to make a unified whole," It was a challenging task for Raja Rao to portray the power of Gandhi's weapons like self reliance, moral resistance , perseverance, through the story of a village."[169] His aim was to emphasize the fact that India is a country of villages and in the deliverance of the villages lies the strength of the nation. "Our villages provide a basic pattern easily discernible all over India…Kanthapura is thus any village in India, India in microcosm."[170] Mukherjee is in support suggesting, " it is therefore in the rural context that the regional reality and the Indian reality more or less merge."[171]

---

[167] Narsingh Shrivastava: *The Mind and the Art of Raja Rao*, Prakash Book Depot , Bareilly (India), 1980, pp. 46-47

[168] Rajesh, K. Pallan. *Myths and Symbols in Raaj Rao and R.K.Narayan*, Jalandhar , ABS Publications, 1994.p.37

[169] Kaushal Sharma ,*Raja Rao: A Study of His Themes and Technique*, New Delhi, Sarup & Sons. 2005. p.12.

[170] Thomas Augustine, "The Village in Raja Rao's *Kanthapura."* in Rajeshwar Mittapalli &Pier Paolo Piciucco. Ed. *The Fiction of Raja Rao, Critical Studies*, New Delhi: Atlantic Publishers, 2001.p.104.

[171] Meenakshi Mukherjee, *The Twice-Born Fiction :Themes and Techniques of the Indian Novel in English*, New Delhi: Arnold Heinemann. 1971, p. 213

Writing the *sthala purana* or legendary history which describes the local significance of a place is an ancient Indian style of chronicling. In this the theme is both mythic and realistic and "the past mingles with the present, and the gods mingle with men" to create the narrative."[172] "Through Kanthapura Rao tries to integrate into his consciousness of the past tradition, his present experience in time,"[173] projecting his vision of the future, hoping that someday his story would become the legendary history of India. The village moving from a static archaic existence to a national awakening and complete annihilation becomes a significant and powerful symbol of political regeneration.

Rao's portrayal of the life and times of Kanthapura is exceptionally vivid, "much of the early part of the book is spent developing a sense of the village itself, establishing its ambience."[174] ... "and the illumination details of the village life, the description of the houses and quarters, the scenic details, the cattle, the annual ceremony of the first ploughing of the fields, the Harikathas and Jayantis and the organizational activities of the women-folk add flesh to it. In *Kanthapura*, Raja Rao has created a veritable Sthala Purana – a legendary history out of the Indian life in the pre-independence era."[175] He divides the village into two mutually exclusive spaces - one the traditional closed social order of Kanthapura and the other enclosed colonial space of the Skeffington Coffee Estate on its outskirts. Kanthapura which represents an archetype colonial Indian village is "unsettled, dynamic, disruptive and dislocating,"[176]

Within this island of misery, Rao creates an oasis – a present and different centre for historical action as opposed to the past and orthodox authority of the Kenchamma temple and the colonial authority of the law courts. Built only three years ago in the middle of the village, Kanthapurishwari temple becomes the

---

[172] Foreword to Raja Rao, *Kanthapura*, New Delhi, Orient Paperbacks. 1971. p. 6.

[173] Esha Dey, *The Novels of Raja Rao, The Theme of Quest*. New Delhi. Prestige Books. 1992..p.25.

[174] Thomas Augustine, "The Village in Raja Rao's *Kanthapura*" in Rajeshwar Mittapalli &Pier Paolo Piciucco. Ed. *The Fiction of Raja Rao, Critical Studies*, New Delhi: Atlantic Publishers , 2001.p. 96

[175] Quoted in Niranjan Rout, The Fictional Work of Raja Rao: A Study of his Mind and Art, Ph.D. Thesis. Magadh University. 1995

[176] Anshuman Mondal, "The Ideology of Space in Raja Rao's *Kanthapura.*" in *Journal Of Commonwealth Literature* ,Vol.34.No.1, 1999,pp. 104.

hub for the "introduction and dissemination of Gandhian thought
…..the scene of crucial happenings."[177] Its presiding deity is the
three eyed Shiva whom Harikatha man Jayaramachar compares
with freedom, "Swaraj too is three eyed, self-purification, Hindu
Moslem unity, Khaddar."[178] Mondal aptly suggests, "it is also
significant that the temple is dedicated to an all Indian deity such
as Shiva rather than to a local deity Kenchamma, whose powers, it
appears have only a limited locally specific purpose…such a
goddess is clearly an unsuitable figurehead for the nation."[179]

Raja Rao exhibited India's resilience when Kanthapura
was purged from its orthodoxy by the exposure of Swami, the death
of Ramkrishnayya, the custodian and interpreter of orthodox texts,
and the departure of moneylender Bhatta, symbolizing the colonial
oppression, becomes a secular space as distinguished from the
colonial space of the Skeffington Coffee Estate. It becomes in
effect, an "incipient Gandhian space," where the "next chapter
opens with a significant alteration in social relations as for the first
time even the women take it upon themselves to be custodians and
interpreters of the sacred texts…The new era is consummated by
the villagers' commitment to Gandhism."[180]

The village *Kanthapura* has a parallel in Ignacio Silone's
Fontamara.. Both the authors, the sons of the soil, using an alien
language but native idiom, narrate the story of the complete
annihilation of their villages by tyrannical forces. In the
Fontamara, "the viewpoint of the writer is that of socialist and an
anti-fascist, in Kanthapura it is that of a deeply religious man and
an anti-imperialist."[181] In the Italian novel, people defend
themselves from oppressive fascist forces but in Kanthapura the
freedom struggle inspires people to sacrifice and selfless action.
Naik points out the differences thus, "Fontamara is a story of
exploitation of the poor by the rich as seen through the eyes of anti-

---

[177] Esha Dey, *The Novels of Raja Rao,* New Delhi: Prestige Books , 1992. P. 32
[178] Raja Rao, *Kanthapura* , Delhi, Hind Pocket Books. 1971..p. 10
[179] Anshuman Mondal, "The Ideology of Space in Raja Rao's *Kanthapura.*" in *Journal Of Commonwealth Literature.,*Vol. 34. No.1, 1999,pp. 106.
[180] Ibid.,p.112.
[181] Thomas Augustine, "The Village in Raja Rao's *Kanthapura.*" in Rajeshwar Mittapalli &Pier Paolo Piciucco. Ed. *The Fiction of Raja Rao, Critical Studies*, New Delhi: Atlantic Publishers , 2001.p. 103.

Fascists and socialists of the 1930s, *Kanthapura* is an account of the renaissance of Indian spiritual life under the impact of the Independence movement."[182]

Raja Rao next upholds another unique aspect of Indian culture, the Indian Feminine principle, which considers women to be the primordial energy. The Village Protector, therefore, is a female divinity Goddess Kenchamma the destroyer of a demon, who demanded young sons as food and young women as wives from the village. The inhabitants of Kanthapura are eternally grateful to her… "Thank heaven, not only did she slay the demon, but she even settled down among us, and this much I shall say, never has she failed us in our grief."[183] Infused with this divine strength, hundreds of village women rise to confront the alien oppressor. This also includes Achhaka of the "Veda Shastra Pravina Krishna Shastri's family"[184] who "taught to uphold the rigid caste system, initially criticizes Moorthy for mixing with the pariahs "Of course you won't expect me to go to the pariah quarters."[185]

Impressed by Moorthy later, she joins the freedom struggle led by pariah women Rangamma and Ratna. Nameless and countless other women become active members of the Congress, spinning the *Charkha* and playing an influential role in bringing social harmony to Kanthapura. Out to destroy the local toddy business, asking people to give up drinking in the name of the Mahatma, they risk their lives to police action. Seeing their womenfolk insulted, the men stop selling toddy. This step exhibits that the women had emerged as leaders taking the freedom struggle forward, especially when Moorthy goes to jail.

Achakka symbolizing the wise old grandmother, is also assigned the critical role of a witness narrator because she is "gifted with a rare insight, intelligence and a sense of discrimination and thus can comprehend the importance of the Satyagraha and the

---

[182] Narsingh Shrivastava: *The Mind and the Art of Raja Rao,* Prakash Book Depot , Bareilly (India), 1980. p.48
[183] Raja Rao, *Kanthapura* , Delhi, Hind Pocket Books. 1971..p.2.
[184] Ibid.p. 12
[185] Ibid.,p. 5

different characters of the village."[186] Despite of her age she is a progressive, practical and considerate woman, who has weathered many storms in life. She is therefore not critical of widow Ratna adorning herself with bangles and collyrium, leaning towards Moorthy or interacting freely with other men. One of the survivors of the carnage, a symbol of rebirth and regeneration, she objectively tells the tale of this village, where the drama of political revolution, social emancipation and economic self-reliance were enacted simultaneously.

Indian tradition reveals an intricate bond between Man and Nature which symbolizes God. Therefore Raja Rao not only describes all "human expression, attitudes ….in terms of forces of nature,"[187] but considers all natural elements as divine symbols. Thus according to Naik "the promontory near the village is an 'abode of Siva', and the river Himavathy is the daughter of Kenchamma, the Goddess of the Hill. Animal creation too shares this divinity in its own way; the eagle is the 'feature of God' and the vehicle of Kenchamma must appear in the sky at the ploughing ceremony so that the Kanthapurians can be assured that the Goddess has blessed their first agricultural operations for the year."[188] He even describes the Gandhian influence in these terms "There is something that has entered our hearts, an abundance like the Himavathy on Gauri's night; when lights come floating down the Rampur corner."[189]

What Raja Rao is essentially trying to show is that," the ceaseless and regular operation of forces of nature is itself an external manifestation of the divine moral law that governs the universe….it is precisely because of this noble nexus that there is perfect empathy between man and external Nature including the animal creation."[190]

Describing the natural beauty and picturesque landscape of Kanthapura, he shows the free villagers revelling in the Vaisakha

---

[186]. Kaushal Sharma ,*Raja Rao: A Study of His Themes and Technique*, New Delhi, Sarup & Sons. 2005.p.17.

[187] Thomas Augustine, "The Village in Raja Rao's *Kanthapura.*" in Rajeshwar Mittapalli &Pier Paolo Piciucco. Ed. *The Fiction of Raja Rao, Critical Studies*, New Delhi: Atlantic Publishers , 2001.p.102

[188] M.K.Naik.*Studies in Indian English Literature*, New Delhi: Sterling Publishers Pvt. Ltd.,1987, p.36.

[189] Raja Rao, *Kanthapura* , Delhi, Hind Pocket Books. 1971.p. 256

[190] M.K.Naik. *Studies in Indian English Literature*, New Delhi: Sterling Publishers Pvt. Ltd.,1987, p.36.

rains, "The rains have come, the fine first footing rains that skip over the bronze mountains, tiptoe the crags, and leaping into the valleys, go splashing and the wind swung, a winnowed pour, and the coconuts and the betel-nuts and the cardamom plants choke with it and hiss back……and people leave their querns and rush to the courtyard, and turning towards Kenchamma temple send forth a prayer saying," There, there, the rains have come, Kenchamma, may our house be as white as silver."[191] The bonded labourers of the Coffee Estate, however, do not welcome it at all, "The darkness grows thick as sugar in a cauldron, while the bamboo creak and sway and whine, and the crows begin to wheel round and flutter and everywhere dogs bark and calves moo, and then the winds come so swift and dashing that it takes the autumn leaves with it, and they rise into the juggling air, while the trees bleat and blubber. Then drops fall…."[192]

Rao has an open mind, and he, therefore, exposes the decadence of the Indian social structure. Convinced about the inherent simplicity and dedication of the average Indian villager, he still does not abstain from exposing their weaknesses, inhibitions, prejudices and material cravings symbolized by Advocate Seenappa, Venkamma, the Chetty brothers. He does not spare Bhatta at all, knowing how much ill-begotten wealth he has amassed in his coffers," He knows how much there is in it. Something around three hundred and fifty rupees. Already a little gone; just ten rupees for Rampura Mala. Nuptial ceremony of some sort, Six per cent interest, and payable in two months."[193].

Realizing how the traditional dowry system oppresses the deprived further, he comments, "And he was telling me how he could find no one for his last granddaughter. No one. Every fellow with matric or inter asks, "What dowry do you offer ? How far will you finance my studies? I want to have this degree and that degree."[194]

---

[191] Raja Rao, *Kanthapura*, Delhi, Hind Pocket Books. 1971.p. 157
[192] Ibid.,p. 76.
[193] Ibid.,p.32
[194] Ibid.,p. 37

The writing was a spiritual exercise for Rao, not meant only to depict the socio-political atmosphere of the nation. So *"Kanthapura* is also an extended metaphor for the search of the author for a Guru."[195] Singh aptly states, "By the end of the novel *(Kanthapura),* it is clear that the novelist Raja Rao shifted his faith from Gandhi to Nehru, from the spiritual to the political leader. This search for a Guru, i.e., a preceptor continued even after *Kanthapura*…. After loitering all over the globe and coming to know from his experiences what life means in the East and the West, he realised that Nirvana is not possible without a Guru. In Mundak Upanishad, it is said, if "I would know the eternal, I would humbly approach a Guru devoted to a Brahmin. In *Kanthapura,* Moorthy had seen a vision of Mahatma Gandhi and accepted him initially as his Guru following him ungrudgingly. By the novel's end he had seen the futility of following that path of truth and non-violence, if his aim was to make people economically and politically happy."[196]

The Gandhian theme has been taken up by other contemporary Indo-Anglian novelists including Mulk Raj Anand and R.K. Narayan. In *Waiting for the Mahatma,* R. K. Narayan's portrayal of Gandhi is too ironic. In Mulk Raj Anand's novels, The *Untouchable, The Sword and The Sickle*, Gandhi preaches truth and non-violence to the disgruntled protagonists Bakha and Lal Singh. Neither is convinced, the former charting his course of action to salvage his people, the latter surrendering to Gandhi only because he was a respectable and wise older man.

Only Moorthy, tremendously influenced by Gandhi, emerged as an ideal selfless leader or *Satyagrahi.* In Moorthy, the author has created an extraordinary character, a cut above the rest, destined to perform unusual feats in a national crisis. Moorthy dreams of the Mahatma and receives initiation by him in his vision. "Thus Raja Rao creates an extraordinary situation to prove the

[195] Singh, R.S. *Raja Rao's Kanthapura An Analysis*, Delhi. Doaba House, 1977, p. 74.
[196] Ibid.,p. 74

extraordinariness of his character making this powerful vision appear as a real experience."[197]

Moorthy's name conveys that he is a perfect replica of Gandhi, and Gandhi's pervasive influence enlivens and overpowers his entire life and, through him, the humble freedom fighters of Kanthapura completely. This character is more significant than life and real. Forester rightly says that in a novel, the character becomes real when the novelist knows everything about it. So Moorthy's life is an open book. Refusing to enter matrimony or taking up a regular job, continuous fasting and meditation for self-purification and strength, each action of such a person is evident and amounts to self-sacrifice. No wonder such people become martyrs after death and thereby immortal.

Thus *Kanthapura's* unique narrative presents the independence struggle in a unique manner through a unique character of an ordinary Indian village. However, Rout argues that "an in depth analysis of the mental, emotional and spiritual conflicts of the characters is lacking severely"[198] Probably, total dedication to a cause leaves no scope for dilemmas of the mind or the heart.

The novel exhibits India's resilience which has the spiritual tenacity to recreate itself. Even in its annihilation, having shaken off its decadence, it holds out hope exhibiting the never say die spirit of the Indian ethos. Sharma concurs that the "total destruction of Kanthapura towards the end of the novel is symbolic of new life emerging out of the dead one. Just as a new phoenix arises out of holy ashes of the burnt one, Kashipura becomes new one. It is a purgatorial process that gives a new life."[199] Charles Larson holds a similar view," the time is propitious, the culture has been renewed, things will never be as they were. The pessimism that has for so long been a controlling factor in Third World fiction has begun to shift towards optimism. Cultural renewal can only

---

[197] Quoted in Niranjan Rout, The Fictional Work of Raja Rao: A Study of his Mind and Art, Ph.D. Thesis. Magadh University. 1995

[198] Quoted in Niranjan Rout, The Fictional Work of Raja Rao: A Study of his Mind and Art, Ph.D. Thesis.Magadh University. 1995.

[199] Kaushal Sharma ,Raja Rao: *A Study of His Themes and Technique*, New Delhi, Sarup & Sons. 2005.p.24.

begin within the culture itself, from within its basic foundations: the village and the family."[200]

Thus "Raja Rao's first novel *Kanthapura* shows him in complete mastery of the various aspects of the novel as a form of art. Never again since this masterpiece of Indo-Anglian fiction on the theme of Indian struggle for freedom has been able to recapture the perfect harmony of plot, character, dialogue and narrative on the one hand and fantasy and realism on the other."[201] Narasimhaiah points out the other uniqueness of Kanthapura. "The novel is a landmark in the history of Indian fiction in English, as it points to a definite stage in the formation of an Indian style of writing in English."[202]

"The novel most artistically and realistically captures the social and political milieu of India during the stirring days from 1919 to 1930. It was during this period that Gandhi transformed the entire nation into an army of disciplined and non-violent freedom fighters,"[203] who like Rao believed in united action, "A cock does not make a morning, nor a single man a revolution, but we'll build a thousand-pillared temple, a temple more firm than any that hath yet been built, and each one of you be ye pillars in it, and when the temple is built; stone by stone, and man by man, and the bell hung to the roof and the Eagle-tower shaped and planted, we shall invoke the Mother to reside with us in dream and in life, India then will live in a temple of our making."[204]

With this vision, Raja Rao began his literary journey of writing the much celebrated Gandhi Purana, conveying his Indian ethos. The political conflict displayed on the surface had a philosophical basis for its action. The novel revealed the intrinsic collusion between materialistic and spiritualistic forces of oppression and emancipation. Following the metaphysical philosophy, the East-West confrontation is resolved through

---

[200] Charles.R.Larson, *The Novel in the Third World*, Washington DC INSCAPE Publishers, 1976, p.142-143

[201] Quoted in Niranjan Rout, *The Fictional Work of Raja Rao: A Study of his Mind and Art*, Ph.D. Thesis. Magadh University. 1995

[202] Quoted in Mallikarjun Patil, "*Kanthapura* :A Portrait of Village Gandhi." in Rajeshwar Mittapalli &Pier Paolo Piciucco Ed. *The Fiction of Raja Rao, Critical Studies*,New Delhi: Atlantic Publishers , 2001.p.112.

[203] Kaushal Sharma,*Raja Rao: A Study of His Themes and Technique*, New Delhi, Sarup & Sons. 2005.p.9.

[204] Raja Rao: *Kanthapura*, New Delhi, Orient Paperbacks. 1971.p. 170

Gandhian ideas and ideals which aim to convert the materialistic west to the eastern philosophy of truth, sacrifice, tolerance, non-violence and universal love. There is no explicit spiritual quest in *Kanthapura*, yet the philosophy of Karma with no expectation of the results derived from the Bhagavad Gita, which inspires all action, is the message of the spiritual East to the Imperialistic West. Nishkama Karma, or selfless action, is the most significant source of deliverance from this mortal life.

"Raja Rao's quest for meaning and his vision of life are fundamentally based on the philosophical tenets of Vedanta as summed up in the Bhagavad Gita. Beginning with Kanthapura, he initiates his quest of the Absolute, which is essential for him, and each of his works moves him further towards realising that truth. Raja Rao, as a grand interpreter between India and the West, wants to make it evident that the real India stands for the highest spiritual value of life- the realization or the redemption of self described as Moksha or Nirvana."

CHAPTER IV: The Discovery of Self

In his magnum opus, the *Serpent and the Rope,* through the themes of love, sex, marriage and death, Raja Rao repeatedly contrasts the western and eastern attitudes by juxtaposing the visual illusion (serpent) and invisible reality (rope). The novel's theme is that valid marriage should lead to the quest for the knowledge of the self and the realization of the eternal self. Raja Rao deals with cultural rites, religious beliefs, intellectual convictions and spirituality, all of which constitute our inner consciousness. *The Serpent and The Rope* is effectively a paranormal novel and Raja Rao the novelist is essentially a metaphysical poet suggests William Walsh[205]. Unlike *Kanthapura* and *The Cow of the Barricades*, where the treatment of this theme is mainly political, the external plane of life, in *The Serpent and the Rope the* East-West phenomena is explained in the context of Indian advaitic philosophy.

Perhaps, through this greatest metaphysical novel ever written in the English language, Raja Rao conveys his idea of the impersonal absolute, using rich Indian mythology, history and culture. M.K. Naik suggests pertinently that *The Serpent and the Rope* " is a highly complex and many-sided work of art, being at once the tragic story of marriage which drifts apart; the spiritual biography of a learned, sensitive and imaginative modern Indian intellectual – a saga of his quest for self-knowledge and self-fulfillment, a memorable statement of the prime value of both the East and the West and a drama enacting their impact on each other; a sustained piece of symbolism and recreation of a valuable ancient Hindu myth; and a conscious attempt both to create a truly Indian novel with its root firmly embedded in native tradition to forge an Indian English style through which alone could its complex vision be authentically and adequately presented." [206]

The novel aims to establish the truth from untruth. The rope signifies reality, and the serpent illusion. The rope appears as

---

[205] William Walsh, *Commonwealth Literature*, London, Oxford University Press.1973, p. 10
[206] M.K. Naik,, *Raja Rao* , Twayne's English Author Series. New York: Twayne, Publishers,1972 p.76-77

a snake because of illusion, but when the illusion vanishes, there is no snake. The rope appears to be a snake only because of ignorance. Since the truth or the reality is projected through Ramaswamy's illuminating ideas after his sojourn in the west, it is essential to unravel his character before analyzing the novel.

Ramaswamy is an ordinary man endowed with an extraordinary mind. As an ordinary man, he is besieged by sensuousness and emotions, but philosophical idealism and psychological detachment characterize his extraordinary mind. He knows the truth, yet suppressed by illusion; he yearns "There must be a way out, Lord, a way out of this circle of life, rain, sunshine, autumn, snow, heat, and the rain once more , in gentle flower like ripples on the Ganges."[207]

This dilemma is not of Ramaswamy alone. It torments every seeker of truth at the initial stage. The knowledge of the truth or the real confronts the fascination for the untruth or the unreal throughout the novel. This truth forms the starting point of the spiritual quest. From his metaphysical understanding, the intellectual Ramaswamy derives his detached and impersonal attitude, which appears to Shepherd as "passivity in ordinary affairs."[208] This is not true. Rama is an average worldly man with typical desires. His sensibilities are essentially Indian. Like a true Brahmin, he chants the Gayatri mantra daily, and a dip in the Ganges always makes him feel very pure. He performs rituals by the force of tradition, realizing their futility.

He loves India and nurtures the ambition of returning home with Madeleine after completing his doctorate and settling down as a Professor at any Indian University. Attracted by the feminine principle, his sensual and romantic escapades with Lakshmi, his fascination for Savithri and his profound and ardent love for his wife Madeleine reveal his emotions and passions. As a family man who shoulders domestic and social responsibilities, he performs his father's last rites in Banaras and even pours oblations

---

[207] Raja Rao,. *The Serpent and the Rope*. New Delhi. Orient Paperbacks.1968 p. 234.
[208] Quoted by Narsingh Srivastava: *The Mind and the Art of Raja Rao*, Prakash Book Depot. Bareilly (India),1980. p.60

in the Ganga for his dead son Pierre. He performs all ceremonies for his sister's marriage as well. According to Madeleine "What really alienates him from the common man is his strange mind making him "one person in ten million."[209]

Ramaswamy is born in a country where there is a fundamental unity amid apparent diversity. It is a land of contradictions where on the Ghats of Banaras, one can see funerals, marriage processions, and the worship of Gods alongside prostitutes soliciting clients. Hinduism is a way of life in this ancient land, and people like their ancestors still seek metaphysical solutions to their problems. Adapting and assimilating Western influences, this land of learning and wisdom maintains continuity with its religious and traditional past. Ramaswamy traces his lineage from famous philosophers like Yajnavalkya, Sankara, Madhava, Vidyaranya Swami and other sages and thinkers who wandered in quest of self-knowledge and self-realization.

Indian philosophy considers life as *Maya* or illusion and each human being a soul on a solitary journey of self- realization, seeking release or *Moksha* from the cycle of birth, death and rebirth. Indians take life seriously, and the truth of human existence imparts them a sense of detachment from worldly affairs. Misunderstood as a sad and melancholic race, Madeleine asks Ramaswamy why there is such acute sorrow behind his laughter. Yearning to listen to some stupid innocent laughter, she tells Ramaswamy that she is not as severe as him, and one day, she may just run away.

Thus what the West calls sorrow is the introspective detachment of the East, oriented towards transcending the self and becoming one with the Creator. This element is an inborn quality of Ramaswamy's intellectual mind, though not perfect from the beginning. Ramaswamy's initiation into theology was quite early. By the time he was four, he had started studying Hindu scriptures like the Brahma Sutras, the Upanishads, and Sanskrit Grammar. Like Raja Rao, his creator, Ramaswamy's inquisitive mind discovered hidden meanings in all objects. He was curious to know

---

[209] Raja Rao: *The Serpent and the Rope*, Delhi, Hind Pocket Books, 1968, p. 28

the meaning of death from the very beginning of his life. Lamenting the death of his mother and grandfather's favourite horse, he exclaims:

> Who is it that tells me they did not die? Who but me....
> ?
> And if they've died, I ask you, where indeed they go?
> Where is Sundar now? Where?
> For I cannot understand what death means.[210]

His character is such a quaint mix of wisdom and innocence that Madeleine observes him as "either a thousand years old or three..." and "he cannot do anything wrong, for he is either so wise or so innocent."[211] He strives to understand the principles of his religion, which later motivates him to find the truth about other religions. No wonder his grandfather says: "I like the way, you go about thinking on the more serious thing of Vedanta."[212] Accompanying his widowed stepmother on pilgrimages adds to his profound understanding of things making him more mature. This external exposure leads to varied experiences, and a constant influx of novel ideas and feelings makes him realize the importance of lasting human values and principles. Like an honest seeker of truth, he reaches that level of spiritual progress where he understands the truth but has yet not realized it entirely within himself. His authentic impersonal self is revealed as he frees himself from prejudices and reactions.

Archetypically, *The Serpent and the Rope* is an Indian story. However, Ramaswamy does not resemble any divine incarnation. He calls himself a holy vagabond and, at best, can be compared to Siddhartha, who leaves home and sets out on a spiritual voyage to discover the truth, which will make him an Enlightened One. Thus Ramaswamy represents a modern-day spiritual initiate who leaves his own country, seeking the truth in a

---

[210] Raja Rao, *The Serpent and the Rope*. New Delhi. Orient Paperbacks. 1968. pp. 5-8 .
[211] Raja Rao: *The Serpent and the Rope*, Delhi, Hind Pocket Books, 1968. p. 140.
[212] Ibid.,p.17

foreign land, only to discover that the answers lie at home. A lifetime dedicated to the pursuit of self-realization, the practice of Yoga and renunciation is a live spiritual tradition in India even today. So like Ulysses leaving behind his wife and son, Ramaswamy embarks on his journey of self-exploration and comes to India repeatedly in search of the Absolute. Shepherd is right is saying "In numerous ways Ramaswamy appears a distinctly Indian character, possessing a symbolic aura which brings to mind a whole culture and tradition and also that he possesses a more immediate and personal presence, a living rather than symbolic being.[213]

Adult Ramaswamy had definite views on philosophical matters and both in life and research "he is always ready to study, analyze and discuss philosophical systems and religious beliefs with people of all types in India, France and England in order to arrive at the truth."[214] Ramaswamy zealously traces the roots of history and unity of cultures. He travels to France to do research on the Albigensian Heresy which influences his thoughts and quest considerably. He aims "to link up the Bogomilites and the Druze and thus search back for Indian background Jain or may be Buddhist – of the Cathars."[215]

Ramaswamy does not entertain contrary views, finding references to prove his conclusions and rejects all evidence that goes against his assumptions. He only appreciates people who do not contradict him and therefore likes Little Mother and his stepsister Saroja, who think he is always right. He is pleased with Savithri, who regards his utterances as gospel truth and considers him her Preceptor, Teacher and God Krishna. Explaining the reasons for her complete surrender to Rama intellectually, Savithri provides an insight into his unique mind: "Ramaswamy has always such interesting things to say about everything", and that "he relates thing apparently so unrelated – for him history is a vast canvas, for the discovery of value, or metaphysical value."[216] Madeleine loves

---

[213] Quoted by Narsingh Srivastava: *The Mind and Art of Raja Rao*. Prakash Book Depot, Bareilly (India),1980. p.61

[214] S.S. Mathur, (ed)., *Guide to The Serpent and the Rope*. Lakshmi Narain Agarwal, Agra, p.110

[215] Raja Rao, *The Serpent and the Rope*, Delhi, Hind Pocket Books, 1968. p.15.

[216] Ibid., p. 182

him very much but being an intellectual herself cannot accept Ramaswamy's dogmatic views on everything, always.

Through this memorable protagonist, Raja Rao carries forward his favourite East-West discourse. From his repeated trips to and from India, this learned and liberal intellectual, interpreting Indian culture, religion and civilization to the west, acquires a new vision of both worlds. His new perspective is not merely of a static East-West confrontation but "a stage in his spiritual evolution, an objectification of his restless intellect, which he appears to have outgrown."[217] This noble Brahmin is loved and admired by all those with whom he interacts.

Evolving as a cultural emissary of the East, Ramaswamy ultimately realizes what India is in the west. Focusing on two contrasting ways of life and thought most dramatically, Rao sincerely believes, "Since the good cannot know itself," it is 'in evil you see good."[218] According to Mathur "to a sensitive and contemplative author like Raja Rao, himself educated both in India and Europe, the theme of dissimilarity, contrast, conflict and essential oneness of the East and the West came naturally and he treated it with a variety and profundity unparalleled in Indo-Anglian fiction."[219]

Perched on the fence surveying two different ways of thought and life, Ramaswamy's "double vision makes him understand one with the eyes of the other."[220] Remembering his formative years in France initially he was so enchanted by the Western civilization that he was "planning to preach its magnificence to his countrymen for the rest of his life."[221] However, even in the midst of this euphoria, his essential Indian sensibilities do not desert him. Ramaswamy's Eastern eye, with great sincerity, clarity and detachment, surveys the Western panorama and as a historian he does it "with no art or decoration,

---

[217] O.P.Mathur, "The Serpent Vanishes: A Study in Raja Rao's Treatment of the East-West Theme." *The Modern Indian English Fiction* New Delhi: Abhinav Publications. 1993. p.102.
[218] Raja Rao: *The Serpent and the Rope*, New Delhi, Orient Paperbacks 1968. pp. 109.
[219] O.P.Mathur, "The Serpent Vanishes: A Study in Raja Rao's Treatment of the East-West Theme." *The Modern Indian English Fiction* New Delhi :Abhinav Pubications. 1993. p.98.
[220] Ibid.,p.10
[221] Raja Rao: *The Serpent and the Rope*, New Delhi, Orient Paperbacks 1968. p.15.

but with the 'objectivity', the discipline of the 'historical sciences.'[222]

Raja Rao firmly believes that a "clearly contrasted portrayal of the West is essential for an understanding of the true spirit of the East."[223] He, therefore, brings out the dualities and the contrasts brilliantly, "India, unlike France, is not a land but 'something other', 'as though the Gods had peopled the land with themselves,' 'something that history has reserved for herself', an area all known but atemporal, where you see yourself face to face'[224]. "Benaras is the sacred capital", "a surrealist city", in which one never knows "where reality starts and where illusion ends."[225] Comparing it to Paris, he says, "Paris somehow is not a city. it is an area in itself, a concord in one's being, where the river flows by you with an intimacy that means to say the divine is not in the visible architecture of the Orangerie or the presence of Pont des Arts, but where the trees would end ... Paris is a sort of Benaras turned outwards."[226]

The novel depicts the physical and material features of France in great detail. However, he describes India metaphysically "India is not a country like France is, or like England, India is an idea, a metaphysic"[227] "a nameless magnanimity, a mystery that has eyes, a sense of existence."[228] It is "like a juice to him, giving him sweetness and the desire of immortality."[229] He finds India to be omnipresent, "wheresoever you see, hear, touch, taste, smell."[230] Thus, discovering India and his own self in a western milieu, Ramaswamy becomes one of the most deeply realized characters of Indo-Anglian fiction. "From the tradition ridden East to the releasing atmosphere of the West and back to the soulful East,

---

[222] Ibid.,p.231
[223] *Quoted in* O.P.Mathur, "The Serpent Vanishes: A Study in Raja Rao's Treatment of the East- West Theme." *The Modern Indian English Fiction* New Delhi: Abhinav Publications.1993. P. 98.
[224] Raja Rao: *The Serpent and the Rope*, New Delhi, Orient Paperbacks 1968. pp.246-247
[225] Ibid.,pp.11-12
[226] Ibid., pp.51-52.
[227] Ibid., pp. 376.
[228] Ibid., p. 193
[229] Ibid., p. 15
[230] Ibid.,p. 349

recalls the famous image of the Wheel or of the serpent eating its own tail."[231]

Thus Raja Rao enables us to comprehend the real India of Ramaswamy. None of his other novels has portrayed India in this unique form. Ramaswamy had a definite purpose in taking the "Albigensian heresy as a subject for research, for he (his father) thought that India should be made more real to the European."[232] Raja Rao, therefore beautifully portrays the accurate picture of spiritual India "Where the past and the present are forever knit into one whole experience", and where "going down the Ganges who could not imagine the Compassionate One Himself coming down the footpath, by the Saraju to wash the mendicant bowl."[233]

The novel begins with a dichotomy "whether the Brahmins of Benares are like the crows asking for funeral rice-balls, saying "caw-caw" or like sadhus by their fires, lost in such beautiful magnanimity, as though love were not something one gave to another, what one gave to oneself."[234] Contrary to the western prejudice of India being a superstitious nation observing black magic, it strives to establish it as the land of truth where religious ideals abound and spiritual quest is still a way of life. The real Benares "was indeed nowhere but inside oneself."[235]India "began where truth was acknowledged."[236]

Identifying it mainly with the truth of advaita or non-duality he says, "Truth is the only substance India can offer and that truth", says Ramaswamy, "is metaphysical, not moral,"[237] This is the reason why "Indian morality was based on an ultimate metaphysic"[238] which recognizes and realizes the oneness of all things. Correcting the popular western notion of India being a polytheist nation he says "Duality is anti-Indian; the non-dual affirms the truth"[239] He strongly feels that this real India "would

---

[231] O.P.Mathur, "The Serpent Vanishes: A Study in Raja Rao's Treatment of the East-West Theme." *The Modern Indian English Fiction* New Delhi: Abhinav Publications. 1993. p.99.
[232] Raja Rao, *The Serpent and the Rope*, Delhi, Hind Pocket Books, 1971, p.17
[233] Ibid., p. 19
[234] Ibid., p. 12
[235] Ibid., p. 50
[236] Ibid., p. 35
[237] Ibid., p. 350
[238] Ibid., p. 349
[239] Ibid., p. 41

never be made by our politicians and professors of political science, but by those isolate existence of India, in which India is rememorated, experienced and communicated."[240]

Ramaswamy strongly feels India's wisdom pervading the Universe makes it limitless and timeless, " Like the Wise bull we laugh at all good men …We Europeans believe in being good … We Indians in being wise."[241] "Besides this august, austere, serene, infinite, eternal India, everything that is West appears to be puny, poetic, feminine, all unreal and illusory."[242]

Missing India in a foreign land, Ramaswamy recreates an Indian environment in his home in France, where "he installs for worship a round and oval Linga found on the banks of Seine"[243] and "imagines a huge flat stone at the edge of his garden to be Shiva's bull"[244], the "pansy to be the 'Buddhist' plant"[245] and "a pine to be the 'Bodhisat Tree"[246], "Mother Rhone"[247] is like the Ganges which flows 'everywhere'[248]. Even Cam 'flows right in herself', outside of history'[249]. These references depict that Ramaswamy approaches the west open-mindedly, trying to perceive the essential oneness with the East. Consciously or unconsciously, he constantly tries to integrate the two cultures by erecting several bridges.

Despite numerous dissimilarities between the customs, religious beliefs and governance of different countries, he finds numerous similarities too. Ramaswamy's quest for real India puts him on a mission to search for the origins of several ancient world cultures which have roots in India, bringing Christianity, Buddhism, Catharism and Hinduism as close as possible. Being a Brahmin, Ramaswamy makes Brahmanism the pivot around which his philosophy and theology revolve. Comparing and contrasting it

---

[240] Ibid., p. 352

[241] Raja Rao. *The Serpent and the Rope*, New Delhi, Orient Paperbacks 1968. p. 338.

[242] O.P.Mathur. "The Indian Protagonist and the Western Experience." *The Modern Indian English Fiction*. New Delhi: Abhinav Publications. 1993. p.10

[243] Raja Rao. *The Serpent and the Rope*, New Delhi, Orient Paperbacks 1968. p. 54.

[244] Ibid.,p.55

[245] Ibid.,p.318

[246] Ibid.,p.321

[247] Ibid.,p.389

[248] Ibid.,p.118

[249] Ibid.,p.167

to Roman Catholicism, Buddhism and Catharism repeatedly, he somehow seems to be convinced that the philosophical world is bipolar where on the one end is the idealism of the Advaita and on the other end is the realism of marxism "there can be only two attitudes to life. Either you believe that the world exists - and so-you. Or you believe that you exist - and so the world. There is no compromise possible. The first is the Vedantin's position –the second is the Marxist – and they are irreconcilable."[250]. 'Buddhism also with its compassion, which presupposes the existence of the world, belongs to this class.'[251] 'The world is either real or unreal –the serpent or the rope. There is no in–between-the-two, and all that is in between is poetry, is sainthood… The actual, the real has no name. The rope is no rope to itself……the rope just is – and therefore there is no world.'[252]

Surpassing these dualities and arriving at the non-duality or advaita, he proceeds to establish that despite the contradictions at personal and social levels, there is an essential oneness at the philosophical plane between the East and the West. Hailing from a liberal background, he sympathizes with the virtuous but heretical Cathars. Trying to prove his metaphysical theory correct by comparing Catharism with Indian beliefs, he says, "To be free is to know one is free beyond the body and beyond the mind; to love is to know one is love; to be pure is to know one is purity…. You need not take Consolamentum and jump into the fire to be a Cathar, for what are you but a Cathar? Everyone beyond his body and beyond his mind is a Cathar. The Ganges dissolves all sin. Even the ashes of the dead but what the fire has burnt must dissolve in the Ganges and have absolution. Benaras is everywhere, where you are says an old Vedantic text, and all waters are the Ganges. To realize this is to be a true Cathar…The rest is heresy."[253]

Roman Catholicism, Raja Rao feels, is quite similar in many respects to Hinduism and even Islam. "I can now understand the Muslim, for Mohammad was the last historical prophet of

---

[250] Ibid,.p. 334
[251] Ibid., p.333
[252] Ibid., pp. 335-336
[253] Ibid.,pp.382-383

God."[254] Leaning toward Christianity, he says, "For these few days how happy I feel in the ancient fold of the church. I feel protected. I feel dominated in my humaneness. I feel truly happy."[255] "He even worships at a church, saying 'inconsequential things', his Latin being too poor."[256] He reveals his liking for British monarchy saying its spirit is Indian. "I am a Monarchist, and I honour the Queen...I belong to the period of Mahabharatha."[257]

Thus Raja Rao perceives the essential oneness of all religions and, through Ramaswamy, wants to synthesize their truths and ideals. He believes the Christian chalice to be a Buddhist artefact that came to Christendom via Persia and thus was "only the mendicant alms-bowl upturned."[258] Madeleine was convinced that the Holy Grail was "part of Albigensian tradition...so she turned her attention more and more to Buddhism."[259] Ramaswamy states, "latter Buddhist phenomena must have fascinated the school of Aristotle."[260] He also points out that "The Swastika, the emblem of Aryans, was brought from central Asia by the Nestorians, the Bogomiles and the Cathars..."[261]

Ramaswamy's research is also "an Indian attempt at a philosophy of history."[262] No one else has tried to focus on the points of unity so well, notwithstanding their contradictions. Staunch Christians like Father Zenobias and Georges, learned Buddhists like Lezo and Sadhaka Vedantist Ramaswamy, all enlightened followers of the world's three great religions, are juxtaposed to each other by the author to prove this phenomenon. Nevertheless, he only projects Rama's wife Madeleine as the one who reveals consistent spiritual progress through her synthesis of the three religious belief systems. The author strongly feels that Marxism, Hinduism, Christianity, Islam, Hitlerism, the British Commonwealth, and the Republic of the United States of America

---

[254] Ibid.,p.82
[255] Ibid.,p.83
[256] Ibid.,p.84
[257] Ibid.,p.351
[258] Raja Rao, *The Serpent and the Rope*, Delhi, Hind Pocket Books, 1971, p. 67
[259] Ibid., pp. 114-15
[260] Ibid., p. 115
[261] Ibid., p. 76
[262] Ibid., p. 103

all are so many voices for some unknown principle, which we feel but cannot name. But according to Holy Gita all rivers "lead but to the Absolute."[263] *The Serpent and the Rope* thus successfully strengthen the oneness of the Eastern and Western cultures, forcing us to change our perception.

After geography and history, Raja Rao's protagonist discovers the true meaning of life and his true self through the love of women appearing on the east-west canvas. By unravelling the secrets of the feminine principle, he provides insight into eastern and western values and their crucial role in his quest for ultimate truth. The novel displays many shades of womanhood, but there are three women Madeleine, Lakshmi and Savithri who are extremely enamoured of Ramaswamy, who in turn is overawed by them, "what a deep and reverential mystery womanhood is." All three women elucidate the limitations and possibilities of the power of love to transform human life.

Profound melancholy characterizes Ramaswamy's character, who considers himself an orphan after his mother's early death. "… I fell before the rice-balls of my mother and sobbed. I was born an orphan, and have remained one. I have wandered the world and have sobbed in hotel- rooms and in trains, have looked at the cold mountains and sobbed, for I had no mother."[264] Hankering for maternal love "has tremendously influenced his view of women and her principle on earth."[265]

By exploring the essential nature, various facets and the changing colours of his relationships, the novel depicts the importance of women without whom man's life is not complete "It is through man's intimate physical union with his woman that he can spiritually realize the great harmony that pervades all aspects of the universe."[266] Asserting the primacy of the female principle, Ramaswamy says, "There is only one woman, not for one life, but for all lives, indeed the earth was created .. that we might seek

---

[263] Ibid., p.90
[264] Raja Rao: *The Serpent and the Rope*, New Delhi, Orient Paperbacks 1968. p. 6.
[265] Kaushal Sharma, *Raja Rao: A Study Of His Themes and Technique.* New Delhi, Sarup & Sons 2005.p.35
[266] Ibid.,p. 32

her."[267] Ramaswamy believes "life is made for woman – man is a stranger to this earth."[268] Only when a man finds himself in his woman does he loves her deeply. The Yajnavalkya-Maitreyi dialogue in the Brihadaranyaka Upanishad establishes, "For whose sake, verily does a husband love his wife, but verily for the sake of the self in her."[269]

All women characters love and admire Ramaswamy in one way or another, but none give him that sense of oneness that he yearns for. He cannot find his authentic self in any of them. Attachment and consequent detachment with these women reveal Ramaswamy's trials and tribulations, challenging his own attitudes and dogmas, which hinder his union of souls. The absence of this soul mate results not only in his intellectual sadness and spiritual loneliness but creative seclusion in the end.

Each woman displaying different physical, intellectual and spiritual attributes becomes a different kind of fulfilment and obstacle simultaneously. Providing the much-needed experience and freedom, their love depicts various stages in the journey of Ramaswamy's self-realization. A Seeker of truth has to liberate himself from all three shackles symbolizing separation, detachment and rejection for self-deliverance. As his spiritual journey advances, Ramaswamy's outlook gradually changes from sensuous to emotional and contemplative. Thus through the nature and meaning of three kinds of love, this metaphysical novel distinguishes the serpent (Illusion) from the rope (reality), revealing the non-dual essence of Indian culture.

Rama's quest for a devoted wife who could be one with him in mind and spirit begins by disregarding Kipling's "East is East, and the West is West, and the Twain shall never meet" and bypassing Forster's cynicism that the earth and the sky were disfavouring an East-West union. Ramaswamy builds the first bridge by marrying Madeleine, a French Christian girl five years

---

[267] Quoted in H.M.Williams, *Studies in Modern Indian Fiction in English* , Vol 1 (Calcutta: Writers Workshop, 1971), p.71

[268] Quoted in M.K. Naik,, *Raja Rao*, Twayne's English Author Series. New York: Twayne, Publishers,,1972, p.139

[269] Raja Rao: *The Serpent and the Rope*, New Delhi, Orient Paperbacks 1968. p.24

older than him and belonging to a totally different socio-cultural and economic background. To Ramaswamy, Madeleine, also a researcher in History with her Cathar-like purity, symbolized the best in Western culture, besides bridging the East-West gap. However, this marriage' "throws Ramaswamy into a jungle of East West dualities, which he, with his deeply reflective nature, a high degree of fervently poetic sensibility and natural and unsophisticated response to life, perceives at all levels of his being and all the while goes on integrating and rationalizing them, consequently finding his own cultural and spiritual moorings."[270]

Ramaswamy and Madeleine's growth of consciousness are explored through the theme of love, marriage and divorce, cultural rites and spiritual faith. As he embarks on his spiritual journey, everything seems like an illusion to him. He, therefore, asks fundamental questions like, "was I really called Ramaswamy or was Madeleine called Madeleine?"[271] On the other hand, by marrying Ramaswamy, Madeleine comes to "know and identify herself with great people."[272]

Their love fructifies in marriage because it is pure and real and there is a complete exchange of sexual, emotional and aesthetic love. Everyone envies this beautiful couple. Tante Zoubie suggests that "never had she seen a couple so happy."[273] Oncle Charles also admits that he has "never seen a European couple act and behave with such innocence."[274] "Above all, and for a Christian what is fascinating is your relationship with Madeleine."[275]

Appreciating Madeleine's sensuous charms, Ramaswamy admits that he loves her "in bits and parts and all, like an antelope does its dove, the elephant does with the ichors dripping from his brows."[276] Ramaswamy's confession in the chapter entitled *Pages from My Diary* gives further details, "I love the curved nape of her neck, so gentle, so like marble for me, almost saffron-coloured

---

[270]O.P.Mathur, "The Serpent Vanishes: A Study in Raja Rao's Treatment of the East- West Theme." *The Modern Indian English Fiction* New Delhi: Abhinav Publications. 1993. p. 103.
[271] Raja Rao: *The Serpent and the Rope*, New Delhi, Orient Paperbacks 1968. p. 14
[272] Ibid., p.18
[273] Ibid., p.91
[274] Ibid., p.82
[275] Raja Rao, *the Serpent and the Rope*, Hind pocket Books, Delhi, 1968, p. 81
[276] Ibid., p. 158

under the light of the moon, or I call her to myself in the day, and take her in my arms, how her throat smells of some known musk.[277]

On the other hand, Madeleine loves Ramaswamy completely, and her love is extraordinary – a form of dedication or worship, where one becomes oneself by becoming another. Ramaswamy knows she wants him to be big and trustworthy so that "She may pour her love on me…"[278] Everything holy to Ramaswamy becomes an object of veneration for her. Displaying deep devotion to his Indian Gods in her garden, she religiously pours holy water on the Shiva Linga, offers grass to Nandi, and caresses his hump, saying, "Here, Bull, here is your feed today."[279] Emotions, Devotion, Understanding- thus moving gradually from the carnal towards the sublime, both cross their first stage of spiritual transformation. Guided by Ramaswamy toward an intellectual quest for Indian thought and philosophy, Madeleine gradually becomes conscious of the true nature of love and the need to attain its highest form.

To remain close to Ramaswamy, who initially symbolised this love, Madeleine wants to become a Hindu Brahmin, discovering one had to be born. Inclined toward Buddhism as the next great Indian religion, Madeleine acquires intense knowledge about Buddhism from Lezo, "She studied Buddhism not for writing a thesis on it but for her own "Spiritual benefit."[280] Becoming a staunch Buddhist out of deep love for Ramaswamy, she admits, "Beloved, it is you who have brought me all this…. I am a Sadhaka now."[281] Her studies, meditation and other spiritual observances make her more rational and impersonal, bringing her closer to the ideal of human perfection of Advaita instilled in her by Ramaswamy. He completely identifies with its principles: "Only true love- the love of souls – reaches fulfillment in their love."[282] Moreover, asserts that "when the ego is dead is marriage true."[283]

---

[277] Ibid., p. 158
[278] Ibid., p. 80
[279] Ibid., p. 65
[280] Ibid., p. 383
[281] Ibid., p. 316
[282] Ibid., p. 310
[283] Ibid., p. 203

The twist in the tale comes when their fiery love ends in a divorce establishing the impracticality of an East-West union. Different upbringing and cultural backgrounds create dissensions, the turning point being the death of their seven-month-old son Pierre. Madeleine had cherished her motherhood and loved the idea of giving birth to Ramaswamy's son. On the other hand, Ramaswamy attached importance to the child, not as Madeleine's son but merely an offspring who would secure his future. While Madeleine is shattered at his death, Ramaswamy takes it as the inevitability of life. Ramaswamy's philosophical attitude toward death and Madeleine's personal and emotional turbulence create a rift between the loving couple. It widens further after the death of their second son, leaving Madeleine completely ravaged.

Meanwhile, Ramaswamy has to go to India to meet his ailing father, whom he never loved. Nevertheless, he expects Madeleine, the family's eldest daughter-in-law, to accompany him hoping it would save him from death. Madeleine is forced to stay back because of a teaching assignment, but she also fails to understand that Indian marriages require adherence to family customs and conventions and are not merely a personal bond between two people as in the West. Psychologically Ramaswamy misses the feeling of kinship in their relationship. Hereafter, Madeleine undergoes radical changes in her character, inner being, and love for Ramaswamy. This is how she crosses the second stage of her spiritual growth. Savithri's ritual marriage with Ramaswamy also creates some alienation between the two.

The rift reaches its culmination with Madeleine's spiritual progress. When Ramaswamy returns from India after a long separation and seeks a reunion with Madeleine, she asks him to leave her house because she has become a Buddhist nun. Following Tibetan Buddhism under Lezo's influence, she practised celibacy, asceticism and extreme mortification of the flesh. Hinduism does not uphold a woman like Madeleine because rejecting a man implies rejecting womanhood and creation. Thus personal tragedy brings to fore the differences between Ramaswamy's and Madeleine's attitude to life, religion and profundity of thought.

Their marriage was a union of minds and not souls since they were both intellectuals and free thinkers with solid personalities who believed in maintaining their individualities.

Ramaswamy, wanting to spiritualize his love, finds the sacred and mystic, which formed a part of his quest for self-realization severely missing in their relationship. "In Indian tradition the woman occupies a cultural place in the family. Man alone can never go for the Absolute." [284] Unlike Savithri, who blindly accepted Ramaswamy's philosophical principles, Madeleine could not always accept Ramswamy's dogmatic views, especially on Buddhism. Ramaswamy, the champion of non-dualism, where the human ultimately becomes one with the divine, could not accept the dualism of Catharism and Buddhism, which treated God and man as separate entities. Had Madeleine followed Catholic beliefs in non-duality, she would have been much closer to Hinduism. Westerners, however, regard Buddhism as the most rational of all Indian religions. It "is the religion of the modern age", as its "intellectual brilliance…has no equal in the world."[285]

As Naik suggests, it is true that in Buddhism, Madeleine finds "a way of escape from her frustration,"[286] Madeleine's spiritual Sadhana "had given her a certain insight into her own nature, a protection from something smelly, foreign and other - it gave her a step, a conscious foothold in India."[287] As Indian spirituality conquers the material West, Ramaswamy and Madeleine are separated and isolated on a physical plane for metaphysical gain. As the search for truth takes them in opposite directions, Madeleine realizing that 'contemplation is the only truth one has"[288], decides to divorce Ramaswamy to wed her true self. A divorce here implies transcending the social and moral values of marriage to liberate the self, those who do not love and those who have realized the truth of love; marriage is a social commitment and bondage.

---

[284] Kaushal Sharma. *Raja Rao: A Study of His Themes and Technique*. New Delhi, Sarup & Sons 2005.p.35
[285] Quoted in Kaushal Sharma. *Raja Rao: A Study Of His Themes and Technique*. New Delhi, Sarup & Sons 2005, p. 301
[286] Quoted by Narsingh Srivastava: *The Mind and Art of Raja Rao*. Bareilly: Prakash Book Depot. 1980. p.70
[287] Ibid. P. 254
[288] Raja Rao, *The Serpent and the Rope*, Delhi, Hind Pocket Books, 1971, p. 334

Before their divorce answering Madeleine's question as to what separated them, Rama opines that "contiguous with time and space, but is anywhere, everywhere", is "Jnanam"[289], or the egoless state "where you dip into yourself, and the eighteen aggregates are dissolved."[290] India symbolizes true love, which is not merely a feeling but a stateless state, the whole condition of oneself. Stepping out from the sensual and the material domain into the realm of reality assimilating all otherness, Madeleine conveys both Advaitic and Buddhist ideals to Rama that "one cannot possibly love a body"[291] and love should not be different from the truth. Realizing the true meaning of love and the message of India, a Westerner like Madeleine had to cross this stage and attain a level of existence where she ceased to be a person. Indifferent to her health, she says to Ramaswamy, "I am no more a person, so why speak of it? Of the body's news let the body hear, and of the rest nobody but oneself can tell oneself. So in fact, there is nothing to say, that is why I do not ask anything of you.[292]

From a metaphysical point, this divorce symbolizes the highest form of love - impersonal love, which enables her to distinguish the rope of love from the serpent. Ramaswamy had once told Madeleine, "There where we love there is not talking. You can but take yourself."[293] Marriage is a sacred act of choosing one person as husband and wife, but when we attain the state of non-duality, all discrimination and distinction between them dissolve, leaving behind only the all-embracing and indivisible self. Ramaswamy says, "Love cannot be added on to love; to know love is to love and to love is just to be.[294] Therefore following her divorce, "Madeleine has reached a state of consciousness in which she alone remains, neither a wife nor a beloved but only she. In this way, India is wedded to Europe, even though Ramaswamy is divorced from Madeleine. The paradox at one level is a truth at the

---

[289]Raja Rao: *The Serpent and the Rope*, New Delhi, Orient Paperbacks 1968. P p. 332
[290] Ibid., p. 388
[291] Ibid., p. 260
[292] Ibid., p. 260
[293] Raja Rao: *The Serpent and the Rope*, Delhi, Hind Pocket Books, 1971 p.363
[294] Ibid., p.134

other, and the two levels cannot be mingled."[295] Contrary to Ramswamy's assumption, Madeleine was not a serpent (unreal) but a rope (hard reality).

Besides Ramaswamy and Madeleine, the author displays meaningful contrasts among other characters on life and religion." Ramaswamy is contrasted to Georges and Lezo in his metaphysical thought and to Oncle Charles and Sigon in the profundity of his approach to life. Similarly the 'emotionalism' of Madeleine is set against the worldly matter-of-factness of Tante Zoubie and Catherine, on one hand and the mystic love and the touch with the traditional that Savithri embodies, on the other. The two 'patriarchs' Oncle Charles and Grandfather Kittanna and the two mother figures, Tante Zoubie and Little Mother respectively embody the materialism and worldly inheritance of the West and the deeply spiritual and ritualistic ,though orthodox, inheritance of India. The pictures of Catherine and Saroja as also their respective marriages are representatives of the two cultures. The mystic marriage of Savithri to Ramaswamy and the atmosphere of sacred ritualism that envelops it are in marked contrast to the initiation of the legal rituals of Ramaswamy's divorce proceedings at the hands of a most worldly and somewhat vulgar lawyer."[296] The position of women is also repeatedly contrasted:

> "In what way, Saroja do you think Catherine or Madeleine is better off than you?"
>
> "They know how to love".
>
> "And You?"
>
> "And we know how to bear children. We are just like a motor car or a bank account. Or better still, we are like a comfortable salary paid by a benign and eternal British Government. Our joy is a treasury receipt.'[297]

---

[295] Quoted in Niranjan Rout, The Fictional Work of Raja Rao: A Study of his Mind and Art, Ph.D. Thesis. Magadh Univerity. 1995

[296] O.P.Mathur, "The Indian Protagonist and the Western Experience," *The Modern Indian English Fiction.* New Delhi: Abhinav Publications. 1993. p.9

[297] Raja Rao: *The Serpent and the Rope*, New Delhi, Orient Paperbacks 1968. p. 257

In sharp contrast to Madeleine, Lakshmi's purely physical and sensuous love appears in the Eastern context, and the two unite only briefly to extinguish their carnal desire. Lakshmi's amorous invitations result in passion meeting passion because Ramaswamy knows that "A woman hates a male when he withdraws."[298] Her ardent calls result in a night when Rama "slipped slowly and deliberately into Lakshmi's bed."[299] Sexually starved, they only meet to pacify their physical urge since Laxmi's husband, Capt. Sham Sunder had other interests and loved white skin after returning from Europe. This raw display of passion for a few days made Lakshmi so attached to Rama that she hated the thought of separation.

She practically began worshipping him till the day she got to know that Rama was returning to Europe. The bubble of pure sensuousness had burst, and the high tidal wave of raw passion had crashed. Distressed and enraged, she showers the choicest invectives of "eunuch" and "lecherous coward" on him. Detaching himself completely, he leaves her. Eros here depicts love as an illusion that confines us to the reality of love. Like Lakshmi, Catherine also simply wanted a mate in Lezo and not a guardian. Thus mere sensuousness leads to casual relationships which, like a river in spate, ebb out in time.

For Ramaswamy, an ideal relationship was one in which his woman would submit to him at all levels. Charmed mainly by Ramaswamy's intellect Savithri accepts his metaphysical statements as gospel truth and Ramaswamy as a Guru. Ramaswamy considers Savithri her natural companion since she embodies both western modernism and conventional Indianness. Experiencing spiritual oneness only with her, he feels that only in this relationship will the masculine (*purush*) and feminine (*prakriti*) principles unite to achieve the Absolute.

Alienated from their partners, Ramaswamy and Savithri are united in a symbolic ritual marriage. Soon Ramaswamy realizes this relationship is incomplete because Savithri's love is platonic,

---

[298]Raja Rao: *The Serpent and the Rope*, Delhi, Hind Pocket Books 1971, p. 163
[299] Ibid., p. 295

and she surrenders to him as Mira or Radha did to Krishna, "I have known my Lord for a thousand lives, from Janam to Janam have I known my Krishna."[300] Real love transcends the body, so feeling content by being her Lord, Ramaswamy still considers her to be "his real woman, a never changing truth, the abiding reality." and believes that like the Savithri of the legend, she will succeed "in leading her eternal lover to the path of the knowledge of the self."[301] Content with his status as a spiritual husband, Rama advises her to return to Pratap, her fiancée, like Krishna asks the gopis to return home and discharge their worldly duties and remain happy being his disciples.

Married only in spirit and not in the body, their union remains only a union of two souls. Savithri worships Ramaswamy but lacks Lakshmi's physical passion and Madeleine's emotional intensity. Her abstract love only gratifies the mind as she was "made of such stuff that for her the real had to be clothed in terms of the illusory to make it concrete; the truth was to be made the revelation of a puzzle, a riddle, a mathematic of wisdom."[302] Madeleine tells Ramaswamy that Savithri " lives in a world of fantasy – a dream."[303] Ramaswamy agrees: "Thoughts intoxicated Savithri as nothing else did; men were just givers of thoughts. Her maidenhood had no physical basis. It existed, just as in fairy tales you cannot win a princess unless you solve a riddle."[304] He knows that "To be in the arms of a beloved, Savithri must have thought, is then just to take delight in one's self, to park the car in the village, go to the top of the mountain in the mist of night, and look out for the sound of the sea."[305]

Ramaswamy's melancholy and seriousness charm Savithri from which Madeleine wanted to escape. Savithri loves for the sake of love, and in his second meeting with her in England, Ramaswamy frankly states, "The fact is, for you, love is an

---

[300] Quoted in, M.K. Naik,, *Raja Rao* , Twayne's English Author Series. New York: Twayne, Publishers,,1972, 212.

[301] Kaushal Sharma, *Raja Rao :A Study of his Themes and Technique,* New Delhi, Sarup & Sons, 2005. p.37

[302] Raja Rao: *The Serpent and the Rope*, Delhi, Hind Pocket Books 1971, p 126

[303] Ibid., pp. 128-29

[304] Ibid., p. 134

[305] Ibid., p. 176

abstraction."[306] This love hinders her marriage with Pratap and Ramaswamy's quest for truth.

Savitri loves Ramaswamy mentally, even if it contradicts social and moral reality because love is a natural phenomenon and is independent of matrimony. Ramaswamy knows that "For her marriage would be to wed anyone, for whatever happened would just happen, and the wedding too would be happening."[307] In his spiritual progress, Ramaswamy easily detaches himself from this kind of love, persuading Savithri to marry Pratap and rejoice in his happiness. Loving one and marrying another tormented Savithri always but "she wanted to hear it proven that Pratap could love her, but that she might not love him and yet marry him."[308] Providing a metaphysical solution Ramaswamy states "…Love can never be movement, feeling, and not", because "All that acts can only be of the body, or the mind, or the ego. Only the selfish can love.

"And the loveless ?"

"They become love." [309]

Ramaswamy believes that "Nobody could marry Savithri; nobody could marry a soul, so why not marry anyone."[310] To her query of what one should do if one is tied to another as "the plane is tied to the radar."[311] Ramaswamy answers, "The plane must accept the direction of the radar, that there be no accident."[312] Accepting the Law (Dharma) is the joy of life, and it is a joy that one can give oneself to another. "Rejoice, rejoice in the rejoicing of another, and know you include the world as joy in the depth of your sleep."[313] Saved from bondage and attachment because "he could only love Savithri and not possess her; therefore, he chooses to remain his own self – pure and free: "I could not possess a Savithri – I become I."[314]

---

[306] Ibid., p. 135
[307] Ibid., p.135
[308] Ibid., p.177
[309] Ibid., p. 177
[310] Ibid., p.197
[311] Ibid. p.363
[312] Ibid., p.135
[313] Ibid., p.365
[314] Ibid., p.171

Savithri is aware that to reach spiritual perfection, love must transcend the body and mind and go beyond that. Nevertheless, like Madeleine, she cannot become love, as she cannot free herself entirely from the idea of personal love. Incapable of annihilating her ego, she chooses to marry Pratap if she cannot marry Ramaswamy. Rama is aware that Savithri must possess the object she loves, but her self-consciousness stands between them, "But we were not one silence, we were two solitudes. What stood between Savithri and me was not Pratap, but Savithri herself."[315]

Savithri is also not able to free herself from her morals and traditions. She, therefore, feels that spiritual love for a married man and physical marriage to another for practical reason can exist simultaneously, without violating the claims of either. Because of some spiritual progression, she easily detaches herself from wanting physical possession of Ramaswamy and is happy having him as a spiritual husband. Therefore on the ladder of selfless love, she is way below Madeleine, who has the strength to go through a divorce to attain spiritual perfection. Savithri achieves spiritual development in love, but Madeleine attains self-realization through love. Madeleine's spiritual progress in love reveals the Advaitic principle that when the truth is born, the person dies, making relative concepts like marriage and divorce irrelevant in the realm of the Absolute. A serpent at the level of the relative becomes a mere rope from the angle of the Absolute. Madeleine has internalized the great Indian principle of the futility of human life if it does not embark on the quest of the Absolute. This is the purpose of this great metaphysical novel.

Ramaswamy may have fallen in love with many women but, like a true Vedantist, detaches himself from their actions. He seldom reacts. Because he knows that "to be free is to know one is free, beyond the body and the mind. Impurity is in action and reaction."[316] Through the Puranic story of Durvasa and Radha, he reveals this truth. Therefore the introspective Ramaswamy - a

---

[315] Ibid., p. 179
[316] Ibid., p. 382.

Sadhaka or spiritual initiate of the Indian tradition is unruffled by mundane things like Lakshmi's abuses, Savithri's wedding and Madeleine's decision to divorce him. Madeleine thus sums up her impression of Ramaswamy, "Your impersonal approach was strange to me, you yourself so impersonal?"[317] Catherine says aptly that "He is not man-man. He is an Indian."[318]

Advaita or non-dualism, achieved through the discovery of self, which forms the novel's core, is the author's message to the West. To this metaphysical truth is wedded the image of real India and the meaning of true love, which is all-absorbing. Ramaswamy, practically born with this metaphysical strain, asserts the importance of self-realization as the highest goal of life in the very beginning. Whatever is not 'self' is mere 'non-self'. Body, Mind, Intellect and Ego, signifying mundane life, comprise the non-self from the Advaitic point of view. This mundane life is the serpent, and the 'self' is the rope.

Referring to the work of Sri Sankaracharya, especially Dakshinamurtyastakam in the beginning, the contrast between 'self' and non-self is depicted clearly by Ramaswamy, "Seeing oneself is what we always seek, the world is like a city seen in a mirror."[319] The same reference in more significant detail appears again in the end:

> "Like a city seen in a mirror, in the universe, seen within oneself but seemingly of Maya born, as in sleep.
> Yet is it reality in the inner self of Him who sees at the Point of Light:
> Within Himself, unique, immutable – To him incarnate as the Holy Guru to Sri Dakshinamurthy be salutation.[320]

The 'inner self' which forms the base for the understanding of the 'self' is clearly revealed as follows:

---

[317] Raja Rao, *The Serpent and the Rope*, Delhi, Hind Pocket Books, 1968, p. 35
[318] Ibid., p. 343
[319] Raja Rao, *The Serpent and the Rope*, Delhi, Hind Pocket Books, 1971, pp. 13-14
[320] Ibid., p.293

"The perfect civilization, then, is where the world is not, but where there is nothing but the 'I'. It is like the perfect number, which is always a manifestation of I. I. I. The Buddhists say the world, the perception is real, 'Sarvam Kshanikam', that everything is minute the moment we see it. The Vedantin says the perception is real. Yes; but that reality is 'my self.'[321]

The Brihadaranyaka Upanishad referring to the Yajnavalkya Maitryi dialogue, emphasises:

"As one embraced by a darling bride, knows naught of 'I', and 'Thou', so self embraced by the foreknowing (solar) self knows naught of 'myself' within or 'thyself' without. Not one is the Truth, yet not two is the truth. Savithri proved that I could be I.[322]

The concept of undivided and invisible self is again explained in the context of a 'brother':

"Brother, have you seen my brother?" I had asked, from kings and going beyond, by the Ganges or the Cauvery, from saints and sages, I had asked, backward in history to the times of the Upanishads, even unto Yajnavalkya and Maitreyi; and as thought at each epoch, with each person, I had left knowledge of myself, a remembered affirmation of myself; and in this affirmation had been the awareness of the presence that I am, that I am my brother.[323]

Here the pattern is distinctly circular, where a circumference encloses all ideas and all religious philosophies. The quest for the centre emerges only at the end when Ramaswamy gives up his initial ambition of returning to India with Madeleine

---

[321] Ibid., p.334
[322] Ibid., p.170
[323] Ibid., p.195

after completing his doctorate and settling down as a Professor at an Indian University.

Trials and tribulations on the path of self-realization make Ramaswamy aware that an initial quest of the mind leads only to the theoretical understanding of the metaphysical truths. However, without translating them into action, progression towards fulfilling the profound need of the soul cannot be achieved. On a worldly plane, a spiritually advanced Ramaswamy, having detached himself physically from Lakshmi, mentally from Savithri and legally from Madeleine and having transformed from Eros into Agape, is ready to embark on this journey. As Savithri becomes a householder *grihastha* and Madeleine turn a nun or *sanyasini,* and Ramaswamy's search for the Ultimate begins. "After years of spiritual quest, and a struggle to lead an authentic life, accepting no suppositions, taking nothing on trust, Ramaswamy in his essential loneliness seems to have created his own value of love."[324] "Left to myself, I became alone and full of love .When one is alone one always loves. In fact it is because one loves and one is alone, one does not die."[325]

Thus through scholar, intellectual and metaphysician Ramaswamy, who chooses to seek liberation of the self through Gyana or knowledge, Raja Rao, the artist of the human mind, successfully projects the Advaitic Indian ideal of the renouncement of the world (non-self) and the attainment of the self (the absolute). For man may be a social animal but an Indian man having overcome his material hunger aspires to quench his spiritual thirst, because he has a life even when his non-self ends. Therefore his restless mind seeks spiritual perfection-a desire to be one with his Creator or attain Moksha. This path chosen by Ramaswamy is an ancient Indian trail traversed by saints like Valmiki, Janaka and Sankara.

No wonder Ramaswamy makes a life-changing decision to lead a solitary and silent life to attain a state of higher being. He

---

[324] O.P.Mathur, "The Serpent Vanishes: A Study in Raja Rao's Treatment of the East-West Theme." *The Modern Indian English Fiction,* New Delhi: Abhinav Publications. 1993. p.102

[325] Raja Rao: *The Serpent and the Rope*, New Delhi, Orient Paperbacks 1968. p. 9

who played a Guru to Madeleine and Savithri now needs a Guru himself, who would resolve all his intellectual conflicts, providing him mental peace and ensuring self-integration. When a vision reveals Guru Atmananda, who lives in Travancore, he exclaims, "Now I think I know, but I must go I must go to Travancore."[326] Only the Guru will lead him to the Absolute because when an ignorant man screams, "ayyo! oh! It's the serpent!" the Guru brings the lantern, the road is seen, the long white road, going into the statutory stars. It's only the rope. He shows it to you. And you touch your eyes and know there never was a serpent. " [327]

The Serpent and the Rope thus describes merely the first stage of the spiritual progression of a seeker of truth whose personal beliefs are still not mature. Synthesizing the cardinal truths of the East and West, Ramaswamy's explications are those of a *sadhaka* or spiritual initiate and not yet of a Siddha or Master. Only after resolving the contradictions at the intellectual and spiritual planes will his transformation complete. "His sensitive nature with inherited Brahmanic 'Samskaras" has drunk deep the waters of the Ganges and the Seine. A full confrontation with the dualities of life, of the East and the West has made him transcend them and now he stands on a higher plane where all the illusions of life and death have been shed and feeling himself an orphan and alone, he goes on seeking truth relentlessly."[328] A product of East-West fusion, this "European Brahmin"[329], is thus made by the West to blossom into one of the finest flowers of Indian thought."[330]

Building the sturdiest bridge between the east and the west through advaita, Raja Rao strongly believes that "when the connection is complete, and all contradictions and differences are resolved, the alien territory conquered even this bridge, the Serpent will vanish "I See I - I See I- I See I."[331] One will be confronted with the absolute reality then, "There never was time, there never

---

[326] Raja Rao: *The Serpent and the Rope*, New Delhi, Orient Paperbacks 1995. P.405

[327] Raja Rao: *The Serpent and the Rope*, New Delhi, Orient Paperbacks 1968. P.335

[328] O.P.Mathur, "The Serpent Vanishes: A Study in Raja Rao's Treatment of the East-West Theme." *The Modern Indian English Fiction*, New Delhi: Abhinav Publications. 1993. p. 108.

[329] Raja Rao: *The Serpent and the Rope*, New Delhi, Orient Paperbacks 1968.p. 283

[330]O.P.Mathur, "The Indian Protagonist and the Western Experience." *The Modern Indian English Fiction*, New Delhi: Abhinav Publications. 1993.p. 11.

[331] Raja Rao: *The Serpent and the Rope*, New Delhi, Orient Paperbacks 1968.p.131

was history, there never was anything but Shivoham, Shivoham, I am Shiva, I am the Absolute."[332] "There is no East and there is no West. All is one rounded like a globe, within your own self. India is infectious, mysterious and infectious."[333] "It absorbs everything and makes it her own."[334] "Only India exists and shall exist. It is the rope, all else is the serpent."[335] M.K. Naik aptly concludes that." All of Raja Rao's powers and interests - his intimate knowledge of India, the west, his immense erudition, his metaphysical quest, his ability to handle myth and symbol; his lyrical and descriptive talent and his experimentation with form and style together found simultaneous fulfillment when he embarked upon this long semi-autobiographical narrative against the vast background of two continents, giving him enough room and scope to express himself fully and satisfactorily." [336]

---

[332] Ibid., p. 197.

[333] Ibid.,p.40

[334] Ibid.,p.137

[335] O.P.Mathur, "The Serpent Vanishes: A Study in Raja Rao's Treatment of the East-West Theme." *The Modern Indian English Fiction,* New Delhi: Abhinav Publications. 1993. p. 108.

[336] M.K. Naik,, *Raja Rao* , Twayne's English Author Series. New York: Twayne, Publishers,,1972, p.76

CHAPTER V: Surrender and Reliance

Raja Rao's novel *The Cat and Shakespeare* portrays the mundane world of man's temporal existence and the need for deliverance from it. Raja Rao, who constantly strived to find oneness in the Western and Eastern traditions, has chosen the Cat as the central symbol. Significant in both traditions, in the west, which perceives the world as real, she symbolizes intellect, and in the East, which regards the world as Maya or illusion, she symbolizes faith. Rao tries to reconcile the two opposites through his narrative, ultimately establishing the Indian view that the Cat alone, as an embodiment of the Supreme Energizing Feminine principle of nature, can take the man to Beatitude.

A sequel to *The Serpent and the Rope,* the central theme again is the quest for reality taking an altogether different path but, "without the sharpness of an invisible encounter, assumes a more meditative and mystic aspect and what is of primary importance, it offers a perennial source of humour which is perhaps the characteristic mark of this novel."[337] Essentially it "is a journey from Gyan Yoga of Sankara to Bhaktiyoga of Ramanuja." [338]

The new direction unwinds itself through sublime and grotesque, "real life situations, metaphysics, irony, fantasy and fact, digressions, tragic and comic situations."[339] It explores various levels of complex relationships to impart a simple message with universal significance that faith drives the Unknown and the Unknown guides the destiny of man. To communicate this message the author chooses the philosophical analogy of cat and kitten signifying total surrender and reliance on the benevolent cosmic mother for salvation.

This idea is derived from the *Vishist Advaita* or modified non-dualistic philosophy propounded by the great saint Ramanuja in the 11th century. Modifying his Guru Sankara's theory of Gyana

---

[337] Esha Dey, *The Novels of Raja Rao, The Theme of Quest.* New Delhi. Prestige Books. 1992.p. 158
[338]. Kaushal Sharma, *Raja Rao: A Study of His Themes and Technique*, New Delhi, Sarup & Sons.2005..p.57
[339]. Ibid.,p.49

Yoga, or the path of knowledge, Ramanuja emphasized Bhakti Yoga or the path of devotion for attaining the ultimate reality. He gave a "new interpretation of Advaita through Bhakti which is complete surrender (*Prapatti*) to the will and grace of God. It is a doctrine of self- surrender or extinction of the self and final merger of the will of man with that of God."[340]

After Ramanuja's death, two schools of thought were developed by his followers. The Northern school or Vadagalai believes in the monkey theory (*Markata Nyaya*) that, like the baby monkey willingly clings to its mother, man, out of his own free will, should surrender himself to the will of God, making individual efforts to attain union with the divine. Nevertheless, Nair is a follower of the Tengalai or the Southern school, which believes in the Cat hold Theory or (*Marjara Nyaya)* in which the devotee seeking deliverance has to remain passive like a kitten, surrendering himself to the Divine Will, which like the Mother Cat takes the responsibility of carrying it in its mouth by the scruff of the neck, softly and safely, wherever it goes.

The novel does not have a structured plot but dwells on some potent symbols and characters whose thoughts, expressions and actions merge to further man's search for spiritual perfection. Govindan Nair is the most powerful of them all who has the "felicity of giving twists to ordinary conversation and relate it to some ontological principle…a highly unpredictable man. What he does or thinks forms the action of the story. Comic fantasy has been very skillfully woven in the narrative through this resourceful and interesting rogue whose actions and statements on one level show his devout prayer, and on the other show metaphysical connotations."[341]

His friend and neighbour, the protagonist, plays no less an essential role in this "unusual narrative, a curious mixture of comic fantasy and deep metaphysics narrated by Ramamkrishna Pai, a clerk in the revenue office. An uproarious funny story, it has deep philosophical implications. For a western reader who has no

---

[340] Ibid.,p.58
[341] Ibid., p.52.

knowledge of Vedanta, non dualism, Hindu scriptures, it should certainly baffle him."[342] For him "it has the illusory non plot ... held together only by ....mystifying points of extreme intensity."[343]

Thus the story revolves around the life of Ramakrishna Pai and Govindan Nair, the two main characters, both clerks belonging to middle-class Brahmin families fused as friends and neighbours. The birth of a child to Shantha, the death of Govindan's son Shridhar, the eruption of killer boils on the body of Ramakrishna Pai, the suspension, trial and acquittal of Govindan Nair, and the sudden death of his boss Boothlingam Iyer are major happenings or non- happenings, which tinge their lives with joys and sorrows.

The two main characters symbolize the polarity of the human predicament. Govindan Nair, "a clever resourceful clerk who works in the ration office and talks about Vedanta in an English flavoured with Shakespearean turns and phrases,"[344] is a complex character. Both the friends represent two states of the human mind. Nair is the -Initiated One who believes in mystery and mysticism, that the unknown takes care of the unknown and that "Life is a riddle that can be solved with a riddle."[345] "the specialness is that it is not special."[346] and "Seeing is sleep."[347] Pai the Uninitiated One, on the other hand, is a dreamer, a realist and an acquisitive man. Narrating the story, he calls himself an average person or everyman, "I am not particularly tall or fair or good or bad, I am just a man."[348] Though a clerk, he is highly ambitious, dreaming of a successful life built around his wife Saroja, his two children – Usha and Vithal and Shantha, his extramarital love.

In sharp contrast, Govindan Nair working in a rampantly corrupt office like a coal cell from where no one comes out untainted is a resigned soul caring for nothing. A man of firm convictions, he staunchly believes in resignation to the Will of God. The idea of surrendering to the Almighty Mother comes to him as

---

[342]Ibid.,p.56

[343] Robert.J.Ray, *The Novels of Raja Rao*, Books Abroad, Autumn, 1966, p.414

[344] Esha Dey, *The Novels of Raja Rao, The Theme of Quest*. New Delhi. Prestige Books. 1992. p.146

[345] Raja Rao: *The Cat and Shakespeare*, Delhi, Orient Paperbacks. 1996. p. 35

[346] Ibid.,p.83

[347]Ibid., p. 104.

[348] Raja Rao quoted in Esha Dey, *The Novels of Raja Rao, The Theme of Quest*. New Delhi. Prestige Books. 1992..p. 206.

naturally as breathing. Nair's unflinching faith in divine grace imparts saintly attributes like inner simplicity, purity and carelessness. On a humane level, he is a carefree, helping and jovial man whose ideal is to work hard and be happy. Nair loves humanity for he believes that "Everybody is half brother to you, man and thing. So why worry?... "I am, so you are my brother."[349] He loved children for their innocence and played with them in the ration shop by weighing them in the great balance. An extremely compassionate man, his benevolence is reflected in his act of slipping small amounts of money through windows "where a child cried because he thought his intentions would help."[350] His knowledge is encyclopaedic, and Pai admires it ardently "he knew everything for he was concerned with everything. Once he talked so much on manure that an agricultural expert asked if he was a Professor at the local college."[351] Thus for Pai Nair is, "a humourist, a humanist and garrulous and a comic metaphysician, all rolled into one,"[352] and though " a terrible man: huge in his sinews but important in his thought."[353] his "instinctive wisdom,"[354] of course is par excellence.

Nair is highly devoted to the concept of "Mother Cat" as the Supreme energizing principle."[355] Parables and fables have been used eternally in India to illustrate divine grace - *The Panchatantra, The Puranas* and *The Mahabharata*. Similarly, *The Cat is* a symbol of Divine Grace, and the novel depicts numerous metaphysical complexities that can be interpreted in various ways. "The centrality of the cat regards, on the one hand, the fact that the animal carries several levels of truth, of understanding, of communication and, on the other hand, it's belonging to different civilizations which correspond to different ways of naming it. The cat incarnates divine wisdom and love." [356] The cat has been held

---

[349] Raja Rao: *The Cat and Shakespeare*, Delhi, 1971. Hind Pocket Books. p.36
[350] Ibid. p. 95
[351] Ibid. p. 18
[352] Kaushal Sharma ,*Raja Rao: A Study of His Themes and Technique*, New Delhi, Sarup & Sons. 2005. p.51.
[353] Raja Rao: *The Cat and Shakespeare*, Delhi, Hind Pocket Books, 1971. p. 13
[354] Kaushal Sharma,*Raja Rao: A Study of His Themes and Technique*, New Delhi, Sarup & Sons.2005,p.55.
[355] Ibid.,p.51
[356] Claudeo Gorlier, "Raja Rao's *The Cat and Shakespeare* ; A Western View" in Rajeshwar Mittapalli & Pier Paolo Piciucco. Ed., *The Fiction of Raja Rao: Critical Studies*. New Delhi: Atlantic Publishers, 2001. p.210

in reverence in many religions since time immemorial. Bastet, from whom the Cat in the novel derives its name, is the sacred cat of the Egyptian tradition. Known as Felinus Persiana or the Persian cat, Islam also venerated it. However, the cat symbolises intellectualism in the west, as in Yeat's poem *Statues,* where the cat crawling under Lord Buddha represents intellect yielding to the power of love.

Dey maintains "that the adoption of the cat symbol according to *Marjara Nyaya* is a means to absorb the ethical essence of Christianity." for "many Indian philosophers trace in this subgenre a recognizable impact of Christianity." and "that the whole background of the Cat and Shakespeare is homogenous only in so far as it is western."[357] Thus *The Cat and the Shakespeare* "is the story of the passion of Christ that underlies the development of the novel as a typical literary form of the West."[358] No wonder the real cat in the novel is called Bastet and has been brought as a gift for Nair by John, a Christian. However, Nair, who regards the cat as "a very God", "Bastet, you are sacred", believes that the sanctity of the cat in Hinduism far predates all other religions.

In Hindu mythology, the cat and its kitten symbolize ultimate devotion and surrender to the Supreme and Absolute will of God. Raja Rao uses it in a novel way as a symbol of impersonal love like the Cow viewed in *The Cow of the Barricades,* where Bain correctly suggests, "What is the secret of the rooted affection of the Aryan and Iranian, the Veda and the Avesta, for the Cow? Partly, no doubt its utilitarian value. But they are deceived, who thinks that this is all. There is religion in it, mysticism and aesthetic affection. The cow is an idea."[359]

Similarly, the Cat is also an idea. Raja Rao regards it "as the purest animal in the world."[360] and has therefore made it the medium for achieving the truth or Ultimate Reality, which is

---

[357] Esha Dey quoted in Claudeo Gorlier, "Raja Rao's *The Cat and Shakespeare* : A Western View." *in* Rajeshwar Mittapalli & Pier Paolo Piciucco. Ed. *The Fiction of Raja Rao: Critical Studies*, New Delhi: Atlantic Publishers, 2001. p.211

[358] Esha Dey, *The Novels of Raja Rao, The Theme of Quest.* New Delhi. Prestige Books 1992. p. 145

[359] K.R.S. Iyengar,1983.*Indian Writing in English*, Delhi: Sterling Publishers. 1983.. p. 389

[360] Raja Rao, *The Cat and Shakespeare*: Orient Paperbacks edition. New Delhi –Bombay, 1971, reprinted 1992. p. 78-80

becoming one with Brahma. The cat-kitten analogy, however reveals the fact that "devotion is a two way traffic - the mother cat always remaining attentive to the needs of the kitten and the latter ever-dependent upon the former for its life and movements."[361] The novel elucidates that only unconditional and ultimate surrender and reliance on the Absolute leads to total deliverance or Moksha.

Govindan Nair himself symbolises a swift cat and taking a massive leap from the material to the spiritual plane, at will opines, "The cat is carrying the kitten. We would all be kittens carried by the cat. Some who are lucky will one day know it …..Others live hearing meow- meow …. I like being the Kitten." [362] He believes firmly in the Mother Cat not only because he seeks divine protection and grace from it, but the sheer joy of being fondled by the mother, "Ah the kitten when its neck is being held by its mother does it know anything else but the joy of being held by its mother? [363] You see the elongated thin hairy thing dangling, and you think, poor kid, it must suffer to be so held. But I say the kitten is the safest thing in the world, the kitten held in the mouth of the mother cat. Could one have been born without a mother? Modern inventions do not as such need a father. But a mother I tell you, without Mother the world is not. So allow her to fondle you and to hold you. I often think how noble it is to see the world, the legs dangling straight, the eyes steady, and the mouth of the mother at the neck. Beautiful."[364]

Pai regards Nair as a Guru, and Nair's constant effort is to impress upon Pai that yearning for material assets is a universal human phenomenon, yet spiritual perfection should also be a part of man's earthly attainments. Nair staunchly believes that unflinching faith and total surrenders, like the kitten alone and not wisdom, can redeem mankind. Pai, a down-to-earth man craving worldly possessions, does not heed Nair's advice. He is desperately chasing his dream to build his own house, knowing full well that

---

[361] Quoted in Niranjan Rout, The Fictional Work of Raja Rao: A Study of his Mind and Art, Ph.D. Thesis. Magadh University. 1995
[362] Raja Rao: *The Cat and Shakespeare*, Delhi, Hind Pocket Books, 1971. p. 13
[363] Ibid.,p.10
[364] Raja Rao: *The Cat and Shakespeare*, Delhi, Hind Pocket Books, 1971. p. 11-12

with his meagre income, he could not afford to do so. Nevertheless, he reveals his big dreams to Nair, "I wanted to become a rich man for then my wife would be so happy that I could do what I liked…I would build a big house, like contractor Srinivas Pai."[365].

Nair is a trustworthy neighbour, who always helps Pai in distress, be it his dreadful skin eruptions or making generous monetary contributions enabling Pai to acquire the rented house of Murugan Mudali in which he lives since his mistress Shantha is pregnant. Pai is grateful for Nair as an ideal neighbour saying, "I sing of man, because he is my neighbour. After all one's big neighbour is oneself. The neighbour's neighbour is always the self ."[366] According to Esha Dey this expression is a western influence on Rao since "Love thy neighbour as thyself forms the basis of Christian humanism for it recognizes plurality as valid. The idea of self (Atman) as the only Reality forms the essence of monist thought and is fundamentally opposed to the Christian pluralism in so far as it is expressed in the concept of the "neighbour. Rao's comedy has therefore to strive for synthesis in the concept of the neighbour to love whom has been so far the duty of the Christian or the Buddhist alone."[367]

Nair's obsession with the cat and Kitten philosophy prompts one of his colleagues, John to gift him a real cat, "Govindan Nair always talks of a mother cat. It carries the kitten by the scruff of its neck. That is why he is so carefree. He says, Learn the way of the kitten, then you are saved. Allow the mother cat, sir, to carry you". [368] Nair quickly replies, "I let the mother cat carry me."[369]

The conviction of this truth provides Nair with a blissful life despite its trials and tribulations. Total surrender to an all-pervasive omnipotent force and the certainty and joy of its total protection stills a restless and rambling mind leading to a state of perfect happiness. Believing firmly that in our strife-torn life today,

---

[365] Raja Rao: *The Cat and Shakespeare*, Delhi, Orient Paperbacks, 1996.p.9.
[366] Esha Dey, *The Novels of Raja Rao, The Theme of Quest*. New Delhi. Prestige Books. 1992. p. 151.
[367] Ibid., p. 151
[368] Raja Rao: *The Cat and Shakespeare*, Delhi, Hind Pocket Books, 1971. p. 74.
[369] Ibid. p. 50

only the Absolute truth (Sat) can ensure bliss (Ananda) or a state of perfect happiness, Nair aptly comments, "The mind that is not when the cat carries kitten; that is happiness."[370] Human beings solely dependent on divine grace, he feels, have nothing to fear, not even Death," What is death to a kitten that walks on the wall? Have you ever seen a kitten fall? You could fall. I could fall. But the kittens walk on the wall. They are so deft.... The mother cat watches them. And when they are about to fall, there she is, her head in the air, and she picks you up by the scruff of your neck. You never know where she is. (Who has seen her? Nobody has). To know where she is you have to be the mother's mother. And how could that ever be ? Mother, I worship you.[371]

The message that reverberates throughout the novel is unconditional devotion and worship of the almighty Mother for benediction and salvation. Pai's love and devotion for Shantha can further explore the idea of the cat-kitten relationship. Though an extramarital affair, "Shantha's unhesitating surrender is symbolic of the devotees surrender to the Will of the Almighty."[372]. Shantha, Lakshmi and Usha all symbolize the Feminine principle, which embodies wisdom and feline grace and eventually the source of spiritual development and deliverance. A pregnant Shantha, who is an integral part of Pai's life, believes that worship and devotion are necessary to know the mother who "is necessary for all children"[373] and also the proof for fatherhood. Pai is elated by the discovery of the phenomenon of protection by women in the form of benign mother, beloved, sister and daughter symbolized by the Cat, "Man is protected. You could not be without a mother. You are always a child. The wife is she who makes you the child. That is why our children resemble us men."[374] Ramakrishna's faith that Shantha's love is absolute and free from all changes exalts their love further, "love is where happening happens as non-happening. What can happen where everything is."[375]

---

[370]Ibid., p. 95

[371] Ibid. p. 68.

[372] Kaushal Sharma ,*Raja Rao: A Study of His Themes and Technique*, New Delhi, Sarup & Sons. 2005.p.61

[373] Raja Rao: *The Cat and Shakespeare*: Delhi, Hind Pocket Books 1971. pp. 93-94

[374] Raja Rao: *The Cat and Shakespeare*, Delhi, Orient Paperbacks, 1996. p. 33

[375] Raja Rao: *The Cat and Shakespeare*, Delhi, Hind Pocket Books, 1971. p. 110

In sharp contrast to Shantha is Pai's wife Saroja, engaged in material pursuits looking after her native home and children. She does not care for his physical welfare, hindering Pai's spiritual quest. Through Shantha and Saroja, the novel reveals the vital message of giving and take, surrender and reliance- the essence of true devotion to God. Nair's conviction that the. "The kitten receives and the mother gives – life, protection and all. To speak the truth, nobody can give. Only the mother cat can give."[376] is revealed through Shantha, who personifies love. No wonder Ramakrishna aptly says, "Shantha worships me and has herself."[377]

When Pai is ill, Shantha weeps in prayer so that he recovers soon. When in need, she sells her land unhesitatingly for him to buy his house, whereas Saroja is busy saving money for her son Vithal not bothering about Pai's health. "This 'giving' of Shantha is greater than taking of Saroja. The two words 'give' and 'take' acquire a rich symbolical significance. The persons like Shantha blessed with spiritual attitude always 'give' whereas, persons, like Saroja, who are deeply entrenched in materialistic pursuits have their palms always extended to "take."[378] Shantha does everything knowing that what belongs to her belongs to Pai and her, "What belongs to you belongs to me, what belongs to the Lord alone belongs. For woman is belonging, as mind is belonging - belonging to me. You can only shine of light. The shine knows its light but to whom does the light belongs? Light belongs to light.[379]

What is missing in the relationship of Ramakrishna and his socially wedded wife Saroja is the incredible intensity and depth – in fact, the reverence that exists in Shantha's love. Ramakrishna knows that Shantha became his mistress "because she felt as his wife. She remained a wife. My feet were there for her to worship."[380]

Shantha lives harmoniously with Pai, understanding even his silence, without demanding marriage because she believes,

---

[376]Ibid., p. 51.

[377] Ibid. p. 23

[378] Kaushal Sharma ,*Raja Rao: A Study of His Themes and Technique*, New Delhi, Sarup & Sons. 2005.p.65

[379] Raja Rao: *The Cat and Shakespeare*, Delhi, Hind Pocket Books 1971. p. 34

[380] Ibid. pp. 23-24

"marriage is not a fact, it is a state. You marry because you see."[381] Shantha finds her fulfilment in surrendering to Pai, considering him the be-all and end of all of her beings. Her self also gets recognized this way, "For a woman love is not development. Love is recognition."[382] Despite her not being wedded ceremonially, this relationship is sacred to her –and she is a wife in the truest sense of the term. The intensity of the love matters because marriage is not a contract and a devoted woman is more valuable than a wife, "To be a wife is not to be wed. To be a wife is to worship your man. Then you are born. And you give birth to what is born in being born. You annihilate time and you become a wife. Wife-hood, of all states in the world, seems the most holy. It lives on even when time dies."[383]

Thus Shantha's love is a perfect analogy to a devotee's resignation to the Almighty Lord or the benign mother. The Masculine and Feminine principles unite in the perfect love of Shantha and Ramakrishna, symbolizing the Advaitic idea of the Purusha-Prakriti relationship, reinforcing the Indian belief that when man and woman unite, they attain the highest and holiest state of self-realization. In this fathomless union, a man aligns with the oneness of life pervading the entire universe. Ramakrishna Pai and Shantha's union was divine, holy matrimony solemnized in heaven as Pai states aptly, "Suddenly I hear the music of marriage, I must go."[384]

For Raja Rao, matrimony means "where there is only perception, and so neither perceiver nor perceived."[385] "You marry because you see" says Pai and transcends duality. Shantha has achieved this state much before Pai, who realizes it only towards the end. No wonder it is Shantha who validates Pai's existence, "I am your proof. You are only seen by me. Who could know you as I know you? …. You made me say I am…..Only I say you. And

---

[381] Ibid.,p. 33
[382] Ibid. p. 24
[383] Ibid. p. 32
[384] Ibid. p. 117.
[385] Raja Rao (Quoted in), M. K. Naik: Perspectives on Raja Rao, op. cit., p. 101.

You say I."[386] Thus feeling illuminated through Shantha Pai proceeds towards divine Grace.

Raja Rao's attitude towards matrimony is quite different from his western counterparts. D. H. Lawrence believes in 'divine otherness' and does not want the woman to surrender to the will of man. He only wants them to unite so that they can experience infinite bliss without annihilating each other's personalities. Where Lawrence believes that the mysterious force of sex unites two people unrelated by blood, Rao believes that karmic connection brings man and woman closer. Bernard Shaw regards woman as a contrivance in the hands of nature and man as an instrument in the hands of a woman. Their union is for the procreation and evolution of the human race. Rao, however, believes them to be divine couples reliving divine roles on earth. Pai, therefore, regards Shantha and not Saroja as Goddess Parvati Shiva's divine consort, who occupies the heart of his temple. Rao's belief synthesizes with western thought in as much as Pai's attraction for women like Shantha "verifies the Jungian paradigm of the male, whose "anima" benefits, in a love relationship, from the woman's "animus", to the point that the feminine "animus" possess a divine omnipotence." [387]

Shantha admires Pai's neighbour Nair also for his philosophizing when she comes to live with Pai after the death of Nair's son Sridhar. A bright young man Nair, despite his marriage to a wealthy landlord's daughter, working as a ration clerk, impresses Shantha with his disposition. Despite his petty monthly salary of forty-five rupees, Nair is a contented man, a true kitten who does not lose his balance ever believing that Mother Cat resides in Heaven so all will be well with him. Divine Grace does give Nair the courage to bear the irreparable loss of his son's tragic death with equanimity. Nair understands that only the personal self has passed from non-being into being. He is aware that by surpassing illusion, human beings thus pass into immortality. What

---

[386] Raja Rao: *The Cat and Shakespeare*, Delhi, Hind Pocket Books, 1971. p. 94.

[387] Claudio Gorlier , "Raja Rao's *The Cat and Shakespeare* : A Western View in Rajeshwar Mittapalli & Pier Paolo Piciucco.Ed.*The Fiction of Raja Rao: Critical Studies*, New Delhi: Atlantic Publishers. 2001. p.210

baffles Pai entirely is Shantha's style of saying two things simultaneously, which resembles Nair's roundabout way of talking. "Indeed she seems to understand Nair's riddles better than Pai and hence has a semblance of individual independence…Unlike Savithri of *The Serpent and Rope* "she is not wholly an object here" and "never seen as a docile disciple of Pai in an asexual role.[388]

Obsessed with building a three-storied house perpetually, Pai tries to convince Nair, "My wife can hire out the first two floors if need be. It would be so much capital invested. A house of three stories is a safe investment."[389] Philosophically a three-storied house, according to Ayurveda, denotes the human body made up of *Vata* (wind), *Pitta* (bile) and *Kaph* (phlegm). It also symbolizes the three primordial human attributes or Gunas, which constitute life. According to Sankhya Yoga of the Gita, these are - *Sattva* (purity, light and upward motion), *Rajas* (luxuries, attachment and downward motion) and *Tamas* (ignorance, negativity and darkness). Only after conquering the Rajas and Tamas can man achieve Sattva and attain Heaven. These Gunas are also associated with the three states of consciousness i.e. *Jagriti* (waking), *Susupti* (sleeping) and *Swapna* (dreaming). Through building this house, Pai desires to consolidate his life on earth.

So important is this symbol that almost all the other characters in the novel discuss their existing houses and their locations or intentions to build one. The different kinds of houses discussed include Boothlingam Iyer's house, located inside a Fort beside the temple. The temple houses divinity; the fort is the home of royalty. Judge Iyengar's house is a hermitage in the Himalayas. Mudali, the toddy seller's house, is a well-equipped structure which brings appreciation from his tenants. Because of inclement weather, the doctor's large house looks dark despite sufficient lighting. Unfortunately, when Nair's son dies, he comments that he has gone to Heaven - a three-storied house.

---

[388] Esha Dey, *The Novels of Raja Rao, The Theme of Quest*. New Delhi. Prestige Books. 1992. p.162.
[389] Raja Rao: *The Cat and Shakespeare*, Delhi, Orient Paperbacks, 1996.p.21.

With his limited means, it is an uphill task for Pai to build this house physically without amassing wealth wrongfully. Using such money does not bring joy, as proved by a member of the revenue department Kunni Kutta Nair, who dies after a fatal fall. To Pai's query about the view from its topmost floor, Nair comments altruistically that he would die the day it is finished. This death implies complete moral devastation, total entrenchment in *Tamas* and the selling of one's conscience for acquiring this ill-begotten wealth.

Shantha, who is quite content with the idea of a two-storied house closer to earth, safer and economically viable, cautions Pai from treading this risky path. Knowing that building the house is a tall order and seeing Pai still clinging to his dream Nair is infused with compassion and love for his deprived neighbour. Probably divinely ordained to be the medium of his salvation, he organizes the money for Pai. Nair also feels that if he helps Pai get his dream house, his ailing son, Sridhar, may gain health because fulfilling somebody's ardent desire brings good wishes. Shantha selflessly sells her land and gives the money to Pai. Thus like the mythical hunter who invokes divine grace by dropping *Bilva* leaves accidentally on the sacred Shivalinga, Pai also receives divine benediction unknowingly because "it's not the way you worship that is important but what you adore."[390]

The *Bilva,* or the wood apple tree here, symbolizes the divine abode of Shiva. As a cosmic tree, it signifies birth, growth, death, and regeneration. The expectant mother, Shantha, relaxes under the tree while Usha and Sridhar play under it. One rainy day getting drenched under it, the latter catches pneumonia and dies, unfortunately. Pai, who had been staring at its falling leaves constantly hoping that divine grace would descend from it very soon, has his prayers answered finally. With the financial help from Nair and Shantha, he decides to build a two-storied house on the latter's advice.

---

[390] Raja Rao: *The Cat and Shakespeare*, Delhi, Hind Pocket Books, 1971. p. 9.

In Hinduism, the two storied houses philosophically symbolize the two paths *Sagun* or with attributes realized through the sensuous world and *Nirgun* or attributeless, which cannot be realized through the senses. The former leads to the latter's attainment, which symbolizes the Absolute or Brahma. "Pai has to pass through the two stages, viz. the feminine wisdom embodied in Shantha and Feline wisdom embodied in Mother Cat. .....Shantha for Pai represents the first stage of building a house, symbolic of the quest for self knowledge. Pai's love for Shantha is symbolic of *Sagun* stage and through this he can comprehend the Ultimate Reality i.e. Mother Cat or Nirgun (Ultimate Reality). Pai plans to build a house of bricks and stone to give it permanence......The investment of money in building this house is symbolic of human values."[391] Therefore it is repeatedly said that, "our houses must look like us just as our ancestors built temples in the shape of man."[392]

Thus to build or rebuild a house satisfies both material and spiritual urges, and therefore it appears as the second most important symbol in the novel, "the house has represented the abode only at face value. Actually, it tends to expand into a status symbol, an ideal stage where the characters play their roles, and the various components may denote the minds, the attitudes, the inclinations, the inner soul of those who inhabit the house; all in all, a bourgeois replica of the temple or of the royal palace."[393] As a metaphysical necessity " this house is also a tabernacle, the symbol of earthly existence of a soul that fundamentally belongs to the divine. "[394] Therefore, like a temple, Pai's small white house displays an ochre band symbolizing spirituality, "the house is like a temple, the temporary abode of a soul whose home is the Lord Himself."[395]

Pai's urge to extend it vertically to three floors is reflected in man's yearning for spiritual perfection in this world and

---

[391] Kaushal Sharma ,Raja Rao: *A Study of His Themes and Technique*, New Delhi, Sarup & Sons. 2005..p.63.
[392] Raja Rao: *The Cat and Shakespeare*, Delhi, Orient Paperbacks, 1996.p.8.
[393] Claudio Gorlier , "Raja Rao's *The Cat and Shakespeare* : A Western View." *in* Rajeshwar Mittapalli & Pier Paolo Piciucco. Ed. *The Fiction of Raja Rao: Critical Studies*,New Delhi: Atlantic Publishers. 2001. p.208
[394] Esha Dey, *The Novels of Raja Rao, The Theme of Quest*. New Delhi. Prestige Books.1992. p 148.
[395] Ibid.,p. 148

transcendence to the Absolute. "To recall a western perspective, the medieval principle of the ascent to the deity (was), often symbolized by the staircase, (*itinorarium mentis in deum*) or, as in George Herbert's Prayer, with its mystic leap to Heaven, from the earth to the "milky ways."[396]

In Pai's house, deities are symbolized by windows which open towards the infinite expanse of the sea, as water symbolizes primordial creation. "So Shantha, carrying four months has a mysterious affinity with the sea (the sea knows me," says Shantha. It is to the swelling crest of the waves that her motherhood supplicates for a child. So, like the sea, her connection with Pai's house is inextricable. She represents in human form this existence, the creative aspect of the Supreme."[397]

Pai's house-building activity on a spiritual level thus denotes his journey toward the Ultimate Reality. He calls his house Kamala Bhawan, which symbolizes purity, and the open garden in front of this house symbolizes Advaita, confirming the divine presence "Thou art there". The ultimate mystical experience which leads to Pai's enlightenment is still to come, "when you can walk to the next garden, you can say, I love the cat." [398]

Moreover, this will happen only when Pai crosses the wall between Nair and Pai's house, which links and separates their identities. Nair and the cat are always going across the Wall. Nair leaps across the wall at will to communicate his teachings and enable Pai to see beyond the wall. Pai will, of course, cross the wall only when the time for his initiation arrives. This wall symbolizes the divide between illusion (*Maya*) and reality. Maya, according to Rao, amounts to misunderstanding, due to which Pai hesitates to cross the wall, afraid that he will never return. "We all know that once we leave personality we cannot come back. There is no personality left after you go beyond it."[399] The ignorant human ego keeps Pai's soul mired in the sufferings of this world, preventing

---

[396] Claudio Gorlier , "Raja Rao's *The Cat and Shakespeare* : A Western View *in* Rajeshwar Mittapalli & Pier Paolo Piciucco Ed. *The Fiction of Raja Rao: Critical Studies*, New Delhi: Atlantic Publishers. 2001. p.208
[397] Esha Dey, *The Novels of Raja Rao, The Theme of Quest*. New Delhi. Prestige Books. 1992.p. 149
[398] Raja Rao: *The Cat and Shakespeare*, Delhi, Orient Paperbacks, 1996.p.92.
[399] Ayyappa Panikar: "A Conversation with Raja Rao on *The Cat and Shakespeare*." *Chandrabhaga* , 2. (1979):. p.15.

him from crossing the wall and passing into completeness. Therefore contrary to Pai suffering with his life partner, the enlightened man Govindan Nair considers his life to be a game that he plays to the hilt .

If it had not been for his roguish philosophy and dedication to the supreme will, Nair could not have survived the fraud and corruption of the ration office- a system introduced during the Second World War. The ration office provides a " microcosm in the microcosm. It stands for daily work and routine, for bureaucracy, for dubious compromise and corruption, for arrogance, for a hybrid of beliefs and allegiances, for the imprint of colonial rule at least "other", remote from a pervasive, omnipresent Britain a travesty and yet an epitome of modern India. Once more it provides the proper stage for a comedy, serious and grotesque, not only for the men who perform it, but the most suitable scene for the epiphany and for its main agent the Cat.[400]"

Despite its negativity, since the ration office provides food grains, sugar, rice, oil and other necessities of life to poor people, Nair perceives it positively, equating it to Kamdhenu, the mythical sacred cow who bestows all boons. Its importance also cannot be undermined because it "determines the action of the novel in two ways. Firstly, it makes Nair's arrest and trial possible and his precept of Cat-and-Kitten is literally translated into reality. He has followed the way of the kitten and has been saved by the Mother Cat in flesh and blood. Secondly, Pai's purchase of the house depends to a large extent on Nair's financial assistance which seems to stem from a mysterious unsuspected source of income."[401]

Like the house, the ration card is also a life-sustaining symbol, the colours green, red and blue symbolizing childhood, youth and adulthood with their infinite wisdom, respectively. "This human world is relative where all our actions or *Karma* are judged and evaluated morally and its fruits carried over from one life into another. So our current life is based on "our karma predestined from

---

[400] Claudio Gorlier , "Raja Rao's *The Cat and Shakespeare* : A Western View *in* Rajeshwar Mittapalli & Pier Paolo Piciucco, Ed. *The Fiction of Raja Rao: Critical Studies,* New Delhi: Atlantic Publishers. 2001. p.209.
[401] Esha Dey, *The Novels of Raja Rao, The Theme of Quest.* New Delhi. Prestige Books. 1992.p 147.

previous births. At a ration shop everybody gets his quota according to the colour of his card, the world offers everyone rewards and punishment according to one's *Karma,* the ration apportioned in this earth. So "we all live on ration " and "life is a ration shop." The scale weighs according to the ration card, "Where is your card, Sir? Green, Red or Blue."[402]

Nair's tribulations begin with his son Sridhar's death is followed by the death of his boss Boothlinga Iyer. While Nair and his colleagues are embroiled in a mock Hamlet scene with to be or not to be stance, the cat suddenly jumps on Iyer's head, who dies on the spot suffering a massive heart attack. Thus through Nair Rao "propitiates the cat's entrance on the scene. The cat is the agent instrumental in reaching the climax of the story, end effecting the epiphany."...In this novel the cat is coherently real even when she performs a factual , but symbolic , ritual action jumping on Boothlinga Iyer's head and officiating , as it were , his astounding death in the reiterated name of Shiva, the destroyer."[403]

Nair is falsely accused of taking a bribe from an old lady and goes to jail "as though in atonement for the whole corrupt life going on in the ration shop as well as for the extramarital propensities of his boss…..this temporary bondage of Nair makes the redemption of Pai, his neighbour possible for Nair's cat is left with Shantha to teach Pai the kitten's way to salvation."[404] While Nair bears his jail term peacefully, the divine mother resurrects him from his predicament. On the day of the trial, the cat is taken to court, and in a mysterious twist to the tale, it points out the incriminating file revealing Boothlinga Iyer's signature establishing his complicity in the case and Nair's innocence. Nair is set free but transferred from Trivandrum. He leaves the Cat permanently with Pai, and Shantha looks after it.

It is Pai's turn to receive divine benediction now. In a magical act, the cat leads him across the demarcating wall where he finds "a truth not as fact but as ignition." Chasing the cat when

---

[402] Ibid., p. 155

[403] Claudio Gorlier , "Raja Rao's *The Cat and Shakespeare* : A Western View." *in* Rajeshwar Mittapalli & Pier Paolo Piciucco, Ed. *The Fiction of Raja Rao: Critical Studies*, New Delhi: Atlantic Publishers. 2001. p.210.:

[404] Esha Dey, *The Novels of Raja Rao, The Theme of Quest*. New Delhi. Prestige Books. 1992.p 151.

Pai crosses over, he finds himself in a beautiful garden, an earthly paradise, fragrant with colourful flowers, herbs and serene water pools. Thus, mere sensory pleasure automatically converts into attainment as Pai instantly feels God's grace being showered on him. Raja Rao opines rightly, "for me it is poor Pai who is only an Arjuna, and Govindan Nair is Sri Krishna. One is the man-man the other is man beyond man."[405]

It seems that Nair's role is of "an agent in action", and "his purpose is to be instrumental in the story of Pai's salvation"… And Pai admits, "he would never have gone to the other side of reality but for Govindan Nair."[406] Thus Nair, a quaint combination of a rogue and a Guru "ultimately proves the efficacy of his teachings in the life of his disciple and thus "Pai's down to earth world view benefits from Nair's metaphysical mastery."[407].The role of the cat in freeing Nair from the prison and leading Pai to his emancipation was to prove to Nair true that the Cat can take a man to beatitude.

Following the technique of contemplative narration, in *The Serpent and the Rope,* Rao reveals the serious through the serious, but in *The Cat and Shakespeare,* it is "a revelation of the serious through the ridiculous."[408] "Humour is as pervasive in the Cat and Shakespeare as melancholy is in *The Serpent and Rope.* Indeed it is the very antipode of its predecessor in which everything is enveloped with sorrow-marriage, childbirth and of course death. In the *Cat and Shakespeare* on the other hand, everything is an object of gentle laughter, not the vindictive satiric demonism, but the quiet humour which indicates distance as well as involvement "[409]

From the trivialities of life often emerge profound philosophical truths. Govindan Nair proves this point beyond doubt. From his perceptions of the humdrum of daily life emerge his thoughts which are echoes of truth perceived and realized as a

---

[405] Ayyappa Panikar: "A Conversation with Raja Rao on *The Cat and Shakespeare.*" *Chandrabhaga* , 2. (1979):p. 16.
[406] Esha Dey, *The Novels of Raja Rao, The Theme of Quest.* New Delhi. Prestige Books. 1992.p.158
[407] Claudio Gorlier , " Raja Rao's *The Cat and Shakespeare* : A Western View." *in* Rajeshwar Mittapalli &Pier Paolo Piciucco Ed.: *The Fiction of Raja Rao, Critical Studies,* New Delhi: Atlantic Publishers. 2001.p.207.
[408] Kaushal Sharma, *Raja Rao: A Study of His Themes and Technique,* New Delhi, Sarup & Sons. 2005. p.53.
[409] Esha Dey, *The Novels of Raja Rao, The Theme of Quest.* New Delhi. Prestige Books.1992.p 159.

matter of faith and felt within oneself, "There's only one depth and one extensively and that's (in) oneself. It's like a kitten on a garden wall.[410]. "Govindan Nair talks of only what he sees. During his trial when the judge asks him the best way to know the truth his simple reply is by "being it." [411]

Thus the expressions of Nair and Pai resound as truths in the novel weaving its metaphysical tapestry. Pai eventually realizes what his Guru always wanted him to realize "only a better union leads to metaphysical understanding which in turn leads to deeper communion with the abstract cosmic reality. Reliance and surrender to this force leads to attainment of protection from it in myriad and mysterious ways- creating and resolving the complexities of our life. The conflict between the mundane and the sublime and the latter's triumph over the former makes this work effective as it is through the conflict of intentions that the fictional medium finds its relevance."[412]

Thus "*The Cat and Shakespeare* proves to be a novel of echoes – echoes of meanings reverberating to consolidate into the philosophic ideal of kitten-like surrender to God. We hear echoes in the Marabar caves in E. M. Forester's *A Passage to India,* too, but the echo there remains just an undefined symbol, whereas in *The Cat and the Shakespeare,* definitions themselves become echoes of truth which can be comprehended fully by being them." [413]

The cat-kitten symbolizes the lover and beloved, the disciple and the Guru, the devotee and God as Bhakta and Bhagwan, in which the substratum of devotion to God is a dual response. The novel emphasizes that one-sided devotion or mere surrender is incomplete and imperfect. The truth is that with surrender, complete reliance on the Absolute invokes divine grace. This is the eternal essence of the Hindu faith. Therefore other characters like John and boss Boothlingam Iyer do not experience

---

[410] Raja Rao: *The Cat and Shakespeare*, Delhi, Hind Pocket Books, 1971. p. 62
[411] Ibid.,p.103.
[412] Quoted in Niranjan Rout, The Fictional Work of Raja Rao: A Study of his Mind and Art, Ph.D. Thesis. Magadh University 1995
[413] Quoted in Niranjan Rout, The Fictional Work of Raja Rao: A Study of his Mind and Art, Ph.D. Thesis. Magadh Usniversity. 1995.

divine benevolence; because they either mock or fear the cat, they neither see nor realize the truth.

In his earlier work, *The Serpent and the Rope* "human suffering and metaphysics clash violently because Western civilizations accept the reality of existence, unlike the East, which considers it a Maya or unreal rejecting suffering as the proof of dualism. "The only way to escape from this impasse, suggests the *Cat and Shakespeare,* is to treat suffering itself as unreal and it seems that only a special brand of humour can shake the irrevocable reality of human misery. So Rao's humour is of that particular variety which …Freud defines as a process permitting 'to refuse to admit that the trauma of the external world can touch one."[414] Raja Rao, therefore, treats the death of a son, dreadful buboes, and corruption charges, which are rationally objects of pain, in a humorous manner.

The narrative and meditative components of the novel seem to be hugely inspired by Shakespeare's to- be or not-to-be, where the "function of the latter is to modify the former……. This grave tomfoolery stems from intelligence which in the form of play of thought performs a surreal function, that of breaking down the barrier erected by rationality between the two states, conscious and unconscious – to be and not-to-be representing different realities."[415] In the novel, therefore "a human situation in fictional reality is presented and immediately rendered unreal through humorous distanciation based on a witty play with metaphysics."[416] No wonder Pai's unconscious body is covered with dreadful pus-laden buboes, or Shridhar's deaths evoke laughter. When Sridhar mistakes Pai's unconscious diseased body as dead, Nair humours reality "When you fall unconscious they say you are dead. In fact where were you brother, when Sridhar thought you were dead? Were you dead to yourself, my friend? You purge to live. You sleep to die. When sleep is life, where is Death? Ha. Ha. Ha." [417]

---

[414] Esha Dey, *The Novels of Raja Rao, The Theme of Quest*. New Delhi. Prestige Books. 1992.p. 160.
[415] Ibid.,pp. 160-161
[416] Ibid,,pp.160
[417] Ibid.,pp. 160-161.

Even Sridhar's death does not sting…. "That is why Sridhar died. Usha spoke over the wall and the cat carried him away. Funny, Sir, that a child is carried away by a Cat." Describing preparations for Sridhar's cremation, the author says, "The bamboos were already in the courtyard. Death had come. It spoilt a nice courtyard, with flower beds of roses. I never went across the wall. How could I? I could hear Tangamma weep, then Govindan Nair say something. Pillai is such an able man. He walked out of the house efficiently. It was a bad case, he said. His Gladstone bag was so knowledgeable. It contained mysterious instruments that spoke Death is such speech."[418]

Rout argues "that the plot is too thin and elusive and the deep truth of total surrender does not impact the readers considerably. Despite of his sincerity and mastery of the medium Raja Rao has failed to create a form of sufficient dramatic intensity. The belated mystical illumination of Ramakrishna Pai goes little beyond metaphysical understanding or enlightened awareness, even as the detection of the real signature in the file remains a mysterious revelation instead of becoming a mystical experience. The novel only resounds with repeated echoes of the highest perception in the form of pronouncements of Govindan Nair, instead of achieving a profound treatment of it…More like an expanded metaphor which is developed in a riddling style of the narrative and dialogue, this novel is closer to an Upanishadic parable and can be rightly branded as a metaphysical comedy or a philosophical fantasy."[419]

Iyengar takes a contrary stand, "If Raja Rao has moved from the *Puranic* 'form' to *itihasic*, from the *itihasic* to the *Upanishadic*, there has been a parallel movement too from Karma in *Kanthapura* to Jnana in *The Serpent and The Rope*, on and onto *Bhakti Prapati* in *the Cat and Shakespeare*…Govindan Nair is no intellectual, he is intelligent, but he is no intellectual, he is no metaphysician. Neither is Ramachandra Pai. They are creatures of common humanity but equally with Moorthy or Rama they too

---

[418]Ibid.,p. 159
[419] Quoted in Niranjan Rout, The Fictional Work of Raja Rao: A Study of his Mind and Art, Ph.D. Thesis. 1995

hanker after fulfillment. For them the path of devotion (*bhakti*) and the path of surrender (*Prapati*) - one shades of into the other – is best; following this path one cannot possibly miss one's goal."[420]

Thus "the mode in which the *Cat and Shakespeare* are presented is more illustrative than imitative, more symbolic than realistic." [421] and "*The Cat and Shakespeare* are justified because it offers a concentrated mystique of the personal faith of an artist astride two cultures. It is a deeply personal correlative for the meeting of opposites, striving towards an objective formulation."[422] Thus, the cat "becomes the central decisive figure, the necessary springboard..., welding together India, the East and the West throughout the timeless history."[423]

"Shakespeare's presence in this book must be seen as functional to the narrative more than to its conceptual structure."[424] For Rao, literature is Sadhana and "it is for this reason that Shakespeare is a saint, a Jnani to him "is almost an Indian of my India so he has too influenced me fundamentally – Hamlet first and foremost then King Lear, and finally The Tempest."[425] "Given that Shakespeare is " the Great Sage" who knew everything of the ration shop i.e. of life he makes possible the shift to a dramatic development and consequently bears on the articulation of Rao's discourse."[426] Rao is convinced that being a Creator, Shakespeare "is someone who has gone beyond duality and as such he is a universal symbol."[427] So, Govindan Nair, the Guru, is full of Shakespeare. Like the Cat, Shakespeare has also been an enigma, a mystery for scholars. In the words of Pai, Nair, who is a true worshipper of the Cat, has a style that "is a mixture of the Vicar of Wakefield and Shakespeare"[428] which makes him an enigma in

---

[420] K.R.S.Iyengar: "A Note on Raja Rao's *The Cat and Shakespeare*, *Perspectives on Raja Rao*, ed, K.K. Sharma Ghaziabad: Vimal Prakashan, 1980.p.107.

[421] Esha Dey, *The Novels of Raja Rao, The Theme of Quest*. New Delhi.Prestige Books. 1992.p.148

[422] Ibid., p.156

[423] Claudio Gorlier, "Raja Rao's *The Cat and Shakespeare:* A Western View." *in* Rajeshwar Mittapalli &Pier Paolo Piciucco: Ed. *The Fiction of Raja Rao, Critical Studies*, New Delhi: Atlantic Publishers, 2001.p.211

[424] Ibid.,p. 211

[425] M.K.Naik: Raja Rao. Twayne's English Author Series. New York: Twayne Publishers. 1972., p. 9

[426] Claudio Gorlier, "Raja Rao's *The Cat and Shakespeare:* A Western View." *in* Rajeshwar Mittapalli &Pier Paolo Piciucco. Ed. *The Fiction of Raja Rao, Critical Studies*, New Delhi: Atlantic Publishers, 2001.p.211

[427] Raja Rao's letter to M.K.Naik quoted in "The Kingdom of God is within a 'mew." p. 143

[428] Raja Rao: *The Cat and Shakespeare*, New York, The Macmillan Company, 1965.p. 110

himself. The symbol of Shakespeare has not been worked out entirely as the Cat has been done in the novel.

However, *the Cat and Shakespeare* is an unusual narrative, a curious mixture of comic fantasy and profound metaphysics. Raja Rao skillfully and artistically weaves myths, legends, fables, and symbols to convey Vedanta and creates characters whose thoughts substantiate the metaphysical content of the novel. This creative technique makes the narrative engaging and profound. The Cat and Shakespeare is thus the story of Pai's quest and attainment of the ultimate reality of total surrender and reliance on God.

Nowhere in Indian writing in English is so much said in so short a space. Nevertheless, 'said' is hardly the right word, for what remains unsaid in this tale is far more critical. Thus according to Rout "Raja Rao has admirably combined realism and fantasy, revealing the a-logical manner of action that suggests the impersonal truth which lies beyond the logic of cause and effect.[429]

---

[429] Quoted in Niranjan Rout, The Fictional Work of Raja Rao: A Study of his Mind and Art, Ph.D. Thesis. 1995

CHAPTER VI: Alienation and Integration

The East-West confrontation in *Comrade Kirillov* is brought to the fore by exploring the complex psyche of Kirillov, the protagonist, who is highly perturbed through individual predicament in a changing complex society. Alienated from this society and disillusioned with the world's sufferings in general, he embarks on an intellectual quest in the west but finds metaphysical solutions for these existential problems in the East. Comrade Kirillov, therefore, " forms a sequel to the earlier masterpieces viz. *The Serpent and the Rope* and *The Cat and Shakespeare* which deal with the quest for Indianness as their theme. *The Serpent and the Rope* explores on a personal level, *the Cat and Shakespeare* on a social level and *Comrade Kirillov* on a political level. It is a fascinating and absorbing story of an Indian intellectual turned communist, a prisoner of ideology, who is lost in his quest."[430] Wavering between his ideological commitments and his quest for his roots, this fundamentally ambiguous character deserves all the sympathy for his noble intentions. Even his Creator, the author does not know what is transpiring in his own hero's mind because he is a soul so ambivalent.

Man, according to Comrade Kirillov, "is an emotional being who has not only material needs but also spiritual hunger."[431] The entire story unfolds as a narration in the third person. The ideological crisis is presented as a dialogue between Kirillov and Rama, the story's narrator. Kirillov was born as Padmanabha Iyer in a south Indian Brahmin family, who received westernized education from early school to college in India. However, emotionally, he is a true Brahmin who takes good care of his sacred thread and adores everything noble and sound in his country, especially literature, tradition and philosophy.

---

[430] Kaushal Sharma ,Raja Rao: *A Study of His Themes and Technique*, New Delhi, Sarup & Sons. 2005..p.70
[431] O.P.Mathur, " Existential Overtones in Raja Rao's Comrade Kirillov."*Modern Indian English Fiction, 1st Edition* New Delhi: Abhinav Publications. 1993.p. 121.

An extremely innocent, loving and honest man ever ready to help others, Kirillov abhors brutality, "You know politics is something I do not fully understand. Human suffering life, birth, death sickness, marriage, love and God, I understand. I hate violence of all sorts, especially political violence."[432] This insight is the cause of his disgust with the Hindu orthodoxy prevailing in modern India, which does not treat human beings equally. His own aristocratic life in his sprawling ancestral mansion, sustained by royal land grants, is in sharp contrast to "the thin–legged Indian driving his miserable bullock, its sides flagging for want of fodder, and its bones speaking of the chemistry of death"[433]

He detests his society which does not respect intelligence and ability, but rewards birth and flattery, "bright limbs and slick tongue.'[434] He abhors Untouchability or the "shameful suppression of the low class people by caste Hindus"[435] and the "way an untouchable has to leap the fence to let your Brahminic presence pass by, or the niggardly twist of dhoti on a ploughing peasant or the brutal bamboo of ancestral masters."[436] This unjust feudal set-up torments Kirillov, who is further rankled by the evil moneylender whose wily ways add "chilly and salt to his small squat unelegant self"[437]. He also detests the spread of British mass education and the subsequent changes, "In new India the university degree spoke the stars and threw in the darkness the horoscope of the ancients. Marriage became a commodity, and European clothes the new uniform. Success waited at your garden gate and the British came and took you away in a landau and tour to a comfortable sub-collectorship."[438]

His criticism of Hinduism is venomous "Indeed, the most reactionary force in world politics today – far more poisonous than Chiang Kai Shek – is your Hindu. He and his metaphysical myths, his Karma and his caste, his I-will-not-eat-this, and I-will-not-

---

[432] Raja Rao, Comrade Kirillov, New Delhi :.Orient Paperbacks. 1976, p.42

[433] Ibid., p.10

[434] Ibid.,p.11

[435] O.P.Mathur, " Existential Overtones in Raja Rao's Comrade Kirillov."*Modern Indian English Fiction, 1st Edition* New Delhi.: Abhinav Publications.. 1993..p. 117.

[436] Raja Rao, *Comrade Kirillov,* New Delhi : Orient Paperbacks, 1976, p.11.

[437] Ibid.,p.11

[438] Ibid.,p.12

touch-that, his superior feeling and impotence – his decadence are the foulest our earth has to bear."[439] He thinks lentils and milk and not mere abstract Vedantic doctrines will sustain the impoverished commoner, "Kalidasa and all that is perfect. But Kalidasa does not produce lentils nor Bharthrihari milk."[440] He is exceptionally hostile to God and religion and feels that metaphysical inquiry "is due to rachitism - it is like a disease caused by vitamin deficiency. God is the fiction of the lazy."[441]

He ridicules the Brahmanic attitude, "What can we do, my friend - the world is all Maya, and why work?'[442] He hates Gandhi and his morality which is, 'fattening itself on the Marwari–capitalist and speaking a brother-brother language'[443] Gandhi, he thinks, is "that old puritan humbug" and "that fine, moral hypocrite," [444] his perfect un-Darwinian enemy… friend and fool of the poor, the sadhu reactionary who still believed in caste and creed "[445]. Kirillov admires Darwin for his survival of the fittest theory, 'Non Violence was a biological lie. Man was born to fight - fighting is an instrument of Darwinian evolution which made dialectics possible. If there were no opposition, there would be no progress."[446] He also ridicules Gandhi's attitude towards sex, "he justifies the sexual act in terms of theological necessities.' Fine, very fine counsels in this age of reason. Ask your Gandhi to read Freud – he would be the wiser for it."[447] Apart from Gandhi, he is also critical of Tagore, "his celebrity is based on the strength of his beard"[448].

Disillusioned with the social, economic and political climate, Kirillov wanders away to distant lands, America, England and Moscow and Peking, in search of truth. "The archetypal, impersonal and abstract quality of Raja Rao's artistic configuration of the quest for reality is unmistakably present in Comrade

---

[439] Ibid.,p.83.
[440] Ibid.,p.83
[441] Ibid.,p.40.
[442] Ibid.,p.85
[443] Ibid.,p.37
[444] Ibid.,p.101
[445] Ibid.,p.33
[446] Ibid.,p. 34.
[447] Ibid.,pp. 35-36
[448] Ibid., p.107

Kirillov."[449] Moving out of the folds of a corrupt and degraded society that derides humanity, he escapes into Theosophy, which takes him to California, where new religions are born. At this stage of spiritual development, he considers Annie Besant as "the great Indian patriot, whose peregrinations across the thundering world cause India to emerge out of the mess of Anglo-Saxon devilry and create a double movement of freedom and prophetic domination."[450]

His experience in capitalist America makes him yearn for material solutions to his people's socio-economic and political impoverishment. Before long, he realizes that theosophy alone cannot provide succour from the festering wounds of Feudalism and Capitalism. Without relinquishing his spiritual life, his quest now becomes intellectual. By reading voraciously, he tries to understand the principles of Capitalism, Hitlerism, Socialism, Islam, and Albigensian Heresy. To comprehend western thought, he successfully learned French to assimilate Fourier and Saint Simon, German to probe Karl Marx and Engels, and as a great admirer of the Russian revolution, he learns Russian to understand Lenin. Without getting overwhelmed by these prominent personalities and their principles, he tries to gain more and more knowledge and formulate his perspectives. His continuous quest for truth manifests in the discovery of progressive western ideologies, especially the communist principles, which he is convinced will change the destiny of humankind.

He goes to England in 1928 to find like-minded Indian friends who zealously study Mahatma Gandhi and Communism. Being a novice, he listens ardently to his friends' lengthy polemics on dialectics. He joins the Labour Party, subsequently discovering the reality of Marxism himself. He feels that its principles are based on argument and logic, and with reason and intellect, one can unravel the intricacies of this discipline. He also studies Gandhism and, despite several doubts, still writes the Marxist interpretation of

---

[449] A.N. Gupta, "Comrade Kirillov. An Appraisal." in *Perspectives on Raja Rao*. K.K Sharma(Ed). Vimal Prakashan. Delhi p. 238
[450] Ibid. p. 9-10

Gandhi. Slowly he understands the indefatigable logic of communism and its possibilities and limitations.

Thus this wandering idealist discovers "joyous knowledge for the neophyte'[451] in Communism, becoming a "Sadhu of communism."[452] himself. He moves to the "safest shores of Marxism"[453] that is Russia "where he finds the Messiah" working for the people, the 'new Ganges' of a new-found faith based on the foundations of 'reason and the steam engine.'[454] He feels that the working classes, whose labour sustains the bourgeoisie, deserved a better deal, "they had a bright messianic future….and the only hope for humanity was better living wages, more muscular ways of thought."[455]

Kirillov meets the narrator Rama during the notorious purges of Stalin. Disregarding Rama's wish, he obeys the party's directive not to join the protests against the Moscow trials. Emerging as a good communist, he also supports the party's policy to oppose Gandhi's Quit India agitation of 1942 against the British. Despite Gandhi's win, he continued to be a devoted communist. Thus completely alienated from Indian society, he takes a new incarnation dropping his Indian identity as Padmanabha Iyer, which has deep religious connotations and adopting the Russian name Kirillov. He also gets married to Irene, a Czech communist nurse. Now "the only morality for Kirillov is scientific, and this is based on the inexorable laws of cause and effect. He dreams of a state of society where no man will be the master of another. He condemns all other philosophies like those of Gandhi and Hitler." and declares his love for the ordinary person, "I know only one God, and that is the common man. I know only one worship that is the party meeting. I know only one morality, and that is a classless society. It will come to India."[456]

He becomes a "Sadhu of communism genuinely believing that Hinduism cannot mitigate the sufferings of mankind and

---

451 Ibid.,p.20
452 Ibid.,p.72
453 Ibid.,p.32
454 Ibid.,p.15
455 Ibid.p.13
456 Raja Rao, *Comrade Kirillov,* New Delhi : Orient Paperbacks, 1976, p.39

provide even the basics of life like food and milk. Hindus are hypocrites merely chanting the name of God and not oriented towards human welfare. They had forgotten to transform noble thoughts into deeds, which was the basis of metaphysics, "Uplift of the suffering masses he thinks is like serving God. Only when all members of a civil society without any distinctions have fulfilled their basic needs can it progress towards total communion with the divine."[457] Obliterating their achievements in both physical and the metaphysical world, the Hindus practice Casteism and Untouchability, which had created an unbridgeable gap in society. Thus while Communism was delivering, Hinduism was only philosophizing.

Confessing his faith in Communism, Kirillov emphasizes the need for material perfection because human progress moves from the carnal to the sublime. Kirillov staunchly believes that physical satisfaction leads to spiritual attainments, and "he who ignores it (communist world), ignores a metaphysical certainty."[458] While traversing new landscapes and interacting with foreign cultures and ideologies, Kirillov undergoes a strange phenomenon. Torn apart between intellectual loyalty to marxism and the emotional pull of being an Indian, he becomes an "inverted Brahmin". Marxism "had given strange ascetic incision to his Brahmin manner", and "the inwardness of his nature gave prominent curve to his chest, which gave that peculiar parabola to his necktie." Though his rational and inquisitive mind reccived uncritically what the West gave him, reforming his Brahmin Indian disposition yet, it could not erasc his love for India. Despite his myriad encounters with western thought, he begins to retain his viewpoint, even trying to impress the Occidentals with his theories.

The irony was that this hard-core marxist preserved in his sub-conscious deep-rooted affiliation to age-old Indian cultural heritage. He firmly believes that they were capable of benefitting not only his country India but the entire humanity. So while on foreign soil, his love for India begins to intensify. Like a true

---

[457] Ibid. p.87
[458] Ibid. p. 44

Marxist, he places the material ends of life over the spiritual but being proper Brahmin guards his sacred thread and chants his daily mantras zealously. Thus his conscious intellectual conviction leads to a commitment to Western thought, and sub-conscious attitudes make him lean emotionally towards the East. A double commitment henceforth characterizes his life and quest wherein conflict ensues between the honesty of mind and honesty of heart. An alien ideology and an inward conflict thus sway his simple and unified personality, making his character very ambivalent - the East-West dissension results in divided consciousness.

Unaware of this dichotomy of the outer and inner self Kirillov reflects the great duality of mind. A committed communist or an idealist, an existentialist who only has his necktie as his companion or a spiritual wanderer, with his multiple identities, Kirillov is considered an alien everywhere he goes because he believes both in God and Communism. However, he is not at ease with either Theosophy or Marxism because "The various influences that Kirillov tried to absorb within himself reveal his extraordinary sensitivity and awareness and his incessant striving after wholeness."[459]. Confronted with the inadequacies of communism which he believed would provide succour to the commoner, he becomes thoroughly disillusioned. Kirillov is a modern "sensitive, innocent and intellectual Brahmin who is thrown off his balance by humanitarian zeal and tries to evolve his own ethical and philosophical values for authentic living"[460]. As his fascination with communism wears-off because of its depredation, he returns to his Indian roots, realizing that Indian spiritualism is the mantra which will rejuvenate humanity eventually.

Thus his alienation and integration caused by Eastern and western ideologies, which give Kirillov a split personality, form the central theme of this novel. Mathur aptly remarks, "the East, an inalienable part of the protagonists' intellectual and spiritual heritage, survives overwhelming waves of Western ideologies,

---

[459] E.J. Kalinnikova, "Ancient Indian Philosophy and Raja Rao's Works." in K. K. Sharma (Ed). *Perspectives on Raja Rao*, Vimal Prakashan. 1980. p. 42.
[460] O.P.Mathur, " The East- West Theme in *Comrade Kirillov*."*Modern Indian English Fiction, 1st Edition* New Delhi.: Abhinav Publications.1993.p. 115.

making him, like his namesake in Dostoevsky, an outsider wherever he goes and creating in him a despair, which is in marked contrast to the conscious levels of faith at which he operates."[461]

His wife Irene's introspective diary entries, jottings, an account of events and comments reveal Kirillov's character, personality, life, attitudes, thoughts and ambitions. Recounting the events of Kirillov's "has given a peep into the inner working of the mind of Kirillov."[462] Raja Rao observes that the Vedanta-based vision of India forms the base of Kirillov's spiritual quest for truth. Since his sensibilities and values are uncompromisingly Indian, it creates his ambivalent character, which amuses people who scorn and ridicule him yet do not lose sympathy and regard for this genuine soul.

Irene, therefore, feels very fortunate to have Kirillov as her man and husband. Like Lord Rama of Ayodhya, Kirillov's ideals are also related to the welfare of his people, "it is because he loved the universal outlook of Marxism" that she feels very proud of marrying an Indian. She is convinced that even though man may not be able to achieve anything, the sheer fact that he strives to achieve his ideals is good enough. Kirillov's thoughts have practically transformed Irene, who thinks like an Indian woman. Like Savithri in *The Serpent and the Rope* and Shantha in *The Cat and Shakespeare,* Irene symbolizes the feminist principle. Like Sita, who, despite being "banished by her husband remained faithful to Rama, Irene also like Sita is true to Kirillov. Both Irene and Sita have the Indian womanly virtue of being faithful to their husbands."[463] Thus totally devoted to Kirillov she says, "I sometimes wish I could kneel and pray, Lord, what gifts thou hast bestowed upon me, I envy Indian women."[464]. Doting on her son Kamal as Bathoska or (*Batasha*) she feels that the absolute joy for a woman is in her womanhood, i.e. being pregnant, "the woman's belly is the seat of natural joy."[465]

[461] Ibid.,p.27

[462] Kaushal Sharma, *Raja Rao: A Study of His Themes and Technique*, New Delhi, Sarup & Sons. 2005.p.74

[463] Kaushal Sharma ,*Raja Rao: A Study of His Themes and Technique*, New Delhi, Sarup & Sons.2005.p.82

[464] Raja Rao, *Comrade Kirillov,* New Delhi : Orient Paperbacks, 1976, p.27

[465] Ibid.,p.43

However, Irene also brings out Kirillov's ambiguities and contradictions very well. She confirms that "Kirillov is completely Indian,"[466] and "is 'racially arrogant."[467] "If Irene does not talk about India positively she becomes his 'enemy'"[468] He raves about Indian classics and poetry and is convinced "from the airplane to the latest theories of democracy, passing through medicine and mathematics, all had one and only one origin – Holy India"[469] Such an ardent devotee of Vedanta was he that even when engrossed in western ideologies his mind resounded thoughts of the Upanishads. Though he had earned his title Comrade, having perfected his understanding of Communism, he could not abandon his Vedic Samskaras and his love for Sri Sankara and his Nirvanaastaka. He would observe traditional rituals and chant prayers every day:

"*Manobuddhi Ahankara Cittani Naham,*
Cidanand Rupam Shivoham – Shivoham.[470]

I am not the mind, neither am I intelligence nor the ego, I am joy incarnate, I am Shiva! I am Shiva! Kirillov believes that *Mun* (mind), *Buddhi* (intelligence) and *Ahankara* (ego), are like piles of dirt and excrement on the soul, which have to be cleaned before a seeker becomes one with the Absolute. Only a Guru can help him conquer his mind, triumph over his intellect and dissolve his ego through various stages of *Sadhana,* before arriving at the kingdom of *Paramatma* (God). The magnitude, mystery, complexity, philosophy and metaphysics of India and the west are juxtaposed by Kirillov whose sensibilities and values are undoubtedly Indian, "I will not be an English man I will be an Indian. An Indian is always a Sadhu, the Buddha, Mahavira, And why not?[471] Irene observes that he has "Oriental masculine psychology–tenderness and tether"[472]His love for his country is "a noble, delicate un-reasoned love"[473].

---

[466] Ibid.,112
[467] Ibid.,114
[468] Ibid.,p.102
[469] Ibid.,p.78
[470] Ibid. p. 86
[471] Ibid. p. 101
[472] Ibid.,p. 104
[473] Ibid., p.86.

He firmly believed in India because "Kirillov was an Indian, and he had peculiar reactions which no dialectics could clarify. He spoke of India as though he were talking of a venerable old lady in a fairytale who had nothing but goodness in her heart and who was made of morning dew and mountain honey. He could not bear a word said against Mahatma Gandhi (though he could sometimes say more severe things than even Churchill might ever about) the saintly Indian leader."[474] Becoming a devout nationalist after the failure of the Russian revolution, Kirillov's Eastern incarnation praises Gandhi sincerely, "the communist party backed Britain, and lost their 1917. Mahatma Gandhi won. He would always win, for he knew India."[475]

Irene rightly comments, "At heart Gandhi is your God. You tremble when you speak of him sometimes. I once saw even a tear, one long tear it was there when you spoke of Gandhi to S."[476] Kirillov admires Nehru and feels that he is, "like most Indians magniloquent. He loves India with a love I often wish I had."[477] Raja Rao, who is himself "a Gandhian and Vedantin and an Indian"[478] views Kirillov's contradictory behaviour as ridiculous. However, he is not surprised because he has known Kirillov to be a true Brahmin who loves India and her new culture, "how you brag about progress and remain a vegetarian. You brag about Islam and Communism and call your son Kamal Dev instead of calling him Stephanovich, or Electricity, as in the earlier days of the revolution … you are an old hypocrite. I am sure, an unrepentant one.[479]

According to Irene his Indianhood would break through every Communist chain"[480] Therefore, despite of his strong Marxist leanings, he did not believe in Marxist domination of India and resisted Mara symbolized by Marxism: "Go, Go Mara,'… I know of your doings … Marx has been suppressed by hagiography, and

---

[474] Ibid., p.58.
[475] Ibid.,p.69
[476] Ibid., p.101.
[477] Ibid., pp. 109.
[478] Ibid.,p.26
[479] Ibid.,pp 85-86
[480] Ibid.,p.91

Lenin is in his tomb. Go, you many- mouthed many armed, you multiple monster, Mara.'[481]

Kirillov's uncompromising Indianness had endeared him to Irene, and this phenomenon ruined their marriage. One trait that Irene detests thoroughly is that Kirillov does not share his anguish, "I dislike his silence when it is to hide the painful from me - more painful."[482] Irene records her thoughts and feelings in her diary: "I need to speak to something…Mother is dead says the news. She alone understood me. P has such infinite love but he completely lacks understanding. Is it difference of race? Will I never understand Kamal wholly? I hope I shall never have to settle in India. I have grown afraid of India. P is completely Indian. "[483] She sadly continues "P left for India without me. He had tears in his eyes…No, I am happy. I am not going to India. I never told him the whole truth. India is now enemy it will eat up P. his Indianness will rise up once he touches the soil of the land and all this Occidental veneer will scuttle into European hatred."[484]

Kirillov had expected that by the time his son Kamal grew up Communism would have come to India and accelerating the development of its people, would have changed the face of the nation "Communism would have purified this ancient, this glorious land of mine."[485] Instead of making him proud of his heritage, the failure of Marxism overshadows his optimism and confidence with existential melancholy and despair. "The earlier Kirillov appears to be a Sartrean 'being for itself 'characterized by the repudiation of the traditional and the orthodox. He feels the burden of freedom, for he is confronted with existential choices. To lead an authentic life he exercises his individual 'praxis' and finally arrives at dialectical materialism."[486]

However, the failed Russian revolution changed Kirillov's perception of the mechanism of Marxist dialectics completely,

---

[481] Ibid.,p.92
[482] Ibid.,p. 106
[483] Ibid.,p.112
[484] Ibid.,p.113.
[485] Ibid.,p.58
[486] O.P.Mathur, "The East- West Theme in *Comrade Kirillov.*" *Modern Indian English Fiction, 1st Edition* New Delhi: Abhinav Publications. 1993.p. 112

"Kirillov's prognostics this time, however, went all wrong"[487] Kirillov's faith in "historical inevitability" and "his hope for the working classes of the Indian cities and landless labour rising in revolt against capitalism on the one hand and imperialism on the other, and Soviet Russia playing the role of a midwife in the rise of a new nation, are shattered.... Indian labour movement fails to bring about a revolution on the model of the Russian revolution, and Kirillov's dream of a classless society does not materialize."[488] He had idealized that communism would usher in a "State of society where no one will be master of another, and where a man like you will sit on some lone hilltop and write beautiful books, instead of wandering in search of metaphysical will-of-the wisp, and a cup of coffee...."[489] He had failed to realize that the individual in a communist society is merely a biological number with an anonymous existence.

The music of Kirillov's sarcasm pours out like a snake charmer playing his bamboo flute, "If the biology of selective killing were understood, humanity might yet attain the clean apex of history...We are the scientists of Man-and our measure is not man, but history. History, said the Mahabharata, is like the collyrium of the feminine eye-your perspective becomes more beautiful, and your nostrils have the camphor of the antiseptic. Deaths, the Moscow deaths, were the anticipation of history-you kill for the beauty of your eyes.[490]

Kirillov attacks communism on the one hand in his paper entitled "India and Our Struggle", criticizing the unholy Russian alliance with the British in the Second World War, which turned the imperialist war into "a revolutionary fight against the bourgeoisie"[491] In India, too, "Comrade and the Collector had now become friends, like the dog and jackal."[492] On the other hand, his Brahmin sensibility had, "such antennae inward and outward that a

---

[487]Raja Rao, *Comrade Kirillov,* New Delhi : Orient Paperbacks, 1976,p.57
[488] O.P.Mathur, " Existential Overtones in Raja Rao's Comrade Kirillov."*Modern Indian English Fiction, 1st Edition* New Delhi: Abhinav Publications. 1993.p. 121.
[489] Ibid. p. 39
[490] Ibid. p. 46
[491] Ibid. p. 64
[492] Ibid. p. 63

fierce anger rose in his belly, and he cursed the British race, wished a sepulchral fire, and the red, ruinous tongues of Hell.[493] Disenchanted completely, he laments, " The bogus Gandhian millennium is over. There is rank riceless poverty in the villages. The population has grown millions and not only is there less rice in our fields, but even less water…. The government of course sits in Delhi, and all is well when Nehru is well. He is such a well meaning, utopian liberal, sitting crosswise on the hedge between socialism and liberalism.'[494]

To relieve him of his dialectical despair when the narrator asks him, "And once you have fed the Indian millions and given them nice houses to live in and railways for their monthly holidays, and sanatoria for their sick, and maternity care for their mothers and the Dnieperstock for the electric illumination of India - what then brother, is to become of your despair, your emotional upheavals, your metaphysical yearning, your Godward beckoning?"[495] Kirillov has no answers. because "his long intimacy with history had now quickly made him into an alien", and he had no illumination-it was the dark night of the soul."[496]

Self-annihilation is the existential answer for such disillusioned comrades, no wonder a desperate Kirillov carries a pistol sometimes pointing at R and sometimes at his head. Raja Rao feels that Kirillov may demand 'the final favour of a quick departure to the other world any day.'[497] "…the western literary tradition has found the very embodiment of self-annihilation as a metaphysical problem."[498] "Rao seems to have arrived at a point where seeming contradictions ceased to be opposed only by denying the whole human experience. Such a summit of self-transcendence may simultaneously indicate the precipice of autodestruction. In fact, the whole avant-garde movement strives to some kind of self-annihilation."[499] "Suicide, symbolic or actual,

---

[493] Ibid., p. 52.
[494] Ibid., pp- 74-75.
[495] Ibid.,p.40.
[496] Ibid.,p.57
[497] Ibid.,p.26.
[498] Esha Dey, *The Novels of Raja Rao, The Theme of Quest,* New Delhi,Prestige Books,1992. p189.
[499] Ibid., pp. 188-189.

becomes the consummation of the avant-garde."[500] Thus "Kirillov stands as an archetype of the modern logical man of the West whose communist dialectic must end in self-annihilation."[501]

In this state of loneliness, and erosion of faith, Kirillov, like an existential man, is groping for companionship and finds only his necktie which emerges "as a symbol of the twist of his thought and psyche."[502] Described in great lyrical and poetic style, it symbolizes his fanatical faith in communism, which hangs around his neck and on his heart, quite indispensable to his existence. "It had such a prater-plus-parenthetical curve, as though much concrete philosophy had gone into its making, and it revealed a soul so ambivalent that I could not gaze on its self-aware turpitudes without human compassion.[503] Lonely and desperate, Kirillov exclaims, "You, you, my noble, secret friend, you lie in the faithfulness of my scholarly solitude. O, go not from my habitation for what shall my destiny be without your contiguous presence."[504]

Thus by using India as the matrix and making Padmanabha Kirillov, "it is made quite obvious that communism can mean only suicide for an Indian."[505] "The only end of such a man is to commit suicide or find "radiance in religion."[506]The narrator sums up, "Suicide is your end —or the Buddhist yellow robe."[507]

"One may wonder if the Buddhist yellow robe the alternative to a Marxist intellectual death, is an equally disastrous end for an Indian or the very hope of redemption…Padmanabha - a hypothetical Buddha defeating the deadly Tempter, now embodied as Marxism ."[508] However, his redemption is not a reality because an orthodox Brahmin hero cannot gain liberation through Buddhism challenged by Brahmanism. "If communism is to be

---

[500] Ilhab Hassan, *The Dismemberment of Orpheus: Towards a Post Modern Literature* Quoted in Esha Dey *The Novels of Raja Rao, The Theme of Quest*, New Delhi, Prestige Books,1992..p.189.

[501] A.Alvarez, "The Savage God :A Study of Suicide." 1971 Quoted in Esha Dey *The Novels of Raja Rao, The Theme of Quest*, New Delhi,Prestige Books,1992..p.190

[502] Raja Rao, *Comrade Kirillov*, New Delhi : Orient Paperbacks, 1976.p.30.

[503] Ibid. p. 25.

[504] Ibid. p. 25

[505] Esha Dey, *The Novels of Raja Rao, The Theme of Quest*, New Delhi,:Prestige Books,1992. p. 190

[506] O.P.Mathur, "Existential Overtones in Raja Rao's *Comrade Kirillov.*"*Modern Indian English Fiction, 1st Edition* New Delhi: Abhinav Publications. 1993.p. 122

[507] Raja Rao, *Comrade Kirillov*, New Delhi : Orient Paperbacks, 1976, pp- 72.

[508] Esha Dey, *The Novels of Raja Rao, The Theme of Quest*, New Delhi,:Prestige Books,1992. p.196

condemned as a specifically alien creed which fails to find roots in the Indian soil, its use of violence and its subordination of a means to an end can be fought not with Brahmanic but with Buddhist weapons alone."[509] The ideals of anti-racism and democracy - the ideals of Indian nationalists can be achieved through Buddhist weapons of non-violence and ethics. Will Brahmanic or Communist Padmanabha salvage himself by donning the yellow robes?

However, standing outside Kirillov's house, ready to knock at his door, R is like Buddha's horse Kanthaka who wishes to take Kirillov to enlightenment. Full of Vedantic wisdom and knowing that Kirillov is an uncompromising Indian at heart, he hopes to convert Kirillov from Communism to Vedantism and bring him back to his estranged Indian roots.

"Like Dostoyevsky Rao regards the present human misery as a spiritual agony caused by the estrangement of the individual. This estrangement is the result of vast cultural failure to recognize the true needs of the essential self. Comrade Kirillov offers a scathing criticism of the Marxist ideals and points out that the modern welfare provisions fall short of the needs of a man who is a citizen of two worlds – material and spiritual. Raja Rao is inclined to believe that man has an inner being which stands beyond the grasp of human intelligence. In spite of all earthly blessings, a man sometimes longs for the most uneconomic nonsense. Raja Rao, like Dostoyevsky, seems to insist on the need for a harmony between the material and the spiritual, the rational and the vital."[510]

Kirillov does return to India because his "soul has a hard Indian core which the crust of western intellectual and spiritual elitism or dialectical materialism can neither destroy nor obscure' ….his tie with India and its pristine culture is unbreakable[511] With his faith fully reconfirmed in Indian ethos, he takes refuge in India to revitalize his inner resources and revive his traditional values. His ardent desire to attain the truth in a western material world fails

---

509 Ibid.,p.197
510 O.P.Mathur, " Existential Overtones in Raja Rao's *Comrade Kirillov.*". *Modern Indian English Fiction, 1st Edition* New Delhi: Abhinav Publications.1993.p.125
511 Ibid.,p.115

miserably as he discovers the ultimate Indian reality of life beyond the non- self, finding solace in his inalienable affinity with the Absolute. A. N. Gupta confirms, " In this journey of Comrade Kirillov (formerly Padmanabha Iyer) from India to California and then to London, followed in the end to Moscow and Peking, we see the passage of a hungry soul who sets himself in search of reality in his country and the other countries of the world – America, England and Russia – and being with an Indian ethos he discovers it ultimately in his own country, India, from the roots of which he cannot completely alienate himself.[512]

"The prodigal son of India finds his spiritual moorings again and recovers his 'native kingdom.'[513] in a transcendental union of Hinduism, Buddhism and Gandhism"[514] "in the deer park of intelligence he set his Wheel of law a turning and wandered over the vast and wondersome land of Hinduism, working the law of non-becoming. The wheel turns like a temple chariot's, and Mahatma Gandhi himself pulls the ultimate cord…"[515]

Kirillov, who began his life as a theosophist, finds an esoteric panacea for the ills of the commoner. Truth alone liberates, and contemplation of truth is a blissful experience. Gupta aptly comments. "He symbolizes his quest for reality and identity in the predicament of the individual in a changing complex society, presenting thus in this process not the discovered truths and tradition but the contemplative sensation of the quest itself.[516]

Immersed in an ocean of thoughts, Kirillov realizes both the physical and the metaphysical truths," What can we do, my friend – the world is all Maya, why work?[517] Despite the world being an illusion, we are sent with a specific mission on this earth. Kirillov does not step back from enacting his part of ultimately seeking spiritual perfection. His fascination with Marxism wears

---

[512] A.N. Gupta, "Comrade Kirillov. An Appraisal." in Perspectives on Raja Rao. Sharma, K.K. (Ed). Vimal Prakashan. Delhi. 1980..p. 124
[513] Raja Rao, Comrade Kirillov, New Delhi : Orient Paperbacks, 1976, p.92.
[514] O.P.Mathur, "The East- West Theme in Comrade Kirillov." Modern Indian English Fiction, 1st Edition New Delhi: Abhinav Publications.1993.p 115
[515] Raja Rao, Comrade Kirillov, New Delhi : Orient Paperbacks, 1976, p.92-93
[516] A.N. Gupta, "Comrade Kirillov. An Appraisal." in Perspectives on Raja Rao. Sharma, K.K. (Ed). Vimal Prakashan. Delhi. 1980. p. 138.
[517] Raja Rao, Comrade Kirillov, New Delhi : Orient Paperbacks, 1976, p. 85

off as he realizes that its theories and principles deal with only transient things. Vedantism, on the other hand, is the highest form of philosophical system recognizing the fundamental reality of the cosmos provides the ultimate solution for man's deliverance. Through meditation, man cleanses his soul and prepares to attain the Absolute. The is-ness of the body disappears into the is-ness of the soul. Motivated by narrator R, Kirillov visits the Guru experiencing real peace and solace.

Thus the rank reactionary, a strange mixture of divergent elements, or a hypocrite comes home to Vedas. He is viewed as an outsider and insider living in self-exile on the East and the West border. The most critical point from analyzing his character is that a total Brahmin –an embodiment of Indianess cannot be converted totally. Kirillov's India has many things that are materially repulsive and wrong, which he criticizes ruthlessly. Yet, no foreign creed, however convincing, can overpower India, transforming it completely, for India is his truth, his real self, his Brahma". Like Ramaswamy, he says, "It was India I wanted to see, the Indian of my inner being. Just as I could now see Antara-Kasi, the "inner Benares", India, for me became no land – not these trees, this sun, this earth; not those ladle hands and skeletal legs of bourgeois and coolie; not even the new pride of the uninformed Indian official, who seemed almost to say, "Don't you see, I am Indian now, and I represent the Republic of India" – but something other, more centred, widespread, humble; as though the gods had peopled the land with themselves, birds winged themselves higher, touched the clouds and soared beyond, calling to each other over the valleys by their names. The India of Brahma and Prajapati; of Varuna, Mitra and Aryaman; of Krishna, Shiva and Parvati; of Rama, Harischandra and Yajnavalkya; this India was a continuity I felt." [518]

Kirillov, like Ramaswamy, realizes that India's unique contribution to the world is not material, "Truth is the only substance India can offer, and that truth is metaphysical and not

---

[518] Raja Rao, *The Serpent and the Rope*, Orient Paperbacks. Delhi. 1968. p. 246.

moral.[519] Adhering to Indian ethos, which mainly contributes to his brilliance, he chooses to devote himself to the Advaita or Absolute.

Unfortunately, Kirillov's serenity is disturbed once again by Irene's death in the second childbirth. This vagabond's ambivalent soul chooses to wander away once again to Moscow and Peking, negating deliverance through Buddhism. Thus, he is 'doomed to remain an alien from his native land- more a freak, a symbol and a warning than an individual."[520] He, however, ensures that his son Kamal should uphold his Indianness by growing up with his Indian grandparents. He, therefore, motivates him to go on a pilgrimage to Kanyakumari, where the Indian continent ends and be acquainted "with the religious and mythical heritage of India".[521]. He uses the myth of Shiva and Parvati to convey the spirit of India since Parvati symbolizes "the endless wait for the sons of the motherland who have gone away to material dualism.'[522]

The narrator initiates Kamal into Hinduism. Draped with sacred silk, wearing a silver waistband, his forehead smeared with sandal paste, Kamal pays obeisance to Mother Kanya Kumari, the beautiful Goddess Parvati, waiting for her marriage with Shiva, which will never be solemnized. Thus Comrade Kirillov is the story of a complex person who wants to escape from the harsh material problems and gets lost in the "ideological contradictions of the modern world."[523] A split between intellectual commitment to the West and emotional dedication to the East leads to his dilemma of divided consciousness, a conflict which remains unresolved till the end. As his conscious mind wins over the subconscious and the rational overpowers the emotional creating a conflict, he prefers to set out on a new voyage.

Now and then, he retraces his steps back like a prodigal son to the ….. " strength and resilience of Hindu culture and '

---

[519] Ibid., p. 350

[520] O.P.Mathur, " The East –West Theme in Comrade Kirillov." *Modern Indian English Fiction, 1st Edition,* New Delhi : Abhinav publications. 1993.p. 115 .

[521] Kaushal Sharma ,*Raja Rao: A Study of His Themes and Technique*, New Delhi, Sarup & Sons. 2005.p.84

[522] Shiva Niranjan, "Myth as a Creative Mode.A Study of Mythical Parallels in Raja Rao's Novels," *Commonwealth Quarterly,* Vol. 4, March, 1980. No.13.p.59

[523] Kaushal Sharma ,*Raja Rao: A Study of His Themes and Technique*, New Delhi, Sarup & Sons. 2005. p.84

Samskaras', as against the mundane life of the west focussed on the visible and the concrete ever in a state of flux. Just as no man can walk except in his own shadow, no Hindu can completely leave the orbit of his traditional culture and philosophy. He even radiates unconsciously an influence which alters the ways of thinking of those like Irene who come in contact with him. The Indian strain is so persistent that it can never die."[524] The author ardently believes that one day when Kirillov "becomes capable of free thinking, if he does not stick to dogma."[525] his essential Indianness will help him genuinely discover himself.

Like *The Serpent and the Rope, Comrade Kirillov* is a spiritual biography of the author himself. Kaushal Sharma aptly says," It follows the evolution and thought processes of the mind of Kirillov."[526]. There is a close resemblance between the protagonist and the novelist; the two have many things in common in their temperaments. "Both are deeply concerned with a spiritual quest for truth, which brings us very close to the Indian and European ways and values of life and varied schools of philosophy.[527] The author firmly believes that "India is the Guru to the World, and "India is culture. "Rao's India has a destiny like Dostoevsky's Russia, to be apprehended with missionary fervour. India will remain India no matter what.

---

[524] O.P.Mathur, "The East- West Theme in Comrade Kirillov." *Modern Indian English Fiction, 1st Edition,* New Delhi: Abhinav Publications. 1993.p.116
[525] Kaushal Sharma ,*Raja Rao: A Study of His Themes and Technique*, New Delhi, Sarup & Sons. 2005.p.83
[526] Ibid., p.77
[527] K.K. Sharma, *Perspectives on Raja Rao.* Delhi. Vimal Prakashan. 1980. p. 25

CHAPTER VII: Raja Rao and the Short Story

Mix beautiful imagery, realistic details, profound thought, intricate description, and intense emotions and top it up with morality and philosophy and sublimate it through powerful words, using alien language but native idiom, tinge it with traditional, cultural and religious ardour and what you get is an outstanding Raja Rao story either so metaphysical that it transports you to a spiritual realm or so stark that its realism shears and scars your soul.

His expressions are the words of a true upasaka for whom Word is mantra and writing is a spiritual exercise. "Raja Rao then becomes a true upasaka, in having a strong desire to communicate and in achieving a mastery over the language to communicate effectively and forcefully."[528] Unless the author becomes an 'upasaka' and "enjoys himself in himself" (which is *rasa*), the eternality of the sound (Sabda) will not manifest itself, and so you cannot communicate either and the word is nothing but a cacophony."[529]

The substratum of all Raja Rao's works is a vision of unity, which he has derived from his deep insight into life. According to Naik, "his literary technique, therefore, can hardly be considered in isolation from his vision. It is indeed a part of the vision and shapes and is shaped by it."[530] A great believer in the fundamental Oneness of the East and West, Rao adopts the form of the western short story but infuses it with his own social, cultural and spiritual concerns; thus, this formidable East-West combination and not confrontation produces some of his most outstanding works.

---

[528] B. Vyaghreswarudu, "The Growth of Mind and Art of Raja Rao: His Short Stories" in Rajeshwar Mittapalli & Pier Paolo Piciucco Ed. *The Fiction of Raja Rao: Critical Studies*, New Delhi : Atlantic Publishers.: 2001. P.229.

[529] Raja Rao , "The Writer and the World," *The Literary Criticism*, Vol VIII, No.1, Winter, 1965.

[530] M.K.Naik, "Raja Rao as a Short Story Writer: *The Cow of the Barricades*." *Books Abroad*. 40.4. 1966 p.394

He is not a prolific short story writer, though the number of stories he writes is fewer than his counterparts, yet they depict "a significant variety of themes and technique. Although the fewer numbers of the stories narrow his range, what he loses in range, he achieves in depth."[531] Therefore, Rao felt that for him," literature is Sadhana - not a profession but a vocation. "That's why I have published so few works."[532]

And these works are the "products of an inevitable stage in the growth of mind, in the evolution of a major novelist who was cultivating his craft with the utmost care."[533] As experiences proliferated, the urge to communicate grew, and as thoughts matured, meaningful words emerged, compelling him to shape them into a story. Rao devised his medium for narrating it as he firmly believed that "the tempo of Indian life must be infused into our English expression, even as the tempo of American or Irish life has gone into the making of theirs."[534] So to an otherwise profound piece of prose, his literal translation of oaths, adages, and famous sayings from rustic Kannada added great colour and meaning, making the narrative very evocative and exciting.

Vyaghreswarudu observes, "Raja Rao, like Chinua Achebe, the Nigerian writer, has demonstrated the compatibility of English with the spirit of the native language and makes it flexible enough to accommodate his varied experiences. It is his experimentation with English and the form of the western short story that makes his art and makes him an outstanding short story writer."[535] When studied chronologically, the stories "reveal the growth of the artist, marked in his firmer grasp of the medium and the better handling of the symbolic language."[536] This experimentation, however, is with the form alone and not the

---

[531] B. Vyaghreswarudu, "The Growth of Mind nnd Art of Raja Rao:His Short Stories" in Rajeshwar Mittapalli & Pier Paolo Piciucco. Ed., *The Fiction of Raja Rao: Critical Studies*, New Delhi: Atlantic Publishers. 2001. p. 223-224.

[532] S.V.V. "Raja Rao: Face to Face" *The Illustrated Weekly of India* , 5 January , 1964. p. 44.

[533] C.D. Narasimhaiah, *Raja Rao, The Short Stories , An After Word*. New Delhi, Arnold Heinemann. p. 127.

[534] Raja Rao, *Foreward Kanthapura*, New Delhi, Orient Paperbacks.1971. p.2.

[535] B. Vyaghreswarudu, "The Growth of Mind nnd Art of Raja Rao:His Short Stories" in Rajeshwar Mittapalli & Pier Paolo Piciucco, Ed.*The Fiction of Raja Rao: Critical Studies*, New Delhi : Atlantic Publishers. 2001. p. 229

[536] Narsingh Shrivastava : *The Mind and the Art of Raja Rao*, Prakash Book Depot , Bareilly (India), 1980 p.140

concerns and contents, "the concerns of the Western short story, motivation or characters are not Raja Rao's concerns."[537]

Experimenting with content and form, he primarily displays the actual human experience, which "establishes itself with a wealth of concrete details and acquires life likeness with the help of realistic linguistic devices."[538] All these devices, whether fable, allegory or symbolism, personify human virtues which alone can lead man to his salvation- the goal of all human life. This reverberating symbolism also makes them "memorable metaphysical documents in fictional form without a parallel in the field of the Indian English short story."[539]

Rao's narrative presents both sides of the spectrum. The stark realism that he depicts to highlight the negative aspects is toned down with poetic imagery. On the one hand are beautiful women compared to "new opened guavas" or "tender as April mangoes," [540]or "as red as the inside of a pumpkin," or with "a heart pure as morning lotus." The picture, on the other hand, reflects decadence, e.g. Kanakapala's "old.. skin shrivelled like the castoff skin of a plantain", or "Akkayya's face all wrinkled like a dry mango."[541]

Naik, who regards him as a master of 'descriptive prose', refers to his graphic description of summer heat and the barren and fissured land in Khandesh as par excellence," *In Khandesh,* the earth floats. Heaving and quivering, rising and shrivelling, the earth floats in a heat flood. Men do not walk in Khandesh. They are carried on the billows of heat ...In Khandesh, the earth is black and grey as the buffalo and twisted like an endless line of loamy pythons, wriggling and stretching beneath the awful heat of the

---

[537] Muralidas Melwani, "Themes in Indo Anglian Literature," p.54 quoted in B. Vyaghreswarudu, "The Growth of Mind nnd Art of Raja Rao: His Short Stories" in Rajeshwar Mittapalli & Pier Paolo Piciucco, *The Fiction of Raja Rao: Critical Studies,*(ed) New Delhi, 2001. p. 229.

[538] Esha Dey, *The Novels of Raja Rao, The Theme of Quest.* New Delhi. Prestige Books.1992. p.246.

[539] B. Vyaghreswarudu, "The Growth of Mind nnd Art of Raja Rao:His Short Stories" in Rajeshwar Mittapalli & Pier Paolo Piciucco. Ed. *The Fiction of Raja Rao: Critical Studies*, New Delhi : Atlantic Publishers. 2001. p. 227.

[540] Raja Rao, quoted in Esha Dey, *The Novels of Raja Rao, The Theme of Quest.* New Delhi. Prestige Books. 1992.p.246.

[541] Raja Rao, quoted in M.K.Naik, "Raja Rao as a Short Story Writer: *The Cow of the Barricades.*" *Books Abroad.* 40.4. 1966 p. 395.

sun....the blood of the earth mingles with the pus of the skies- to bear cotton."[542] A further reference to 'thin unmoving bonelike plants' with little 'skulls of cotton,' according to Esha Dey establishes Raja Rao, essentially as a "sensitive observer of the reality around" offering "glimpses of a dying world – sometimes even deprived of nature's vital bounty-ruthlessly exploited by a rapacious foreign rule as much as by its own proto feudal socio-economic system."[543]

Thus, Rao's stories reveal his complete vision of life, reflecting contemporary social, political and economic realities, ideologies, radicalism and social commitment. Essentially Indian in spirit, they portray rural and urban concerns but convey relevant messages nationally and internationally. Like his counterparts, some of them depict his intense zeal for social reform feels Esha Dey, "Raja Rao's short stories, however, are expressions not only of an inner joy but also something more too- a desire to satirize, a desire to reform the social scene all around."[544] Wadia seems to concur," Like many Indians he adopts the art of the short story to Indian condition and uses it as a vehicle of new ideas and means of accelerating reforms."[545]

Their characteristic feature, however, is the portrayal of Raja Rao's quest for the absolute. He desires to transcend the external plane and attain the metaphysical divine plane through them. Revealing Indian attitudes, beliefs, customs, conventions and traditions through myths, legends, metaphors and symbols, he unfolds the great metaphysical truth of India's eternal existence and how its hoary past in continuum still casts an immense influence on our present. According to Venugopal, " Raja Rao stands out among the Indian short story writers in English in more ways than one, "He shares with Isvaran a tenderness of approach, with Anand a

---

[542] Ibid., p. 395.

[543] Esha Dey, *The Novels of Raja Rao, The Theme of Quest*. New Delhi. Prestige Books. 1992. p.246.

[544] B. Vyaghreswarudu, "The Growth of Mind nnd Art of Raja Rao: His Short Stories" in Rajeshwar Mittapalli & Pier Paolo Piciucco Ed. *The Fiction of Raja Rao: Critical Studies*, New Delhi : Atlantic Publishers. 2001.p. 223.

[545] A.R. Wadia, *The Future of English in India*, Bombay,1954.p. 118. Quoted in B. Vyaghreswarudu, "The Growth of Mind nnd Art of Raja Rao: His Short Stories" in Rajeshwar Mittapalli & Pier Paolo Piciucco Ed. *The Fiction of Raja Rao: Critical Studies*, New Delhi: Atlantic Publishers. 2001. p. 224

deep awareness of the contemporary situation, with Narayan an ease of narration, and combining them treats his themes with the objectivity of a philosopher."[546] His sole aim is to expose the intense and "inevitable impact of India's cultural past and its tradition, its people's attitude to life's ups and downs."[547]

Rao's form of narration is derived from the famous ancient Sanskrit classic lore, which influenced him immensely, "The mythological framework in some and the folklore technique in others also contribute to the obvious Indianness of the stories."[548] Following the traditional style of beginning and ending them with quotations, invocations and benedictions have a vast cultural, and metaphysical impact on the readers "for such stories have about them a finality of upanishadic or epical sayings." Sometimes when he ends them in a mundane manner with a personal comment, like," and way, "here I have written the story of *Akkayya* may be her only funeral ceremony,"[549] it hits the readers with its starkness who are left craving for some artistic relief.

In keeping with the spirit of the epigraph, on the title page, a quotation from Kabir, the 15th-century saint-poet, reads, "when I tell them the truth they are angry. Moreover, I cannot lie". Raja Rao constantly seeks and speaks the truth through his stories. As reflected in *Kanthapura* his overriding concern for humanity reverberates in *The Cow of the Barricades* published in 1947. Bearing his inimitable stamp, his stories strive to maintain a delicate and perfect balance between myths and reality to reveal the sublime truth. They can be divided into three groups "a) Realistic, e.g. *Javni, Akkayyu, A Client. The little Grain Shop, In Khandesh.* B) Mythic e.g. *Companions, and The True Story of Kanakapala.* C) Realistic - Mythic, e.g. *Narasinga, and the Cow of the Barricades.*"[550]

---

[546] C.V. Venugopal, *The Indian Short Story in English*, Bareilly: Prakash Book Depot. 1976. P. 74.

[547] B. Vyaghreswarudu, "The Growth of Mind nnd Art of Raja Rao: His Short Stories" in Rajeshwar Mittapalli & Pier Paolo Piciucco Ed. *The Fiction of Raja Rao: Critical Studies*, New Delhi: Atlantic Publishers. 2001. p. 224

[548] Ibid.,p. 223

[549] Ibid .,p. 229

[550] Esha Dey, *The Novels of Raja Rao, The Theme of Quest*. New Delhi. Prestige Books. 1992. p. 60

His existential stories are based on the realistic western model, and to temper his grave concerns, he also pens mythical stories which are alienated from this mode, "This serious concern with the contemporary existence expressed in a form which drew heavily on the western realistic mode is complemented by a complete distancing of reality."[551]

The Cow of the Barricades is a collection of powerful stories that perfectly reveals the truths of Indian village life, making it very appealing. Set in the thirties, the eventful period of Gandhian struggle for freedom, they are "by no means of merely topical interest. For through the impact of modern Indian resurgence brought about by the contact with the West is very much in evidence in them, they also reveal how the traditional mores of Indian life are still a vital force working for the good as well as to the detriment of the community."[552]

The canvas is of rural South India, barring in *In Khandesh,* Maharashtra. The setting shifts north in *The Companions* and *A Client* as it moves to the city. The context may be Indian, but the "heartbreak at the heart of things" they depict highlights the unusual tragedies of human life anywhere.

The *Cow of the Barricades, Narasinga* and *In Khandesh* picture the unrest of the most eventful period of modern Indian History. They study the struggle of the Indians against the Redman and the role of Gandhian philosophy in the national resurgence of India. In the first story, Gauri, named after Goddess Gauri, consort of Lord Shiva, is a mysterious holy cow symbolising Mother India. She is a powerful Indian synthesis of a martyr "carrying on the old tradition yet adapting it to changing times."[553] Visiting Master the Mahatma's disciple, she tries to harmonise the relationship between human beings and animals in a household. Traditionally in India, the sacred cow is either officially dedicated to a temple or God. Gauri is not so, yet she has some strange saintly traits in her," She

---

[551] Ibid.,p. 246.

[552] M.K.Naik, "Raja Rao as a Short Story Writer: *The Cow of the Barricades.*" *Books Abroad.* 40.4. 1966 p.392

[553] Jawaharlal Nehru, *The Discovery of India,* Bombay, Asia Publishing House.1961.p. 477.

came every Tuesday evening before sunset to stand and nibble at the hair of the Master...ambled round him and disappeared among the bushes . And till Tuesday next she was not to be seen. And the Master's disciple gathered grain and grass and rice-water to give her every Tuesday but she refused it all and took only the handful of grain the Master gave. She munched it slowly and carefully as one articulates a string of holy words, and when she had finished eating she knelt again, shook her head and disappeared."[554]

The freedom struggle in her village grew increasingly intense. "she looked very sad and somebody had even seen a tear, clear as a drop of the Ganges run down her cheeks, for she was of compassion infinite and true."[555] Though sacred, Gauri is killed in a firing by a British Officer during riots at the barricades put up by the agitating freedom fighters, saving many villagers' lives. Becoming a martyr in the national cause, she thus infuses patriotic feelings in both the soldiers and the freedom fighters. A colossal statue larger than her size is installed to pay tribute to her supreme sacrifice and immortalise her in public memory. This makes her a legend and the source of income for many who make her toy replicas and sell them for a living. Thus *"The Cow of the Barricades,* a study of yet another facet of the nationalist movement, presents a unique combination of symbol and reality."[556]

Narasinga pictures how Gandhi created and raised the national consciousness to such an extraordinary level that infused by it, a small illiterate orphan Narasinga imagines the great man going in the air with his wife Sita in a flower-bedecked chariot drawn by 16 steeds. Weaving myth and legend with Gandhi's life and character, "Narasinga is undoubtedly the best example of Raja Rao's ability to capture a whole society with sustained brilliance. His (Gandhiji's) fight against poverty, untouchability, drinking and

---

[554] Raja Rao, *The Cow of the Barricades* quoted in M.K.Naik, "Raja Rao as a Short Story Writer: *The Cow of the Barricades." Books Abroad.* 40.4. 1966 p.394

[555] Ibid., p. 394.

[556] B. Vyaghreswarudu, "The Growth of Mind nnd Art of Raja Rao: His Short Stories" in Rajeshwar Mittapalli & Pier Paolo Piciucco Ed. *The Fiction of Raja Rao: Critical Studies,* New Delhi: Atlantic Publishers. 2001. p. 226.

illiteracy are all taken up with the thread of the narrative most naturally."[557]

In Khandesh illustrates the vanity of the rulers who force loyalty out of their subjects, "a witty and energetic satire on the defunct feudal system,"[558] which expects people to demonstrate their loyalty even if it is fake. "The story depicts the transition from the era of unquestioning loyalty to the British to the beginning of organised opposition to the alien rule."[559] Ridiculously, the village headman orders the villagers to stand with their back to the special train carrying the Viceroy to express their loyalty to the British Emperor, fearing, "you know how some devilish prostitute born, scoundrels tried to put a bomb beneath the train of the representative of the most high across the seas."[560] The havoc wrought by the British rule and the end of loyalty is graphically compared to nature's fury. The " pattern of broken and unconnected lines add a visual dimension to the description of the confusion of the storm.[561] According to M.K. Naik, it "shows the descriptive power which is a mark of Raja Rao's later and mature works."[562]

Distancing himself from reality, Rao writes *The True Story of Kanakpala*, Protector of Gold and *Companions,* "which utilise the indigenous oral technique of narration." Cast in the ancient mythic mould, "in this other world of Rao, animals play no less an important role than human characters."[563] Each fable has moral content, and the situations are not specific in time.

Companions is a mysterious and philosophically complex story about Hindu-Muslim unity. Moti Khan, the snake charmer and his companion snake, a reincarnated fallen Brahmin, liberate each other, "one is redeemed in helping the other in his redemption

---

[557] Ibid.,pp.225- 226.

[558] Ibid.,p. 226.
[559] Ibid.,p. 226
[560] Raja Rao, *The Cow of the Barricades* quoted in M.K.Naik, "Raja Rao as a Short Story Writer: *The Cow of the Barricades." Books Abroad.* 40.4. 1966 p.392.

[561] L.S.R. Krishan Sastry, "Raja Rao," *Triveni,* January. 1968. Quoted in B. Vyaghreswarudu, "The Growth of Mind and Art of Raja Rao: His Short Stories" *in* Rajeshwar Mittapalli & Pier Paolo Piciucco Ed. *The Fiction of Raja Rao: Critical Studies,* New Delhi: Atlantic Publishers 2001. p. 226.
[562] M.K.Naik, "Narrative Strategy in Raja Rao's *Cow of the Barricades and other Stories."* (U.P.P) quoted B. Vyaghreswarudu, "The Growth of Mind and Art of Raja Rao: His Short Stories" in Rajeshwar Mittapalli & Pier Paolo Piciucco Ed. *The Fiction of Raja Rao: Critical Studies,* New Delhi: Atlantic Publishers. 2001. p. 226.
[563] Esha Dey, *The Novels of Raja Rao, The Theme of Quest.* New Delhi. Prestige Books. 1992.pp. 246-247

"[564] Moti Khan eventually becomes a Sufi mystic and attains healing powers. The moral is "when Islam gets Indianized, its spiritual force manifests itself."[565] This story aims at liberating the two characters from the bondage of life and death by ending the cycle of Karma. The symbols used "heighten the mystical experience"[566] imparting it a "profound spiritual significance,"[567] which "forces ordinary mortals entwined in the coils of flesh to look for God."[568]

The True Story of Kanakpala or the protector of gold is a story of greed for family wealth. It vividly portrays the kin's hatred over acquiring material assets and how one friendly serpent fights the vices of greed and crime. The benediction, "May those who read this, be beloved of Naga, King of Serpents, destroyer of ills." establishes its folk style. However, to make it realistic and authentic, Rao " gives a vivid description of the sentiments and stories with snake motif. His graphic description of the scene and setting, results in "willing suspension of disbelief and "acceptance of fiction as truth."[569]

The stories that depict contemporary life in a realistic manner deal with child marriage and the status of women in traditional society. *A Client* exposes the ills of child marriage in which a wicked marriage broker Nanjundia, chases a simpleton Ramu, still in school for marriage. The story depicting the tussle between the unwilling boy and the crooked matchmaker, who goes all out to ensnare him "like a patient hunter luring his prey into his trap,"[570] exposes a grave, although illegal, problem prevalent in our society till today.

---

[564] B. Vyaghreswarudu, "The Growth of Mind nnd Art of Raja Rao: His Short Stories" in Rajeshwar Mittapalli & Pier Paolo Piciucco ed., *The Fiction of Raja Rao: Critical Studies*, New Delhi : Atlantic Publishers. 2001. p. 226.

[565] Makarand Paranjape, *The Best of Raja Rao*, (selected and edited).New Delhi, Katha Classics, 1998. p . x.

[566] B. Vyaghreswarudu, "The Growth of Mind nnd Art of Raja Rao: His Short Stories" in Rajeshwar Mittapalli & Pier Paolo Piciucco Ed. *The Fiction of Raja Rao: Critical Studies*,New Delhi : Atlantic Publishers. 2001. p. 226.

[567] Narsingh Srivastava, *The Mind and Art of Raja Rao*, Bareilly, Prakash Book Depot,1980.p. 135

[568] Esha Dey, *The Novels of Raja Rao, The Theme of Quest*. New Delhi. Prestige Books. 1992.pp. 246-247

[569] B. Vyaghreswarudu, "The Growth of Mind and Art of Raja Rao: His Short Stories" in Rajeshwar Mittapalli & Pier Paolo Piciucco Ed., *The Fiction of Raja Rao: Critical Studies*, New Delhi: Atlantic Publishers 2001. p. 225

[570] Narsingh Shrivastava : *The Mind and the Art of Raja Rao*, Prakash Book Depot , Bareilly (India), 1980 p 122.

Javani is the sad tale of a low caste widow who is despised and ill-treated by her own family. Her sister-in-law does not allow her to touch her child, cursing her as " a witch and an evil spirit."[571] *Javani* is fortunate to be working in a caring Brahmin household, where her status as a widow does not come in the way of her being loved by the mistress of the house. *Javani* works in this household not for earning a livelihood so much as for the affection that is bestowed on her. The mistress is "a veritable goddess"[572] , and *Javani* is "Good like a Cow"[573] to her. This unusual bond of love prospers without any discrimination of caste or creed. Seeing *Javani*'s plight, protagonist Ramappa vociferously condemns the evils of the caste system throughout the story.

On the other side of the spectrum is the high caste child widow *Akkayya* who, unlike Javani, is not loved at all but barely tolerated. This little bride fails to comprehend the implications of her husband's death, not wearing the vermilion mark and other deprivations. As a child, what engages her attention is the doll show. All her life *Akkayya* brings up other people's children with no gratitude at all. She becomes resigned to her fate, as in life, so in death, she is only a burden on her relatives.

Even though *Javani* and *Akkayya* belong to two different castes, they equally suffer the adversities of widowhood - simple living, complete self-denial and lifelong drudgery. Raja Rao advocates a "through overhauling of the Indian attitude to the widow and exposes the hollowness of some of the superstitious customs down the ages."[574] *The Little Grain* shop tells the story of a miser and greedy Bania couple, Motilal and Beti Bai, where the latter is beaten up, hoping that she will turn into an ideal wife. Amassing wealth by illegal means, Motilal becomes a

---

[571]Raja Rao, *The Cow of the Barricades* quoted in M.K.Naik, "Raja Rao as a Short Story Writer: *The Cow of the Barricades.*" *Books Abroad.* 40.4. 1966 p.394.

[572] Raja Rao, *The Cow of the Barricades* quoted in B. Vyaghreswarudu, "The Growth of Mind nnd Art of Raja Rao: His Short Stories" in Rajeshwar Mittapalli & Pier Paolo Piciucco. Ed. *The Fiction of Raja Rao: Critical Studies,* New Delhi : Atlantic Publishers. 2001. p.224.
[573] Raja Rao, *The Cow of the Barricades* quoted in M.K.Naik, "Raja Rao as a Short Story Writer: *The Cow of the Barricades.*" *Books Abroad.* 40.4. 1966 p.394..

[574] B. Vyaghreswarudu, "The Growth of Mind nnd Art of Raja Rao: His Short Stories" in Rajeshwar Mittapalli & Pier Paolo Piciucco ed. *The Fiction of Raja Rao: Critical Studies,* New Delhi : Atlantic Publishers. 2001. p. 225

moneylender, but this ill-begotten wealth ultimately spells his doom.

Most of the stories in this collection thus illustrate the traditional Indian life in the thirties. Rao not only brings out the negative side in the economic, political and social afflictions, e.g. the "stranglehold of superstition and ignorance upon the rustic mind", [575] the Brahmin being the "Chosen One,"[576] the women, especially the widow's lot, caste system and the position of women in Indian society,"[577] but also reflects the positive by showing," the heroism, courage, wisdom and loyalty of its common folk."[578] "Local colour is not the only force of Raja Rao's style. He is a master of descriptive prose."[579] With keen insight and incredible detail, he thus shows the face of rural India in the pre-independence era.

So graphic and realistic is his portrayal of the Indian village that many villages still resemble them today or bring vivid memories from our parents' childhood. Long cycle rides on empty, dusty roads to access a village, the village crier making official announcements on his drum like a walking gazette, and the practice of remembering significant events by connecting them with essential happenings like harvest, festivals, and ceremonies, all reflect the rural Indian ethos accurately. Religion here is a way of life which is characterised by rampant poverty. *Javani* eating a frugal meal in the dark portrays her utter deprivation, "because the oil is too expensive ... it costs an anna for a bottle apart from the fact that there is no necessity to see what you are eating."[580]

In this society which follows the rigid caste system, the "twice-born" Brahmins, keepers of the sacred books, do not work as they are the "Chosen One." [581] The lowly-born *Sudras* are destined to serve them. However, people believe in Dharma- an

---

[575] M.K.Naik, "Raja Rao as a Short Story Writer: *The Cow of the Barricades*." *Books Abroad*. 40.4. 1966 p.394.
[576] Raja Rao, *The Cow of the Barricades* quoted in M.K.Naik, "Raja Rao as a Short Story Writer: *The Cow of the Barricades*." *Books Abroad*. 40.4. 1966 p.394.
[577] M.K.Naik, "Raja Rao as a Short Story Writer: *The Cow of the Barricades*". *Books Abroad*. 40.4. 1966 p.394.
[578] Makarand Paranjape, *The Best of Raja Rao*, (selected and edited).New Delhi, Katha Classics, 1998. p . ix.
[579] M.K.Naik, "Raja Rao as a Short Story Writer: *The Cow of the Barricades*." *Books Abroad*. 40.4. 1966 p.395.

[580] Ibid., p.393

[581] Ibid., p. 393.

ideal way of life in which selfless action or Karma assumes prime importance. Rebirth, reincarnation and transmigration of souls are popular beliefs. Women's lives are miserable with rampant child marriages, wife beating and child widows. Ghosts, witchcraft, magic and superstitions rule their lives, as evident from the villager's gossip, "with these very two eyes, I have seen the ghosts of more than a hundred young men and women. All killed by magic."[582] *Javani* cautions Ramappa, "never to go out after sunset, for there are spirits of all sorts walking in the dark."[583] In this village, plague is considered the curse of the Goddess, a badly burning kitchen fire and the morning view of the cat is treated as evil omens, and the lizard falling on the right shoulder is a good omen.

However, change is on the horizon in sharp contrast to the elders Govindopant and Dattopant, who still dream of showing allegiance to the Maharaja in return for bags and bags of gold, the young Vithobopant and Pandopant reveal nationalistic fervour and discuss freedom from foreign rule. While *Javani*'s mistress, despite loving her, thinks it is irreligious to eat with a lowly born, her brother Ramappa disregards the rigid caste system. The motley group of villagers include the Gujarati grocer poor as a cur and later a prosperous moneylender, the professional matchmaker adept at the art of catching eligible bachelors, the snake charmer, the saintly Brahmin, the Sadhu in the Ashram, the simple peasant boy and the city-bred young man questioning archaic norms are all worth remembering.

The women characters that live a life of utter exploitation are demonstrated both by the poor maid *Javani* and the rich wife Rati, whose mother-in-law treats her as her slave because her son is involved in an extramarital affair, and disrespects Rati thoroughly. On the other side of the spectrum are *Narasinga*'s nasty aunt and wicked Sata, who is said to have poisoned and killed her old husband.

---

[582] Ibid., p.394
[583] Ibid., p.394

All these images are of pre-independent India, and though independent India has changed rapidly, some of these images have not been obliterated. There has been remarkable economic and social development, untouchability has been abolished, witchcraft, child marriages, bigamy, and domestic violence are illegal, illiteracy has been considerably reduced, and widow remarriage is not taboo. The Brahmin holds an important position but is not the Chosen One. Women have equal social status with men and equal opportunities for education and employment. A lot remains to be done even today. One cannot help but validate M.K. Naik's statement of 1972, "Yet there is much in the picture that is more or less true, even today."[584]

He was portraying an incredible picture of this quintessential rural India.- Rao's most remarkable distinction, the query that naturally confronts us, is how Rao compares with his counterparts, Rabindranath Tagore, Mulk Raj Anand and R.K.Narayan. M.K. Naik states that "... he clearly lacks their range and variety. In his wide sweep, Tagore ranges over themes as diverse as the decadent Bengali aristocracy ... Mulk Raj Anand is equally at home with rural or urban life...and with his socialistic sympathies he is a committed writer ...Narayan with his delicate touch brings out both the humour and the pathos in the lives of ordinary men and women both rustic and city bred,...But none of these writers has felt the pulse of village India with a surer touch, nor seen the traditional and transitional and the universal in it more clearly than Raja Rao has done in his one book. This is perhaps the reason why he has the most distinctive style of all the Indo-Anglians."[585]

The Policeman and the Rose, the second collection published in 1978, is another set of stories revolving around the East-West theme, which uses many symbols and is essentially

---

[584]Ibid., p.394.

[585] Ibid.,p. 396.

metaphysical. "It utilizes the theme of human bondage quest and liberation in an extravagant surreal-symbolic narration."[586]

It is a symbolic story with a complex philosophical theme. According to its subtitle, it is a "True Story" which " suggests a deeply personal tale, narrated in an elliptical, allegorical manner." the policeman symbolises pride or Ahankara - He and I, i.e. the Ego and the self, which arrests all human beings as soon as they are born. The Red Rose symbolises the Rajoguna, the passionate mind that drives man relentlessly all his life. [587] The story illustrates the Advaitic concept of the Jiva and the Atman through a beautiful woman who secures release only after meeting her Guru, symbolised by the policeman. Jiva imprisoned in the human body is an illusion, and the Atman or self - the liberated life force is the reality.

To secure release from the iron grip of this policeman or the bondage of the self, one has to surrender the Red Rose to a Guru, who symbolises the Lotus of Truth. He alone can remove *Avidya* or ignorance residing in the consciousness of the Ego. As the Guru reveals the ultimate truth, "one becomes a liberated soul free from the recurring cycle of time." After several reincarnations, the policemen is born as a human being to be freed by his Guru, from the prison of existence by showing him the path of liberation. "The theme and the style both evidence how philosophy can successfully be turned into art and in this respect this story is a unique example of Raja Rao's maturity as a writer."[588]

Nimka depicts the protagonist marrying a foreigner, the death of their child and a marital breakup. On a trip to India, this disillusioned man takes refuge in his Guru, who leads him to spiritual perfection. The story reveals how the author sublimates his thwarted emotions and feelings into art." This story, with its unique poetic style based on a harmonious blend of emerging sentiments of the movement and dazzling ideas, foreshadows the

[586] Esha Dey, *The Novels of Raja Rao, The Theme of Quest*. New Delhi. Prestige Books. 1992.p. 247

[587] Makarand Paranjape, *The Best of Raja Rao*, (selected and edited).New Delhi, Katha Classics, 1998. p. x

[588] Narsingh Shrivastava : *The Mind and the Art of Raja Rao*, Prakash Book Depot , Bareilly (India), 1980 p. 136.

typical narrative style of "*The Serpent and the Rope* and *The Cat and Shakespeare.*"[589]

India: A Fable is about the author distant from its soil and missing home; this story showcases India's great charm and magical effects, where fantasy and realism merge to create a most incredible nation. Initiating a French child Pirrot into this fascinating world, the Indian narrator grips his imagination so well that Pirrot becomes highly interested in knowing more about India, its varied landscape - the dense forests and the winding rivers, its people, its gods and goddesses, and even its animals. Pirrot first loves the camel, but the majestic Indian Elephant overpowers his desire eventually. This suggests "that India offers non-duality which is preferable to the monotheism of semitic religions."[590]

Both these stories " explore the human condition in multicultural encounters where the state of exile provides a constant framework of reference and grounds the presentation to a semblance of actuality. The same India whose absence in life turns the experience as distant as a fabular world of prince and princesses resides ironically at the core of the self as a source of atrophy to resist any alien touch and impedes the growth of a lasting relationship with a foreigner, hence the white Russian Nimka is left alone with her identification of Gandhi, India and the Indian hero."[591]

"Although Raja Rao's early short stories often find place in different anthologies, his fame rests on his novels.... his stories were regarded largely as by products of the novels. [592] However, his third collection, *On the Ganga Ghat,* published in 1989, changed that notion forever. The "prose in this collection is exquisitely chiselled, sparse yet evocative."[593] It has eleven stories which are so structured that they could form a novel. Some critics

---

[589] B. Vyaghreswarudu, "The Growth of Mind nnd Art of Raja Rao: His Short Stories" in Rajeshwar Mittapalli & Pier Paolo Piciucco Ed. *The Fiction of Raja Rao: Critical Studies*, New Delhi : Atlantic Publishers. 2001. p.225.

[590] Makarand Paranjape, *The Best of Raja Rao,* (selected and edited).New Delhi, Katha Classics, 1998.p.ix.

[591] Esha Dey, *The Novels of Raja Rao, The Theme of Quest.* New Delhi. Prestige Books. 1992.p. 247

[592] Ibid.,p. 246

[593] B. Vyaghreswarudu, "The Growth of Mind and Art of Raja Rao: His Short Stories" in Rajeshwar Mittapalli & Pier Paolo Piciucco Ed. *The Fiction of Raja Rao: Critical Studies*, New Delhi: Atlantic Publishers. 2001. P. 227

like Esha Dey feel that this "new form emerges as a fusion of the short story and the novel...a neat circular arrangement of imaginary characters round a central theme."[594] Others feel that a new form of the novel has been introduced but without the main protagonist and independent themes in which each story is complete and interlinked. Each picture forms a part of the bigger collage, and according to B. Vyaghreswarudu "Each story is a Jerk of the Kaleidoscope when a new engaging pattern emerges to hold our attention."[595]

Paranjape feels that "the real protagonist of these stories appears to be their setting Banaras."[596] B. Vyaghreswarudu disagrees, saying, "Like Malgudi of Narayan the Ganges is the real hero of the eleven stories."[597] Both statements are fallacious since Banaras and Ganga are inextricable. They are both conjoined, and together they symbolise the bridge of salvation crossing which man passes from the dual to the non-dual from mortality to eternity.

The stories candidly depict the varied elements of Banarasi life, the holy city of Death, cherished by countless Indians since time immemorial, as their final resting place or home on the Ganga Ghat, where the river "Ganga purifies all." Death dominates all characters, Bhola loses his family in an epidemic, Muthradas and Ranchoddass lose their wives, the taxi driver Motilal talks about his son who " died of death," and Rani Rashomani stocking sandalwood for her cremation "waited for death as a baby- bird awaits his mother's beak." Only Shankar, whose wife is expecting, will transcend death, as he was awaiting life

The novel depicts how death in the holy city secures Moksha or is a release from the cycle of birth and rebirth. Thus from the opulent to the indigent, be it the royalty and the nobility, beggars and merchants, crooks and simpletons, courtesans and

---

[594] Esha Dey, *The Novels of Raja Rao, The Theme of Quest*. New Delhi. Prestige Books. 1992.p. 248-249

[595] B. Vyaghreswarudu, "The Growth of Mind and Art of Raja Rao: His Short Stories in" Rajeshwar Mittapalli & Pier Paolo Piciucco Ed. *The Fiction of Raja Rao: Critical Studies*, New Delhi: Atlantic Publishers. 2001. P. 228.
[596] Makarand Paranjape, *The Best of Raja Rao*, (selected and edited).New Delhi, Katha Classics, 1998.p. xxii.
[597] B. Vyaghreswarudu, "The Growth of Mind and Art of Raja Rao: His Short Stories" in Rajeshwar Mittapalli & Pier Paolo Piciucco. Ed. *The Fiction of Raja Rao: Critical Studies*, New Delhi: Atlantic Publishers. 2001. p. 228

charlatans, all classes, castes and creeds, even animals assemble here, all inadvertently preparing for the same final journey - the only truth of life. Thus this ancient spiritual destination provides refuge to outsiders like business people Muthradas from Vrindavan and Ranchoddass and his ascetic daughter Sudha from Bombay, widow Rani Rashomoni from Bengal, all having retired from life engage in penance and prayer, preparing for their inevitable end.

Even the saintly parrot Bhim, the brahimini cow Jhaveri Bai, besides pilgrims and Sadhus of all hues, collect on the Ghats in Banaras, seeking redemption from life. "The characters are bound together only by the tie of deliverance as preceptor and disciple or pilgrims on the same journey towards nothingness."[598] For life is nothing before birth or beyond death. All assembled on the Ganga Ghat with a fervent prayer, "Mother give us no birth or death," for birth is so mean and death is so low."[599] "What we see is not only a rich and diverse picture of society but, in a sense, of the cosmos itself, both human and animal and extending further, the animate and the inanimate everything seeking the same Truth or emancipation."[600]

The stories also highlight the life of people flocking to the Ghats for religious observances and invoking the benevolence of the river which also gratifies all wishes giving " songs to songsters, limbs to brave, paddle push to the boat and child to wife."[601] The river and its environs sustain the lives of the locals immensely. So the bachelor Madhoba who loves the spirit Mohini carries logs for a cremation to the ghats, the tramp Bhedia, Putli the street juggler and her snake charmer father, petty thieves Mohendra and his gang, motor mechanic Bhula, pimp Shivlal, the fallen concubine Nanna all wander in and around the river for some income.

These characters pursue religious observances (Dharma) and material objectives (Artha and Kama) amidst all the humdrum

---

[598] Esha Dey, *The Novels of Raja Rao, The Theme of Quest*. New Delhi. Prestige Books. 1992.p.255.
[599] Ibid.,p. 253.
[600] Makarand Paranjape, *The Best of Raja Rao*, (selected and edited).New Delhi, Katha Classics, 1998.p.xxiii

[601] Raja Rao, *On the Ganga Ghat*, as quoted in B. Vyaghreswarudu, "The Growth of Mind nnd Art of Raja Rao: His Short Stories" in Rajeshwar Mittapalli & Pier Paolo Piciucco. Ed., *The Fiction of Raja Rao: Critical Studies*, New Delhi: Atlantic Publishers. 2001. p. 228.

of daily life, intentionally or unintentionally seeking the ultimate liberation (Moksha) from this very mundane existence. Exploring the myths and realities encompassing Mother Ganga, the novel exposes the soul of this ancient spiritual sanctuary. "In these stories the Indian philosophy, ethics and metaphysics, converge into a unified whole and flow along the Ganga Ghats as the Mother Ganga does."[602] "It marks a brilliant achievement as a classic of fabulation."[603]

Paranjape observes further that Rao is obsessed with Banaras "both as a real location and as a symbol.... and it figures in one way or another in nearly every novel of his. Banaras seems to stand for non duality, for that principle which overcomes death. Death of course, is a constant presence in this holiest of holy cities. But unlike elsewhere, death here is not just welcome, but auspicious- a release, a liberation, moksha. In fact what dies in Banaras is death itself. That is why it is so important in Rao's scheme of things. It is Banaras, as a sort of miniaturised India that stands for the truth of the world. It can unveil the mystery of human life and misery by showing the way to transcendence through the dissolution of the Ego."[604]

Thus these are "compelling stories with their photographic realism, comic and irreverent element, metaphysical and philosophical content."[605] "A meeting of the artist and the pilgrim brings to life India as a timeless existence, ruled by orthodoxy, peopled by men and women content to live in an age old hierarchy of structure. For the lifelong exile in the modern West, India is all that the contemporary age is not – a mythical entity in wish space and wish –time built with deliberate simplicity and apparent innocence that mark the height of Rao's success as India's greatest anti-modern modern writer in English."[606]

---

[602] B. Vyaghreswarudu, "The Growth of Mind nnd Art of Raja Rao: His Short Stories" in Rajeshwar Mittapalli & Pier Paolo Piciucco Ed. *The Fiction of Raja Rao: Critical Studies*, New Delhi : Atlantic Publishers. 2001. p. 228

[603] Esha Dey, *The Novels of Raja Rao, The Theme of Quest*. New Delhi. Prestige Books. 1992.p. 248

[604] Makarand Paranjape, *The Best of Raja Rao*, (selected and edited).New Delhi, Katha Classics, 1998.p. xxiii.

[605] B. Vyaghreswarudu, "The Growth of Mind nnd Art of Raja Rao: His Short Stories" in Rajeshwar Mittapalli & Pier Paolo Piciucco Ed. *The Fiction of Raja Rao: Critical Studies*, New Delhi,: Atlantic Publishers .2001. P. 227.

[606] Esha Dey, *The Novels of Raja Rao, The Theme of Quest*. New Delhi. Prestige Books. 1992..p. 249.

Thus the series begins with *The Cow of the Barricades*, followed by *The Policeman and the Rose* ends abruptly on *The Ganga Ghat*. Naik regrets that "Raja Rao has written so few short stories. The comparatively freer form of the novel has been a fatal Cleopatra to him......Indo Anglian writing is certainly the poorer because Raja Rao did not submit himself oftener to the relatively more exciting discipline of the short story."[607]

---

[607] . M.K.Naik, "Raja Rao as a Short Story Writer: *The Cow of the Barricades.*" *Books Abroad.* 40.4. 1966 p.396.

CHAPTER VIII: Conclusion

To bring this work to a close, it is important to reify the main thrust of our arguments. The prime context of Raja Rao's writing was his diasporic context defining his spiritual quest which led him to his expositions of Indian cultural, intellectual and spiritual life which he was keen to share with the west where he lived[608]. Paranjape also confirms, "Rao has lived abroad for the greater part of his life, yet he has continued to live in the greater India of his imagination which he espouses so ardently." [609]

His quest for this truth had begun on foreign soil, where Rao had taken refuge, disillusioned with the misery of pre-independent India. However, there was a definite purpose in exploring the mysticism of the west and studying the Albigensian heresy, for his grandfather thought that India should be made more accurate to the Europeans. Since Rao was an academic, an intellectual, the urge to discover his own identity in an alien milieu and the yearning to reveal the eternal truth of India initiated him into the creative art of writing.

Kumar suggests, "But what does chain him to India, as in the case of migrant Brahmins is the Brahmanic tradition. If one is a creative writer like Rao, the wish fulfillment takes the form of creative works. The material comforts of the west and the privileged position that India offers them are fused artistically in these works. Thus most of his characters like Rama in *The Serpent and the Rope* are nostalgic about India."[610]

In self-exile, even though he was far from home, he could not emotionally alienate himself from the reality of India. Iyengar commenting aptly on his diasporic locus as a write, "Raja Rao hails from Mysore State, and the action of his novels strays far afield-as

---

[608] Mambrol, N. Analysis of Raja Rao's Novels. Literary Theory and Criticism. July 29, 2020. URL: https://literariness.org/2020/06/29/analysis-of-raja-raos-novels/. Consulted on 29-11-22; Sethi, R., Letizia, A. Reading India in a Transnational Era
The Works of Raja Rao. Routledge India. 2021. URL: https://www.routledge.com/Reading-India-in-a-Transnational-Era-The-Works-of-Raja-Rao/Sethi-Alterno/p/book/9781138550292. Consulted on 29-11-22
[609] Makarand Paranjape, *The Best of Raja Rao*, (selected and edited).New Delhi, Katha Classics, 1998. p.xxiii.
[610] G. Thirupathi Kumar, *Conceptualising Tradition: A Study of Raja Rao, R.K. Narayan and Mulkraj Anand..* New Delhi. Research India Press. 2007.p. 70

far indeed, as France, England and Moscow – his heart is effectively tethered to his immutable ancient moorings with the strong invisible strings of his traditional Hindu Culture."[611] Personified by his protagonist Ramaswamy of *The Serpent and Rope* he battles to keep Indian culture alive be it installing for worship "a round an oval lingam found on the banks of the Seine"[612] and imagining "a huge flat stone at the edge of the garden to be Shiva's Bull,"[613]and "Mother Rhone" as Ganges which flows everywhere."[614]

The profuse use of sanskrit in his writing is a way feels Kumar, that "places him on a pedestal in India and abroad, his knowledge of European languages like English and French secure a high amount of respectability among his relatives and friends in India. If he had only used Sanskrit in India he would have been treated like any traditional Brahmin and if it was a European language alone abroad, he would not have created that mystic aura around himself. Thus language plays an important role in establishing Rama as he proudly calls himself a "wise man."[615]

The first instance of a close East-West encounter is when Ramaswamy marries a French lady Madeleine. His Indian ethos charmed her as Rama admits "that he has won Madeleine through the demonstration of his metaphysical Brahmanic knowledge and by chanting slokas with a full breath."[616] Madeleine is undoubtedly impressed in the beginning calling herself a pagan, "She is not happy with her given identity as a European woman nor is she satisfied with her Christian God."[617] Rama gradually inculcates the love of Indian thought and culture, initiating the search for Truth in Madeleine, which eventually enables her to embark on a journey for spiritual perfection.

The East-West interaction profoundly influenced Rao, who tried to understand the West with an open mind, committed as

---

[611] K.R.S.Iyengar, *"Raja Rao", Indian Writing in English*, Bombay, Asia Publishing House, 1973. P. 386
[612] Raja Rao, *The Serpent and the Rope*, New Delhi, Orient Paperbacks. 1968. p. 54
[613] Ibid., p. 55
[614] Ibid. p. 118.
[615] G. Thirupathi Kumar, *Conceptualising Tradition: A Study of Raja Rao, R.K. Narayan and Mulkraj Anand.*. New Delhi. Research India Press. 2007.p. 73.
[616] Ibid.p. 73.
[617] Ibid.p. 90

he was to living abroad. Perceiving an essential oneness in all religions and through Ramaswamy, he wanted to synthesise both cultures' truths and ideals. Sharma aptly states that "Raja Rao though firmly rooted in Indian metaphysics and culture, could not be indifferent to writers and cultures of the west. An expatriate who has spent major period of his adult life in the west....who first married a French lady and later an American has studied western culture and thus is competent to speak on both the oriental and the occidental literature."[618]

Rao saw much opposition in the east and the west in his initial years. A modern Indian intellectual, he oscillated between the west's materialism and the east's spiritualism. However, when the gloss and glamour of the materialistic west faded away, his intercultural western encounters resulted in the rediscovery of the brilliance of his heritage and his "inextricable and living bond with the language, literary tradition, and a whole ethos",[619] which was his metaphysical, eternal India. He faced the challenge of preventing alienation from his ancient moorings and protecting his Indian identity

Esha Dey suggests "the problem of identity for a Hindu magnifies itself for another inexplicable mystery - the intimate relation between the Indian soil and the Hindu roots which stubbornly refuse transplantation anywhere else in the world. Indeed Hindu tends to be a geographical concept which seeks to disregard time. So the Mahabharata points out that a happy Hindu is one who is never in exile. The fear of extinction strikes the modern Hindu who has chosen the west with an atavistic force, which seeks desperately to resist the undeniable impact of what is assumed to be an alien culture. This complex love hate syndrome is particularly noticeable in a generation of Indians belonging to a privileged class with sophisticated western academic background and nationalist aspiration – a class of which Raja Rao may appear as a representative."[620]

---

[618] Kaushal Sharma, *Raja Rao: A Study of His Themes and Technique*, New Delhi, Sarup & Sons. 2005.p.5.
[619] Esha Dey, *The Novels of Raja Rao, The Theme of Quest*. New Delhi. Prestige Books.1992. p. 231
[620] Ibid.p. 231

Chitra Sankaran also supports the idea of his writing representing strongly of his diasporic persuasion and questions Rao's "Indianness". To her, Rama, as its epitome, is a typical 'post-colonial' Hindu, and his Brahmanism or spiritualism is not the unsullied tradition of the yore. Rao simply accepts the colonial discourse of the artificial divide of the West and East regarding the material/spiritual."[621] Kumar concurs, "Raja Rao is very selective in his definition of tradition totally excluding many major traditions. What Rao praises in the name of spirituality – the Brahman is not ancient traditions but the modern colonial presumptions. Rao's whole endeavour...is to celebrate the hegemony of the Brahmans in the name of India and tradition. Thus Ramaswamy starts as a born Brahmin, leads his life as a Brahmin, and by the time the novel ends (even until the last page) he still remains a Brahmin celebrating Brahmanism."[622] Thus vacillating between two worlds, the impersonal and personal, the believer and the non-believer, the modern and the traditional, moralistic and theistic, Rao endeavoured to find the meaning of his life. Compelled to soothe the existential torment of the West by reconciling it with the spirituality of the East, he created a significant body of literature whose form and content were remarkably Indian and which conveyed his profound view of life, especially his spiritual message perfectly. His quest for spirituality lent a magical aura to his writings.

He chose English as the medium of expression so that he could communicate better with the west also. No one ever Indianized English the way Raja Rao did. He devised a particular usage for a unique story he wanted to narrate. This innovation was a tightrope walk indeed for him because the response of the Indians used to write in Standard English was unknown. Literal translations and usage of typical Indian vernacular idioms and phrases, words and terms, oaths and imprecations, expressions and adages

---

[621] Chitra Sankaran, *The Myth Connection:The Use of Hindu Mythology in Some Novels ;Raja Rao and R.K. Narayan.*Ahmedabad, Allied Publishers.1993.p. 100.
[622] G. Thirupathi Kumar, *Conceptualising Tradition: A Study of Raja Rao, R.K. Narayan and Mulkraj Anand..* New Delhi. Research India Press. 2007.p. 99..

imparted great colour and spirit to his narrative. His selection was very judicious as he never used Kannada words or exclamations. Instead, he used Sanskrit words, mantras and quotations to create Indian fervour. Altering the typical structure of English syntax also enhanced the impact of his narrative. He successfully used different techniques for different narratives. He used a poetical style in *Kanthapura*, a riddling and syllogistic style in *The Serpent and the Rope*, an allegorical, black humour style in The Cat and Shakespeare, and a violent, ironic style in *Comrade Kirillov.*

Whether he excelled in all forms or whether they were Eastern or western can be debated, but for one, they were apt and effective. Sharma is convinced that "The value of technique in fiction has been recognized by the novelists as well as the critics alike, it is considered as an important tool in the presentation, interpretation and evaluation of a novel. The choice of the narrative technique depends upon the kind and quality of experience, the novelist wishes to communicate and the thematic, artistic and psychological effects he wants to produce. Its judicious employment, therefore, goes a long way in determining the success of a novel."[623]

In the methodology of the novel, symbols, legends and myths are used to convey abstract thoughts. Timeless myths have always remained an integral part of literature since they are considered a store and blend of fact and fiction, conveying the inner meaning of the universe and human existence. Esha Dey rightly points out, "the metaphysical attitude of a traditional and (primitive) society, towards time as a cyclical occurrence as distinct from the Judaeo- Christian concept of time as a straight line. The action narrated in a legend or myth always happens in the "Holy time of the Beginning."[624] Holy Time belongs to Cosmos, and thus the repetition of archetypes in the form of recurrent myths and legend represents the cosmic rhythm...Repeating the myth in actual life in the form of recital of the deeds of mythical heroes, the

---

[623] Kaushal Sharma, *Raja Rao: A Study of His Themes and Technique*, New Delhi, Sarup & Sons 2005.,pp 3-4.
[624] Mircea Eliade , *The Myth of the Eternal Return or Cosmos and History* ,1949,trans, 1954, p. xii. quoted in Esha Dey, *The Novels of Raja Rao, The Theme of Quest.* New Delhi. Prestige Books 1992.p25

archaic man lives in "sacred time."[625] Therefore in the storytelling tradition of India Rao found a "feasible narrative structure to present an "Indian identity"… not in the Holy Time, but in the historical present."[626]

Through myths, the author not only "communicates his vision of life but also imparts form and compactness to his novel."[627] Raja Rao, therefore, made them "an integral part of the organic structure of the novel,"[628]   He also knew that "Indian people were very close to their myths." because they symbolized the essence of Indian life. He, therefore, realized "the inadequacy of the western model for portraying true Indian ethos and sensibility and thus resorts to the traditional Indian form…Raja Rao emerges as the foremost exponent of the Puranic model of storytelling, the oldest technique of narration."[629] This uniquely Indian traditional form of storytelling is "written from the point of view of "I" as witness narrator" who "weaves the past and present gods and men together in her narrative,"[630] employing myths "to extend our understanding of a particular situation or give meaning, symbolic meaning to the theme"[631].

The result of all these innovations and combinations was incredible. Rao's fictional world encompassing the " story, fable, myth, religion, philosophy and politics"[632] of both the East and the West made his exemplary works a virtual repository of Indian culture and tradition. Alternating between fantasy and realism, they revealed his ideas, experiences and emotions - his complete vision of life and his universal message of deliverance.

Given his background, Raja Rao's message was essentially a metaphysical, an Indian mantra which exhorts release from worldly dualities and a progression towards spiritual perfection. This process, however, suggests Paranjape "does not

---

[625] Mircea Eliade , *Myths, Dreams and Mysteries:The Encounter between Contemporary Faiths and Archaic Realities,* 1957, trans. 1960.p. 23 quoted in Esha Dey, *The Novels of Raja Rao, The Theme of Quest.* New Delhi. 1992. Prestige Books.p25

[626] Esha Dey, *The Novels of Raja Rao, The Theme of Quest.* New Delhi. Prestige Books. 1992.p. 25

[627] Kaushal Sharma ,*Raja Rao: A Study of His Themes and Technique,* New Delhi, Sarup & Sons. 2005.p.20.

[628] Ibid.,p. 21

[629] Ibid.,p. 20.

[630]. Ibid.,.p. 16.

[631] Ibid.,p. 22.

[632] Makarand Paranjape, *The Best of Raja Rao,* (selected and edited).New Delhi, Katha Classics, 1998. P. vii

preclude any action in the world. The choice is ours...the world can be negated even as we participate in it, just as it can be negated when we withdraw from it." In both conditions, Moksha or Oneness with the Absolute remains the ultimate goal of human life in this illusory world. This truth of salvation, according to Esha Dey, is his message to the "Christian West which believes in a personal God and in the existence of the individual in his own right at a level qualitatively different from the Divine."[633]

She, however, rejects Rao's idea that "Duality is anti-Indian, the non- dual affirms the truth with Rabindranath Tagore's statement," that complete and fulfilled love between the Divine and the human of which duality and non-duality are the two aspects, one complementing the other." Dey feels that this stand may have helped Rao to establish his Indian Identity with the Western readers for whom he writes, "obliterating the Indian truth that this is a stand no Indian thinker or artist has ever struck in the whole course of the history of the subcontinent because it reduces spirituality to the level of a mere attribute of nationalism and above all its rigidity denies that core of heterogeneity which is the dominant motif in the vast and variegated Indian culture. ...Exile, therefore, is destined for Raja Rao, his *Karma*."[634] Although, Parthasarthy differs strongly, "Rao is one of the most innovative novelists, now writing. Departing boldly from the European traditions of the novel, he has indigenized it in the process of assimilating material from the Indian literary tradition."[635]

Sharma suggests Rao's distinction is that "instead of a well-developed plot in the traditional sense, his novels, appear to be books of philosophy and metaphysics, chiselled with Encyclopaedic knowledge."[636] Raja Rao combines "Western" (historic, romantic, personal, poetic) and the "Indian" (traditional, classical impersonal, antipoetic)"[637] elements, as Narasimhaiah

---

[633] Esha Dey, *The Novels of Raja Rao, The Theme of Quest*. New Delhi.. Prestige Books. 1992...p. 232.
[634] Ibid.,p..233
[635] R. Parthasarathy, quoted in Makarand Paranjape, *The Best of Raja Rao*, (selected and edited).New Delhi, Katha Classics, 1998.p..ii
[636] Kaushal Sharma ,*Raja Rao: A Study of His Themes and Technique*, New Delhi, Sarup & Sons. 2005.p. 1.
[637] Esha Dey, *The Novels of Raja Rao, The Theme of Quest*. New Delhi. Prestige Books 1992..p.223

opines, " is the greatest English novelist."[638] Verghese concurs "Undoubtedly with Raja Rao Indian English novel has come of age."[639]

Rao's stories are not merely spiritual and metaphysical interpretations of ancient Indian thought but enmeshed in these ideas they reveal nuances of multilayered human relationships. His characters transcending time and space and their individuality illustrate not only his profound thoughts, beliefs, and exhaustive experiences but also social and political concerns. Hence they cannot be described by simple social epithets like father, mother, sister, brother, uncle and friend. Apart from themselves, they are also symbols demonstrating the third dimension. Thus the women, despite being sisters, mistresses, wives, daughters, followers, friends, and workers, are also women in their own right.

Representing Indian womanhood, they display independent personalities with independent consciousness, striving knowingly or unknowingly towards their salvation. *Javani,* for instance, highlights the plight of a maid servant and throws light on the caste system and the position of low caste widowed working women in pre-independent India. Her cordial relationship with her high caste mistress displays a unique bond of solidarity between them. This humanness borne out of spirituality is the third dimension of Raja Rao's characters - the distinguishing mark of the Easterner, which elevates him and sets him apart from his Western counterpart. India has not held its unique position in the comity of nations since time immemorial.

The appeal of a writer lies not only in appreciation from his lay readers but also in the connoisseurs of his art. Since creative writing and literary criticism proceed parallelly, the critic's touchstone has also to be applied to an artist's art. Divided into the introductory and the comprehensive, both categories have antagonistic and sympathetic critics. Rao's form and content- his language and style, his themes and techniques, his ideas and

---

[638] Paul Verghese. Quoted in Makarand Paranjape, *The Best of Raja Rao,* (selected and edited).New Delhi, Katha Classics, 1998. P. iii.

[639] Paul C. Verghese, *Problems of Indian Creative Writer in English,* Bombay Somaya Publications Pvt. Ltd. 1971.p. 99.

emotions and most importantly, his metaphysical viewpoint, which flows as an undercurrent in all his works, were subjected to severe critical examination by both the Eastern and the Western readers. His works demanded a close look for greater clarity of thought because if the metaphysical aspect which forms the backbone of Raja Rao's Indian ethos is not interpreted in a proper perspective, his basic premise, which lends distinction to his works, would be severely challenged. For this, the great body of criticism on the fictional world of Raja Rao, both negative and positive, has to be explored.

However, we also conclude that Raja Rao was a pioneer, and it would not be an exaggeration to say that Raja Rao was a pioneer in making Indian writing, especially fiction in English, emerge as the essential genre in Indo-Anglian literature. Before him, the Indian novel for long suffered the stigma of lack of originality. It failed "to emerge as an original and characteristic genre of literature." The authors were not "able to evolve any distinctive Indian form in consonance with their artistic instincts"[640] feels Sharma. Bhattacharya also felt the same, "In one respect, Indian fiction in English does not seem to have made any appreciable progress- here, I use the word progress with some hesitation. They have clung, as a rule, to conventional moulds and patterns. There is a lack of inspired experimentation."[641] Voicing the same concern Rajan suggests, "Indian novelists tend to write as if the development of the novel ended with Trollope." [642] In fact, most of them have "adopted the traditional nineteenth-century western form of the novel in presenting the varied colours of Indian life."[643]

In terms of Jhabvala's very rigid framework for the ideal novel," Indian novel cannot become a distinctive genre, and its creator cannot be true to their basic artistic instincts until they produce novels which would be bits of prose, poetry, anecdotes,

---

[640] Kaushal Sharma ,*Raja Rao: A Study of His Themes and Technique*, New Delhi, Sarup & Sons. 2005.p.4
[641] Bhabani Bhattacharya, "Indo Anglian", *The Novels in Modern India*, ed Iqbal Babhtiyar, Bombay: The P.E.N. ,All India Centre 1964. P. 46.
[642] B. Rajan, "India". *Literature of the World in English*, ed. Bruce King, London, Routledge and Kegan Paul.1974. p. 84.
[643] Kaushal Sharma ,*Raja Rao: A Study of His Themes and Technique*, New Delhi, Sarup & Sons. 2005..p.4.

lots of philosophizing, and using an oblique kind of wit, and an ultimate self surrender, a sinking back into formlessness, into eternity…something like Indian music."[644] Along with G.V. Desani, S.N. Ghosh and Ananatnarayanan Raja Rao passed this acid test proving to be an exception by his innovations, making the Indian novel a different genre today. "The most important thing for an Indian English novelist is to have his roots deep in Indian soil."[645] With this realization, Sharma feels that Rao combined the modern western experiments in novel writing, reorienting the Indian traditional style of storytelling popular in the epics Ramayana and Mahabharata, the Puranas and Panchtantra, to evolve an entirely new form.

Thus "a blend of metaphysical tradition and his susceptibility to western culture has made his novels philosophically complex."[646] In Rao's words, "the Indian novel can only be epic in form and metaphysical in nature."[647] Kumar disagrees that this "precludes the vast multiculturalism and the oral tradition and literature that represent the life of the Indian masses. He finds it strange that it comes from a person who experimented with orality in his first novel Kanthapura."[648] Sharma puts up a strong defence "no one can deny the fact that Raja Rao is so original that his artistic achievements both in the sphere of content and technique cannot be ignored."[649]

Taking note of his excellence, Naik suggests, "Raja Rao has also brought to the Indian novel in English many elements, to which it had been previously deficient, an epic breath of vision, a metaphysical rigour and philosophical depth, a symbolic richness, a lyrical fervour and an essential Indianness of style."[650]

By winning international recognition, Rao also made Indian English Fiction an integral and outstanding part of the commonwealth literature. As a result, the growth of Indian English

---

[644] Quoted in M.K.Naik, *Raja Rao*, Bombay,. Blackie and Sons Pvt. Ltd.1982..pp. 159-160,

[645] Kaushal Sharma ,*Raja Rao: A Study of His Themes and Technique*, New Delhi, Sarup & Sons. 2005..p. 4

[646] Ibid.p. 5

[647] Raja Rao Quoted in G. Thirupathi Kumar, *Conceptualising Tradition: A Study of Raja Rao, R.K. Narayan and Mulkraj Anand..* New Delhi. Research India Press. 2007.p. 67

[648] Ibid.p. 67.

[649] Kaushal Sharma ,*Raja Rao: A Study of His Themes and Technique*, New Delhi, Sarup & Sons. 2005..p.4

[650] M.K.Naik, *Raja Rao*, Bombay, Blackie & Son Publishers Pvt. Ltd. 1982. p. 160..

fiction received great impetus by gaining its rightful place among lay readers and becoming a part of the English literature syllabus of Indian universities. Today global acclaim and the spurt of creative writing in English by Indians everywhere has given Indian English Fiction a thriving presence and a bright future.

One of the three greatest Indian novelists in English compared to Mulk Raj Anand and R. K. Narayan, Raja Rao is a choice of both serious students and eminent critics of Indo-Anglian literature. His themes and their treatment are quite different from theirs. Raja Rao's works relate to philosophical consciousness, while Anand and Narayan's works relate to social realities. Raja Rao is concerned with man's spiritual quest and his quest for selfhood. Paranjape aptly comments that compared to the other two, "neither, their stylistic and poetic depth or dexterity can compare with the best of Rao's writing. Thematically also Rao is different from them….He is a metaphysical novelist whose concerns are primarily religious and philosophical."[651]

A significant criticism of Raja Rao is available through reviews, interviews, research and full-length articles. Iyengar, Naik and Narasimhaiah emerged as pioneer critics in introductory criticism, demonstrating a balanced and considerate approach, writing extensively on Raja Rao's craft. Derret in his book *The Modern Indian Novel in English* appreciated the original form of Kanthapura and The Serpent and the Rope. Examining his style, Ray observes a definite evolution in his successive works. Despite these sympathetic criticisms, two prejudices worked against Rao, one of a serious overload of ideas and the other his consistent metaphysical strain. The initial neglect and ignorance of the new genre were replaced by gradual discernment and sensitivity by the critics who sacrificed Rao's rigidity of ideas to his vigour and vision of India.

Razdan and Ranchan were the first to identify the particular diasporic vein in raja Rao's writing and reviewed the theme of East-West confrontation in three issues of *The Illustrated Weekly of India* (March-April, 1996). They took a sympathetic

---

[651] Makarand Paranjape, *The Best of Raja Rao*, (selected and edited).New Delhi, Katha Classics, 1998.p.ii

view discussing the aims and achievements of the author and his works. A similar strain is visible in the two articles in the *New Literature Review* (Australia, 1978). R. Shepherd, in his detailed analysis of Ramaswamy, appreciates his mind and metaphysics in *The Serpent and the Rope.* O.P. Mathur gives a deep insight into the existential dilemmas of *Comrade Kirillov.*

On the other hand, the formless structure of his novels, particularly *The Serpent and the Rope* and *The Cat and Shakespeare,* have been severely criticized. Mulk Raj Anand, talking about *The Serpent and the Rope,* describes Raja Rao as "an anti-novel novelist, self-consciously using the philosophical essay as part of the bardic recital form" and as a novelist who "defies the novel form and uses it for philosophical essay."[652] Rajeev Taranath also comments on the structural deficiency of *The Serpent and the Rope.*

However, this great novelist of ideas gets his due from the noted critic. In his monumental work *Indian Writing in English,* Iyengar recognizes Rao's distinction as a novelist and short story writer, clearly asserting that "all his writing is part of Raja Rao's sadhana or spiritual experience, and so *Kanthapura, The Serpent and the Rope* and *The Cat and Shakespeare...* should be viewed as steps – or paths – towards realization." Thus he is the first critic to recognize Rao's first three novels as a 'Trilogy' which presents "a steady progression in Raja Rao's sadhana,"[653]

He first distinguishes Raja Rao from R. K. Narayan and Mulk Raj Anand, regarding Rao's art as having an 'enchanting prose style'. Analyzing the themes, he praises the form and content in the most evocative manner. However, he does not abstain from criticism finding Rao's approach to Gandhian politics as "half poetical and half-whimsical". He probably fails to perceive that the poetry reinforces and intensifies the dreary reality of the theme. Iyengar also feels that the physical and the psychological aspects in *The Serpent and the Rope* have not been harmonized with the

---

[652] Mulk Raj Anand, *"Old Myth-New Myth: Recital Versus Novel"*, in M. K. Naik, *Raja Rao,* Bombay, .Blackie & Sons Publishers Pvt. Ltd. 1982.P.. 147

[653] K.R.S. Iyengar, *Raja Rao, Indian Writing in English,* Bombay, Sterling Publishers. 1983.. p.411

metaphysical aspects adequately, presenting a half-truth. However, his candid remarks that "grumble though we may we do not actually run away from the book"[654] reveal a judgment which suitably silences most critics who cannot accept the ideational structure of Rao's works.

His appreciation of the narrative of *Kanthapura* is entirely objective, "And the manner of her telling too is characteristically Indian, feminine with a spontaneity that is coupled with swiftness, vivid with raciness suffused with a native vigour and exciting with rich sense of drama shot through and through with humour and lyricism.[655] He also comments on the narrative of *The Cat And Shakespeare* in a similar vein which he thinks "is more like one of the bigger Upanishads, part narrative, part speculation, and part dialogue or discussion", and "…The description zigzags rather than progresses straight on, the speculation is not so much analytical as a series of spasmodic lightening flashes, and the dialogue is dialectical rather than an exchange of confidence."[656]

Meenakshi Mukherjee, in her remarkable book *The Twice Born Fiction,* provides a rare insight into Rao's vision with regard to the novel *The Serpent and the Rope* finding Ramaswamy and Madeleine to be "completely convincing and recognizable as individuals,"[657] The portrayal of Ramaswamy as an exponent of Advaitic principles, a spiritual aspirant in quest of the ultimate truth, personifying Rao himself leads her to opine that, "The East-West theme assumes a depth and validity not achieved before in Indo-Anglian fiction"[658]. She extols the use of myths which augments our understanding of the present situation. Legends are used to connect belief and reality and reinforce the realism of the national uprising. Myths have been used as a fictional technique to reveal contemporary events' historical significance and establish intercultural links in both Kanthapura and The Serpent and the Rope. They also symbolize eternal Indian values still thriving

---

[654] Ibid., p. 405
[655] Ibid. p. 390
[656] Ibid. p. 390
[657] Meenakshi Mukherjee, *The Twice Born Fiction,* New Delhi. Arnold Heinemann. 1974..p.91
[658] Ibid., p.89.

today. However, her opinion that Kanthapura essentially follows a legendary pattern instead of a realistic one is fallacious.

Being the first to comment positively and objectively on Rao's innovation of Indian English and the 'Indianess' of his style, she says "It should be emphasized, however, that creating an 'Indian English' is by no means the primary duty of the Indo-Anglian writer. His success or failure will be judged not by the amount of Indian imagery he has used in his novels nor by his capacity to capture the rhythm of the vernacular in English. These images and rhythm become important only if they serve some purpose in the context, becoming integral to the total pattern and if they perceptibly enhance the scope of the language.[659] On Raja Rao's literal translations and usage of typical Indian vernacular idioms and phrases, she rightly observes that the writer has "to make sure that the translated idioms or images do not go against the grain of English Language."[660]

P. P. Mehta's (1979) book *Indo-Anglian Fiction: An Assessment* considers Rao among the three greatest novelists of modern India, along with Mulk Raj Anand and R. K. Narayan. Highlighting his philosophical insight and metaphysical ideas, he regards that it is due to Rao's significant contribution that Indian fiction in English, since its beginning in the nineteenth century, has grown significantly. Unlike the majority of Raja Rao's readers who are enamoured by his ideas alone, Mehta finds the ideational structure of *The Serpent and the Rope* "mystifyingly dull". Though he feels the basic premise of total self - surrender to the divine will practised in *The Cat and Shakespeare* is borrowed from Ramanuja. However, he finds Rao's creative exercise praiseworthy. He describes Kanthapura as a poetic novel.

Naik's *Raja Rao* (1972) is the first comprehensive critical study of the artist and his art. Commenting positively, he lauds the innovations which have shaped his 'epic breath of vision' and 'metaphysical rigour and depth of thought' and the 'essential Indianness', all contributing to the fantastic originality of his style.

---

[659] Ibid., p.167
[660] Ibid. p.168

Perfectly balanced and considerate in approach, his perceptive criticism embodied in this book surpasses all critical works on Raja Rao, becoming an ideal sourcebook for the serious student of literature. Contradicting antagonistic critics like Mulk Raj Anand, he emphasizes that *The Serpent and the Rope* is not "a philosophical essay but a philosophical novel"[661]

It "is not a didactic tract, but, among other things, an intensely human document."[662] His analysis of Raja Rao's style in Kanthapura is also entirely objective. His review of *The Cat and Shakespeare* where philosophy is concealed within the folds of humour, is comprehensive and insightful. However, being realistic, he points out the inadequacy of its plot construction as not being a coherent whole. His view of Ramaswamy and Madeleine's breakup as "an unbridgeable gulf between two kinds of cultural ethos"[663] is debatable. He considers *The Serpent and the Rope* to be " a kind of Indian Maha Purana (Major Purana) in miniature."[664] His analysis of Rao's short stories, focusing both on their motif and the narrative strategy is quite enlightening.

Narasimaiah's book *Raja Rao* touches on various aspects of the novelist's life and works themes and techniques. It provides deep insight and a better understanding of Rao's vision of India's social and political predicament and the universal values that have enabled her to tide over her miseries. The note of idealism in Kanthapura and growth of Moorthy's character, on religious, social and political all three planes, who seems "to slip out of the clutches of convention and go his own way, to fulfill his destiny"[665] is regarded by Narasimhaiah to be quite a just portrayal. He focuses on the spiritual and metaphysical planes of reality existing in *The Serpent and the Rope* and *The Cat and Shakespeare*. He admires the creative use of English for the depiction of true Indian sensibility and his usage of "the fantastic to serve a metaphysical end."[666]

---

[661] M.K.Naik, *Raja Rao*, Bombay, Blackie & Son Publishers Pvt. Ltd. 1982. p. 147
[662] Ibid.p. 147
[663] Ibid. p. 83
[664] Ibid. P.106
[665] C.D. Narasimhaiah, *Raja Rao, Indian Writers Series*. Sterling Publishers, New Delhi. 1988. p.46
[666] Ibid. pp. 134-35

Venugopal's commendable book *The Indian Short Story in English* regards *The Cow of the Barricades*, Raja Rao's experiment with the folk-tale form of narration to, "present an intimate yet comprehensive picture of rural India of the nineteen thirties and the 'forties'"[667] Venugopal feels that Raja Rap's distinction lies "in that he views the contemporary events against the background of the saner aspects of our cultural heritage."[668]

However, it is this "Indianness" that Esha Dey severely criticizes in her book *The Novels of Raja Rao.* She believes that in Kanthapura and *The Serpent and the Rope,* Rao follows the "very authentic tactics of western realism, that of opposition between appearance and reality, ideal and achievement, great expectations and lost illusion. It is perhaps ironic that his admirers cherish these two novels that incorporate the western traditional poetics of fiction as profoundly "Indian."

The relative lack of enthusiasm in his later works indicates how pathetic the whole fallacy of "Indianness" in the concept of the Indian novel in English, for Rao's "Indianness" is no less a controlling force in the later works than it is in the beginning." [669] She further argues that to achieve greater freedom of expression, he combined many elements borrowed from the western tradition, which created certain anomalies in his Indian style. Strangely, he rejected the time when the West considered India timeless, yet he adopted the realistic mode of personal biography from the west. His attitude towards orthodox and humanist life was also dual.

Naik refutes her stand by saying, " Rao has consistently tried to modify the western form of the novel to suit his Indian subject matter. In fact it would not be incorrect to say that he reinvents and Indianizes the novel as no one else does. He accomplishes the feat by using traditional Indian genres such as the Puranas, the Sthalakatha and the beast fable to structure his works. Furthermore, they are written in an English that is uniquely Indian in style, tone, mood and rhythm. The Indianess of style is achieved

---

[667] C.V. Venugopal, *The Indian Short Story in English,*.Bareilly, Prakash Book Depot. 1976. p .55
[668] Ibid. p.60
[669] Esha Dey, *The Novels of Raja Rao, The Theme of Quest.* New Delhi. Prestige Books.1992 .p. 228

by relying heavily on translation, quotations and the use of Indian proverbs, idioms and colloquial patterns. Rao adroitly manipulates vocabulary and syntax to enhance the Indian flavouring of his English. The result is a style which although distinctly Indian is evocative and perfectly intelligible to western readers as well. The language is unique to Rao, a highly refined medium of expression which suggests truths beyond those normally available in our everyday speech. To put it somewhat dramatically Rao has restored sacredness to the Word."[670]

Paranjape in support suggests "Even his short stories and non-fictional prose is imbued with the spirit of inquiry into the meaning of things. It is both playful and serious at the same time creating not merely discussing philosophy. Thus in Rao's works there is an ongoing discussion of major systems of thought chiefly of India but also of the west."[671]

Esha Dey ultimately relents, saying that the reconciliation of two opposed styles - the traditional and the modernist - resulted in some great literature. She appreciates Rao's strength of synthesizing the Eastern and Western linguistic forms and disapproves it in the same breath as ironical, "the direct borrowings from the French, the sprinkling words, and unusual frequency of certain English words related to inner life produce altogether an atmosphere exotic and spiritual. This does not therefore ostensibly conflict with the use of literary devices at every level of the total construct –vocabulary, syntax and imagery. The poetic devices do reveal a greater mastery over the English literary tradition in the sensitive manipulation of rhythm, combined with whole paraphernalia of rhetoric, synaesthesia, inversion, parallel construction, repetition in syntax and vocabulary, from which quite often emerge strong and definite symbolic motifs. The irony lies in this very excellence, this successful assimilation of the western tradition by an Indian." [672]

---

[670] M.K. Naik, *Raja Rao* quoted in Makarand Paranjape, *The Best of Raja Rao*, (selected and edited).New Delhi, Katha Classics, 1998 p. ii-iii.
[671] Ibid.,p. iii.
[672] Esha Dey, *The Novels of Raja Rao, The Theme of Quest*. New Delhi. Prestige Books. 1992..pp. 224-225.

She agrees that Rao matured with each work; however, *Kanthapura, The Serpent and the Rope were* the best. Only Raja Rao, she is convinced, had the calibre to produce such outstanding art, "the much sought for synthesis between orthodox values presented as truth or wisdom and the humanism felt to be essentially moralistic and western is achieved by turning both into pure conceptual pattern revealed as symbols some of which are traditional and others personal. Thus Rao's metaphysics of truth as transcendental reality or Absolute consciousness has to seek expression in a personal symbol of Shakespeare, who as an artist is a creator and in his negative capability is beyond the relative existence of the world, which is like a ration shop ruled by scales. This cross-cultural stasis is typical of Rao in his maturity as an artist, so an ostensibly Indian symbol derived from a minor subgenre of one particular system of Vedanta serves as a means to approximate the West. In contrast, the western symbol, Shakespeare, is built into the structure as a symbol of another system of Vedanta. Both Cat and Shakespeare mean what they are not or to put it another way they are meant to suggest far more than the normal connotation can logically conceive of."[673]

Ivar Ivask also concurs, "On the whole Rao's life and writing have evolved in the direction of increasing openness from the archetypal village of Kanthapura, to Paris London America, from village realism to a Joycean polyphony of language, languages and mythologies."[674] Sharma agrees that "Raja Rao in his works endeavours to collate Indian philosophical strands with the corresponding western ideas to experiment and innovate and finally to synthesize them. Though his debt to the west is considerable yet he is essentially Indian in thought and spirit."[675] Thumboo emphasizes that "Rao's greatest achievement which I suspect only he can surpass is the degree to which his works ...contain the insights, emblems, mantras, metaphors, and other carriers of meaning and instruction that enable the individual to

---

[673] Ibid.,p. 222-223.
[674] Ivar Ivask,quoted in Makarand Paranjape, *The Best of Raja Rao*, (selected and edited).New Delhi, Katha Classics, 1998.p. vii
[675] Kaushal Sharma ,*Raja Rao: A Study of His Themes and Technique*, New Delhi, Sarup & Sons. 2005.p.3.

achieve, through his own meditations, a better understanding of self through Knowledge and Truth."[676]

However, critics and studies in Indo-Anglian fiction have concentrated more on the themes. However, a thorough study of his medium, his innovation of fictional forms, language, the blending of the temporal and the metaphysical, and a study of his characters' varying levels of consciousness need to be pursued further.

In any case, Rao's literary genius is unquestionable, even if he is wavering between being a "thorough realist or a metaphysical idealist. An American reviewer's remarks on the publication of *The Cat and Shakespeare* in the U.S.A is quite apt, "The greatness of a writer lies not in the number of works he has produced but in the varied dimensions and levels at which his works can be interpreted; and in this respect Raja Rao has every claim to greatness. The function of future criticism will be to bring out this greatness, and also establish that Raja Rao has neither performed "Metaphysical rope tricks" nor created "pseudo-profundities." through the ideas in his novels.[677]

According to Paranjape, "ultimately Raja Rao is an artist and not a philosopher. It is as an artist that he has to be judged and understood. And as such he has been true to his calling. In terms of language, style and theme, he has been perfectly consistent fulfilling the promise he made in his foreword to Kanthapura. It is this consistency, the integrity of purpose, this concern with the ultimate reality coupled with stylistic innovation and inspired use of language that makes him one of the most significant and interesting writers of the world."[678]

In this book, we have thus attempted to study how Rao created something authentically eastern to reconcile different cultures and worldviews, as a diasporic author. His legacy consists of his explorations in the diasporic literary, intellectual, and cultural space, reflected in the fact that many of his characters tend to

---

[676] Edwin Thumboo quoted in Makarand Paranjape, *The Best of Raja Rao*, (selected and edited).New Delhi, Katha Classics, 1998.p. xvi.

[677] G.J. Advani, *"Pseudo-profundities"* cited in *"Raja Rao's The Cat and Shakespeare* in the U.S.A."* by Ray Lewis White, *The Journal of Indian Writing in English*, Vol. 7, No. 1, January 1979, p. 28

[678] Makarand Paranjape, *The Best of Raja Rao*, (selected and edited).New Delhi, Katha Classics, 1998.p. xxv

struggle in the diasporic space. They attempt to resolve interpersonal, intellectual, philosophic and even civilizational dilemmas between themselves. To that extent, his works are also an ethnography of the west and the east, with westerners as actors in Indian cultural and social realms and vice-versa, an ethnography he, as an author, performs surrogately through his characters.

Follies of Indian life, society and philosophy do not escape his attention. However, his unique position as a diasporic author also places him suitably for an ethnography of the east, explored from a western vantage. Nevertheless, this ethnography of two worlds results in a history of morality, the intellect and spirituality of the east and west documented from the mid-twentieth to the early twenty-first century. Other than in the Kanthapura, most of the leading characters of his novels, like his, travel abroad, hoping to make their fortunes there. Like him, they marry into local society, philosophy and life with varying degrees of success. Raja Rao presents a view of all these worlds, which he represents to his readers both in the east and the west, making his works a historical ethnography performed through his novels.

In the words of Kathleen Raine," Raja Rao is much more than an apologist for India who also loves and understands the best in Europe; he is a universal writer who brings the Water of the Ganges to heal the ills of the modern world."[679] In his own words, Rao says that in *Kanthapura,* he was a Gandhian, in *The Serpent and the Rope* he was searching, and *The Cat and Shakespeare* is the conclusion of *The Serpent and the Rope.* Like in *The Cat and Shakespeare,* Ramakrishna Pai, who having believed that he is 'neither Indian nor spiritual but just a man' finds deliverance in the end. What matters ultimately for the ordinary human being is that all his duality should cease. Eventually, his self is also effaced. He attains divine union forgetting all otherness. Rao's quest for the realization of truth thus culminates with the attainment of the ultimate reality of the Absolute, and this is the universal message - the Idea of India.

---

[679] Kathleen Raine. Quoted in Makarand Paranjape, *The Best of Raja Rao,* (selected and edited).New Delhi, Katha Classics, 1998.p.xxii

For Rao, who carried his India wherever he went it remained an actual entity all his life, his cherished destination to which he always wanted to return, "I would go back to India, for the Ganges, and for the deodars of the Himalayas and for the deer in the forests, for the keen call of the elephant in the grave ocellate silence of the forests. I would go back to India for India was my breath my only sweetness, gentle and wise, she was my mother."[680] Wasn't it the spirit of his long-lost mother beckoning him back?

Paranjape feels that "Rao succeeds in capturing the spirit of India in his works….there is no one else who has even attempted to do what Rao has accomplished to portray and justify the wisdom of traditional India to the modern world. No one moreover has even approached, let alone reached his heights of spiritual illumination. The aesthetic delight in his works is as rare as it is authentic."[681]

C.D. Narasimhaiah aptly says, "Raja Rao is the greatest Indian English novelist is as true today as when it was first made, twenty-five years ago." [682] To a discerning reader, Raja Rao is and will always remain a writer for all seasons and reasons.

---

[680] Raja Rao, *The Serpent and the Rope* , Orient Paperbacks, New Delhi 1968.p. 376.
[681] Makarand Paranjape, *The Best of Raja Rao*, (selected and edited).New Delhi, Katha Classics, 1998.p.iii.
[682] Ibid.,p. iii.

BIBLIOGRAPHY: PRIMARY SOURCES

Fiction

Novels

Rao, R. *Kanthapura*. New Delhi. Orient Paperbacks: 1971. Bombay, Blackie & Son Publishers Pvt. Ltd. 1982. Delhi: Hind Pocket Books 1971.
Rao, R. *The Serpent and The Rope*. New Delhi. Orient Paperbacks. 1968. Delhi, Hind Pocket Books, 1968.
Rao, R. *The Cat and Shakespeare*. Delhi: Hind Pocket Books. 1971.
Rao, R. *Comrade Kirillov*. New Delhi: Orient Paperbacks. 1976.
Rao, R. *The Chessmaster and His Moves:* New Delhi. Vision Books. 1988.

Short Stories

Rao, R. *The Cow of the Barricades and Other Stories:* Bombay. Oxford University Press: 1978
Rao, R. *The Policeman and The Rose*. Bombay. Oxford University Press: 1978.
Rao, R. *On the Ganga Ghat*. New Delhi. Vision Books: 1989.

Non Fiction

Books

Rao, R. *The Meaning of India*: The Collection of Essays. New Delhi. Vision Books: 1996.
Rao, R. *The Great Indian Way: A Life of Mahatma Gandhi.* New Delhi. Vision Books: 1998.

Essays

"Pandit Taranath," *Asia*. Jan. 1935, 10-15.
"Varanasi," *The Illustrated Weekly of India:* LXXXII. 36, Sep 3 1961, 12-15.
"Trivandrum," *The Illustrated Weekly of India:* LXXXIII. 25 Feb. 1962: 12-16.
"Aurobindo Ghosh: An Anniversary Meeting Address. *"Arts and Letters: Journal of the Royal India and Pakistan Society* 31-2. 1957: 4-6.
"Fables for the Feeble," *The Illustrated Weekly of India:* Dec. 9. 1982. 46-47.
"The Gandhian Way: Replies to Questionnaire on Gandhi," *The Illustrated Weekly of India.* 14th Feb. 1965: 39.
"Books Which Have Influenced Me," *Aspects of Indian Writing in English:* Ed. M. K. Naik. New Delhi: Macmillan, 1979, 45-49.
"E. M. Forster," *A Tribute with Selection from his Writings on India:* Ed. K. Natwar Singh, Delhi. Clarion Books 1969, 15-32.
"Jawaharlal Nehru: Recollections and Reflections," *The Illustrated Weekly of India:* Nov15 1964, 64-67.
"The Writer and the Word," *The Literary Criterion*, VII,1, Winter 1965: 30-31.
"Irish Interlude," *The Saturday Review* XLIX, 26, June 25, 1966: 37-38
"The Climate of Indian Literature Today," the Literary Criterion, X,3, 1972: 1-7.
"The Caste of English," *Awakened Conscience: Studies in Commonwealth Literature*. Ed. C.D. Narasimhaiah. New Delhi: Sterling Publishers. 1978:420-422.
"Entering the Literary World," *The Journal of Commonwealth Literature*. XIII. 3, April 1979: 28-32.
"Creatures of Benaras," *World Literature Today:* Vol 62. No,4. Autumn 1988: 540-546.
"Autobiography: Entering the Literary World," *The Journal of Commonwealth Literature*. 13.3 London. Apr. 1979: 28-32
"The Cave and the Conch: Notes on the Indian Conception of the Word," *The Eye of the Beholder: Indian Writing in English* Ed. Maggie Butcher. London: Commonwealth Institute, 1983: 45.

SECONDARY SOURCES

Interviews

A.S.R. "A Meeting with Raja Rao Recalled 1 and 2," *The Illustrated Weekly of India*, 25 Sep. 1966: 13-15.
Balu, S. "Meeting Raja Rao." Interview. *Economic Times*. 25 Jan.1987: 3
Balu, S. "Eternal Quest of Raja Rao." *The Times of India*, Patna, 30 Jan. 1987
Bhattacharji, S. "Interview with Raja Rao," *The Book Review*.VII, No. 2 Sep-Oct. 1982, 63-68.
Brierre, A. "An Interview with Raja Rao." *The Illustrated Weekly of India*. LXXIV, No. 10,10 March. 1963: 26-27.
Eskay. "Raja Rao: Man and the Mask," Interview. *Patriot* (mag). 25 Apr. 1982: IV
Elizabeth Wohl, "Raja Rao on America," Span Jan 1973, 35-37.
Kaushik, A. "Meeting Raja Rao." *The Literary Criterion*. July 1983: 33-38.
Kohli, S. "Raja Rao: Ambivalence and Individuality" Interview. *The Indian and Foreign Review*. 15 June. 1969: 11.
Kohli, S. Interview with Raja Rao. *Times Weekly*. 13 Sep. 1970: 4.
Kohli, S. "Views of an Indian Novelist." Interview. *The Times Weekly* Supplement. 18th April. 1972.

Niranjan, S. "An Interview with Raja Rao," *Indian Writing in English*. Ed. Krishna Nanda Sinha. New Delhi: Heritage Publishers 1979: 19-29.

O'Brien, A.P. "A Meeting with Raja Rao". *Prajna* XI, 2 (Benares) 1966: CLXXX-IV

Pais, A, Radhakrishnan, R.. "Award Winning Raja Rao Likened to Joyce, Proust." *India Abroad* 27 May 1988: 134-135.

Panniker, A. "A Conversation with Raja Rao on The Cat and Shakespeare." *Chandrabhaga* 2. 1979:14.

Paranjape, M. "Art of the Matter: Raja Rao's The Meaning of India The Collection of Essays." An Interview. *Indian Review of Books* 16 Nov- and 15 Dec. 1976:.6-7.

Parthasarathy, R. "The Future World Is Being Made in America: An Interview with Raja Rao," *Span*. New Delhi. Sep. 1977: 30-31

Parthasarathy, R. "Raja Rao: A Brief Encounter". *India Express* 28 April 1982.: 3.

Raman, A.S. "Chiaroscuro: A Meeting with Raja Rao Recalled," *Illustrated Weekly of India*. 25th Sep. 1966: 15

Ranchan, S. P. "A Meeting with Raja Rao." *Thought*. Delhi.13th July 1968: 14-16.

Rangra, R. "Beyond the Body and Mind: An Interview with Raja Rao." *Interview with Indian Writers*. Delhi. B.R. Publishing Corporation. 1992.

Reddy, P. B. "A Conversation with Raja Rao." *Studies in Indian Writing in English*. New Delhi. Prestige Books. 1990: 88-92.

S.V.V. "Raja Rao: Face to Face." *The Illustrated Weekly of India*. LXXXV, 1, 5th Jan. 1964: 44-45.

Shankardass, R. "Face to Face." *Weekend Review*. 15th June. 1968:16-17.

Shekhar R. R. "Seventy- Six Years of Solitude," *Society*, Aug. 1985: 30-33

Subrahmanian, K. "Meeting Raja Rao." *Kakatiya Journal of English Studies* 3.1. 1978: 70 A.

Vaiju, M. "Raja Rao A.Y.T Interview," *Youth Times*, May 1978: 13.

Bibliographies

Bhattacharya, P.C. "Select Bibliography." *Indo-Anglian Literature and the Works of Raja Rao*. Delhi. Atma and Sons. 1983. 379-395.

Celly, A. "A Selected Bibliography." *Women in Raja Rao's Novel: A Feminist Reading of The Serpent and the Rope*. Jaipur. Printwell. 1995.117-124.

Dey, E. "Bibliography." *The Novels of Raja Rao*. New Delhi. Prestige Books. 1992. 256-264.

Hardgrave, R. L., "Selected Bibliography," Ed. *Word As Mantra: The Art of Raja Rao*. New Delhi: Katha Publications in association with The University of Texas at Austin. 1998.

Jamkhandi, S. R. "Raja Rao: A Selected Checklist of Primary and Secondary Material." *Journal of Commonwealth Literature*. 15.1.1981. 132-139.

Mittapalli, R and Piciucco, P. P."Select Bibliography," *The Fiction of Raja Rao: Critical Studies*, (Ed) New Delhi, Atlantic Publishers and Distributors. 2001. 234- 273.

Naik, M.K. "Bibliography." *Raja Rao*. Madras. Blackie and Sons. 1982. 157-160.

Nanda, N. "Bibliographies." *Raja Rao and The Religious Traditions*. New Delhi. Anmol. 1992. 115-119.

Narayan, S. A. "Selected Bibliography." *Raja Rao. Man and His Works*. New Delhi. Sterling Publishers. 1988. 134-139.

Niranjan, S. "Select Bibliography." *Raja Rao: Novelist as Sadhaka*. Ghaziabad. Vimal Prakashan. 1985. 139-148.

Paranjape, Markarand. "Selected Bibliography," Ed. *The Best of Raja Rao:* New Delhi: Katha Publications. 1998.

Sharma, K.K. "Select Bibliography." *Perspectives on Raja Rao*. Ghaziabad. Vimal Prakashan. 1980. 231-234.

Sharma, K. "Select Bibliography," Raja Rao: A Study of His Themes and Technique. New Delhi. Sarup & Sons. 2005. 127-134.

Sharrad, Paul. "Bibliography." *Raja Rao and Cultural Tradition*. New Delhi: Sterling Publishers. 1989. 171-189.

Singh, P. "Bibliography." *Semiotic Analysis of Raja Rao's The Serpent and The Rope* Delhi: Bahri Publications. 1991.

Srivastava, N. "A Select Bibliography." *The Mind and Art of Raja Rao*. Bareilly: Prakash Book Depot. 1980. 154-157.

Srivastava, R.K. Comp. "Selected Bibliographies: Raja Rao" *Six Indian Novelists in English*. Amritsar: Guru Nanak Dev University. 1987. 329-333.

Special issues

World Literature Today 62.4: A special issue on Raja Rao as an award winner of the Tenth Neustadt International Prize for Literature. 1988.

Books

Abraham, T.J. *A Critical Study of Novels of Arun Joshi, Raja Rao and Sudhin Ghose,* New Delhi: Atlantic Publishers. 1998.

Agnihotri, G.N. *Indian Life and Problems in the Novels of Mulk Raj Anand and Raja Rao and R.K. Narayan,* Meerut: Shalabh Book House. 1993.

Amur, G.S. *Images and Impressions*, Jaipur: Panchsheel Prakashan. 1979.

Belliappa, K.C. *The Image of India in English Fiction: Studies in Kipling, Myers and Raja Rao*. Delhi: B.R. Publishing Corporation. 1991.

Bhattacharya, B. "Indo Anglian", *The Novels in Modern India*, Ed Iqbal Babhtiyar, Bombay: The P.E.N. All India Centre 1964.

Bhattacharya, P.C. *Indo-Anglian Literature and the Works of Raja Rao*. Delhi: Atma Ram and Sons, 1983.

Celly, A. *Women in Raja Rao's Novels: A Feminist Reading of the Serpent and the Rope*. Jaipur: Printwell. 1995.

Coomaraswamy, A.K. *The Figures of Speech or The Figures of Thought*. London: Luzac Co.1946.

Dayal, P. *Raja Rao: A Study of His Novels*. New Delhi: Atlantic Publishers. 1991.

Dey, E. *The Novels of Raja Rao*. New Delhi: Prestige Books. 1992.

Donne, John. *Death Be Not Proud: The Complete English Poems*, Penguin Classics, Paperbacks. U.K. 2004.

Hardgrave, R. L., Ed. *Word As Mantra: The Art of Raja Rao*. New Delhi: Katha Publications with The University of Texas at Austin. 1998.

Herbert, George, *The Pulley: The Complete English Poems*, Penguin Classics Paperbacks, U.K. 2005

Iyengar, K.R.S. Indian *Writing in English*. New Delhi: Sterling Publishers. 1983.

Krishnamurthy, Shantha. The Women in Indian Fiction in English, New Delhi: Ashish Publishing House. 1984.

Kumar, G. T. *Conceptualising Tradition: A Study of Raja Rao, R.K. Narayan and Mulkraj Anand*. New Delhi: Research India Press. 2007.

Larson, C. R. *The Novel in the Third World*, Washington DC: INSCAPE Publishers, 1976.

Mathur, S.S. ed., *Guide to The Serpent and the Rope*. Agra: Lakshmi Narain Agarwal,

Mehta, P.P. *Indo-Anglian Fiction: An Assessment*. Bareilly: Prakash Book Depot. 1968.

Mukherjee, Meenakshi. *The Twice Born Fiction*, New Delhi: Arnold Heinemann. 1974.

Mittapalli, R & Piciucco, P. P, (Ed). *The Fiction of Raja Rao: Critical Studies*. New Delhi: Atlantic Publishers and Distributors. 2001.

Naik, M.K. *A History of Indian English Literature*. New Delhi: Sahitya Akademi.. 1982.

___ *Dimensions of Indian English Literature*. Delhi: Sterling Publishers. 1984.

___ *Raja Rao*. Twayne's English Authors Series. New York: Twayne Publishers. 1972.

___*Aspects of Indian Writing in English*. Delhi, The Macmillan Company of India Ltd. 1979.

___& Shyamla,A, Narayan. *Indian English Literature 1980-2001*. Delhi: Pencraft International.2001.

Nanda, N. *Raja Rao and the Religious Traditions: Study of The Serpent and the Rope*. New Delhi: Anmol. 1992.

Narasimhaiah, C.D. *Raja Rao*. New Delhi: Indian Writer's Series. Arnold Heinemann. 1973.

___*Indian Literature of the Past Fifty Years 1917-67:* Mysore: Prasaranga, University of Mysore. 1970.

___*Fiction and the Reading Public in India* Mysore: University of Mysore, 1967.

Narayan, A.S. *Raja Rao Man and His Works*, New Delhi: Sterling Publishers. 1998.

Nehru Jawaharlal, *The Discovery of India*, Bombay: Asia Publishing House. 1961.

Niranjan, S. *Raja Rao: Novelist as Sadhaka* Ghaziabad: Vimal Prakashan. 1985

Niven, A. *Truth within Fiction: Raja Rao's The Serpent and The Rope*. Calcutta: Writer's Workshop. 1987.

Pallan, R. K. *Myth and Symbols in Raja Rao and R.K. Narayan*. Jalandhar: ABS Publication. 1994.

Parameswaran, U. *A Study of Representative Indo- English Novelists*, New Delhi: Vikas Publishing House. 1976.

Raizada, Harish. *Indian English Novelist: Some Points of View*, Delhi: K.K. Publications, 1996.

Rajan, B. "India". *Literature of the World in English*, ed. Bruce King, London, Routledge and Kegan Paul.1974.

Ramchandra, Ragini. Ed. *Raja Rao: An Anthology of Recent Criticism*. Delhi: Pencraft International, 2000.

Rao, A.S. *Myth and History in Contemporary Indian Novel in English*, New Delhi: Atlantic Publishers and Distributors. 2000.

Rao, K.R. *The Fiction of Raja Rao*, Aurangabad: Parimal Prakashan. 1980.

Rao, S. *Socio-Cultural Aspects of Life in the Selected Novels of Raja Rao*, New Delhi· Atlantic Publishers. 1999.

Shankaran, C. *The Mythic Connection: The Use of Hindu Mythology in Some Novels of Raja Rao and R.K. Narayan*, New Delhi: Allied Publishers. 1993.

Sharma, J.P. *Raja Rao: A Visionary of Indo-Anglian Fiction*. Meerut: Shalabh Book House. 1980.

Paranjape, M. (Ed).*The Best of Raja Rao*, New Delhi. Katha Publications. 1998.

Sharma, B.D. *Contemporary Indian English Novel*. Delhi: Anamika. 1999.

Sharma, Kaushal. *Raja Rao: A Study of His Themes and Technique*. New Delhi: Sarup & Sons 2005

Sharma, K.K. *Perspectives on Raja Rao*, Ghaziabad: Vimal Prakashan. 1980.

___*Four Great Indian English Novelists*, Delhi: Sarup and Sons, 2002.

Sharrad, P. *Raja Rao and Cultural Traditions*, New Delhi: Sterling Publishers, 1988.

Singh, Parminder. *A Semiotic Analysis of Raja Rao's The Serpent and The Rope*. New Delhi: Bahri Publications. 1991.

Singh, R.S. *Raja Rao's Kanthapura: An Analysis,* Delhi: Doaba House Booksellers and Publishers. 1977.

___*Indian Novel in English*, New Delhi: Arnold Heinemann. 1977.

Srivastava, N. *The Mind and Art of Raja Rao,* Delhi: Prakash Book Depot. 1980.

Venugopal, C.N. *The Indian Short Story in English*. Bareilly: Prakash Book Depot.

Verghese, C. Paul. *Problems of Indian Creative Writer in English* Bombay: Somaiya Publications, 1971.

Williams, H.M. *Indo-Anglian Literature 1800-1970:A Survey*. Calcutta: Orient Longmans, 1975.

___*Studies in Modern Indian Fiction in English,* Calcutta: A Writer's Workshop Publications. 1973.

William Walsh, *Commonwealth Literature*, London, Oxford University Press.1973.

Advani, G.J. *"Pseudo-profundities"* cited in *"*Raja Rao's *The Cat and Shakespeare* in the U.S.A." by Ray Lewis White, *The Journal of Indian Writing in English*, Vol. 7, No. 1, January 1979, p. 28.

Aithal, S.K. and Aithal, R. "Inter-racial and Inter-cultural Relationship in Raja Rao's *The Serpent and the Rope.*" *International Fiction Review* 7.2 (1980): 94-98.

Alam, Q. Z. "*Kanthapura*'s Style: A Point of View." *Language Forum* 5.2 (1979): 27-37.

Ali, A. "Illusion and Reality: The Art and Philosophy of Raja Rao.*" Journal of Commonwealth Literature*, July (1968): 16-28.

Alvarez, A. "The Savage God: A Study of Suicide." 1971 Quoted in Esha Dey *The Novels of Raja Rao, The Theme of Quest,* New Delhi, Prestige Books,1992..p.190.

Amur, G.S. Raja Rao: "The Kannada Phase." *Journal of Karnataka University* (Humanities) 10 (1966): 40-52.

Amur, G.S. "Self-Recognition in Raja Rao's *The Serpent and the Rope.*" *Kakatiya Journal of English Studies* 3.1(1978): 71-82.

Anand, M.R. "Roots and Flowers: Two Lectures on the Metamorphosis of Technique and Content in the Indo-English Novel." *Littcrit* 8.1 (1982): 47-60.

Anjeneyulu, D. "The Art of Raja Rao." *Thought.* 9th May. (1964) 12-14.

Augustine, Thomas. "The Village in Raja Rao's *Kanthapura*," in Mittapalli, R. and Piciucco, P. *The Fiction of Raja Rao: Critical Studies,* (Ed) New Delhi, Atlantic Publishers and Distributors. (2001):

Badve, V.V. "The Use of Mythology in Raja Rao's *Kanthapura.*" *Journal of Shivaji University,* 10.16 (1977): 45-51.

Balla, Brij, M. "Quest for Identity in Raja Rao's *The Serpent and the Rope.*" *Ariel.* 4 (4) (1973): 59-105.

Belliappa, K.C. "The Question of Form in Raja Rao's *The Serpent and the Rope.*" *World Literature Written in English* 24.2 (1991): 407-416.

Bourton, T.D. "India in Fiction." *Critical Essays on Indian Writing in English,* Ed. M.K. Naik, S.K. Desai and G.S. Amur, Dharwar: Karnataka University (1968):51-61

Chandrika B. "Gender and Resistance: A Reading of Raja Rao's *The Cat and Shakespeare.*" *Indian Journal of English Studies* 32 1994: 80-86.

Chari, V.K. "Rama's Tragic Quest: A Reading of *The Serpent and the Rope* in the light of Rasa theory." *Littcrit* 36, 37, 19. 1-2 (1993): 5-20.

Chase, Richards. "Notes on the Study of Myth," Twentieth Century Criticism, Ed. William. J. Hardy, New York. The Free Press. 1974, 244-51

Curtis, C. "Raja Rao and France." *World Literature Today* 6.2(4): (1988): 595-598.

Daniel, E. M. "A Writer of Purana." *Tribune,* 8th March. 1987

Das, Elizabeth. "The Choric Element in *Kanthapura.*" *Panjab University Arts Research Bulletin,* (Arts) 15.1 (1984): 53-58.

Dayal, P. "The Influence of Vedanta on Raja Rao." *Punjab University Journal of Medieval Indian Literature* 7.12(1983): 62-74.

____ "The Image of Woman in the Novels of Raja Rao." *Punjab University Research Bulletin.* (Arts) 16.1 (1985): 54-53.

____ "All Brides be Benares Born: An Interpretation of The Serpent and the Rope." *The Journal of Indian Writing in English.* 13.1 Jan (1985) : 64-68.

___. "The Tantric Elements in the Novels of Raja Rao." *Literary Half-Yearly* 28.1(1987): 105-118.

___ "Raja Rao and Romain Rolland." *Literary Criterion* 22.3 (1987): 65-72.

____ "Raja Rao and Fyodor Dostoevsky." *Punjab University Research Bulletin* (Arts) 18. 1 (1987): 11-18.

____ "Raja Rao and the Charles Baudelaire: An Affinity." *Literary Half Yearly* 30.2 (1989): 54-65.

· "Raja Rao," *Bharati Journal of Comparative Literature*, 1.1 (1985):27-40.

____ "The Concept of "Shivoham" in Raja Rao's *The Serpent and the Rope,*" *The Journal of Religious Studies,* XII.1, (1984): 109-17.

____ "The Image of Women in the Novels of Raja Rao," *Punjab University Research Bulletin* (Arts) XVI.1, April (1985): 45-53.

____ "The Influence of Vedanta on Raja Rao," Punjab University Journal of Medieval Indian Literature, VII 1 and 2, Mar-Sep, (1983):62-74.

Devi, D. D. "From Quiescence to Self-Action: A Study of Raja Rao's *Kanthapura* in the Light of Gandhian Thought". *Commonwealth Quarterly* 11.32 (1986): 31-49.

Dey, E. "A Hindu Critique on *The Serpent and the Rope.*" *Bharati* 6.10 (1972): 27-36.

___. "Myth and Metaphysics in *The Serpent and the Rope.*" *The Journal of the Department of English of Utkal University.* 2.1(1974): 10-25.

____ "Fissures in Being: Anguish and Alienation in The Serpent and the Rope." *Littcrit* 12.7.1(1981): 62-73.

____ "Raja Rao's India: The Axis of *Comrade Kirillov* - An Anti-Novel." *Commonwealth Quarterly* 5.20 (1981): 24-43.

____ "A Baroque Stylization: A Note on *The Serpent and the Rope*". *Language Forum* 6.3-4(1981): 1-15.

____ "Woman as Object: The Feminine Condition in a Decadent Patriarchy (Raja Rao's *The Serpent and the Rope* and Shouri Daniels's *The Salt Doll* ." *Literary Criterion* 20.4(1985): 9-19.

Dissanayake, W. "Questing Self: The Four Voices in *The Serpent and the Rope.*" *World Literature Today.* 62.4 (1988): 598-602.

Dooley, G. "Attitudes to Political Commitment in Three Indian Novels: *Kanthapura, Train to Pakistan and Rich Like Us.*" *Littcrit* 39. 20.2 (1994): 30-39.

Dutta, S. K. "A Stylistic Study of Raja Rao's English." *Journal of the Maharaja Sayaji Rao University of Baroda* 31-32 (1983): 17-27.

Dwivedi, A.N. "*The Serpent in the Rope*: Symbolism in *Kanthapura*." *Ravenshaw Journal of English Studies* 6.2 (1996): 1-17.

Eliade, M. *The Myth of the Eternal Return or Cosmos and History,* 1949, trans, 1954, p. xii. Quoted in Esha Dey, *The Novels of Raja Rao, The Theme of Quest.* New Delhi. Prestige Books (1992):25

Eliade, M. *Myths, Dreams and Mysteries: The Encounter between Contemporary Faiths and Archaic Realities,* 1957, trans. 1960.p. 23 quoted in Esha Dey, *The Novels of Raja Rao, The Theme of Quest.* New Delhi. Prestige Books (1992):25.

Eliot, T.S. "Tradition and the Individual Talent", *Selected Essays,* Faber and Faber, London, (1951): 21

Eng, O. B. "Making Initial Innocent Sense of *The Serpent and the Rope.* "*Journal of Indian Writing in English* 8.1-2 (1980): 53-62

Gondal, Y. "Raja Rao: Obscure but Rhythmic Writer." New Delhi 3.7. 18th to 31st August (1988): 60-64.

Gorlier, C. "See What I am: The Figure of Beatrice in *The Serpent and the Rope.*" *World Literature Today* 62.4 (1988): 606-607.

Gorlier, C. "Raja Rao's *The Cat and Shakespeare* : A Western View" in Mittapalli R. & Piciucco, P.P. Ed. *The Fiction of Raja Rao: Critical Studies.* New Delhi: Atlantic Publishers and Distributors. (2001): 204-213.

Gowda, H. H. A. "Raja Rao's *The Serpent and the Rope.*" *Literary Half-Yearly* 4.2 (1963): 36-40.

Gowda, H. H. A. "Phenomenal Tradition: The Case of Raja Rao and Wilson Harris." *ACLALS Bulletin* 9 (1972): 28-48.

Gregor, A. "An Introduction to Raja Rao's *The Cat.*" *Chelsea Review* 5 (1954): 16.

Gupta, A.N. "*Comrade Kirillov*: An Appraisal." Ed. Sharma, *K.K., Perspectives on Raja Rao.* Ghaziabad. Vimal Prakashan, (1980):120-139.

Guruprasad, T. "Reflections on Rama: India as Depicted in *The Serpent and the Rope.*" *Journal of Indian Writing in English* 1.1 (1973): 19-28.

Guzman, R. R. "The Saint and the Sage: The Fiction of Raja Rao". *Virginia Quarterly Review.* 56.1 (1980): 32-50.

Harris, W. "Raja Rao's Inevitable Style and Art of Fiction." *World Literature Today.* 62.4 (1988): 587-590.

____"Typology and Modes: Raja Rao's Experiment in Short Stories" *World Literature Today* 62.4. (1988): 591-595.

Hiatt, S. T. "Oral Tradition as a Nativization Technique in Three Novels." *Journal of Indian Writing in English.* 14.1(1986):10-20.

Hassan, I. "The Dismemberment of Orpheus: Towards a Post Modern Literature." Quoted in Esha Dey *The Novels of Raja Rao, The Theme of Quest,* New Delhi, Prestige Books, (1992):189.

Ivask, I. quoted in Makarand Paranjape, *The Best of Raja Rao,* (selected and edited). New Delhi, Katha Classics, (1998): vii.

Issac, S. "Two French Elements in *The Serpent and The Rope.*" *Journal of Karnataka University.* (Humanities) 18 (1974): 138-147

Iyengar, K.R.S. "Literature as Sadhana": A Note on Raja Rao's *The Cat and Shakespeare.* " *Aryan Path,* 40.7. (1969):301-305.

Jamkhandi, S. R. "*The Cat and Shakespeare*: Narrator Audience and Message." *The Journal of Indian Writing in English.* 7.2 (1979); 24-41.

Jha, A. K. "Identity and Its Quest in Raja Rao's Later Fiction." *Language Forum.* 1. 1-2 (1992): 29-37.

John, J. "Ramaswamy's Quest: Explorations of Love in *The Serpent and the Rope.*" *Journal of South Asian Literature* 26. 1-2 (1991): 277-292.

Kalinnikova, E.J. "Ancient Indian Philosophy and Raja Rao Works," Ed. Sharma K.K. *Perspectives on Raja Rao,* Ghaziabad, Vimal Prakashan, (1980): 23-31.

Kachru, B. B. "Toward Expanding the English Canon: Raja Rao's 1938 Credo of Creativity." *World Literature Today.* 62.4 (1988): 582-586.

Kamath, M.V. "The Brahmin and the Rabbi." *Illustrated Weekly of India.* 24th Aug. (1980): 47.

Kantak, V.Y. "The Language of *Kanthapura.*" *Indian Literary Review* 3.2 (Apr.1985): 15-24.

Karnani, C. "From Sense to Nonsense: The Case of Raja Rao". *Thought.*" 17th Aug. (1974): 15.

Katamble, V.D. "*Kanthapura* and Things Fall Apart as Sthalapuranas." *Littcrit.* 22&23 12. 1-2 (1986): 56-78.

Kaul, R.K. "The Problem of Speech in Indo-Anglian Writing. R.K. Narayan and Raja Rao." *Quest* 85. Nov-Dec. (1973): 65-87.

Kaul, R.K. "*The Serpent and the Rope* as a Philosophical Novel," *The Literary Criterion,* 15. 2. (1980):32-43.

Kirpal, V.P.K."*Comrade Kirillov.*" *The Journal of Indian Writing in English* 5.2 (1977): 46-48.

Knippling, A. S. "R.K. Narayan, Raja Rao and Modern English Discourse in Colonial India." *Modern Fiction Studies.* 39.1 (1993): 169-186.

Krishna Kutty, G. "From Indulekha to Shanta: A Lineage of Coconuts." *Literary Criterion* 20.4 (1985): 26-68.

Krishnamurthi, M.G. "Indian Writing in English", *Humanist Review.* 1:4. (1969)

Kumar, B. "Theosophy in the Fiction of Raja Rao." *Contour.* 1.2-3 (1992): 16-19.

Kumar, S. K. "In Search of Excellence: A Tribute to Raja Rao on Receiving Neustadt International Prize." *Hindustan Times.* 4 Dec. (1988): 13

Kumar, S. " Reading Raja Rao's The Meaning of India." *New Quest.* 126, Nov-Dec. (1997): 337-340.

Lal, P. "Indian Writing in English," *Harvard Educational Review,* 34:2.(1964)

Lalitha, J. "Politics of Freedom: Gandhi in *Kanthapura* and A Bend in the Ganges." *Kakatiya Journal of English Studies* 10 (1990): 32-40.

Latha, K.S. "Rural Ethos in Indian Novels in English: Kamala Markandaya's Nectar in a Sieve, Raja Rao's *Kanthapura,* Mulk Raj Anand's The Village". *Triveni* 61.2 (1992): 53-56.

Laxmana Murthy, S. "Raja Rao. A Note on the Philosophy. " *Journal of English Studies*." 8 (1988): 9-18.
Laxmi, M. "Voices and Vision in Raja Rao's Fiction". Journal of *South Asian Review*. 4.1(1980): 1-11
Lehmann, W. P. "Literature and Linguistics: Text Linguistics." *Literary Criterion*. 17.1(1982): 18-29.
____ "The Quality of Presence." *World Literature Today*. 62.4 (1982): 578-582
Mambrol, N. Analysis of Raja Rao's Novels. Literary Theory and Criticism. July 29, 2020. URL: https://literariness.org/2020/06/29/analysis-of-raja-raos-novels/. Consulted on 29-11-22
Maini, D.S. "Raja Rao's Vision, Values and Aesthetics, *Perspectives on Raja Rao*. Ed. K.K. Sharma. Ghaziabad. Vimal Prakashan. (1980): 1-22.
Mani, R. "*The Cat and Shakespeare*: Dialectics of Inclusiveness." *Language Forum*. 24.1-2 (1998): 193-199
Mani, K. R. S. "The Use of Myth in Raja Rao's *The Serpent and the Rope*." *Triveni*. 60.3 (1991): 9-17
____ "Mythic Form in Raja Rao's *The Cat and Shakespeare*." *Triveni*. 67.2 (1998): 42-44.
Mani, Laxmi. "Voice and Vision in Raja Rao's Fiction." South Asian Review, 4, Jacksonville, FL. (1980):1-11.
Mansur, R. "Why Does *The Cat and Shakespeare* Fail? A Linguistic Approach," *Journal of Karnataka University:* Humanities 26 (1982.): 68-75.
____ "*Kanthapura* and *The Princes:* A Study in Contrasting Modes of Political Fiction." *Journal of Karnataka University:* Humanities 30 (1986): 43-56.
Maratha, S. M. "Three Indian Novelists. *Life and Letters*. Dec. (1948.) 187-192.
Mathur, O.P. "The Serpent Vanishes: A Study in Raja Rao's Treatment of East-West Theme". *Modern Indian English Fiction*. New Delhi. Abhinav Publications. (1993): 98-108.
____ "The East-West Theme in *Comrade Kirillov*." *Modern Indian English Fiction*. New Delhi. Abhinav Publications. (1993): 109-116.
____ " The Indian Protagonist and the Western Experience." *Modern Indian English Fiction*. New Delhi, Fp in India. Abhinav Publications. (1993): 1-29.
____ " Existential Overtones in Raja Rao's *Comrade Kirillov*." *Modern Indian English Fiction*. New Delhi, Fp in India. Abhinav Publications. (1993): 117-125.
Mathur, O.P. and Rai, G. "Existential Overtones in Raja Rao's Comrade Kirilov." *The Journal of South Asian Literature,* 17.1. (1982):264.
McCutcheon, D. "The Novel as Sastra." Writers Workshop, Miscellany,8. 1961, 91-99.
Meera Bai, K. "The Theme of Marital Disharmony in *The Serpent and the Rope* and *The Guide*." *Triveni*. 64.3 (1995): 23-25.
Mehta, P.P. 1979. Indo-Anglian fiction: an assessment
1979, Delhi: Prakash Book Depot.
Melwani, M.D. "The Experimental Story in English." *Thought*. 15th May. (1971):14-15.
Menon, A.M. "Indian Writers in English Literature: Raja Rao." *Akashavani*. 4th July (1971): 344.
Menon, K.P.K. "*Kanthapura* as a Political-Religious Novel". Paniker, *Contemporary Indian Fiction* in English 68-75.
Mishra, G. "The Search for an Idiom. A Study of *Kanthapura* and *Nectar in a Sieve*." *Mahanandi Review*. 3.2. (1983)
Mishra, G. "The Novel as Purana: A Study of the Form of *The Man-Eater of Malgudi and Kanthapura*". *Journal of Literary Studies*. (1978): 1-24
Mondal. Anshuman. "The Ideology of Space in Raja Rao's *Kanthapura*", *Journal of Commonwealth Literature* 34.1 (1999): 103-114.
Monti, Alleggandro. "A Plea and a Cheer for Indian English: A Note on Raja Rao". *Journal of Literature and Aesthetics* 7.1 (1999): 7-11.
Moorthy, S.S. "Beyond the Gandhian Dimension: Mythical and Folklore Elements in *Kanthapura*". *Commonwealth Novel in English* 5.1(1992): 20-26.
Mukherjee, Meenakshi. "Raja Rao's Shorter Fiction" *Indian Literature* July – Sep. (1967): 66-76.
Muller, Ulrich and Willian C. McDonald. "Tristan in Deep Structure: Raja Rao's *The Serpent and the Rope* – A Paradigmatic Case of Intercultural Relations". *Tristania: A Journal Devoted to Tristan Studies* 12.1-2 (1986-87): 44-47.
Nagarajan, S. "An Indian Novel: *The Serpent and the Rope*" Sewanee Review 72.3 (1964): 521-517.
Nagarajan, S. "A Note on Myth and Ritual in Raja Rao's *The Serpent and The Rope*". *Journal Commonwealth Literature* 4.1 (1972): 45-48.
Nagarajan, S. "Little Mother in *The Serpent and the Rope*". *World Literature Today* 62.4 (1988): 609-611.
Nagpal, L.R. "Home Coming in *Comrade Kirillov*" *Awasthi* 123-131.
Naik, M. K. "*Kanthapura*: The Indo-Anglian Novel as Legendary History. "*Journal of Karnataka University*. (Humanities) Volume 10. (1966): 26-39.
____ 1966. "Raja Rao as a Short Story Writer: *The Cow of the Barricades*". *Books Abroad* 40.4: 391-96.
____ 1968. "*The Serpent and the Rope*: The Indo-Anglian Novel as Epic Legend." *Indian Writing in English* Ed. M.K. Naik, S.K. Desai and G.S. Amur, Dharwar, Karnataka University (1968): 214-248.
____ "The Kingdom of God is Within a Mew A Study of *The Cat and Shakespeare*". *Journal of Karnataka University* (Humanities) 12 (1968); 123-150.
____"The Achievement of Raja Rao". *Banasthali Patrika* 12 (1969) : 44-56.
____ "Influences on Raja Ral". *Triveni* 41.1 (1972) : 68-75.
____"Narrative Strategy in Raja Rao's *The Cow of the Barricades and Other Stories*". *Indian Writing Today* 5.3 (1971)
,____ "In Native Accents, The Juvenilia of Raja Rao". *Aryan Path* 43 (1972): 74-80.
____ "Feline Felicity: On the Meaning of *The Cat and Shakespeare*". Ed. K.K. Sharma *Perspectives on Raja Rao*, Ghaziabad: Vimal Prakashan (1980): 93-102.

___ "The Short Story as Metaphysical Parable". Raja Rao's *The Policeman and the Rose*". *Language Forum* 7.14 (1981-82): 110-122.

___ "Coils of the Serpent: Raja Rao and the Unreal World". *Naik, Studies* 34-45.

___ "Raja Rao's *Comrade Kirillov*". *The Indian Journal of English Studies* 21 (1981-82): 107-116.

Naikar, Basawaraj S. "Coming Together: The Central Problem in *The Serpent and the Rope*". *Journal of Karnataka University* (Humanities) 22 (1978): 114-122.

Nair, Rama. "Maya as Narrative Structure: A Study of Raja Rao's *The Cat and Shakespeare*" *Osmania Journal of English Studies* 25 (1989): 18-29.

Narain, Lakshmi. "Raja Rao: Indian Novel in Three Languages". *Asian Student* 6 Feb. (1972.)

Narasimhaiah, C.D. "Raja Rao's *The Serpent and the Rope*: A Study". *Literary Criterion* 5; 4 (1963): 62-83.

___ "Raja Rao's *Kanthapura*: An Analysis" *Literary Criterion* 7.2 (1966): 15-77.

___"*The Cat and Shakespeare*: An ad hoc Assessment". *Literary Criterion* 8.3(1968): 65-95.

___ "National Identity in Literature and Language: Its Range and Depth in the Novels of Raja Rao". Paper delivered at the Commonwealth Literary Conference on National Identity at University of Queensland, Brisbane on August 9th-15th, 1968. Goodwin 153-164.

___ "The Metaphysical Novel: *The Serpent and the Rope*" Narasimhaiah, *The Swan and the Eagle* 150-202.

___"Raja Rao: Novel as Magic Casement of Celestial Concerns and Social Transactions" *Literary Criterion* 33.3 (1998): 37-47.

Narayan, Shyamala. "Social Concerns in the Fiction of Raja Rao." *Gray Book* 3 (1973): 42-46.

___ "East-West Encounter in Raja Rao's *The Serpent and the Rope* and Victor Anant's *The Revolving Man*". *Indian Literary Review* 1.5-6 (1978): 50-55.

___."Ramaswamy's Erudition: A Note on Raja Rao's *The Serpent and the Rope*" *Ariel* 14.4 (1983): 6-15.

___ "Tender Confrontation between East and West" *Hindu* 20 Nov. (1983):18.

___ "Women in Raja Rao's Fiction" *Literary Criterion* 20.4 (1985): 35-47.

___"My Language, Your Culture: Whose Communicative Competence". Kachru. 327-339.

Nasimni, Reza Ahmad. "*Kanthapura*: Language as Convulsions of Consciousness." *Nasimi* 56-75.

Nath, Suresh. "Gandhi and Raja Rao." Ed. Sharma, K.K. *Perspectives on Raja Rao*. Ghaziabad. Vimal Prakashan. (1980): 55-66.

Nelson, Cecil. "Syntactic Creativity and Intelligibility." *Journal of Indian Writing in English* 12.2 (1984): 1-14.

Niranjan, Shiva. "The Nature and Extent of Gandhi's Impact on the Early Novels of Mulk Raj Anand and Raja Rao." *Commonwealth Quarterly* 3.2(1979): 36-66.

___ "Myth as a Creative Mode: A Study of Mythical Parallel is in Raja Rao's Novel" *Commonwealth Quarterly* 4.13 (1980): 49-68.

___ "Philosophy into Fiction: A Study of the Thematic Aspects of Raja Rao's Novels." *Responses: Recent Revelations of Indian Fiction in English*. Ed. Harimohan Prasad Bareilly: Prakash Book Depot. (1983): 94 -112.

Niven, A.1974."Any Row over Rao?" *Commonwealth Newsletter* 6 (1974): 34-35.

Ojha, U.S. "Gandhian Ideology: A Study of Raja Rao's *Kanthapura*" in Mittapalli, R. & Piciucco, P. P: *The Fiction of Raja Rao, Critical Studies*, (Ed) New Delhi, Atlantic Publishers and Distributors, (2001):107-111.

Pai, Arthur and Radhika Radhakrishnan. "Award-Winning Raja Rao Likened to Joyce and Proust". *India Abroad* 27 May (1988): 134-135.

Pallan, Rajesh K. "The Feminine Principle in Raja Rao's *The Cat and Shakespeare*". *Mothers and Mother-figures* 70-86.

Paniker, Ayyappa. "The Frontiers of Fiction: A Study of Raja Rao's *The Cat and Shakespeare*". *Journal of Literary Studies* 2.2 (1979): 39-56.

Paniker, Ayyappa ."Man and God in Indian and African Fiction: A Study of Raja Rao's *The Cat and Shakespeare*". *Journal of Literary Studies* 2.2 (1979): 39-56.

Paniker, Ayyappa "On Translating Raja Rao's *The Cat and Shakespeare*", *Changing Traditions* 13-22.

Parameswaran, Uma. "Karma at work, The Allegory in Raja Rao's *The Cat and Shakespeare*". *Journal of Commonwealth Literature* 7 (1969): 107-145.

___ "Without Women, the World Is Not: Shakti in Raja Rao's Novels." *ACLALS Bulletin* 9 (1972): 4-72.

___. "Excelsior Raja Rao" Parameswaran, *A Study of the Representative Indo- English Novelists*.141-171.

___. "Siva and Shakti in Raja Rao's Novels" *World Literature Today* 62.4 (1988): 574-577.

Paranjape, Makarand. *The Best of Raja Rao* ed. New Delhi. Katha Publications. (1998)

___. "Critique of Communism in Raja Rao's *Comrade Kirillov*" *Pandey & Raja Rao* 69-83.

___. "Raja Rao". *Critical Survey of Long Fiction*. Ed. Frank N. Magill. Englewood Cliff (New Jersey): Saleem Press, 1983. Vo. 6. 2205-2215.

Parashar, B.P. "The Cow and the Herd: The Image of Plurality in *Kanthapura*". *Ken* 2 (1986): 35-54.

Parera, Senath W. "Towards A Limited Emancipation: Women in Raja Rao's *Kanthapura*". *Ariel* 23.4 (1992): 99-110.

Parthasarathy, R. "Tradition and Creativity: Stylistic Innovations in Raja Rao". *Smith* 157-165.

Parvathi Devi, M. "Threefold Path to Fulfillment: A Note on Raja Rao's Fiction". *Triveni* 53.1 (1984): 46-52.

Pati, M.S. "Rope in the Serpent", *Sambalpur Studies in Language and Literature* 2 (1981): 10-30.

Patil, Chandrasekhar B. "The Kannada Element in Raja Rao's Prose: A Linguistic Study of *Kanthapura*" *Journal of Karnataka University* (Humanities) 13 (1969): 143-167.

Patil, Mallikarjun. Raja Rao: A Philosophical Novelist." in Mittapalli, R. and Piciucco, P.P. *The Fiction of Raja Rao: Critical Studies*, (Ed) New Delhi, Atlantic Publishers and Distributors. (2001):1-12

Pousse, Michel. "So Many Freedoms." *Commonwealth Essays and Studies* 12.1 (1989): 30-38.

Powers, Janet M. "Raja Rao". *Encyclopaedia of World Literature in the 20th Century*. ed. Wolfgang Bernard Fleischmann. New York: Frederick Ungar, 1985.

_____. "Initiate Meets Guru: *The Cat and Shakespeare* and *Comrade Kirillov*". *World Literature Today* 62.4 (1988) : 611-616.

Prabhat, Swarna. "The Use of Myth in *Kanthapura*". *Quest* (Ranchi) 5.2 (1991) : 25-27.

Prakash, Ravendra. "Indian Element in the Style of *The Serpent and the Rope*". *Rajasthan University Studies in English* 13 (1980): 96-102.

Prasad, Baidya Natha. "The Language of Raja Rao's *The Serpent and the Rope*". Sinha, K.N., *Indian Writing in English* 92-41.

Prasad, V.V.N. Rajendra. "Raja Rao and the Imperial Self." Prasad, V.V.N. Rajendra 43-70.

Raizada, Harish. "Literature as Sadhana: The Progress of Raja Rao from *Kanthapura* to *The Serpent and the Rope*" Sharma, K.K., *Indo-English Literature* 157-176.

_____. "Point of View, Myth and Symbolism in Raja Rao's Novels". Sharma. K.K. *Perspectives on Raja Rao* 189-204.

Raine, Kathleen. *"On The Serpent and the Rope."* *World Literature Today* 62.4 (1988): 603-605.

Raine, Kathleen. Quoted in Makarand Paranjape, *The Best of Raja Rao* (selected and edited). New Delhi, Katha Classics, 1998.p.xxii.

Rajan, B. "*Kanthapura.*" King, *Literature of the World* 87-97.

Rajan, P.K. "An Introduction to *Comrade Kirillov*". *Littcrit* 3.1 (1977): 51-54.

"Raja Rao" *World Authors, 1950-1970.* 1183-1185.

Ram, Atma. "Peasant Sensibility in *Kanthapura*." Sharma, K.K., *Indian English Literature* 193-200.

_____. "Raja Rao: The Philosopher Novelist." *Perspective* May (1978) : 49-50.

_____. "The Linguistic Devices in Indian English of Raja Rao and Mulk Raj Anand" Ram, *Essays* 8-25.

Ramachandran, G. "Promotion of Gandhian Philosophy," Mysore (1973): 33

Ramachandraiah, P. "The Journey Motif in *Kanthapura*". *Indian Review of English Studies* 1.1 (1989): 61-65.

Ramamurthi, K.S. "*Kanthapura, Kedaram, Malgudi* and Trinidad as India in Miniature: A Comparative Study". Srivastava, A.K., *Alien Voices* 61-74.

Rama Moorthy, P. "Death in Raja Rao's *The Policeman and the Rose* and Witi Ihimaera's *Pounamu*". *Commonwealth Literature* 127-136.

Ramanan, Mohan. "Rao on Gandhi: A Method of Reading." *The Journal of Indian Writing in English*. Ed. G.S. Balrama Gupta 29.2. (2001)

Ramaswamy, S. "Self and Society in Raja Rao's *The Serpent and the Rope*." *Aspects of Indian Writing in English.* Ed. M. K. Naik. Delhi: The Macmillan Company of India, (1979): 199-208.

_____. "India and France in Raja Rao' *The Serpent and the Rope*". Ramaswamy, *Explorations* 179-185.

_____. "The Sanskrit Charge" in Raja Rao: The Word and 'Sabda Tattva". Rao, A Ramakrishna, *Comparative Perspectives* 103-112.

Ranchan, Som P. "Ramaswamy's Dilemma: An Analytical Interpretation of *The Serpent and the Rope*". *Language Forum* 7-14 (1981-82): 101-109.

_____. "*The Serpent and the Rope:* India Made Real". *Illustrated Weekly of India* 13 Mar. 1966: 45-47

Rao, A. Ramakrishna "Kirillov in the First Circle". *Literary Endeavour* 6.1-4 (1985) : 45-54.

Rao A.V., Krishna. "Raja Rao: The Novel of Prophecy". Rao, A.V. Krishna *The Indo-Anglian Novel* 107-133.

Rao, J. Srihari. "Concept of Time and Death in Raja Rao's *The Cat and Shakespeare*". *Littcrit* 3, 2.2 (1976): 35-38.

_____. "Image of Truth: A Study of Raja Rao's *The Cat and Shakespeare*". *Journal of Indian Writing in English* 5.1 (1977): 36-41.

Rao. K. Ramachandra "Raja Rao's *Kanthapura*" Raghavacharulu, *Two Fold Voice* 99-113.

_____. "The Novelist as a Marxist: A Study of Raja Rao's *Comrade Kirillov*". *Triveni* 49.1 (1980): 47-50.

_____. "Raja Rao and the Metaphysical Novel". Amur et al. *Indian Readings* 87-93.

Rao, N. Madhava. "*Kanthapura*: An Appreciation". *Triveni* 44.3 (1975): 55-59.

_____. "The Experiences of Renaissance in *Kanthapura*". *Triveni* 49.4 (1981): 29-32.

Rao, M. Subba. "Raja Rao : The Path Breaker" Rao, M. Subba Vol. 1. 130-140.

Rao, C. Vimala. "Love and Marriage in Raja Rao's *The Serpent and the Rope*" *Littcrit* 33, 17.2 (1981): 12-21.

Ray, Robert J. "The Novels of Raja Rao". *Books Abroad* 40.4 (1966): 411-414.

Reddy, K. Venkata. "An Approach to Raja Rao's *The Cat and Shakespeare.*" *World Literature Written in English* 20.2 (1981): 344-350.

Rothfork, John. "Religion and Culture in Raja Rao's *The Serpent and the Rope*" *Journal of Literary Studies* 4.2 (1981): 24-44.

Sambarmurthy, Indira. "The Divine in their Human Abode: Mythical Lore and Metaphysical Quest in the Novels of Raja Rao". *Quest* (Ranchi) 4.2 (1990): 25-33.

Sanyal, Samaras. "Gandhi as Prominent Myth in *Kanthapura*". Sanyal, *Indianness in Major Indo-English Novels* 128-130.

_____. "Raja Rao and His Experiment with New Technique and Vision in Style". Sanyal, *English Language in India* 77-85.

Sarachchandra, Edirwire, "Illusion and Reality: Raja Rao as Novelist". Amirthanayagam and Harrex 107-117.

Sastry, L.S.R. Krishna. "Raja Rao" *Triveni* 36.4 (1968): 16-30.

Seshachari. Chandadai. "The Gandhian Dimension: Revolution and Tragedy in *Kanthapura*". *South Asian Review* (Jackson Ville, F1) 5.2 (1981): 82-87.

Sethi, R., Letizia, A. Reading India in a Transnational Era: The Works of Raja Rao. Routledge India. 2021. URL: https://www.routledge.com/Reading-India-in-a-Transnational-Era-The-Works-of-Raja-Rao/Sethi-Alterno/p/book/9781138550292. Consulted on 29-11-22

Shahane, Vasant A. "Raja Rao's *The Cat and Shakespeare*: A Study in the Form of Fiction". *Journal of Indian Writing in English* 3.1 (1975): 7-91.

_____. "Quest for Reality in Patrick White and Raja Rao: A Comparative Appraisal". *Orbit* 1.1 (1982): 1-12.

_____. "Raja Rao's *The Serpent and the Rope* and Patrick White's *The Solid Mandala*". Nageswara Rao 177-192.

_____. "Raja Rao's *Kanthapura*". Pradhan, 22-40.

_____. "Fiction and Reality in Raja Rao." *Journal of South Asian Literature* 22.2 (1987): 34-42.

Sharma, Atma Ram. "Raja Rao: Cats, Serpents and Comrades of the Human Condition". *Perspective* 1.1 (1978): 59.

_____. "Raja Rao's Prose Style". Sharma, K.K., *Perspectives on Raja Rao* 204-214.

Sharma, B. D. "Mothers and Mother Figures in Raja Rao's Fiction". Bande, *Mothers and Mother-figures* 87-94.

_____. "Victim of Colonial Oppression in Raja Rao's *Kanthapura*". Bande, *Victim Consciousness* 17-27.

_____"Raja Rao's *Kanthapura*: A Plea for the Nehruvian Socialism." *Points of View*, Vol 6, Summer 1999.

Sharma, Jatindra Kumar. "Responses to Alien Culture in Henry James and Raja Rao: Comparative Observations on *The American* and *The Serpent and the Rope*". *Panjab University Research Bulletin* 15.1 (1984): 11-25.

Sharma, K.K. "The Philosopher as Novelist: Raja Rao's Preoccupation with Philosophy". *Rajasthan Journal of English Studies* 13 & 14 (1981): 40-41.

_____. "Introduction". Sharma, K.K., *Perspectives on Raja Rao* i-xiv.

_____. "Raja Rao: A Reappraisal". Pathak, *Indian Fiction in English* 55-70.

Sharma, P.P. "Quest for Wholeness: A Central Pre-occupation of Raja Rao's Fiction". Sharma, K.K., *Perspectives on Raja Rao* 32-43.

Sharma, R.S. "The Rope without the Serpent: Reading Raja Rao's Classic". *Osmania Journal of English Studies* 25 (1989): 1-17.

Sharma, Roshanlal. "The Enlightenment Theme: A Study of the Motifs in Raja Rao's *On the Ganga Ghat*". *Revaluations* 6.1 (1995): 53-54.

Sharma, Som P. "Raja Rao's Search for the Feminine". *Journal of South Asian Literature* 12. (1977): 95-101.

Sharrad, Paul. "Aspects of Mythic Form and Style in Raja Rao's *The Serpent and the Rope*". *Journal of Indian Writing in English* 12.2 (1984): 82-95.

_____. "A Sense of Place in Raja Rao's *The Serpent and The Rope*". Nightingale 86-96.

Shepherd, Ron. "The Character of Ramaswamy in Raja Rao's *The Serpent and the Rope*." *New Literary Review* 4 (1978): 17-24.

_____. "Symbolic Organization in *The Serpent and the Rope*". *Southern Review* (Adelaide) 6.2 (1973): 93-107.

_____. "Raja Rao: Symbolism in The Cat and Shakespeare". *World Literature Written in English* 14.2 (1975): 347-356.

_____. "The Conservative Rebel: A Type of an Indian Hero". Sharma, K.K., *Perspectives on Raja Rao* 171-180.

Shirwadkar, K.R. "Literature as Ideology: Raja Rao's *The Serpent and the Rope*". *Pandey and Raja Rao* 1-12.

Singh, Avtar. "Raja Rao's *Kanthapura*: A Study on Technique". *Sinha & Sinha* 123-135.

Singh, Brij Raj. "Looking for a Classic in Indian English Writing". *Humanities Review* 2.1 (1980): 15-21.

Singh, J.P. "The Serpent and the Rope Dancer". *Indian Journal of English Studies* 16 (1982): 53-76.

Singh, R.S. "Raja Rao's India: Fact or Fiction?" *B.I.E.T. English Association Journal* (1971): 14.

_____. "A European Brahmin". Singh, R.S., *Indian Novel in English* 73-95.

Singh, Satyanarain. "A Note on Raja Rao's World View in *The Serpent and the Rope*." *Kakatiya Journal of English Studies* 3.1 (1978): 253-256.

Singh, Sunaina. "*The Cat and Shakespeare*: Metaphysical Reality or Surrender to Destiny." *Kakatiya Journal of English Studies* 8 (1987-88): 156-162.

Sinha, R.K. "Oral Tradition in *Kanthapura* and *Arrow of God*". Sinha & Sinha, 136-143.

Sitaramayya, K.B. "The Narrator in Raja Rao's *Kanthapura*". *Journal of Literature and Aesthetics* 2.2-3 (1982): 67-73.

Sivaraman, S. (Mrs.) "Archetypal Experience in *The Serpent and the Rope*," Pathak, *Indian Fiction in English* 71-78.

Soni, N.C. "The Achievement of Raja Rao." Sharma, K.K., *Perspectives on Raja Rao* 215-230.

Srinivas, V "Tradition and Experiment in *The Cat and Shakespeare*". *Kakatiya Journal of English Studies* 11 (1991): 119-124.

_____. "Myth and Experiment in *Kanthapura*". *Kakatiya Journal of English Studies* 13 (1993): 74-80.

Srivastava Narasingh. "Love and Divorce in *The Serpent and the Rope*". *Quest* Sept.-Oct.1975: 58-62.

_____. "Image of India in the Novels of Raja Rao". *Indian Scholar* 2.1 (1980): 57-69.

_____. "Raja Rao's *Comrade Kirillov*: The Dilemma of a Divided Consciousness" *Journal of Commonwealth Literature* 16.1 (1981): 8-15.

_____. "The Narrative Technique of Raja Rao". Dwivedi, *Studies in Contemporary Indian Fiction in English* 173-190.

Srivastava, Ramesh. "Structure and Theme in Raja Rao's Fiction". Sharma, K.K., *Perspectives on Raja Rao* 140-170.

_____. "Raja Rao's *Kanthapura*: A Village Revitalised". Srivastava, R.K., *Six Indian Novelists* 3-16.

Subramanyam. Ka. Naa "On Reading Raja Rao's *The Cat and Shakespeare*". *Thought* 16 Apr. 1966: 16-17.

_____. "Raja Rao and Current Literature". *Hindustan Times* 6 June 1969: 7-4.

Sundaram, P.S. "Single and Double Vision: Anand, Raja Rao and R.K. Narayan". *Rajasthan University Studies in English* 7 (1974): 68-78.

Taranath, Rajeev. "A Note on the Problem of Simplification." *Fiction and the Reading Public in India*. Ed. C.D. Narasimhaiah, Mysore University. (1967): 205-212.

Tiffin, Helen and Arvind Sharma. "Advaita Vedanta in Three Novels. Of Raja Rao". *Religion* 13 Oct. (1983): 359-379.

____. "The Word and the House: Colonial Motifs in *The Double Hook* and *The Cat and Shakespeare*". *Literary Criterion* 20.1 (1985): 204-226.

Thumboo, E. quoted in Makarand Paranjape, *The Best of Raja Rao*, (selected and edited). New Delhi, Katha Classics, (1998): xvi.

Tikoo, Swaraj Krishna. "Raja Rao's *The Serpent and the Rope*: The East-West Cocktail". Rao, Visheswara 83-94.

Tiwary. R.S. "Tolerance and Accommodation in *The Serpent and the Rope*" *Language Forum*. 24.1-2 (1998): 177-191.

Usha, V.T. "Raja Rao and Jhabvala Two Variant Visions of Indian Widow". *Journal of Indian Writing in English* 21.1 (1993): 13-20.

Vanita, Ruth. "Ravana Shall be Slain and Sita Free – The Feminine Principle in *Kanthapura*." Chatterjee 188-193.

Venkatachari, K. "Raja Rao's *The Serpent and the Rope*: A Study in Advaitic Affirmation". *Osmania Journal of English Studies* 8.1 (1971): i-xii.

____. "The Feminine Principle in Raja Rao's *The Serpent and the Rope*". *Osmania Journal of English Studies* 8.2 (1971): 113-120.

Venugopal Rao, C.V. "Raja Rao: A Short Story Writer-- A Study" *Journal of Karnatak University* (Humanities) 14 (1970): 159-170.

Verghese, C. Paul. "Raja Rao, Anand, R.K. Narayan and Others". *Indian Writing Today* 3.1 (1969): 31-38.

____. "Raja Rao: An Assessment". Verghese, *Problems of Indian Creative Writing in English* 142-154.

Vijayasree, C. "The Philosophy of Womanhood in Raja Rao's *The Serpent and the Rope*". Rao, Ramakrishna & Sivaramkrishna 106-114.

Visweswariah, H.S *"The Serpent and the Rope*: A Stylistic Approach". *Literary Endeavour* 1.1 (1979): 49-62.

Vyaghreswarudu, B "The Growth of Mind and Art of Raja Rao: His Short Stories" in Mittapalli, R. & Piciucco, P.P. *The Fiction of Raja Rao: Critical Studies*, (Ed) New Delhi, Atlantic Publishers and Distributors. (2001): 223 - 230.

Wasi, Jehanara. "Metaphysical Novelist". *Link* 19 May 1985: 41.

____. "Metaphysical Quest". *Economic Times* 16 Nov. 1986. 4.1.

Westbrook, Perry D. "Raja Rao". *Contemporary Novelists*. 5th ed. (1991): 756-757.

____. "Theme and Inaction in Raja Rao's *The Serpent and the Rope*". *World Literature Written in English* 14.2 (1975): 385-398.

____. "Raja Rao's *Comrade Kirillov*: Marxism and Vedanta" *World Literature Today* 62.4 (1988): 617-620.

White, Ray Lewis, "Raja Rao's *The Cat and Shakespeare in the U.S.A.*" *The Journal of Indian Writing in English* 7.1 (1979): 24-29.

____. "Raja Rao's *The Serpent and the Rope* in the U.S.A." *Journal of Indian Writing in English* 10.1-2 (1982): 41-50.

Williams, H. M. "Raja Rao: The Idea of India". *Miscellany* 61 (1973): 10.

____. "Raja Rao's *The Serpent and the Rope* and the Idea of India". *Rule, Protest, Identity: Aspects of Modern South Asia*. Eds. Peter G. Robb and David D. Taylor. London: Curzon, 1978: 206-212.

Walsh, William. "The Indian Sensibility in English." *Awakened Conscience*. Ed. C. D. Narasimhaiah. New Delhi: Sterling Publishers (1978):65-70.

Yok, Choi Kim. "The Concept of Love in Raja Rao's The *Serpent and the Rope*". *Triveni* 44.4 (1976): 39-47.

REVIEWS

Advani, "G.J. Philosophical Novel" Rev. of *The Serpent and The Rope*". *Baltimore* Sun (MD) 14 April 1963.

____. "Pseudo Profundities." Rev. of *The Cat and Shakespeare. Baltimore* Sun (MD) 14 Feb. 1965.

B.J.R. "Rao Explores Oriental Mind" Rev. of *The Cat and Shakespeare. Birmingham News* (AL) 4 Apr. 1965.

Badve, V.V. Rev. of *Comrade Kirillov. New Quest* Mar. – Apr. 1979: 121-128.

Barkham, J. "Hindu Widens Gulf Between East West". Rev. of *The Serpent and the Rope. Philadelphia Bulletin* (PA) 17 Feb. 1963.

____. "India's Gifted Raja Rao Wins Acclaim with Brilliant *The Serpent and the Rope*" Rev. of *The Serpent and the Rope. Youngstown Vindicator* (OH), 2 Mar. 1963.

Bergamo, R. "A Piquant Fable About India in War." Rev. of *The Cat and Shakespeare. Atlanta Journal and Constitution* (GA) 31 Jan 1965.

Bloom, E. A. Rev. of *The Serpent and the Rope. Providence Journal* (RI) 10 Mar. 1963.

Bosworth, G. "Near East Revealed". Rev. of *The Cat and Shakespeare.* Norfolk Pilot (VA) 31 Jan. 1965.

Brandt, J. D. "Wedding of Two Worlds." Rev. of *The Serpent and the Rope. Wilmington News* (DL) 11 Mar. 1963.

Clifford, William. Rev. of *Kanthapura. Saturday Review* 11 Jan. 1964: 62.

Dimock, E.C. Jr. "The Garden Wall Between Worlds" Rev. of *The Cat and Shakespeare. Saturday Review.* 48.3 New York. 16 Jan. 1965: 27-28.

Fremont-S, E. "Books of the Time." Rev. of *The Cat and Shakespeare. New York Times* 20 Jan. 1965.

Glauber, R. "A Story of Two Worlds". Rev. of *The Serpent and the Rope. Chicago Daily News* (IL) 15 June. 1963.

Godsell, G. "Novels From India and Japan". Rev. of *The Serpent and the Rope. Christian Science Monitor* (Boston, MA) 14 Feb. 1963.

Hill, William, B. Rev. of Raja Rao's *The Serpent and the Rope. Best Sellers: The Monthly Book Review* 15 Feb. 1963: 429-430.

"Indian Writer Honoured". Rev. of *The Serpent and the Rope. New York Times* 4 Apr. 1964.

Jackman, F.P. "The Flower of India". Rev. of *The Serpent and the Rope. Worcester Telegram* (MA) 17 Feb. 1963.

King, Terry Johnson. "Tender Love Story in Eastern Setting." Rev. of *The Serpent and the Rope. Miami News* (FL) 17 Feb. 1963.

Krishnama, B.G.R. Rev. of *The Policeman and the Rose. Hindu* 8 Aug. 1978: 5.

Leland, J. "Indian Novelist Raja Rao's Book Gains High Praise". Rev. of *The Serpent and the Rope. Charleston; News and Courier* (SS) 10 Mar. 1963.

Mann, C, W. Jr. Rev. of *The Serpent and the Rope. Library Journal* 1 Feb. 1963.

____. "Rev. of *Kanthapura. Literature East and West* 8.4 (1964): 154-155.

May, C. "Novel with East Flavour Ranks High." Rev. of *The Serpent and the Rope. Nashville Tennessean* (TN) 2 June 1963.

McLaughlin, R. "*The Serpent and the Rope*: A Notable Indian Novel". *Spring Field Republican* (MA) 10 Mar. 1963.

McMurtry, L. "Subtle East-West Tale". Rev. of *The Serpent and the Rope. Houston Post* (TX) 27 Jan. 1963.

Morgan, J. G. "Conflict Between Cultures" Rev. of *The Serpent and the Rope. Charleston Gazette* (SC) 17 Feb. 1963.

Nagarajan, S. "An Indian Novel: *The Serpent and the Rope*". *Sewanee Review* 72.3 1964: 512-517.

Naik, M.K. "Not Quite Pandit Jagannath". Rev. of *On the Ganga Ghat. Indian Literature* 136, 33.2 1990: 151-155.

Narasimhan, R. Rev. of *The Policeman and the Rose. Hindustan Times* 11 June 1978: IV.1.

Orth, J. "New Novel is Strange Experience". Rev. of *The Serpent and the Rope. Charlotte Observer* (NC) 24 Feb. 1963.

Panikar, A.K.C. Rev. of *The Cat and Shakespeare. Quest* 57, Apr.- Jan. 1967: 101– 102.

Ray, Robert. Rev. of *The Serpent and the Rope. Mahfil* 1.3 (1965): 47-51.

Reif, J. "Hindu Mysticism Sets Mood." Rev. of *The Serpent and the Rope. Norfolk Pilot* (VA) 3 March 1963.

Rev. of *The Cat and Shakespeare. Chicago Tribune Books Today* 31 Jan. 1955.

Rev. of *The Cat and Shakespeare. Times* 5 Feb. 1965: 85-114.

Rev. of *On the Ganga Ghat (Short Stories). Times of India* 10 Dec. 1989 : 3.

Ross, N. W. "Subtle Marriage of East and West" Rev. of *The Serpent and the Rope. New York Herald Tribune Books* 7 Apr. 1963.

Rothschild, S "The Book Shelf." Rev. of *The Cat and Shakespeare. Jewish Advocate Boston* (MA) 16 Sep. 1965.

Ryan, Charles. " Of Brahmins and Bromides". Rev. of *The Serpent and the Rope. San-Francisco Chronicle* (CA) 17 Feb. 1963.

Schroetter, H. N. "Indian Author Produces Quiet Warm Simple Tale". Rev. of *The Cat and Shakespeare. Richmond Times-Dispatch* (VA) 14 Mar. 1965.

Singh, K. N. "Return Passage to India". Rev. of *The Serpent and The Rope. Saturday Review* 16 Mar. 1963: 88-89.

Thorpe, Michael. Rev. of *The Policeman and the Rose. Literary Half-Yearly* 29.2 (1978): 160-162.

"Truth and All that" Rev. of *The Serpent and the Rope. Times* 22 Feb. 1963.

Tucker, M. "Cultures in Conflict" Rev. of *The Serpent and the Rope. Commonwealth:* 25 Jan. 1963.

Watts, A. "Indian Novel Has Metaphysical Bent." Rev. of *The Cat and Shakespeare. Fort Worth Star* (TX) 7 Feb. 1965.

Wood, P. "Beautifully Written Tale of Brahmin Folkways." Rev. of *The Serpent and the Rope. Chicago Tribune* (IL) 10 Mar. 1963.

Yadav, R.S. "Cat Gut" Rev. of *The Cat and Shakespeare. Thought* (India) 3 Aug. 1974: 18.

Dissertations and Theses

Bhattacharya, P.C. "Study of the Works of Raja Rao to Assess his Contribution to Indo-Anglian Literature". Gorakhpur University, 1978.

Choudhary, Shashikala, "Raja Rao's Novels: A Transmutation of Philosophy". IIT Delhi, 1988.

Devi, Deena. D. "Raja Rao: A Study in the Light of Indian Thought". Banaras Hindu University, 1981.

Mishra, S.K. "The Destiny of Man in the Novels of Raja Rao". Banaras Hindu University, 1988.

Niranjan Rout, The Fictional Work of Raja Rao: A Study of his Mind and Art, Magadh University 1995.

Niranjan, Shiv. "Raja Rao: Novelist as Sage". Bihar University, 1983.

Singh, Ashok Kumar. "Quest for Truth in the Novels of Raja Rao."Magadh University , 1988.

Srivastava, Girish Chandra. "Raja Rao as a Novelist: A Study of Themes and Techniques in His Novels". Gorakhpur University. 1983.